I0460715

#1 in The Heaven's Pond Trilogy

The Master
and
The Maid

Laura Libricz

Blue Heron Book Works, LLC
Allentown, Pennsylvania

Cover design: Angie Zambrano
Cover photography: Paul Heller
Stylist for the cover: Rose Ellen Moore of RC Moore Boutique for the Unique Individual

Blue Heron Book Works, LLC
Allentown, PA
www.blueheronbookworks.com

"We are not doomed to make history repeat itself; it is open to us, through our own efforts, to give history, in our case, some new and unprecedented turn. As human beings, we are endowed with this freedom of choice, and we cannot shuffle off our responsibility upon the shoulders of God or nature. We must shoulder it ourselves. It is up to us."

—*Arnold J. Toynbee*

Table of Contents

ACKNOWLEDGMENTS

What started as a casual inquiry into the German psyche turned into a full blown investigation of a certain fascinating yet tragic period in German history: the Thirty Years War. Known as the Great War up until the first World War, this catastrophe desecrated much of the German territories, leaving those who survived with a justified lack of trust in the ruling forces of Europe and a even stronger lack of faith in the natural forces of the world.

This trilogy is my attempt to fill in the blanks left by the gaping hole that is the voice of women in history, their story screaming to be told. Through my research I have tried to make an accurate portrayal of what their lives could have been like.

I would like to thank those scribes who took the time to put down written accounts of their lives and the current events of their ages and also the historians who attempted to piece together the events for posterity. Please refer to my bibliography for reference material. Without these records, any study of history would be impossible. How accurate these accounts are, though, remains shrouded in the misty depths of what those writers wanted us to believe. *Papier ist geduldig* is a German saying that means 'paper is tolerant.' Anything can be written down or printed, no matter if it is true or complete nonsense. We can only imagine what future societies will think of our age judging by the written records we are leaving them!

I would also like to thank Bathsheba Monk from Blue Heron Book Works. She 'gets it' and knows where I want to go with this project and has been instrumental in molding this book into its present state. Big thank-yous to my supporters from early on, Kay Thomas-Sukrow, Graham Stockley, Nicole Weber, Betsy Souders, Wolfgang Mazkal, Regina Holm, Jane Kovalchick as well as those who had to put up with me on a daily basis, my wonderful children, Jan and Yvonne Mazkal.

This is a work of fiction and similarities to those living or dead is purely coincidental.

Part 1

Chapter 1

Nuremberg, Germany — May 1616

Katarina twisted the tap on the wooden barrel of beer. Foam spluttered into the tankard and sprayed the white apron covering her coarse brown dress.

"Willi, get me another barrel," she shouted over the heads of three men sitting at the table nearest her.

The three men swayed from side to side singing a drunken song: "*Ich bin a mal auf fischn ganga, in a sumpfig Weier, hockt a Frusch auf meiner Stanga…*"

One man lifted his tankard, slammed it on the table and hit the rude bit of the song, "*…zwickt mi in die Eier.*"

The tallow lamp spun across the table and onto the floor. The new barmaid, Lily, stomped on the burning oil, proving herself quite useful on her first night serving drinks at The Stork's Nest.

"Willi can't hear ya," Lily said. "I'll get cha one."

She swung her wide hips around the three drunk men, waddled behind the bar and heaved the empty wooden barrel onto her shoulder. It was the same size as her stomach. She disappeared into the storeroom.

Katarina grabbed her wooden spoon and whacked the drunk at the bar who dared put his head down on the smooth wooden surface.

He raised his head, rubbing the crown. "*Hör auf*, Katarina. What was that for?"

"Either you're here to drink, or you're here to drink. You can sleep at home," she said.

Near the back door of the tavern, a woman shrieked and a man laughed. Katarina looked up and saw Willi Prutt catch the still-shrieking woman, set her on his lap and kiss her on the lips.

"Katarina, bring us some beer," the butchers yelled from the table by the door.

Lily rolled back into the taproom and plunked the full barrel onto the short wooden stool. She bent at the waist and hammered the tap into it, sending foam flying everywhere.

"Hand me some tankards there Katarina, be a dear," Lily said.

Like a practiced team, Katarina passed Lily empty tankards, Lily filled them and Katarina grabbed the full ones back, banging them down on the counter. Lily straightened, heaved five full tankards in each hand and rolled back towards the table of butchers.

The drunk at the bar took a swig and said, "They say the butchers feed her fat to keep her that fat. They just love her young skin. She's probably carrying another one of their bastards."

The tavern door opened, letting in a chill evening breeze. In the street beyond, a group of vagrant boys taunted passers-by. The scent of late spring fleeted by her. As the season headed towards the solstice, the evenings seemed to go on forever. And here she was, in this smelly, dark tavern bettering neither herself nor her purse.

She and Willi had been working this tavern since his mother died two years ago. As a result of them working hard together, they had great turnover and they were making more money than when they were weaving cloth and selling fabrics on the market. He promised they would get married when they had the money. But the money they took in made him giddy, like sweet wine. He forgot his promises. He forgot the reason he'd gotten so far was Katarina. He'd forgotten Katarina it seemed.

She would run this tavern by herself if she could. She'd surely be better off without him.

A man who didn't belong entered the taproom. Katarina pictured a rose growing amid a field of wheat. He closed the door. The flames from the tallow lamps on the tables nearby flickered. He pulled the thin black cape off his shoulders and removed his hat. His dark smooth hair was caught in a black ribbon at the base of his neck. He moved between the full tables to an empty one at the back of the tavern. He caught Katarina watching him. She poured him a cup of port and silently moved to his table.

Katarina set the ceramic cup on the table in front of him. "Good Evening Herr Tucher."

"You look wonderful tonight, just like always," Herr Tucher said.

"You look drawn and pale, like always," she said.

"I can always rely on you for uplifting conversation, Katarina."

He smirked in a way Katarina found maddening, as if he were making fun of her. As if he saw something in her that she herself was blind to and she wanted to know what it was.

"That must be why you always end up here," she said, tersely. "For the conversation."

"The scenery mostly. But it's a wonderful place to have a strengthening drink, if not always prudent," he said.

The shouting escalated as a disagreement erupted around the dice table. Two men who were losing money rose from their seats hissing and poking each other in the chest.

"Maybe not prudent but certainly entertaining." Herr Tucher shook his head. "My dear Katarina. There is a matter at hand I need to discuss. When your man is in any position to speak with me, that is."

Willi, his arms around two women who were enthralled by the animated story he illustrated with vigorous hand movements, joined in as the men in the bar sung louder: "Went a fishin' all alone, by the muddy falls, sat a frog up on my bone, and bit me in the balls!"

Katarina felt her face redden with shame. "I will see if he's available," she said, purposely ignoring the scene she already knew by heart.

"Do send him over, when he's *available*," Herr Tucher continued. "We have, yet again, a problem with the rent. My uncle has given me the task of reminding you that it is due."

"That can't be, Herr Tucher, I gave Willi all the money last week. He paid you, he told me that much."

Katarina wanted to believe Willi even if the evidence usually betrayed him. She had to stand behind him. Together they would show this patrician that they could play his game and win. A crash caused Katarina to wince. One of the dice players had tipped the table. Willi stood in the middle of it and they all had a good laugh. When he saw Katarina standing next to Herr Tucher's table, he sauntered towards them.

"A lovely evening, Herr Tucher," Willi said, laying an arm on Katarina's shoulder.

"Marvelous," he said.

"Those dice players are always trouble," Willi said.

"Always something," Herr Tucher said, uninterested. "Speaking of trouble…"

"Nope, no trouble this month." Willi pounded the table, making the cups bounce. "I paid you last week."

"You most certainly did not." Herr Tucher rose from his seat.

"Liar," Willi said, the word an audible breath.

He pushed a chair out of the way and walked to the other side of the bar, disappearing into the store room.

Katarina looked to see if Herr Tucher caught that last comment.

"See, Herr Tucher? You've been paid. Maybe the memory is going?" She was breathing heavily.

"Katarina, he is the liar."

"You seem to always forget about uplifting conversation at the beginning of the month," Katarina said, trying to make light of it. "Only thinking of your money tonight."

"You should be thinking of your money," Herr Tucher said. "You do realize how serious this has become?"

"There must be an oversight. We've been paying you! You know, without Willi, we would never have as many guests."

"There's only one, no, maybe two reasons why they drink here. One: you have drink. For another, you, Katarina, make sure their cups are full. You are the reason. Not him."

"I would run this place by myself if I could," she said, resolutely.

"Is that what you really want? I could certainly find a better place for you." His whole manner softened.

Katarina felt her face flush and hurried away from the table. His comments irritated and intrigued her. What did a man like him care about what she wanted? She should challenge him sometime. And where was this better place he spoke of, then? He would back down, just like the rest of these men who came to the tavern. All they wanted was recognition and affirmation from her, like little boys trying to get their mother's attention. She knew better than to have her head turned by his casual concern, but it was heartening to indulge her fantasy of a man who actually looked out for her.

The door opened and slammed shut. A large robust young man, the tanner who lived opposite her and who worked for Herr Tanner, moved through the taproom. She nodded and smiled to greet him. He made his way to the table in the back of the tavern and sat at Herr Tucher's table with a thud.

"Good Evening, Tanner," Katarina heard Herr Tucher's voice over the din.

Katarina could see the excitement in Tanner's smiling, boyish face. He pushed his dark-blond waves away from his forehead as his words bubbled over but she could not understand what he said. She flitted closer. Herr Tucher leaned towards Tanner and lowered his voice.

"…Liar…," Herr Tucher said.

Katarina made an abrupt stop at their table. She lit a fresh candle from the sputtering flame of the spent one and placed it in the wooden holder.

"I have waited for two weeks and he will not so much as look at me," Herr Tucher continued and turned to Katarina. "I will be leaving here shortly and he can meet me at my home when you close up. My uncle and I will tolerate this no more."

"I don't believe you," Katarina said. "And I will sort this out. It must be just a misunderstanding."

She marched back to the bar, picked up the wooden spoon off the counter and whacked that sleeping drunk on the head. He didn't move.

Katarina filled ten empty tankards and passed them off to Lily who grabbed four in each hand and delivered the drink. Katarina grabbed the last two and moved closer to Herr Tucher's table so she could hear their conversation.

"I've packed most of my things, Herr Tucher," Tanner said. "I have the coach ready and we should be able to leave the city tomorrow afternoon."

"What can I get you to drink, Tanner?" Katarina asked.

Herr Tucher's eyes reflected the dancing light from the candle. "Katarina, you know what happens next. You will have to leave the premises." Herr Tucher's voice lowered to a whisper. "I dare not think of what other options you have."

"I said I would sort this out," she hissed under her breath.

"A woman like you? No family. No money."

Katarina froze at Herr Tucher's accurate assessment. Yes, a woman like her. A simple woman, alone in the city of Nuremberg, now playing the barmaid for a gaming drunkard. At an age of four and twenty years, her options were limited: soldier's wife, rich man's maid and a whole slew of unsavory occupations.

"Your eyes burn like coals when you're angry," he said, reaching out to touch her hand.

She wrenched it away.

He turned his attention back to Tanner. "Excellent! You are packed. I am packed."

"I need to help my father in the morning, but we'll be finished with our chores early afternoon," Tanner said. "My wife is also very excited."

"Lucky man," Herr Tucher said. "A pity, but my wife is not. She just told me she is pregnant again. After losing the last child, she is not traveling." Herr Tucher motioned casually to Katarina, who had made no effort to move on. "I have one last stratagem to sort out these two here and then I will be ready to leave. You'll be impressed, my boy, when you see the countryside."

Katarina fought down the despair swelling in her throat. Willi always had some excuse not to get married; if she only worked harder, if they had some extra money, if she could give Willi a child. But all the work was wearing her down and Lily said it was probably the reason she could not conceive. Any signs of fertility Katarina had when she came to the city disappeared when she started working at the tavern. Willi said she was barren. Lily said Katarina needed help with all the work and would come over evenings to help out, now that the old butcher Lily worked for had died and she was on her own. But if they lost the tavern and Willi turned Katarina out, who would have her? At this age, barren and no longer pure. The fear that she would have no place to go was too real to ignore.

Herr Tucher spoke directly to Katarina. "Will there be anything else?"

A thud and a crash forced them all to abandon the conversation. Willi had fallen off his chair and crashed against the table of butchers.

The men had a good, hearty laugh at the escapades.

"Du ehlender Hund!" Katarina marched over and pulled him up by the arm. *"Verfluchter Mistkerl!"* Stand up you, you, good-for-nothing…"

She dragged him behind the bar towards the steps leading to the garret room upstairs. He shook himself free from her grasp. She climbed the steps, his laughter echoing off the walls.

The only light in the meagre, musty garret room came from two small openings in the stone wall. The sloping roof darkened the space even more. She turned her back, rubbed her eyes and picked up a mug from the worm-eaten table. She sipped at the cold herb tea, set it back down and pulled the leather cord out of her hair. Russet curls fell around her face and the cord fell to the floor. Willi's boots clumped up the steps. The light from his lamp entered the room first.

"Katarina?" he said, stopping at the top of the steps and setting the lamp onto the table. "Come here, *Schatz.*"

His boots rang out as he crossed the floor. His arms circled around her waist, pulling her in. His lips touched her neck and lingered for a moment.

She pushed him away. "Where is that money, Willi? We are earning a lot of money. He says the rent wasn't paid. I gave you that money two weeks ago!"

Willi smiled. He pulled off his leather doublet and threw it on the table, knocking over the mug. He was wearing a new shirt.

"I'll go talk to him," he said. "You see, he's raised the rent, the lying, old dog. He got his money, now he wants more."

"Who is lying to me?" she cried.

She stomped over to a straw pallet in the corner of the room, pulled a metal till out from under the mattress and let it fall back with a musty cloud of dust. The till rattled quite promisingly.

"There's enough here to pay Herr Tucher in full," she said.

Willi grabbed at Katarina's prize but she was quicker. She moved to the wall and grabbed a cloak off the peg.

"I'll go pay him myself," she said. "You are drunk."

"No woman settles my business for me, ever."

His body pinned hers to the wall before she even realized he was near her. He had the till in his hands and pressed it against her upper chest. She gasped for breath and looked up at his face, trying to deny he was treating her with such disregard. He wouldn't meet her gaze.

Katarina let the till go and dropped the cloak.

Willi straightened and moved a step back. "Don't you worry, Katarina. I'll talk to him. I'll bring him around."

He pulled her into an embrace, his body tense and suddenly foreign to her. He leaned down and kissed her softly on the lips, his breath a mingle of beer and tobacco.

"This isn't the first time we've had problems," he said.

Willi released Katarina, turned and grabbed a leather pouch from the table and poured the coins out of the till into the pouch. She grabbed the pouch out of his hand and held it behind her back.

"Give that back!" A dark flash crossed Willi's face, like a dangerous thought took hold of him, a look she tried hard not to see.

She wanted to trust him but here was the nagging truth she had to face. He was a thief and he was using her. Had she misread him all along? Had he only told her lies? As if he saw mistrust in her eyes, he grabbed a handful of her hair and pulled her head back. She mustered all the strength she could and managed a whisper.

"You're not ruining everything I've worked for."

"Give me that." He grabbed the pouch out of her hand. "It's my money. You do as I say."

"Why should I? I'm not your wife."

He kissed her hard and bit her lip, let her go, grabbed his doublet and turned to walk down the steps. She followed him down into the tavern. He bent over one of his wenches and kissed her lips. He said a few words to the remaining guests and left the tavern. She grabbed her wooden spoon and whacked the drunk at the bar.

"Oww-ah, Katarina," he said, sitting upright, rubbing his head.

Few guests remained. It was late indeed. She grabbed a basket and cleared the sticky mugs from the just-as-sticky tables, wooden chair legs scraping the floor as she pushed them out of the way with her hip. The last guests headed towards the door. In the quiet, fear and despair threatened to render her lame and unable, all fight gone. Her hands trembled.

Lily stood still in the shadows next to a table with the last burning tallow lamp. "Don't you worry about Willi. He's a good man. They're all the same, you know."

"Aren't they, though," she said.

Lily laid an arm on her shoulder. "Let's leave this for tonight, shall we? I'll come early tomorrow and clean up. You can come later."

"Are you sure?" Katarina said, already grabbing her shawl and moving towards the door.

They left the tavern, locking the door to the building. The night was chilly and they both pulled the wraps over their shoulders. They joined arms and walked silently along the Findelgasse, past the orphanage and across the Fleischbrücke, the new, solid, stone bridge. The river Pegnitz flowed under their feet towards the executioner's house. At this late hour they passed only shuttered houses on the Winkelgasse, walked by the St. Sebaldus Church and turned onto the Weinmarkt, stopping in front of the crooked little house where Lily had her new room on the second floor.

Lily came to Nuremberg a few years ago to work for the old butcher. She'd been a wisp of a girl from a farm family in Tennenlohe that had too many children and not enough to eat. The old butcher fattened her up and the others passed her around. Lily didn't seem to mind her lot.

"Thanks, Lily." Katarina gave her the key to the tavern door and kissed her on the cheek.

Katarina crossed the Weinmarkt and walked along to the bowed row of half-timbered houses making up the Tannery Row, towards their house. The road was dark except for a lantern still burning outside the young tanner's house. The rotting smell of tanning hides had mercifully let up this time of night. But over the street there still hung the odor of dung-scrubbed skin soaked in a solution of animal brains that made her gag. She looked over her shoulder as she opened the door and went into the dark house, shuddering at the empty chill. He should have been home long before.

She stoked the embers on top of the kitchen hearth and threw two split logs into the glow. Sparks illuminated the tiny kitchen that was her refuge. This was the beating heart of every home. She wondered where she went wrong. She had wanted no more than to belong here, to have a real home and a family and she'd worked like three to accomplish that. But no matter how angry she was at what Willi had done, the idea she had failed and was to blame fought its way through her rage.

Suddenly this house felt as foreign as Willi's embrace. Tying a leather band into her hair, she climbed the creaking steps into their little room and opened the window to the street below. She took off her dress, which smelled of stale beer, and lay on the bed they had shared if and when he came home.

Chapter 2

Katarina woke with a start to the sound of *thunk, thunk* out on the street. It was well into the morning. Worker's shouts sounded along the street. Logs thunked as they hit the woodpile. Horse's hooves clattered on cobblestones. The repulsive smells from the carcasses and tanning hides filled the room. She stood, bent out of the window and looked up and down the street. Her hands shook with anger as she pulled her hair back as tight as she could. The bun wouldn't hold and strands fell in her face.

"Katarina! Are you waiting for him?" Tanner yelled up to her.

He ducked a log that his father threw from the wagon of firewood they were unloading and pointed down the bowed Tannery Row. Willi Prutt appeared, finally, staggering up to the front door. He swayed and tried to pull the door handle this way and that. Tanner jumped down from the wagon and opened the door for him.

"You shouldn't leave that pretty lady alone all night, my friend!" Tanner said, backed into the road and waved up at Katarina.

She smiled and slammed the window, ran down the steps and rounded on Willi the moment he shut the door. He was so drunk he could hardly stand.

"Katarina, come here, *mm*, give me *mm* kiss." He swayed and fell against the wall.

She turned her back on him, folded her arms over her chest and closed her eyes a moment to compose herself. After taking a deep breath, she stomped down the hallway and heard him following, slobbering like a dog. They turned into the dusty sitting room dominated by a massive loom. He fell onto one of the two chairs next to a table stuffed in the corner by the open window. The chair banged against the wall. His head scraped the window pane.

"Horrible wretch, you are," Katarina said and went into the adjoining kitchen.

She stirred what embers had survived the night and laid kindling over the top. The dry branches began smoking immediately.

"You'll be the death of me, you drunken ox," she said, loud enough for him to hear.

She hung a pot of water over the meager fire to heat and added poppy with a bit of fennel seed and anise to brew him a tea. From the shelf, she pulled a jar of valerian root, added a pinch to the potion, thought again and added a handful. The day was warming quite pleasantly but if she smelled the reek of urine, excrement and leather any longer, she would heave. She poured him a cupful, squeezed past the loom carrying his tea and tried to close the window. The handle broke off in her hand. She shut her eyes and inhaled sharply.

"*Mm*, come here, *Schatz*," he said and grabbed her waist.

She set his tea down and slapped his ear with a crack that startled her more than him. He slapped her back. She ran off into the kitchen. The fire smoldered and a dense smoke filled the room. It was impossible to get the smoke to go up the flue on such a warm morning. She coughed and waved the towel, checking the shelves for something more potent than valerian root.

"Did you pay that Tucher?" she called from the kitchen.

"Wha…?"

"I'll kill you if you didn't," she added in a whisper.

"What, *mm*, *sch*…? Can't hear you."

She stood in the doorway. "He'll evict us, damn you!"

"*Mm*, rent, *mm*…"

"What about the rent?" Katarina stood over Willi and shook his shoulders. "Where is that money?"

"Money, *sch*…"

Someone was at the door, pulling on the bell. Jolted to his senses, Willi staggered up and shoved Katarina aside. Still wearing his doublet and boots, he clump-clumped on the wood floor down the hall. He opened the door and leaned against the wall to steady himself.

"Herr Tucher, good *mm*, morning," he slurred.

"Good Day, Prutt. I'm sorry to intrude but I need to speak to the two of you. You are expecting me, I believe?" He shoved past Prutt, walking directly to the kitchen and Katarina.

Startled, she tried to look past him to see Willi, but he filled the doorway.

"Good morning, Herr Tucher," she said, as if his visit were a pleasant occurrence. Truthfully, though, she was shocked at his appearance. She'd never seen Herr Tucher in the daylight. He looked so drawn. Those tired, dark-shadowed eyes aged him considerably even though he was only about ten years older than she was. He was a handsome, neat man; his dark, smooth hair groomed, his face clean shaven but a bit pale. Without that smug smile, he would have had a likable expression.

"Katarina, nice to see you again. You look well," Herr Tucher said.

He smiled down at her and his scrutiny pierced though to her soul. She felt like a curious carnival act and had to look away. Embarrassed, she moved aside to let him enter. He walked towards the sitting room, watching her over his shoulder.

"I don't believe we should air such differences to the whole neighborhood," he said, pointing to the open window.

"Differences?" Katarina said. "Willi said you raised the rent. We pay enough."

"When you pay."

"What?" she said. "I gave him that money last night. He brought it to you."

She frowned at the landlord. His hands were stained brown with ink, as if he spent all his time over ledgers. He moved into the sitting room and considered the loom as if he analyzed its workings.

"Look in your books, sir," she said. "You've been paid."

Willi clumped into the sitting room and slid between Herr Tucher and the loom. He removed his doublet and let it fall to the floor. He pressed Katarina into the chair and motioned for her to stay quiet. His eyes were half closed, grey and unfocused. Foreign. Once they were blue like the cornflower; she fell in love with him because of those eyes.

"I think we ought to try something else Herr Tucher," Willi said. "How about we roll for it."

Willi pulled a flat leather cup out of his trousers pocket. Dice rattled as he reformed the cup and his face lit up in a mad sort of passion. He rolled the cup back in forth in his two hands, savoring the sound of the dice and the thrill of the wager.

Herr Tucher smoothed his hand over his simple black jacket. But he, like Willi, seemed impassioned at the idea of a wager. "What do you have that I could possibly want to win? You have everything to lose…"

"Three sixes wins. Three tries. No sixes, the next best three of a kind. No three of a kind, then the highest roll added together."

"Willi stop!" Katarina stood and lunged for the cup.

Willi pushed her into the kitchen. "This is none of your business, woman."

"Name your stakes, Prutt," Herr Tucher said.

"I win, I go rent free. Let's say, for a year, shall we? You win, you get…"

"What do I get Prutt? What do you have that would interest me?"

Katarina stood in the smoky kitchen doorway and dabbed her burning eyes with a towel. Could she only stand by and watch these two crazed men wager her fate?

"What do you want from us?" she said. "To squeeze every penny from our bent backs?"

"What my uncle really wants is to see you both led away in irons and thrown into the Debtor's Tower!" Herr Tucher said directly to Katarina. "They have a tower especially for women, my dear."

He smiled and held her gaze, forcing her to look away.

Herr Tucher clapped his hands together. "Yes, that is settled then! I win, Prutt, I lead the two of you away in irons."

"Dear God, no," Katarina said. "Willi, no! Think about what you're doing!"

Willi rattled the cup and turned it upside down on the table. "Three, four, five," he said.

Herr Tucher grabbed the cup and dropped the three dice into it, shook it twice and let the dice spill on the table. "Five, five, six."

Willi grunted, swept the dice into the cup and turned it upside down. "Two, two, four."

Herr Tucher smiled. "Is the lady lucky today?"

He gathered the dice, rattled the cup, let the dice spill onto the table. Willi looked down and slumped onto the chair. Katarina shot out of the kitchen, looked at the table and at Herr Tucher.

"Three sixes," Herr Tucher said. "So, Katarina, irons it is."

Katarina had an overwhelming rush of warmth as her body readied itself to bolt.

"Though maybe I shouldn't be so hasty," he continued. "Even though I would like to see you both squirm."

He paused for effect and took Katarina's hand. She tried to pull away.

"We may have another solution, Herr Prutt. Yesterday, I became the proud owner of a quaint country estate. This will interest especially you, Katarina. It is your birthplace. The farm called Sichardtshof."

"Sichardtshof?" She yanked her hand free. "Have you been there?"

"Not recently. The last time was in the autumn. Kunigunda is your grandmother, is she not? She was fragile then but she still got around. She asked if I knew of you. I told her I did. But the Old Widow Hansen was bed ridden. The entire property was run down. Decrepit, really. That is why it is being sold. I am traveling out there this afternoon and I need a *Magd* to help me get the place in order."

Katarina was never allowed to call her grandmother anything but Frau Kuni. The day she left, four years ago, was the last time they had spoken. They had argued. Frau Kuni made her promise to send money. Katarina never did, never thinking she would have to face her again.

Willi stood up, suddenly awake and sober. "That's it! You win, you get Katarina!"

"Willi stop!" she said.

"Yes, my solution exactly," Herr Tucher said. "The girl will be my maid and you, Herr Prutt, can avoid eviction."

She glared at one man and the other, speechless.

"But that only solves the one month's rent," Herr Tucher said.

Willi sat back down. "I think Katarina is worth two months."

She sat down in the other chair, numb. The nagging fear and despair that Willi was tired of her dissipated as the realization of its truth poured over her like a pail of cold water. This was the man she thought she loved. She would have defended him, would have gone through fire for him, fought any battle by his side.

"So, settled!" Willi said and rubbed his hands together. "Not so bad, eh?" he said, but when he saw the look of utter disbelief on her face, his expression changed to that of a puppy that had piddled on the floor.

Herr Tucher turned towards the hallway. "I'll be back in an hour," he said over his shoulder. "Be sure you are ready to travel, my dear."

Katarina couldn't move after Herr Tucher left. He'd mentioned something about having a "stroll 'round town, a drink, maybe a chat." He seemed to enjoy the little confrontation. It was just business for him. And Willi acted as if it didn't involve him. He sipped his tea. He stammered and slurred, peeled off his boots and let them fall on the floor. His head dropped to the table. Katarina shook his shoulder and he struggled to his feet, ignoring her as he left the room. She listened to him gingerly climb the creaking steps and close the door to the room they'd shared after his mother died.

She needed to pack her things and wait for her coach.

She stood and walked towards the doorway of the windowless kitchen, lit only with the glowing embers of a dying fire. She was going home. Her last and final defeat: to return to Frau Kuni with her tail between her legs. She laid a few branches on the embers, out of habit.

"Nein!" she whispered as smoke filled the room again.

Willi was leaning in the doorway, watching her. She hadn't heard him come back down the steps.

"Don't worry, you'll be back as soon as he gets tired of that prattle of yours," he said.

"Willi, how could you do this to me?"

"I'll come get you. I promise." He grabbed a bottle of down off the shelf, uncorked it and took a steadying gulp. "Play along for now. I'll get you out of this."

"You got me into this!" she said.

"Your place is in the tavern, he knows that. Don't worry. He won't keep you too long, you're a nag."

"Willi, I thought…"

"You thought what," he said.

"I thought you wanted to bring me here to be your…"

He put the bottle down and rested his fists on his hips like a defiant boy who'd been challenged to a fight.

"To be my wife? You thought I was going to marry you?" he snorted, swayed and swirled up a cloud of ash as he hurried out of the kitchen.

"Yes," she said, quietly to herself. "I did. I thought I was going to be your wife. How could I have been so wrong about my instincts?"

There was no purpose in looking back. That much she was sure of. She had to leave. Searching for something, maybe a piece of cloth to bundle her belongings, she found a wooden box the size of a baby's bed in the corner of the kitchen, forgotten under a shelf of odd pots. It was the box she had brought from Sichardtshof. She pulled it across the floor, nearer to the firelight, pried the rusted latch open and rummaged through the contents. Under some scraps of fabric, she found her cherished healing herb pamphlets, an old moth-eaten blanket and the few coins Frau Kuni gave her the day she left for the city. The coins were still wrapped in cloth, so they wouldn't jingle in their leather pouch and attract bandits. She slipped the leather cord attached to the pouch around her neck and secured the pouch under her dress. This was all she had left. She was right back where she started from.

Down at the bottom of the box, she found a blue tablet-woven band that Willi had made for her hair. Two summers ago, they had collected cornflowers in a field beyond the city walls and prepared a light-blue dye for some leftover flax. She had cornflowers stuck in her hair. He had cornflowers stuck in the hole in his shirt. His skin was so warm she could taste the salt on his cheek when he pulled her close. He smelled like wood smoke and wine.

That evening, Willi and Katarina had sat shoulder-to-shoulder at the table. He strung the blue-dyed flax and a few brown strands for contrast around the two dowels on the weaving board, threading the yarn through the tablets' holes. As he turned the tablets this way and that, they clicked on the weaving board. His nimble fingers fed the yarn through the two rows of threads. He pressed the woven fibers back with a bit of wood and turned the tablets for the next pass. A diamond pattern emerged. He finished the ends of the band and placed it around her head like a crown. The room had grown dark and one candle burned low. They were expensive and they only had the one. He kissed her long and warm. She wanted him to have the only gift she could give him: her innocence. He made love to her that night and promised they would marry.

Chapter 3

The coach kept a cheery pace along the unusually dry road. The rains the ground needed in the spring never came. They passed through villages, the farm houses safely clustered together, their red tile roofs under the shadow of the barns towering over the cottages. Katarina stuck her head out the window from time-to-time to watch the two Friesian stallions pulling the coach, their black manes blowing in the breeze. She loved to watch their rippling muscles, smell their sweet sweat. And she liked the distance she had from them, sitting in this coach. She never intended to sit atop a horse again.

They passed a church under construction, the half-built tower surrounded by wooden scaffolding. Another village passed on the left, only three houses and a barn surrounded by fields of grain. Beyond the hedgerow, the bleating of sheep rose from a field. A barefoot boy herded a flock of goats towards yet another village as they sped by. The sun drew towards the western horizon, still hot and dry. A few wisps of cloud blushed pink. Although late in the afternoon, a pair of hawks circled lazily overhead on the rising current.

The coach slowed and entered the forest. The air cooled, the sound of pounding hooves muffled in the soft soil of the forest floor. The trees smelled dewy and damp despite the lack of rain. After the long silence, Herr Tucher cleared his throat and spoke softly, as if approaching a delicate subject.

"You do understand that this is temporary. I felt the need to get you out of there for your own good. The situation between you and Prutt is unacceptable. A respite in the country will do you some good. You know, get away from the city."

"I could have stayed and taken care of the tavern. He could have had the respite in the country."

"It is not your tavern. It is his. And, yes, I do regret taking you out of there."

"Why must I leave?"

"I want you to accompany me. I can think of no better-qualified person to help me with this endeavor."

"I feel like I'm being punished for someone else's crimes."

"You, my dear, are being justly rewarded for your perseverance."

"That tavern was all I had." Katarina turned away.

"But it isn't yours," Herr Tucher reminded her.

He was right of course. All she had was nothing to show for two years of hard work. Herr Tucher would regret leaving the tavern in Willi's care. He never served drinks or collected payment from customers. His skill was drinking on the house and entertaining the guests. And squandering the money. Both Tucher and Willi would be begging her to come back, if Tucher's uncle ever wanted to see another penny from The Stork's Nest. But what if Willi got along fine without her?

"You still have your husband," Herr Tucher said.

"He's not my husband."

He smiled and sat back, surprised, and dismissed her comment with a wave of his hand. He seemed pleased. Most of her neighbors had thought she and Willi had married and she'd never corrected them.

"I have learned over the years to value what others cannot take from me," he said. "I store it here."

He tapped his forehead and put his hand over his heart. Katarina readied herself for a sermon. He could save his pious ramblings. The coach hit a bump in the road and Katarina held onto the white linen cap that Herr Tucher insisted she wear.

"I am talking about knowledge," Herr Tucher said. "I study certain philosophers and write my own philosophies. *Ideas Regarding the Ordered World*, I call my latest work of essays. I also have a volume of my own verse. Would you like to hear some of them? Can you read?"

"A bit," Katarina said, not pleased to have *Ideas Regarding the Ordered World* forced on her when she had real problems to think about. The month ahead of her seemed to stretch out indefinitely.

"How did they raise you out here in the province?" he asked. "I assumed these villages were Protestant even though we are so close to Höchstadt and Bamberg and they are firmly in the grip of the Papists."

Frau Kuni had told Katarina to never discuss religion or beliefs with anyone. Katarina could recite the right prayers if need be, answer questions correctly if challenged and lived a charitable existence so as not to attract unwanted attention. The difference between the Protestants and the Catholics seemed minute to her. Both religions wanted only power as far as she could tell. And both sides would happily tie her atop a bundle of kindling if they knew she got her inspiration from the earth, not the heavens.

"Do you have a bible?" Herr Tucher said. "I have two of Luther's if you would like one."

"Yes, I have a bible. A German one from Luther."

"Then you are a Protestant?

Katarina mumbled and hoped he would change the subject.

"You have been baptized, haven't you?" he said.

Katarina didn't know if she'd been baptized or not. Nobody paid any attention to the children born to the maids on these provincial farms and she was the bastard child of a bastard child. She'd been raised to keep her head down and her eyes to the ground, unless she was alone. Then she was free to watch the clouds and the changing of the seasons and the phases of the moon. Frau Kuni taught her how the years were divided: winters gave way to warmth; blossoms gave way to ripening fruits; budding leaves gave way to herbs that needed gathering; cold, rain, snow and death giving way to new life. Light and dark. Herbs that healed. Fruit that nourished. This was life. There was truth and a rhythm, a reality, a usefulness.

In the cities, people were no longer aware of their roots; torn from their natural conditions, from their true origins. In these artificial communities full of disease and filth, void of trees and nature, worshiping doctrine and rules and rituals in church filled the hole in people's souls. But many men of the churches were seduced by money and power. Katarina saw how these men kept people afraid of damnation, afraid for their souls and afraid for their very lives. Katarina loved living in the city but the constant fear was draining; the fear of someone accusing her of being an unbelieving heathen, an unmarried woman living in sin, a tainted unbaptized thing no better than afterbirth, cap on her head or not.

"We can discuss these things in depth in the next few months," Herr Tucher said. "I intend to use the Estate as my *refugium*. I will be bringing my books, my paintings and my writing things out when I come for good."

"What about your wife? I thought you were married."

"My wife?" He smiled. "She is pregnant and has no need for me. Well, she needs me to conduct my businesses in a respectable fashion and she needs me for her weekly allowance, and now and again to sire a child, but otherwise she cares nothing for art and has no ear when it comes to vigorous verse and witty wisdom. She stifles my creativity. I must say we desist from spending much time with each other."

"Hmpff."

They traveled on through the woods in silence. Katarina pulled off the linen cap and laid it in her lap. Only a virgin could flaunt her bare head but it was far too warm to keep her head covered. She was no longer interested in making a good impression on Herr Tucher. He seemed to take no notice of her now that the coachman slowed the horses to a walk and the path wound and turned. Katarina's thoughts of what he might expect from his life in Sichardtshof and what he expected from her were as unsettling as the sound of the wooden coach creaking in protest as it bumped over tree roots.

The coach began a descent. The trees receded as if the coach had passed through a great gateway and they both looked out the window. The Aisch River valley opened up before them.

"Splendid," Herr Tucher whispered.

The day was clear; the sprawling landscape a masterpiece dotted with tiny villages, smoke rising from chimneys. The hot breeze carried distant hums of life.

"It is not far now. We need to ride beyond those hills. And then we shall see what awaits us. The Old Widow's trustees told me the place has become even more run down after the cold winter."

The coach traveled north along a wide, straight road. After a spell, they turned off the main road and onto a small track dividing the fields of the Edelgraben, a hollow at the base of the low mountain range called Steigerwald. The green hills rolled away as far as the eye could see. Atop the North Hill stood a shock of forest. To the south an indigo shadow in the middle of a field must be where the secret meadow was; an orchard Katarina played in as a child. Her heart rose as they rounded the first bend and a noisy flock of waterfowl flew up from the string of ponds at the deepest point of the hollow. *Himmelsweiher* they were called, Heaven's Ponds, because there was no influx, no source of water except for what the heavens gave: rain. Here they farmed carp.

The coach slowed as they rounded the second bend. Katarina leaned forward and stuck her head out of the window to look for the house. The tiny spruce she remembered was now a thick tree that hid the house from view. The jolt of joy was replaced with misgiving; an icy shiver at the thought of returning home. The coach stopped alongside the tree. She reached through the window, undid the bolt on the outside of the coach door, swung it open and jumped off.

"Is anyone expecting us?" Katarina said.

"Stay where you are, Tanner, I'll only be a moment," Herr Tucher called to the young tanner on the coach box as he opened his door and climbed out.

Katarina noticed who was driving the team of horses. She waved up at him and he smiled. She turned and walked to the wooden fence and lifted the latch from the garden gate. Herr Tucher helped her pull at the stubborn gate. He was more than a head taller than Katarina and had good posture. Together they tugged until the hinge's top anchor bolt pulled out of the moldy, wooden post and the gate sank in the mud. No matter how dry the weather, that mud never dried. He helped her pull the gate up out of the mud and together they wrenched it ajar, enough for them to slip through.

"What has happened here? Have I been gone so long?" Katarina said.

"How rundown indeed," Herr Tucher replied. "More than I was led to believe."

The half-timbered house was built on a stone foundation, the upper two thirds of the house constructed of exposed beams filled with plaster panels. The beams were weatherworn—not so bad, the wood could be stained—but the plaster panels on the east side of the house buckled under the weight of the sinking roof.

"Yes, there is a hole in the roof. And it did not take long to rot the beams, I see. I need to get some men out here to fix that. Otherwise the roof will fall on your head," Herr Tucher said.

"On our heads, you mean?" Katarina said. "Is Frau Kuni still living in there? And the Old Widow?"

"I assume so. I have not yet been inside. That is why I brought you out here."

"Where are the farmhands?"

"Are there farmhands?" Herr Tucher asked.

She frowned at his incessant sarcasm. "When I left there was one old farmhand still living back there." He was so old when Katarina lived here, she'd be surprised if he was still alive.

The outbuildings of the oval farmyard stood silent and dark in the shadows of the evening light. She pointed to the small, crooked house with a narrow, slanted thatched roof that stood beyond the well and the biggest barn.

"There is a workers' house back there by those bramble bushes," she said.

"You can put the workers' house in order, too, for the men I send. But now I must leave and sort out all the formalities of owning the property."

"You're leaving?"

"I must still take care of the documents. The Old Widow's trustees have arranged the transfer of the property now, under the condition she be allowed to live here until she dies."

"You're leaving me here alone in this place with two old women?" Katarina felt as if her feet were stuck in mud. She would never get the traction to leave here again.

"I am spending the next few days in Lonnerstadt with acquaintances," he said. "Then I must settle the property, as I told you. I will send word when I am to return. Please prepare my rooms. Within ten days or so."

Katarina shook her head. "What have they been living on? No animals. It looks like no one has lived here for years."

"Then you have your work cut out for you!" Herr Tucher said and marched towards his coach. "Adieu, *Magd*."

Chapter 4

Ralf jammed the key into the iron lock, turned it and opened Andra-Angela's bedroom door. The window was wide open and white silk curtains that had seen better days hushed in a slight breeze. Ralf wiped the sweat from his forehead with the sleeve of his black monk's robe. He was sure his was the only key to this lock. He had not allowed her to have one. He had not allowed her to leave.

He slammed the window shut. A round, fist-sized pane popped out of its lead fitting and shattered on the floor. He kicked at the glass, stubbed his toe, cursed and pulled the silk curtains from the window. Andra-Angela von Obereierhofen was due to have her illegitimate baby any day now. Her father, Friedrich von Obereierhofen, once adamant that no one was to see his daughter in this condition, seemed to be banding together with her late in the pregnancy, rekindling their strained relationship. Ralf only hoped that when she labored, complications would take care of her and the baby.

He ran back down the bowed stone staircase and stopped in the estate's entrance hall. The once well-kept and proud estate of Upper Eierhofen smelled of mold and sad neglect. The floor of the entrance hall was covered with ash and dried leaves. Cobwebs hung from the rough-hewn sandstone walls. A few of the fist-sized panes of glass that formed the high windows were missing. The oak doors that lead into the great hall were in desperate need of staining. Ralf leaned his weight on the one door, pushed it open and entered.

He rushed to the end of the hall where Friedrich von Obereierhofen sat behind a heavy dark-stained wooden desk in a high-backed chair. A plump, ginger-haired man, Friedrich stared at a dusty wooden chess game, his feminine hands folded over his massive belly. His ancient *Magd* sat across from him with her fingers on a bishop as if she'd held this pose the last century. Ralf had wanted to replace her since he came to Upper Eierhofen a few years back. He would soon have the chance.

"Andra's gone, Herr Friedrich," Ralf said to his master. "I locked her in but she must have a key as well!"

"I let her out, Father Ralf," Friedrich said. "She whined so. It broke my heart to hear the girl. She wanted to go into the garden and collect herbs for the meal. Check out there."

Ralf swallowed an oath. His raging anger should be turned towards accomplishing great deeds, not wasted on this oaf. He prayed for the strength to compose his thoughts and concentrate on his goals. He ran from the great hall, through the entrance hall and bounded out the front doors, down the few front steps into the courtyard. The wooden gate in the sandstone wall surrounding the estate stood firmly latched. A breeze fluttered the fronds on the two exotic potted trees that flanked the wooden gate.

Ralf heard a hoof kick the wooden barn wall. His young stallion was getting impatient. All ready midday and the horse was still in his box. He tried the other stable doors and they were all locked. He ran along the path towards the back garden. A few of Friedrich's hired black-clad soldiers lounged next to the door to the kitchen. Two of their wenches knelt in the herb garden but Andra-Angela was not among them. Ralf had taught Andra-Angela everything she knew about herbs and together they'd cultivated this garden to rival any monastery garden.

Ralf crossed himself at the sight of a large wooden cross at the end of the garden under which Andra-Angela's mother was buried. Friedrich had never recovered from the loss of his wife after she died birthing Andra-Angela and he might very well have to face his daughter's death today. The girl was nowhere to be found.

He pushed past the black-clad thugs into the kitchen. Another wench tended the smoldering fire on the wide, low fireplace. Smoke streamed up the open flue. A few more thugs played cards at the long working table lit by high windows and a single candle. Ralf ignored the men as he grabbed the candle off the table and ducked through the passage to the cellar. A door at the far end of the earthen cellar stood ajar. It led to a tunnel system dug long ago that allowed the inhabitants of Upper and Lower Eierhofen to get off the hilltop and into the forest unnoticed.

He ducked and squeezed through the tight tunnel. The wooden door at the end of the passage came into the candlelight. It had been recently opened judging from the footprints in the mud. Damp always collected by the tunnel opening. The hinges squealed as he opened the door and looked out into the forest. She had been using this tunnel all along.

Rage fueled his mission now. The candle blew out as he reached the cellar, so brisk his pace. He ran through the kitchen, up the stone stairs and into the entrance hall. He burst into the great hall and obviously scared Friedrich and the ancient maid.

"Your daughter is gone," Ralf yelled. "Do you realize what could happen should someone see her? In her condition? What were you thinking?"

Friedrich blubbered and coughed.

"I will not look for her alone," Ralf continued. "I am taking the men. If I meet up with that Protestant heretic…"

"Yes, Father Ralf, do what you must," Friedrich said. "Just bring her back."

"That heretic boy has poisoned her mind! He is only after your estate."

"Calm yourself. It is not as dire as you think. Just bring the girl back and we will remedy the situation after the child is born."

"Where is your honor, master?" Ralf said. "No one can know about the child. The community will shun you."

"I won't be the first to man in the Catholic community to have an illegitimate grandchild. Calm yourself. I have half a mind to allow her to marry Hans-Wolfgang. That way I can assure the estate has a male heir. I have been thinking, Ralf."

"Allow her to marry that Protestant heretic? That you cannot do! They are expecting Andra-Angela at the convent in Bamberg. They have agreed to take the child too."

"I cannot take care of this estate any longer on my own, Ralf."

"But that has all been settled. We cannot renounce our plans. The Jesuit school is to commence in the summer. We have promised the children, the men!"

"Yes, Ralf, but I have been thinking. I would rather see the estate stay in the family. Now that I am to have a grandchild…"

"The Jesuits are counting on this school!" Ralf forced his fists to open.

"If they have one house fewer, the society will not collapse. As if the Catholic faith would not survive with one less Jesuit school. The most important thing now is you are to go find my daughter and bring her back."

Ralf twirled and stomped out of the hall, out of the house and down into the courtyard. The stallion whinnied now, a mirror of Ralf's spiralling impatience. He stormed back out behind the house and into the garden. He heard drunken revelry behind the stone wall. He slipped behind some shrubs that hid a spot in the wall where a man could easily climb over. Four soldiers sat around a crude table. One man snatched three dice off the table and shoved them in his mouth. Six more men reclined in the grass.

"Men! I need five riders. This instant!" Ralf said. "We have work to do!"

One man looked at the next as if none of them wanted to admit they were riders.

"You five! On your feet!" Ralf commanded.

Five grumbling men, each clad in black with black boots and black woolen jackets, stood and climbed over the wall to join Ralf. The men laughed and growled in a mix of Slavish, Italian and German as they walked to the front of the house, into the barn and led the horses out into the courtyard with no sense of urgency.

"Don't waste any time with saddles, men," Ralf said.

Ralf's young dark bay stallion stamped and puffed and pulled against the rope as Ralf tethered him to the barn wall. He bit Ralf on the shoulder. Ralf slammed his open hand against the stallion's sleek neck. It took all of Ralf's strength to hold the stallion's head and slide the bridal over his ears. Another soldier opened the estate gates and joined them; a man with light-brown hair and a spritely face.

"He's a barrel of gun powder, Padre." The man laughed at Ralf. "You sure you can ride him without a saddle?"

"I am sure, Elis, and I will show you I can ride him!"

Ralf could only think of one place to look for Andra-Angela. That meadow he had spied her in so often. How she might have walked that far in her condition baffled him. One after another the men swung up onto their horses and they bolted out of the estate gates. They rushed out through the forest, down the hillside and across the flood plain. Next to the river, they stopped at a spot where they could pick a path across the low water.

The men followed Ralf as he continued through the village and up the hill, along the main road. They turned onto a narrow track in the Edelgraben and rode towards that indigo shadow of shrubs to the south; towards the secret meadow behind the wall of sloe bushes where the herbs grew. A strange orchard, Ralf thought, and the hair on his arms stood up. It was bewitched, a place of curious, pagan happenings. No wonder the girl gravitated here.

They rode around the perimeter once, twice and looked for a way in. The sloe bushes grew dense and thorny. The soldier named Elis dismounted and led his horse around. He ducked down and peeked through the bushes.

"Look harder, Elis," Ralf said.

"What am I looking for?" Elis asked, his German flattened by his Scandinavian accent.

"A way in," Ralf sneered.

Another man whistled like a hawk. He motioned towards the bushes and disappeared as if he passed into another realm. The others dismounted, tethered the horses to some branches, grumbled in their mixture of languages and followed him in one at a time. Elis hung behind until Ralf prodded him into motion.

One of the men who spoke German said, "I found the master's daughter!"

Ralf's heart began to pound. He pushed Elis through the sloe bushes and followed him. There was something incorporeal here, Ralf could feel it, but it was unchaste. Devilish. He crossed himself. Fruit trees stood in rows in the middle of the meadow. The twisted apple trees reminded him of cripples. Herbs grew unrestrained. A strange smell like fermented fruit turned Ralf's stomach.

Andra-Angela lay on the ground under a tree that was just past its bloom. Her legs were stretched out in front of her; her light blue dress and the grass around her stained with blood. Crumpled underneath her head like a pillow lay her costly light blue cloak. She propped her upper body up on her elbows and watched Ralf approach.

"What has happened here?" Ralf asked her, familiar, as if he was her parent.

"Ralf, help me sit up, I am not well," she said.

Ralf knelt at her side. He'd presided over enough childbeds to perform last rights to know what had happened here. She had birthed the baby. Alone? Where was the baby? Andra-Angela looked at him like she could read his mind. Her sort of intelligence was malicious and dangerous and only found in a stained woman. Sly and unforgiving, Andra-Angela preyed on his worldly weaknesses and his thoughts turned impure. Ralf's mother had only looked at him with reverence and tended to his every need, as a woman should.

Andra-Angela played him for a fool. Because he had taken the three oaths of the Jesuits, she would tease him for his oath of celibacy. She would chide him as to why he wouldn't want to be a Protestant and marry like some other priests had done. She would give him suggestive, seductive looks and it would enrage him. Now she was trying all her wicked tricks to command him.

"Help me sit up," Andra-Angela said. "Do you have any water?"

"Yes, Andra," Ralf said and motioned to Elis to bring him his skin.

She drank and pressed the skin back to Ralf's chest. "You may go now."

"I will not be dismissed," Ralf said. "You will come home with me. Your father sent us to bring you and the baby home."

"No I will not come. Not with you," Andra-Angela said.

A man called Andra-Angela's name from beyond the wall of sloe bushes.

"Ralf, go now. Leave me be," she said.

Ralf slid one arm under her bent knees and another around the small of her back and attempted to stand and lift her at the same time. Andra-Anglea straightened her body, fell out of his grasp and rolled onto her side. She summoned strength from somewhere, got onto her hands and knees and began to crawl away.

"Andra!" the man's voice from beyond the bushes cried out again. It was Hans-Wolfgang.

"Help me, Hans-Wolfgang!" Andra yelled to him.

She slumped forward and tried to kneel again like she wanted to run away. She crawled along the sloe bushes towards the sound of Hans-Wolfgang's voice. Ralf would not have any of this. This lewd slut and her bastard child and her heretic lover would not force him to lose the estate he had won for the Jesuits. Friedrich had promised the estate to Ralf. He had agreed to sign the lands over to him. Only then did Andra-Angela begin this ploy to wriggle back into her father's good graces. Ralf stood, walked over to Elis and pulled the sword from Elis's sheath.

Andra-Angela crawled farther still. Hans-Wolfgang's frantic cries fell flat beyond the bushes as he tried to find a way into the meadow.

"One more chance, Andra-Angela von Obereierhofen. Come home with me and do what I say," Ralf commanded.

"Ralf, go home yourself and leave me alone!"

"Your father will be angry."

"No, father will be angry if you can't find me." She stuck her hand through the bushes and tried to stand. "You're only out to save your own skin."

"I'm out to save your soul."

"My soul?" Andra-Angela said. "You're only here to clear me out of the way so you can take over my estate."

"The devil has taken hold of your senses again, child." Ralf stood over Andra-Angela's kneeling form and crossed her, as if he had given her the host.

"You know yourself that the devil is only a fabrication of your evil mind. Hans-Wolfgang and I will marry. I will live in my estate. You are now dismissed!"

"You are wrong, child, that heretic is only out to rob you of everything you have."

"Never, Ralf, never. I will see to it that my child is the heir. You will never see one stone of the estate, God as my witness."

"God is the only witness here," Ralf said and grabbed a handful of Andra-Angela's hair.

Andra's eyes opened wide. Ralf looked over his shoulder as Elis came up next to him.

"Finish this, Padre," Elis said.

Elis grabbed the sword from Ralf's hand. Ralf shied and fell to the side as Elis swung the sword two-handed and swept Andra-Angela's head from her neck. She slumped forward. Elis smiled at his sword, nodding his head at the good fortune he had. Separating a head from a body was no easy task.

Elis pulled up her slumped-over body and threw it backwards. "Where I come from, that's what we do to witches."

Chapter 5

Magd, Herr Tucher called her. Katarina was not his maid.

She watched his coach disappear around the bend. Tanner was in a hurry to get away before night fell. She didn't blame him. The beautiful sky of an hour ago had turned inky black and the wind had come up out of nowhere as if summoned from another world. The brown-leaved branches from a not-so-recent storm were swirling angrily in eddies from the new storm.

She turned back to the Sichardtshof property that appeared abandoned, the chicken coop empty and in disrepair. No sign of life anywhere. The house looked like it was a mountain she was to climb. After their harsh parting, she didn't know what kind of welcome to expect from Frau Kuni. She climbed the few steps to the double front doors, shoved the doors open and heaved as she pushed them closed against the strengthening wind. She pushed her back against the doors and listened.

"Frau Kuni?" she called.

She thought she heard someone holler beyond the South Hill. The sound echoed through the hollow. It must be the wind, she thought. Turning to have a look around, her ears filled with the familiar sounds of a country storm—winds whipping through the spruce tree, loose hinges squealing from untethered windows. While eerie, it was better than the disturbing din she could never escape in bustling Nuremberg.

Katarina seemed to be truly alone. Herr Tucher and Tanner wouldn't be back for ten days. She had not yet seen Frau Kuni, if Frau Kuni was even still alive. Katarina's heart pounded and her courage begged to be heard. She could slip away and nobody would even notice. Yes, it was foolish for a woman to travel by herself but villages were situated all along the Aisch River. To the south she could reach Neustadt in a day. She could work in any mill or tavern and she could work hard. Even Würzburg was only a few days' march away.

She opened her wooden box and pulled out that moth-eaten blanket. She grabbed a few things she deemed important and laid them in a compact fashion onto the fabric: her pamphlets, some bundles of healing herbs, a blunt knife, a flint stone, the only other dress she owned, her cloak. She tied the bundle tight and made a strap with the leather cord.

Even more foolish was to begin her journey at the end of the day and in a gathering storm no less. She straightened her shoulders, heeded that little brave voice and slung the bundle over her back. This was her chance to escape and it might be the only chance she would ever get.

She pushed her way out of the front doors, through the garden gate and started along the track. The roar of the wind was accompanied by a throbbing, a pounding, maybe the racing of her heart? Or was that thundering hooves? No, she could see it now through the dust whipped up by the wind. One horse at a frenzied speed. She forced herself back inside the gate and crouched behind the fence. A horse with rider appeared, racing up the path towards the house. They neared the fence. Too fast. Towards her hiding place. She dove to the side, fell on her knees and rolled onto her back. The horse jumped over the fence. The rider pulled the horse around. The horse reared. The rider saw Katarina laying there, jumped down from the sorrel stallion and advanced, drawing his sword.

"You, *Magd*, on your feet! I have a task for you," the rider said, feet braced in a fighter's stance, sword pointed at her throat.

The wind caught the hem of his brown rider's cloak, exposed his armless leather jerkin and his strong, stocky form. His leather trousers were oily and stained. His brow and short-cropped dark-blond hair were wet with sweat.

Katarina stared at this wild man, afraid to move. He panted as if he had run a long distance. The sword sagged in his grip as he struggled to pull a package wrapped in an ornate, light-blue fabric from under his riding cloak. Something inside writhed. He reached towards Katarina. Her arm snapped up instinctively to shield her face and she heard her own breath huff in short, quiet gasps, like a wounded lamb.

"Stand up!"

He grabbed Katarina's arm and wrenched her up onto her feet.

With the same hand he tried again to free the parcel from under his cloak. Allowing the sword to droop in his grasp, he thrust the parcel with both hands to her chest. It smelled of blood.

"Open it!" he demanded.

Katarina undid the blue ribbons and unrolled the bloody fabric. A tiny finger appeared and a little nose. A wisp of white hair. A strange smell: the mixture of life and death. She touched its cheek. It was still and unmoving. But it was warm and obviously alive. Trembling, Katarina dared not meet his gaze again. He was still speaking, his words garbled rantings in the wind. The blood pumped in Katarina's ears. More muffled words. The man called himself Hans-Wolfgang. The baby's mother was dead. All she understood was some fantastic story about witches and executions. He even said he saw the great seer Sybilla Weiss!

"She told me to bring the baby to the *Magd* at Sichardtshof!" Hans-Wolfgang said.

"I am not the maid," Katarina said.

"Sybilla Weiss was there. She sent me and my horse in the direction of your farm. She told me you would take the baby."

"She is only a legend!" Katarina screamed. "No one has ever seen her."

He allowed the sword to roll in his hand, agilely and artistically. Katarina backed up as the blade swung dangerously close to her face. He gripped the hilt with both hands and pointed the sword to her chest.

"Listen to me!"

Katarina flinched and stared at him like an obedient daughter. He looked familiar. He was nearly the same age as she was.

"Listen to me! You see this child? If they find the child, they will kill her. If they find me with this child, they will kill me. They've already killed her mother. Sybilla saw them do it. But they won't kill you. I'll see to it. But you must swear to care for the child as your own. Never tell a soul where she came from or I will slit your throat."

"Who killed the baby's mother?"

"I'm not sure myself. But the baby's family is behind this. Of that I am sure."

Katarina took a step back.

"Swear on your own life that you will care for her!"

Katarina's head shook slowly from side to side. She refused to believe what he was demanding of her. To accept and raise this baby as her own illegitimate child was like a *Todesurteil*. This was her sentence to death. She could just as well confess she had a pact with the devil as to admitting she was unmarried with child. She would not be accepted into any village and she'd be shunned no matter where she went. Willi would never believe this story and he'd never take her back. What would Herr Tucher do with her?

"Swear you will take her!" he shouted. "Swear to me!"

What choice did she have?

"I swear," she whispered and lowered her head.

He backed up and lowered his sword. He reached in his pocket and handed Katarina something. "Take this ring. It belonged to her mother. The child's name is Isabeau."

Katarina took the ring and turned it around in her fingers; a simple silver band stamped with a worn coat of arms. When she looked up again, Hans-Wolfgang had taken the reins and, with one fluid movement, mounted the horse. The horse protested and danced on the spot. He kicked the horse's flanks. They turned a lap around the farmyard to gain speed, jumped the fence and rode off into the stormy night.

Katarina moved slowly to the house, let herself fall onto the landing outside the double front doors, the bundled baby on her lap, its head cradled in her hand. She tugged at the leather cord that bound her hair so tightly against her scalp. Her head hurt as her hair fell heavy around her neck. She took the leather pouch that hung around her neck from under her dress and dropped the ring in with the wrapped coins and became aware suddenly that the wind had died down.

The baby's face was barely visible in the dark. Katarina moved the costly, light-blue fabric aside and wished for a lantern. She leaned over trying to see the unmoving child. Taking the corner of her dirty skirt, she wiped the tears and sand out of the baby's eyes.

Something moved in the trees. Katarina's head shot up, eyes flicking from side-to-side. She grabbed the baby and jumped up, about to push the doors open and look for Frau Kuni. Next to the fence, a dark hump caught her eye. Her bundled belongings! She walked over and retrieved the bundle.

Now the severity of the situation became clear. Alone she could move freely, work where she wanted, caring only for herself. But with this child, she was condemned. Nobody would believe this story. No village would allow her refuge. She had no chance of survival.

The second time today, an overwhelming rush of warmth gripped her as her body readied itself to bolt. An involuntary resolution possessed her like a demon. She would end this madness now. When she was a girl, she would help the farmhands do this to sick lambs: end their misery. And this baby would die anyway. Heartbreaking. This was a tragic child, yes, but Katarina couldn't feed or care for it either. Who would know if it died? And she would be gone before anyone could find her.

She squinted through the darkness in what she remembered to be the direction of the well. No one would be the wiser. She could drown the child, bury it and she would be on her way tonight.

The sound of wood creaking in the house made her swallow hard. It felt like the blood drained from her face. She threw her bundled belongings onto the ground, slumped with the baby like a stealing thief and scurried towards the barn before her conscience could talk her out of the deed. She would end this now. She tripped over tangled branches and regained her balance.

"Who's there?" a gentle voice said out of the darkness.

Katarina looked around, startled and gasping for breath.

Carrying a hanging clay lantern and a small pitcher, Frau Kuni took stiff, careful steps through the low brush from behind the barn. She must have been fetching water from the well.

"Katarina, it's you! What in the devil's name are you doing back here?" Frau Kuni set the pitcher on a tree stump and moved towards her.

"What are you doing back here?" Katarina said.

Her hands tightened around the bundled baby. The baby emitted a peculiar tone.

"Katarina, what have you got there?" Frau Kuni said. "Let me see."

Frau Kuni held her lantern up and closed her eyes against the acrid smoke from burning animal fat. She leaned in before Katarina could object and caressed the baby's cheek. The baby opened its mouth, awaiting a nipple. Katarina's face was burning, her jaw clenched. Frau Kuni focused her eyes on Katarina's face, reading her crazed expression in the lantern's weak glow.

"What are you doing, child? Whose baby is this?"

"Frau Kuni just now a man came by and told me to take care of this baby because its mother is dead and he can't be seen with the child he and the baby are in danger he told me if I fail he will kill me!" Katarina shouted at her. "You must have seen him if you were out here!"

"Oh, Katarina, don't make up such stories," she said. "Is this child from that man Prutt? Or do you have another lover?" She smiled knowingly. "Oh! Is this why you had to leave the city?"

"No, I..." Katarina began. She knew how unbelievable this story sounded.

Frau Kuni's disapproving face twisted into a devilish mask in the flickering lamplight. Katarina fought the urge to drop the baby and run away. She gritted her teeth together and held the baby out towards Frau Kuni. The baby made a weak grunt and contracted inside itself. Something warm landed on Katarina's bare foot. Frau Kuni directed the lamplight down. A slimy black mass slid off Katarina's foot.

"*Säuglingspech*," Frau Kuni said. "That's a newborn's stool. You don't look like you just gave birth, girl."

"It's not my baby," Katarina said. "Didn't you see..."

The baby made weak, cranky moans.

"We need to get you inside so you can nurse your baby," Frau Kuni said.

"It's not my..."

"No matter." Frau Kuni walked towards the house. "Let's get you inside."

Katarina hung her head and followed her grandmother.

Chapter 6

Katarina woke the next morning in the tiny alcove next to the kitchen, where she had slept as a child. The moldy smell of the damp straw mattress stung in her nose. Her clothes and hair smelled of mold, too. The kitchen was filthy. No fire burned and it was cold. She tried to brush the moldy smell from her clothes, knowing it was fruitless.

The cold stone floor chilled her bare feet as she walked through the kitchen and opened the door to the adjoining low-vaulted stable. Two chickens clucked and a goat bleated a plea for feeding. So here were the animals she didn't see last night. The air flowed fresh through the openings in the sandstone wall. She walked across the straw-strewn stable floor to the door that led to the paddock, opened the door and breathed in the clean spring-morning breeze.

Frau Kuni hobbled towards the paddock. She was coming back from the well, carrying a pitcher of water. The last four years had aged her considerably. Her hair was now completely white, the thin strands braided and fastened to the back of her head. Years of farm work had bent her back; years of hunger had wasted her away.

"Where is the baby?" Frau Kuni said.

Katarina frowned at her. "It must be in its basket."

She ducked back into the alcove and reached her hand into the basket where the baby slept. The baby was warm but lethargic. Katarina pulled it out of the basket, laid it on the straw sack mattress and undid the cocoon-like swaddling clothes.

"What are you doing?" Frau Kuni shouted behind her.

"I may have no experience with children, but I assume it is wet and needs to be changed."

"Give her to me," she said. "Milk the goat and get a fire going."

"With what? You have no wood stored."

"Go find some," Frau Kuni said. "That's what I have to do."

Katarina grabbed a basket and walked towards the barn. The unused hinges squealed as she opened the door. She scoured the earthen floor for some bits of wood. Wood chips and old rotted logs lay under a moldy sack, enough to get a fire going. She piled the bits of wood into her basket and brought it back to the kitchen.

"Do you have a fire going upstairs? Embers maybe?"

"No, there's a flint stone by the fireplace. Use a knife."

Katarina scraped a knife along the flint stone and as sparks ignited, the old straw glowed pathetically. She nursed the smoking straw until it produced a real flame. When she felt she could leave the burning to its own devices, she milked the goat and brought the milk into the kitchen to heat.

"And how are we supposed to feed it?" Katarina asked.

"I found this bottle last night." Frau Kuni held up a small ceramic flask with a thin neck. "I used this when your mother dumped you on me." She snorted and shook her head. "After you hid in that alcove last night, I stretched a bit of cloth over the opening and let your baby suck on the cloth. I thickened the milk with flour and egg so the milk wouldn't flow too fast. That's what I did with you and it didn't seem to harm you at all."

"It's not my baby," Katarina said.

Frau Kuni took the baby and went out of the kitchen and up the steps to the floor above. The floorboards creaked overhead as Frau Kuni walked across her room. Katarina sat on the low stool next to the smoldering fire, added some egg to the milk to thicken and prepared the bottle like Frau Kuni told her; a bit of cloth over the narrow opening, secured with twine.

Frau Kuni came back into the kitchen with the swaddled baby. It squirmed inside and mewed like an impatient, hungry kitten. She handed the baby to Katarina, who brought the bottle to its mouth. It accepted the hard opening of the bottle and suckled on the cloth quite happily.

Sitting on the stool by the fireplace, listening to the feeding baby, Katarina looked around at the state of the kitchen. This was once the beating heart of the farm. It was the center of her childhood. How she wished she could still feel the warmth of the crackling fire, hear the clanging of the iron lid on the heavy pot hanging under the open flue and the lowing of the cows in the stable. But the comforting smells of stewing meat with vegetable root were replaced by stale wine and damp. In spite of the smoldering embers and the doors open to the May morning, the stone walls and floor radiated a chill. A thick, sooty dust settled on every surface and the table was smeared with some animal's blood, flies hanging lazily over the worktop.

Frau Kuni's sharp voice sliced through her memory. "You can collect wood today. Then check the elder bushes up the North Hill and see how far along the blossoms are. It's been warm and you may be able to collect some the next few days. You have to bring the Old Widow something to eat and then you must..."

Katarina turned away and looked at the baby. She had never known her mother. Yes, she ran away. She dumped Katarina on this woman who had no desire to care for her. And now this child was left alone with someone— Katarina—who didn't want to care for it either. Why wouldn't its father even keep it?

"Are you listening to me?" Frau Kuni barked. "Now you know how it feels to have to care for a child!"

"I'll treat her better than you treated me," Katarina said under her breath.

"What did you say?"

"I'm eternally grateful, Frau Kuni!"

Outside in the paddock, Katarina straightened her aching back. She loaded the last of the split logs onto the top of the woodpile she'd been stacking all afternoon. Frau Kuni called from in the kitchen. Katarina cursed under her breath. The shadows grew longer and she still had so much work. She threw the last of the wood into a basket.

"Katarina, where are you? The baby is hungry. Take her so I can go to bed."

She darted back in from the paddock carrying the basket full of firewood, stomping her feet, hoping Frau Kuni noticed she was slowly losing her temper. In the low-vaulted stable, the two chickens clucked in protest. The baby's cries echoed off the stone walls of the kitchen. Even though the doors from the kitchen to the stable and to the paddock outside were open all day, the warm breeze could not be tempted to pervade the dark, dank room.

"I haven't finished my chores yet," Katarina said. "Give me some more time. You could help me, you know."

"Why did you remove the baby's swaddling clothes?" Frau Kuni said. "I had her snug and quiet. Now I've wrapped her back up, she still won't stop crying."

"Exactly. The child is crying because you bound it up in that cocoon again."

"If I must have the child all day, I will care for her how I see fit!"

"Give it something to eat, then," Katarina said.

Katarina rushed back out to the paddock and returned with a basket full of elder blossoms she'd collected earlier. The kitchen filled with the penetrating, fruity-floral aroma. Busying herself with laying the blossoms out in flat baskets along the back wall behind the fire, she breathed in the heady perfume. The fire glowed low with enough heat to dry the blossoms so they could store them. In a small ceramic pot resting on another tripod over the embers, Katarina stirred the honey dissolving in water. She took a ceramic pot down from the shelf, cleaned it, put a few handfuls of blossoms in and poured some honey water over them.

"You can finish that in the morning. I am tired. Take this child!" Frau Kuni said.

With the back of her hand, Katarina brushed loose strands of hair out of her face. Her fingers were covered with sticky, yellow pollen. "Remember you used to say, 'When you see the elder tree, tip your hat and get on your knee?' And, 'We are to be grateful to God for such gifts, like the elder blossom'?"

The baby's cries steadily increased in pitch. "Katarina..."

"I was careful not to let anything metal touch the blossoms, like you taught me. I broke them off with my fingers, not a knife. The smell is making me giddy!"

"Take the baby!"

Katarina felt her face flush. "For the love of God, can't you see I need to finish this now? This was one of your orders today, remember? The blossoms will be ruined in the morning. Take off its swathing and put it in that basket. I'll feed it when I'm done here."

"Maybe it's time for you to face responsibility for what you've done! Other women have a whole brood by the time they are your age."

"Hand me another one of those ceramic pots. Can you get the lids down from that shelf, too? They're filthy. Please wipe them off. Better yet, wipe the pots out and fill them with these blossoms. I'll pour the honey water over them to make some syrup. Then we can actually drink that horrible sour wine from Herr Tucher with the syrup."

Frau Kuni, still holding the baby, handed Katarina a ceramic pot with her free hand. "You're not listening to me! You didn't have to go to the city. Never sent word. We wondered what happened to you. Last fall, Herr Tucher said that man Prutt never married you. You lived with him like a whore."

"I thought we had more of these ceramic pots with lids. I have some *Korn*. I can make us some elder schnapps with it. Isn't it funny, we have hardly anything to eat, but plenty of wine and schnapps?"

"That's the problem with you. Can't accept your position in life. You'll never understand. You could have moved to my sister's house. Married her neighbor. But, no. Not Katarina. You're just like your mother."

Something in Katarina's ears popped. She threw the pot she held against the wall. Ceramic shards rang out and skidded across the stone floor.

"I should have married that ancient old man?" Katarina's head jerked.

The baby wailed.

"He had acreage," Frau Kuni said. "And he's dead now, anyway. And, you might have inherited his farm. What has that Prutt given to you?"

"We were going to marry," Katarina said, barely audible over the screeching baby.

"Why didn't you demand he marry you? You never had any trouble talking back to me."

"He wanted to wait. He said it was because of his mother. I never knew why."

Katarina threw a log onto the hearth will such vehemence that a clump of glowing embers flew onto the stone floor. The dust on the floor smoked and smoldered. Katarina brushed the embers onto the ash shovel and dumped them onto the fire.

"Probably because you speak your mind and you don't know your place," Frau Kuni said. "That's not good for a woman your age."

Katarina yelled over the baby's cries. "I did everything they told me to! I learned to weave, probably too well. My fabrics were top quality. They couldn't bear to hear that from our customers. And after she died, he changed. Drove my customers away. Got involved in that tavern. Drinking, staying out all hours of the night."

"So you found a lover and had a child."

"No, I slogged away night after night like a work horse to help him build up that tavern. It was fast money compared to textiles."

"Then you found a lover and had his child."

Katarina jumped up, wrenched the sobbing baby from Frau Kuni's grasp and held her next to her own face. "Look here! Look at the two of us! The baby is fair, with white wisps of hair and her strange grey eyes will turn blue, you said. I am red haired, dark eyed with sallow skin! You always complain that I'm just like my mother. This baby is not mine!"

Frau Kuni turned to leave and over her shoulder she said, "The baby is your responsibility. For once, finish a task you started."

Katarina waited until the old woman left the kitchen to tend the sobbing baby. She unwrapped the swaddling clothes and laid her in her basket. Isabeau relaxed, breathed deep and even. Katarina grabbed a small pot, sneaked out of the kitchen and into the stable to milk the goat.

Frau Kuni had probably swaddled Katarina, too. She wondered if that was the reason for the trapped feeling she often had. She would trade her soul for her freedom if she could. How long would she last, snared here like a pigeon, caged, wings clipped? Was she going to bow down now like she had always done and let others decide her fate? Maybe that was the reason her mother had to leave, too. She pulled on the goat's teat, who objected by brushing Katarina's arm with her hind leg. The goat tossed her head and the chain around her neck clanked against the stone floor.

"We are much the same, you and I," Katarina said to the goat.

Maybe she could let the goat out into the paddock tomorrow. Frau Kuni had been hiding the goat and the two old chickens in the stable next to the kitchen for quite some time now, because of the wolves. Wolves are so populous, they would come right into the farmyard, even in broad daylight. She latched the paddock door and went into the kitchen.

Katarina set the pot of milk on the tripod over the embers. While the milk warmed, she pulled the small wooden box with her belongings out from the corner. The box smelled like the house on Tannery Row. She opened her traveling bundle and laid those things on the floor next to it. Amid a few other pamphlets and bundles of herbs, she found an ample swatch of fabric. She had seen women in the fields who secured a baby to their back, allowing the mother to work. Kneeling now, she crossed the fabric around her shoulders and secured it behind her waist, making a sort of sling. That way, during the day while she worked, she wouldn't have to leave the baby, swaddled, in that dark room. Frau Kuni reasoned she did this to keep the baby from hurting herself. She also said the baby would get sick if they took her outside. Katarina had never cared for a child before, nor had she grown up with other children. But one thing she knew: that woman could never know what was best. She was a fool.

Frau Kuni wanted Katarina to collect snails tomorrow morning down by the river. The baby could lie on a blanket in the grass. Maybe she could walk up to that secret meadow she played in as a child. Herbs and fruit trees grew there and in the fall, an assortment of mushrooms. Katarina would take the baby with her. She allowed herself a moment to savor the thought.

The smell of milk boiling brought Katarina back to the task at hand. She added an egg to thicken and bound a morsel in a sucking rag. She gave the sucking rag a dip in elder blossom tea with honey, for taste, and lifted the baby up out of the basket like she was made of porcelain. Her head flopped to the side and Katarina struggled to support her head and not drop her by doing so. She took her out onto the front step, slid her hand behind her head, sat down and cradled the baby in her lap. These balmy evenings before the summer solstice could go on forever as far as Katarina was concerned. A blackbird sat on the barn's roof, singing a lonely bed-time melody. Clouds of gnats swarmed in the slanting sun's warm rays.

Isabeau suckled contentedly on the sucking rag and her eyelids became heavy. The blackbird sang on as the baby fell asleep. Katarina held her tight, stood and slipped back into the kitchen. She put her in her basket and set it in the alcove, the space really intended for storing firewood. The little alcove stayed cool in the summer and was close to the fire in the winter. She went into the kitchen and opened a bottle of that horrible sour wine and added some elder blossom syrup she had made today. At this rate there would be none for the winter.

Chapter 7

The messenger bowed and took his leave. Katarina leaned against the door jamb and watched him mount his heavy brown horse and trot off down the track. She opened the letter sealed with a waxy 'T' and read the fine-flowing script. Herr Tucher would be coming in two days' time.

Eight days she had woken up here at Sichardtshof. She'd made a mark on the wall of her alcove each morning with a charred twig. Herr Tucher said he'd return in ten days. That meant she had to get the Old Widow Hansen out of that room today and prepare it for him.

When Katarina went in yesterday to start moving the Old Widow's things, she wailed and was having nothing to do with any sort of upheaval. After a long, warm march this morning, Katarina had found some valerian root along the roadside by the forest on the North Hill. She crushed it and soaked it in *Korn*, mixing in some elder syrup for taste. Valerian should calm the Old Widow down enough to move her. What else was Katarina to do? Drag the limp yet very vocal woman down the steps?

She pushed the creaky door open to Old Widow Hansen's dark, musty room. The smell of sick, decaying flesh nauseated her. She set the baby basket in the corner on the floor, pushed the two tiny windows open and turned to look at the old woman, droopy and white on the bed, the morning sun illuminating her motionless face. At first, Katarina thought the woman was dead. She felt the Old Widow's forehead and neck and the woman opened her eyes. Katarina shuddered, remembering the last months of old Frau Prutt's life.

The Old Widow blinked and she spoke weakly and dry lipped. "Maria, is that you? Get me some water, dear, I'm so thirsty."

"It's me, Katarina. I'm Maria's daughter. I've told you this before." She tried to help the Old Widow sit up but she sunk back onto her pillow. "We need to move you out of this room, Frau

Hansen. We have a new master."

"This is my farm. This is my room."

Katarina sighed. "I have some tea and a few eggs for you."

"Get me some bread, Maria. I want bread and butter."

"I'll go make some bread once we have you in your new room," Katarina lied.

"Maria, I'm cold, close the window."

"Frau Hansen, it's me, Katarina. And we need some air in here. It's a wonder you don't suffocate."

"Maria, why do you always have to argue with me? You are so difficult. I say it all the time: you'll come to no good end."

The Old Widow wrenched her limp frame back and forth, the bed creaking under her weight, until she managed to sit up alone. Katarina held out the cup. She grasped it with two hands and drank some tea. Her eyes widened in approval when she tasted the elder blossoms. Isabeau gurgled and moved in the basket. She probably smelled the cooked egg Katarina peeled. That child was insatiable.

"Little Katarina is waking up, dear," the Old Widow said.

"Her name is Isabeau. I'm Katarina!"

"Where's Kuni? Kunigunda!" she yelled. She seemed frightened and confused.

Katarina went to the door and yelled for Frau Kuni, too. "Come up here and talk to this old woman. I need help moving her."

Frau Kuni moved gingerly into the room, as if her knees pained her, still clad in her night dress. She gave Katarina a sidelong, disapproving glance. Katarina sneered and turned away. Why did she feel guilty? This wasn't her idea. None of this was, for that matter.

"I'll get some water and you can clean her up," Frau Kuni said and left the room.

"Widow Hansen, I have your medicine."

Katarina sat on the bed next to her, holding the small bowl of valerian tincture. She spooned some of the liquid into her mouth and the Old Widow took it obligingly.

"One more. That's right, you'll feel better in a moment, I promise. One more spoonful."

Katarina stood and set the small bowl on the chest of drawers and turned back to the old woman. She exhaled, collapsed and drooled out the side of her mouth. Panicking, Katarina grabbed the woman by the shoulders and tried to straighten her up. She slumped forward again like an under-stuffed sack of straw.

"What have you done?" Frau Kuni hollered, rushing in from the doorway.

"She's just sleeping," Katarina said.

Frau Kuni shook the Old Widow. "Oh Lord, the woman is dead!"

Katarina's heart raced. She laid the old woman on her back and arranged her in a peaceful position.

"See?" Katarina said. "She's breathing."

Frau Kuni slapped the widow's cheek. "If you've hurt her, you will be one very sorry girl."

"Let me give her some water," Katarina said.

"Leave the poor woman alone!" Frau Kuni yelled. "Get out of this room! You come here after all this time and try to rearrange everything to fit your scheme. I don't know what you're after, but I will not stand by and watch you ruin everything!"

Katarina grabbed the baby, stomped down into the kitchen and tied her into the sling. Her head flopped to the side so Katarina stuffed a balled-up swatch of cloth alongside her head for support. She stomped out of the kitchen, through the paddock and set off, pulling a light handcart behind her.

"You're out to kill that child, too!" Frau Kuni yelled out the window. "You can't schlep her around like that."

Walking would clear Katarina's head, order her thoughts, help her let off some steam. When she was a child, she often fled to the secret meadow to collect herbs or fruit. Up the bank from the road, to the south of the village called Mailach, the meadow was completely hidden from view by a thick wall of sloe bushes. She found a break in the thorny bushes, ducked down and passed through the opening.

An odd assortment of straggly, lichenous apple and plum trees stood in neat rows in the middle of the meadow amid trim, soft grass imbued with the smell of fermenting fruit. Frau Kuni said the trees were planted by Roman soldiers who brought all these trees and herbs up from Italy years ago. It's a wonder they grew here at all but frost never seemed to touch this protected sanctuary. Herbs grew wild, spreading their seeds at random. Chamomile, red clover, yarrow, hyssop—Katarina walked among the wild plants and named them, stopping to smell the peppermint. Telltale signs that deer frequented this hiding place were evident; trails through the high grass, greenery flattened where they bedded, selected spots where they deposited their droppings.

Katarina untied the baby from her front, laid her on the warm, dry grass next to an apple tree and undid the makeshift diaper of cloth and a bit of sheepskin. A warm breeze carried the smell of elder blossoms. Goat's milk had filled out Isabeau's now-plump cheeks and she'd taken to sucking her finger. Her eyes were still an other-worldly grey and she looked off into the distance as if she were remembering another time, another life.

Katarina tried to forget the tone of Frau Kuni's voice. Even in the stillness of the meadow—her sanctuary—she could hear her accusing words ranting on: *You don't know your place. You'll never understand. You're not listening to me!* She lay back and covered her eyes with the baby's sling. It felt so good to just let go.

As she opened her eyes again, she sat up with a start. The shadows had grown long and there was a chill in the air. They had fallen asleep and the afternoon had passed! A herd of petite roe deer fed in the early evening shadows of the trees. Katarina and Isabeau had been lying so still and quiet the deer hadn't seen the two. Katarina hurriedly tied the diaper around the chilled baby and secured her to in the sling. Isabeau laid her head on Katarina's chest and suckled her finger.

The deer heads shot up simultaneously as Katarina stood. But they were not interested in her. Katarina followed the deer's gaze towards the trees. In the woods, something heavier moved with slow footfalls. Katarina feared a visit from a wild boar but, hardly visible in the woods, a man clad in brown appeared on horseback. He looked familiar and she knew where she'd seen Hans-Wolfgang before. As children, she had seen him hunting with his father in the woods.

Katarina met Hans-Wolfgang's gaze, determined not to act afraid. She waited straight and still. He drew his bow, took aim and let the arrow fly. The herd of deer dispersed at the sound of the whizzing arrow. He strung a second arrow and pointed it at Katarina. She raised her chin, daring him to shoot her. She slowly turned her back on him.

"You shouldn't come here," he said, approaching.

Katarina held the child tight and made her way towards the spot where she'd entered through the sloe bushes. The entranceway was no longer open. It was as if the bushes had grown shut after she had entered. She moved around the periphery and searched for another way out.

"It's not safe here." Hans-Wolfgang stood right behind her. "This is where she died."

Katarina stopped. "I used to come here as a child."

"This place has been desecrated," he said. "I'll help you find the way out."

Hans-Wolfgang pointed to an opening. "There, that's where I came in," he said. "Follow me. You can get through there."

Katarina stopped before she ducked through the hole in the sloe. "May I ask how long you need my services? You know, I won't be here much longer. What are you going to do when I go back to the city? I'm only here until the master is done with me."

"Sybilla Weiss sent me to you. You will raise Isabeau."

"Firstly, Sybilla doesn't really exist," Katarina said. "And second: I am not going to raise this child for years to come."

"I have seen her. And she did not randomly choose you to care for Isabeau. You are destined to teach her what she needs to know."

Hans-Wolfgang pulled Katarina through the sloe bushes and out of the meadow. "Her grave has moved away from the churchyard wall. Do you know what that means?"

Katarina shook her head.

"You must not be seen out here alone with the baby," Hans-Wolfgang said. "I will walk you partway home and tell you the proper story.

"Behind Lonnerstadt is the old Oak Forest. There between Siebenmorgen and Thonbruck is the spot where once a castle stood in Wolf's Hollow. Its well had the best water and its landlady was the well-known sage, Sybilla Weiss.

"Sybilla Weiss foretold many things. She said that one day women will wear trousers like men. She said that one day, monsters made of iron will roam the earth and wagons will propel themselves across the land without beasts of burden. A great war will destroy what we know as Franconia.

"When she died she wanted her body to be put into a coffin and strapped to a donkey's back. The donkey would carry her up the hill called Lauberberg to the Antonikapelle, a chapel above the Aisch flood plain, where she should be buried next to the churchyard wall. The mound marking her grave should always touch the wall. If at any time, the mound should erode away from the wall, Judgement Day would be at hand.

"Sybilla died one day. The men of Lonnerstadt bound her coffin to a donkey's back. The donkey carried her body up the Lauberberg. He stopped in the middle of the river and had to be prodded to continue on. The donkey did move on and finally stopped up at the chapel. At that very spot she was buried."

Hans-Wolfgang stopped walking. They stood looking down the South Hill at Sichardtshof. He grabbed Katarina by the shoulders and turned her to face him.

"The men have always tried to insure that the mound touches the churchyard wall," Hans-Wolfgang said. "They had even rebuilt the wall so that it actually stood on top of her grave. But to no avail. The wall is now so far away from her grave that a rider can easily ride around it. Judgement Day is at hand."

Chapter 8

Sebald Tucher XI von Simmelsdorf und Sichardtshof took a deep breath. The familiar smell of old books forced him to crack a painful smile. Dull pain roused him as he stretched his limbs. Eyes closed, he began a slow inventory from top to bottom, starting with his face. His fingers moved in the direction of the throbbing ache in his head. He tenderly touched the welt on his forehead and the scrapes on his cheek. His nose hurt but wiggling it proved it to be unbroken. His lip was split. Again he inhaled the scents of the library at the end of the wing in his family's Nuremberg manor, the wing he shared with his wife. She had begun storing her old clothes in this room and it was only termed "the library" because here he was allowed to keep reference books and his writing things.

The thought of the wife made him cringe. The respectable Frau Tucher scoffed at his books, what she called silly writings and unorthodox opinions. His views would only get him into trouble, she said. No, his views would get *them* into trouble. He wondered if she saw him when he came home last night and if she had him put in this room. He thought not. She was too immersed in her pregnancy to pay attention to him.

Cautiously he moved his shoulders. No damage there. His fingers moved now towards his upper arm; a slash in his shirt and his skin caked with blood. Knife cut. The slightest movements caused the scrapes all along his backbone to sting. He stretched his legs and dried blood tightened around his knees. His head drummed when he sat up so he let himself fall back onto the settee and again closed his eyes.

The next step of the inventory was to piece together the day before. He remembered taking leave of his counterparts in Lonnerstadt after delicious days of drawing up official-looking papers, exchanging quirky quips and drinking dry wine. The yesterday had promised to be clear and crisp. After Tanner woke him, the two of them hoped to get an early start towards Nuremberg. Herr

Tucher truly felt he was beginning a new facet in his life. After dwelling his whole life in this great city, he would become a country nobleman, or so he would feel. Noble, that is.

Those were the same counterparts who had urged him to buy the quaint country dwelling called Sichardtshof in the first place. The idea allowed him to rest no more until he had the property in his possession. So, today, on this great day, he would uproot his tradition-rich existence and prepare to move his most personal belongings, that is, his writings and art collection, out to the farm. But first he must get off this settee.

Country estates were becoming quite the fashion. But the farm was no *Schloß*, a castle, as his counterparts liked to call theirs. The term *Schloß* only meant it was a building one could lock. The term was used loosely by other contemporaries for their country dwellings they would like to refer to as their castles. Herr Tucher considered himself a bit more humble. He liked to have both feet on the ground, his shirt sleeves rolled up and himself thrown into the thick of it.

Yesterday, after Tanner hitched the horses and a meager breakfast with the counterparts in Lonnerstadt, they embarked immediately for the city, determined to make good time. They were eager to get to the city, retrieve their things and return to Sichardtshof. Herr Tucher mulled over the new beginning, hoping he had not overburdened dear Katarina. She looked like a lost child on the journey but in the same instant she would breathe fire like a miniature dragon, strands of russet hair dangling in front of her glaring black eyes. When he thought about it, and he did a lot, he decided it was this maddening juxtaposition that he found so provocative.

His proposed life in Sichardtshof was shaping up nicely. Tanner had agreed to accompany Tucher, leave his life on the Tannery Row, and Tanner's wife and son Falk would join them later. Herr Tucher wanted to hunt. He himself could skin and preserve meats. Tanner, of course, would tan the hides. He would also herd and shear the sheep. Bright boy and strong, too. They would also gather up the Knecht, who was out in the Tucher family stables here at the Nuremberg manor. Dirty man, but that was what he was needed for. He'd lost an eye but he seemed fit enough for the journey.

Late yesterday afternoon, after a bumpy ride, Herr Tucher and Tanner finally approached the Neutor, the massive round tower at the gate in the northwestern section of Nuremberg. They were admitted without ado. Herr Tucher wanted to spend as little time as possible in the city home and remove his things before his pregnant wife caught wind of his presence.

Tanner had steered the coach along the city wall. Herr Tucher strained his neck to watch the Imperial Castle built up on the sandstone outcropping pass by the left side. They approached the Webersplatz and the Seven Rows of weaver's houses where Prutt had lived as a child. Around the corner stood the Tucher family's city dwelling. Tanner alighted from his coach box and was greeted by two *Knechte* who opened the gates to the courtyard. Tanner climbed back onto his coach box and drove the coach toward the stables.

"Sir, if we get fresh horses, we can be back to the country before it gets dark," Tanner said as he opened the coach door.

"Say, my boy, good idea. But first, I need to stretch my legs after that ride. I will take a stroll, if I may. Maybe stop for a drink before we get underway."

"I'll be waiting here, sir."

"Come with me, we will only be a short while."

The evening air was a mere breeze, dry and inviting. The sun hung low, casting shadows around the courtyard of the Tucherschloss. They meandered out of the gate, along the Hirschelgasse to the Webersplatz, down towards the river, passing the Lauferschlagturm, a tower in the old city wall. A harried man and his young worker, a boy no older than ten, loaded manure from the cobbled street onto a horse cart. Hordes of children skittered in every direction like a host of chirping sparrows. Standing on the Heubrücke, the bridge by the Debtor's Tower, they saw the doors to The Stork's Nest stood open.

"Come Tanner, I want to have a look in on that Prutt and see how he is. He has received a month's advance on beer and wine and a lovely sweet wine for special guests, like me."

They had crossed the bridge and entered an unusually quiet tavern. Herr Tucher's feet stuck to the floor and announced his entrance with a stick-stick-sticky stride as he walked alongside the counter. So close to the river, it was impossible to get the damp smell out of this room. At best it could be replaced with the smell of stale beer. The only other guests, two shabby men quietly conversing in the shadows, looked up as Tucher and Tanner passed. Such a shame.

This tavern usually bustled with better sorts.

"Good evening, Prutt. Please get me some wine," Herr Tucher said and pulled a chair up to his table in the corner. "Get Tanner a beer, too, would you be so kind?"

Prutt had given him a weary but lucid smile. A bit thin, face drawn, his curls hung limply around his shoulders. He kissed Lily as she poured drinks. So, Prutt wasted no time finding a replacement for his bed. Lily gave Herr Tucher a toothless grin as she rolled towards the table carrying a tankard and a wine cup.

"There you go, Herr Tucher. A port and a beer," Lily said, setting the drinks on the table.

"Thank you, my dear. Business a bit slow tonight?" Tucher asked.

"Like every night," she said.

Here in the safety of his library this morning, a chill of dread ran up Herr Tucher's mangled backbone as more memories returned. The evening had worn on, and a few more of those shabby sorts turned out. An odd, volatile group had gathered. Usually, he regarded himself as a fairly reserved man. But when the wine flowed, his confidence peaked and he summoned the courage to actually tell people what he kept secret: his thoughts.

The idea of moving to Sichardtshof and breaking away from the rigidity of his family was like sheading a constricting armor. He'd said he was too '*novellus*' for Nuremberg. He snorted at how clever his pen name was, *Sebaldus Novellus*, keeping with the times and latinizing his name. He winced, remembering he had told the group this last night too. He told them he would publish his writings and possibly move about unobserved using an alias instead of his real name. They had laughed at him.

Herr Tucher covered his face with his hands, hoping the others had imbibed last night as he had. Hopefully they were in their beds nursing their own drink-induced diseases, forgetting most of what he had said. As the fog lifted he wished more and more it would stay intact.

The memory of holding a speech flooded back; a monologue regarding his humanistic views on social structures, the role women play and the less fortunate. He was embarrassed at making a spectacle of himself, but he was glad he said it. Maybe an odd member would heed what he had said. He found harsh treatment of women appalling. Coming from an influential family, he was shocked at how subordinates and the less fortunate suffered, especially unfortunate women. No, especially unfortunate women with children.

Nuremberg rarely persecuted young women for witchcraft, certainly not on the grand scale of cities like Bamberg or Würzburg. But an unmarried mother, whose child had died under unexplainable circumstances, faced the danger of being flogged, banished or even executed under brutal conditions. No matter she had most likely nothing to eat or lived in appalling conditions. This would be the topic of his next essay.

At one point he stood to leave and go home. But he was no longer in the tavern. He had been in a private residence. Where did Tanner get to? Herr Tucher had opened the door and a rush of cool night air filled his nostrils. He was still whole and uninjured at that point. A man blocked his way, no, two men. Those two shabby fellows.

"The Patrician Herr Sebald Tucher," the one man spelled out in an odd dialect.

Herr Tucher was surprised to be recognized at a patrician. He did not dress as a patrician should, according to the strict code of dress. He politely bowed and answered, "At your service."

The bowing proved fatal. His senses reeled and that was the last thing he remembered.

Now, still trying to sit up on this settee, he stretched his legs again and his calves cramped. The door slowly squeaked open and it made him jump. "Please let this be someone other than my wife," Herr Tucher whispered like a prayer, his mouth dry and fuzzy. He opened his eyes, and breathed a sigh of relief to see Tanner.

"You in one piece, sir?" Tanner asked, clear eyes and red cheeks adding such vitality to his strong appearance.

"Oh, I envy your fresh, healthy exterior," he said. "Please call the *Magd*, Tanner. I shall want to leave for the country."

Tanner turned and froze in place when more than one pair of footsteps clacked on the stone floor in the hallway downstairs. Women's voices cackled like excited chickens.

"*Halt!*" Herr Tucher motioned to Tanner to wait a moment. "Were we not together last night?"

"Yes, sir, but you sent me to fetch the coach and I never found you again. I finally found you this morning in front of the house. I heard the merriment must have continued up the street, behind locked doors. Afterwards someone dragged you down the steps."

"So, that explains the scrapes on my back."

"I don't know how you got back here, though, sir."

"And my wife?"

"She wanted to leave you out on the front step. She didn't want me to bring you in. You must have fallen right before you opened the front door, then you never got back up. You were still on your knees, propped up by the door."

"That explains the lump on the head and the wounds on my knees," Herr Tucher said.

"She opened the door and you fell on your face. She was quite angry."

"Tanner, quick! Shut the door," he hissed.

Tanner closed the door quietly and pressed his ear against the wood.

"Is that your wife, sir?"

"Worse. My wife and my mother."

The two women discussed a heated topic outside the room in tones that would make the devil turn tail. More feet stomped up the wooden steps and creaked all along the hallway beyond the safely-closed door. Tanner and Herr Tucher stayed quiet like trapped mice. The trampling receded back down the steps where it came from, like an ogre descending into Hell. Quiet reigned like an angel's soft breath.

"How much time do you need to get ready?" Herr Tucher asked.

"Sir, I'm ready to leave. I was ready yesterday."

"Yes, of course." He made a silent vow to remain focused on his task at hand.

Slowly Herr Tucher stood and bent down to look under the settee for a chamber pot. The blood pumped into his head and he lost his balance. Tanner silently understood, was away in a heartbeat and brought a pot from the room next door. Bright boy, the compliment cannot be said too often. He stepped outside the door and allowed Herr Tucher some privacy.

A few moments later, Tanner knocked softly on the door. He entered, carrying a pitcher of water and some clean linen, set the things aside and helped Herr Tucher out of his shirt. Tanner cleaned the wound on his arm and wrapped the arm in torn linen.

"Here are some clean clothes, sir. I found them in the *Magd's* room."

"You slept in the *Magd's* room?"

Tanner smiled and helped Herr Tucher into the clean shirt that smelled like it had hung in the fresh air. Herr Tucher breathed in the clean, untainted smell.

"Ah, my boy, today is the start of a new life. We need to have these few trunks moved down into the courtyard and that Prutt should be picking these up and traveling with us today."

"What? Prutt's coming too?" Tanner said.

"Yes, he still has quite a bit of debt to work off. Has he sent word this morning?" Herr Tucher needed to keep a short rope on that man. He would also remind his Uncle Paul to keep him shadowed until Herr Tucher could take care of him once and for all.

Chapter 9

It was late in the afternoon when Katarina heard the teams of horses and the carriages approaching. She laid the ash shovel under the wood stove, wiped the ash from her face with her apron and leaned out the upstairs sitting room window. Dust billowed up from the track. She grabbed the ash bucket, ran down the steps, out of the double front doors and down the steps into the farmyard. She dumped the wood ash under the spruce tree and threw the bucket aside. Wiggling the gate free from the dried mud, she pulled it open. Even with the dry weather, that mud puddle never dried out. The lower anchor bolt on the gate loosened from the wooden post and the heavy gate slipped and slit her leg. She cursed and leaned the gate up on the fence.

Three coaches trundled along in a slow parade. The waterfowl took to flight from the ponds. Herr Tucher's coach, driven by the young tanner, was in the lead. Willi drove the second cart, pulled by Vulkan, a heavy-bred Noriker gelding, who was anything but the explosive volcano that his name implied. The cart was loaded with barrels of provisions and sacks of dried goods. From the distance, Willi looked fresh.

Katarina had been so busy she rarely even thought about him. Only late at night, alone in her bed, had she longed for some company. As if he'd ever been there to comfort her. Still, seeing him now, as angry and lonely and exhausted as she was, she yearned for him and her old life.

Katarina hadn't eaten at all today but there would be no time for eating now. After a glance down at her soiled dress and the bleeding slit on her leg, she ran a hand over her tangled hair and realized how disheveled she was. This was how Willi would see her.

Behind Willi's cart, a burly man wearing a hat pulled low over his eyes drove a team of grey horses hauling an enclosed cart full of bleating sheep. A woman Katarina recognized from the Tannery Row and a young boy traveled on the coach box next to him.

Herr Tucher's coach pulled up. He opened the door, jumped down and winced. He pulled a crossbow from the coach and with one arm in a sling, had trouble navigating it onto his shoulder. He dressed more simply than the other men of his standing, wearing black breeches, black boots and a white shirt with the sleeves rolled up. Without his usual cloak and hat, Katarina found herself admiring him.

"Can you please take this for me, my boy?"

The young tanner relieved him of his weapon.

Herr Tucher turned to Katarina. "Looking forward to a bit of hunting. The laws against shooting big game don't apply here. This is my land now. Let some margrave tell me what to do on my land."

He smiled at Katarina and scrutinized her appearance. His quick stare pricked her like a needle intent on extracting her thoughts. "Now, you look a mess, *Magd*."

Katarina didn't dare say aloud what she was thinking: up close Herr Tucher looked a mess. His lip was split. There were bruises all about his face and his arm was in a sling. His usual smooth, dark hair was tangled and caught behind his head with a black ribbon. His simple but finely-woven white shirt was rumpled.

"Is everything in order, Herr Tucher?"

The baby's cries echoed in the house.

"Is that a child?" He looked puzzled.

"Yes, sir," Katarina said.

"Does that child have anything to do with me?"

"No, sir."

"Safe to say, then, that it is not my child," he said.

"No, it's not your child." Katarina blushed, relieved he didn't seem more concerned with the baby than the fact that it wasn't his.

Satisfied with her answer he turned and watched the other two harnessed teams pulling around in the yard. Tanner jumped from his coach box and he and Willi undid the tarpaulin from Willi's cart, revealing a large amount of baggage. Katarina wondered where he would put it all.

"By the way, sir, the Old Widow is still in the master's bedroom, I couldn't get her out."

"Do I still have a room?" Herr Tucher said.

"More than one, actually. The upstairs sitting room with a wood stove, alongside that a small room to sleep in. And an extra room up under the roof."

"All I need is a place for my desk, my writing things, and my books. And a bit of light."

Willi was smiling, walking towards her. Katarina turned before he could see what a mess she was and ran down to the kitchen, fetched a bowl of warm water from next to the fire and went into her alcove. The baby cooed. Katarina pulled her soiled dress over her head. She shook out the other, less soiled dress. It would have to do.

It was a spring evening, just like this one, four years ago, when Katarina met Willi at the market in Lonnerstadt. She had returned on foot back to the farm to warn Frau Kuni that he was coming back for her at dawn and she was going to leave with him and move to the city. Frau Kuni had been waiting on the front step. When Katarina told her she was leaving, Frau Kuni's face flushed red in the bright moonlight. She ranted on because, without Katarina knowing, she had promised her to her sister's neighbor, the old Farmer Zimmermann. She forbade Katarina to leave in the morning and said she had to do her bidding, lest she be cast in a bad light. Katarina refused outright and they argued.

"*You're just like your mother,*" Frau Kuni had said. "*Do you have any idea what you're getting yourself into?*"

"*Anything is better than staying here with you or marrying someone you approve of!*"

"*You'll come to no good end. You'll come crawling back to me or end up a whore or dead like your mother!*"

No one had told Katarina that her mother was dead. "*Rather be dead than stay here with you!*"

Katarina had run into her alcove, much like she was doing this evening, to wash and change into the only other dress she had. She collected the wooden box with her things and without saying a word, Frau Kuni handed her a pouch with a few coins.

"*I'll write,*" Katarina said, her voice pleading.

They didn't embrace. They never said goodbye. Katarina went to sleep that night angry. She woke up the next day angry. Willi came as promised at dawn and his fresh smile was a warm change to the sour old woman and her oppressive ideals. Katarina left angry and swore she'd never return.

Now Katarina had returned and she wondered how much longer

she would be here. She laughed ruefully. The baby made an insistent sound. Katarina finished washing and threw her dress on. She smiled down at the baby and ran out of the kitchen and up the steps. Walking out the front door and down the steps into the yard, she watched Willi unhitch Vulkan from the cart and secure his reins to a post. It appeared that he hadn't drunk for a few hours. He saw her finally and smiled wide as he approached. He'd lost a tooth on the right side.

"Katarina, I... well, I don't know what to say." He lowered his eyes and his voice and took her hands. "Katarina, I miss you so. I've been such a fool."

He locked her in a cornflower-blue gaze and charm poured out honey thick. It was as if he'd rehearsed this scene.

"I can't go on like this without you," he said. "I'll come out and help you here. Let me stay with you."

He sounded so sincere and Katarina wanted to believe him so badly that it was as if he held a magic wand over her and she was fated to follow it where ever it pointed. She clenched her eyes shut. No! He'd used the same tricks on other women. Katarina would watch him in the tavern and pity the dumb hussies. In the end he was forever the huckster.

Still, her heart raced and her knees weakened. Willi ran his finger along her cheek. She drank in his sweet, subtle touch and it filled that hole in her soul.

"I'm so sorry," he said.

She wanted him to kiss her. She wanted to leave here, now, with him. Never come back here. He was really all she had. This time it would be different. That was it. Katarina had to give him a chance. She would work harder this time.

"I haven't been opening the tavern," he said. "I'm staying away from the drink."

"Take me with you tonight," she said. "Tonight, Willi."

"I have to leave this evening. Business for Tucher. But I'll come back tomorrow or the day after."

Tanner prodded a few sheep into the dilapidated paddock. "Katarina! Don't let my friend here get the better of you," he said and laughed heartily, red cheeks glowing in the warm sun.

Willi waved him away like he was swatting at flies. "This time I'm serious. I've missed you so. I haven't been myself these past few months." He closed his eyes and bent in to kiss her.

Herr Tucher was suddenly standing behind Willi. "What could be sweeter than young love?"

Katarina breathed in sharply.

Herr Tucher spoke. "Prutt, please take those trunks to the first floor. Those paintings are going in there, too. Follow the other men." He watched Willi walk away. "I do not want him here. He is leaving this afternoon. He…"

He never got to finish expressing his opinion of Willi because at that exact moment the baby's cries flooded the front hall like those of a beast being slaughtered. Katarina ran into the house and down the steps into the kitchen. She picked her up. Her blue eyes were wide, red rimmed and full of tears. Katarina smiled down at her and she quieted, still taking short, teary breaths. What had startled her so? Katarina looked up and jumped herself. Willi was standing right beside her.

"Whose baby is this?"

He seemed to read Katarina's hesitation as guilt. He changed his tone, his face twisted and he demanded, "Whose baby is this?"

Herr Tucher came up behind him and led him away, out of the house and down the front steps into the yard. Katarina followed them and watched from the front door as they quietly conversed.

Willi came back to Katarina and touched her hand. Katarina stroked Isabeau's cheek as Willi looked on.

"Looks like a devil child," he said.

"It's not my baby," Katarina said.

"I know, Tucher just said you take care of it for him. So he's got you here tending his bitch's brat. Just be careful with him, Katarina, he'll be after you next."

"Take me away from here, Willi," she said. "Wait until it gets dark. Come back tonight, please."

He jumped back down the steps. "I have to run some errands for Tucher. I'll get back in a few days, I promise. Bring you home. I don't care what he says."

He ran back up the steps, kissed her cheek and jumped back down with more vigor than she had seen in a long time. He turned towards his horse. Katarina turned away and took Isabeau back to the kitchen. Willi would come and get her out of here.

Chapter 10

Summer Solstice 1616

Katarina threw the last pitchfork of hay into the paddock, jabbed the tongs into the dry earth and watched Herr Tucher march down the North Hill, crossbow leaning on his shoulder. That burly Knecht followed close behind, a dead roe deer thrown over his shoulder. She had not been able to sleep early this morning and heard them set off. It was the summer solstice and although late in the afternoon, the sun was still high. Dawn seemed to break in the middle of the night this time of year, the birds chirping and fluttering under the ivy covering the outside wall.

Without that hat pulled low over his eyes, Katarina could see Knecht's black, burnt socket where his right eye had been. He was an older man and took stiff, rocking steps on thin bowed legs. His barrel chest heaved and, with hands the size of small iron skillets, he patted his dead deer. Both men looked quite pleased with themselves.

"Now my dear, this calls for a feast," Herr Tucher said. He straightened himself and his self-satisfied smirk. "I was afraid we would be living on acorns and snails all summer. We also brought some vegetable root when we came out with the sheep. You will find them in those barrels of sand in the cellar by the wine. They are from last fall so they may be a bit soft, but when they are cooked, they will taste fine."

He hung ropes from the two wooden pegs protruding over the crooked shed's door and made slipknots. "Knecht, help me hang this beast up. I need to get the skin off. Katarina, fetch me a few vessels for the innards, would you be so kind."

"I'll fetch a few vessels, sir," Katarina said.

She dashed to the kitchen and found two wooden bowls. The baby fussed in her basket, screwed her face into a grimace and stretched her legs. Each week Isabeau lost that crushed up, newborn look. She must be about five or six weeks old now. After her second week here, Katarina had forgotten to mark off the days so she abandoned the count.

In Nuremberg, the time of day and the days of the week were closely measured. The church bells pealed differently depending on the day of the week, the time of day and the service being celebrated. Every Sunday morning, they announced the Lord's Day and the beginning of another week.

In the country, gauging the passing of time had little importance. The bells in Lonnerstadt might carry on the wind, but not always. Katarina's day was determined by the weather, who needed feeding, and what tasks she could do with the amount of light she had.

Katarina took her wooden bowls and ran back outside. The two men tied the deer's back legs up to the ropes and hung it head down. Herr Tucher made an incision along the belly to the throat in order to remove the innards. The intestines flopped out into the bowl. Knecht quickly set the next bowl down to catch the blood.

"We will grind the innards up and make hash. I have a book with some other recipes, too. Knecht wants the intestines. Please set them aside somewhere."

Herr Tucher handed Katarina the bowl with the heart, liver and kidneys and she set off for the kitchen. "Katarina, bring me some of those greens, please?" he yelled after her.

The baby kicked and flung her arms. Katarina set the bloody bowl aside, bent in over Isabeau's face and the baby smiled! Katarina had never seen a baby smile before. She must have made a surprised expression because Isabeau opened her eyes wide and her mouth formed an O. Katarina laughed and did the same. Isabeau smiled again wide and fidgeted like she wanted to get out of the basket.

Katarina took a pitcher down from the shelf by the fire, grabbed some of the extra greens and put them in an empty bowl—stinging nettles, some white dead nettles and sorrel leaves that she'd collected earlier today—and brought all of it outside. She set her things aside and poured the collected blood from the other bowl into the pitcher. Blood made gravy thick and tasty. Herr Tucher expertly began to remove the deer's skin, cutting around each hind hoof and making incisions down the legs, separating the hide from the meat with his knife.

"Knecht, help me pull the rest of the hide off," he said.

After the hind legs were skinned, the two men slowly pulled the skin from the torso like they were removing a tight sock. The hide hung half removed when Herr Tucher straightened up, stretched his back and wiped his bloody hands on a rag.

Katarina grudgingly admired him. "Where did a spoiled city businessman learn to hunt and prepare his own meat?"

"I had a wonderful governess as a child who taught me to be self-sufficient. I spent summers with her at my family's country home north of Nuremberg. She told me I should always be in a position to feed myself. You know, not always be dependent on the market. After the last few winters, I see why. We have no means of being self-sufficient in the city."

He turned to the deer and they pulled the hide off completely down to the neck.

"I brought some salt," he said over his shoulder. "By the barn in that sack. Can you bring it here? We'll salt the animal's cavity here and stuff it with the extra greens."

"I had no food of my own in the city," Katarina said. "I had to buy everything we ate. No matter what the price."

She fetched the sack of salt, set it at his feet and untied the sack.

"Precisely. And the situation worsens. Because of all this strife between the Catholics and the Protestants and everyone up in arms about the Catholic Revival or Counter-Reformation, whatever they call their movement today, people are flocking to whatever city will tolerate them. Nuremberg is overridden with people seeking some sort of haven where they can live in peace. But who will feed them all, I say!"

Knecht brought a spit from the wood shed, the two men speared the carcass and together they rested the spit horizontally on two dowels standing astride over a wood pile. Knecht busied himself with lighting the fire.

"I hope no one ever strings me up like this, you know, impaled on a skewer to be roasted," Herr Tucher said.

"Don't say such things, even in jest," Katarina said.

"I'm not jesting." He smiled at Katarina, no smirk this time, and wiped the sweat from his forehead with his shirt sleeve.

"What happened to Knecht's eye?" Katarina whispered.

"A neighboring landowner took exception to him hunting too close to his land," Herr Tucher said. "He was caught and punished before my family could do anything about it. Must have been painful.

Knecht said the meat was worth it."

Katarina remembered a farm hand who had lived here at Sichardtshof when she was a young girl. Frau Kuni had taken her to watch the man be hanged for poaching. Frau Kuni said the laws against poaching were strict and Katarina had better keep her head down and stay out of trouble or she would be next.

She retied the sack of salt and took it into the barn and up the ladder to the hay loft to store it in a dry corner. There she found an empty crate and went down into the cool cellar to collect a few onions, parsnips and what other soft, shriveled roots they had stored in sand. They weren't moldy, so they would do. She lugged the crate full of vegetables up the steps, out of the barn and into the main house, down into the kitchen. Katarina poured a mouthful of wine into a mug, sipped at it, washed the root vegetables in clear water, cut them small and set the potful on the flame to cook. She sorted through the rest of the greens and decided to blanch them.

"I have a present for you," Herr Tucher said, coming into the kitchen and holding out a small muslin sack. "Pepper. Grind some up and put it on the vegetables. Carefully. Not too much."

He sat on the low stool by the fire and watched Katarina try to grind the pepper in a wooden bowl with a pestle. The tiny pellets shot from the worktop like bullets.

He laughed. "Carefully I said. Pepper is expensive, you know."

They collected the little balls from all over the floor together. Katarina made a heap on the worktop and crushed them carefully this time. She sniffed the black powder and sneezed.

"Biting? Pungent? How would you describe the aroma?" he said.

Katarina sneezed. He laughed. The baby cried a sleepy reproach.

"She's hungry again," Katarina said.

She washed the pepper from her hands and lifted Isabeau out of the basket. Isabeau rubbed her eyes and laid her head on Katarina's chest. Katarina shifted the baby onto her hip so that her right arm was free and set a pot of milk over the embers to warm.

Frau Kuni limped into the kitchen, her expression both sour and lightheaded. Her wrinkled face was crumpled from sleeping deep and unbothered. She'd taken the trouble to re-braid her hair and fix her bun. She went right to the stove, saying nothing, no greeting, nothing. Herr Tucher finished grinding the pepper and wiped his hands on a towel.

"Good evening, my good woman," he said. "We shall be eating soon. You are coming to dinner?"

"Let me take something up for the Old Widow," Frau Kuni said.

"She won't be able to keep it in, but she'll appreciate it."

"Is the woman sick?" he said.

"She can't seem to keep any food in. She's weak and looks so dried out."

"I have a wonderful tincture that's just the cure for an upset stomach. I'll fetch it for you."

He left the room and Frau Kuni and Katarina were alone. Frau Kuni made a bowl of vegetables for the Old Widow and Katarina prepared the baby's bottle. Katarina wanted to ask her grandmother what she thought of Herr Tucher, but Frau Kuni's expression warned her off.

Herr Tucher came back and handed her a little ceramic flask, stopped with a cork.

"Laudanum is bitter," he said. "Give her a few drops on a spoon. It works wonders."

Katarina carried the rest of the cooked vegetables in bowls out to the fire, handed them to Tanner's wife who in turn handed Katarina a wooden plate covered with meat she'd taken from a huge platter. The others had assembled around the fire and loud laughter drifted along on the smoke. The whole yard smelled of charred wood and roasting meat.

They now numbered nine souls living on the farm, counting the Old Widow and the baby. Sitting around the fire, Katarina thought they could pass for a motley family—of sorts—except for the fact that no one knew the other at all.

"I was telling Falk that you could read and he should learn to read, too," Tanner's wife said, slopping a spoonful of vegetable puree onto Katarina's wooden plate. "Can you write, too?"

"A bit. I haven't had much practice, but I could write once," Katarina said.

"Where did you learn how to write?" Herr Tucher asked.

"When I was young, a woman lived here with us for a few years and she taught me to read and to write," Katarina said, sitting down on a log next to him. "I don't remember too much about her, though." The woman was kind to Katarina and sometimes she would pretend that the woman was her mother.

"She was a nun who ran away from the convent," Frau Kuni said. "She wanted to leave the Catholic faith and then she was shunned by her family. She passed through here and lived with us a few years."

Tanner and Knecht each threw a log on the fire that sent an eruption of sparks into the evening sky. Tanner's wife gave her husband some food on a platter and a kiss. Falk sat down next to him on the log by the fire and stole a slice of meat from Tanner's platter. Tanner shoved the boy with his shoulder and the boy rolled off the log. Falk laughed and sprung back onto his feet and sat back down and Tanner's wife handed him his own platter.

"We'll have plenty of time for reading in the winter," Herr Tucher said. "I intend to get this place into a condition that we can even spend the winter here. By the way, Tanner and I are traveling to Amsterdam for the next few weeks. I must accompany a shipment of goods for my uncle. Katarina, I'm leaving a horse for you and you are then free to travel about, if you need to. Knecht can help you harness up, if you need help."

Katarina froze.

Frau Kuni laughed. "Katarina and a horse? She likes to look at horses and maybe stroke its mane, but she's no good to you riding on the thing."

"Surely Katarina can ride," Herr Tucher said. "Tanner's wife can help you, too. Then you can get to town together, if need be."

Herr Tucher studied Katarina's face like he was trying to decipher a foreign language. These piercing looks were making her uncomfortable.

Frau Kuni continued, "Katarina, tell him about the time you fell off that horse. She made such a fool out of herself, didn't you Katarina?"

"I almost died that day," Katarina said. "Making a fool of myself was the least of it."

"*Quatsch!*" Frau Kuni said, "Nonsense! Always making up stories, you are. I'll tell you how it really happened: Katarina was to take the old nag to my sister and collect something or other, I don't even remember what. When she got on the nag's back she was so afraid, no matter how I tried to get her to relax. She tensed her body up on the nag and, of course this was his signal to jump. Katarina knows that, don't you?"

She glared at Katarina and continued. "Away he shot out of the open gate and down the road, Katarina hollering her head off." Frau Kuni took a moment to enjoy a belly laugh at the memory. "Of course this scared the horse more than anything. Katarina didn't listen when we tried to tell her how to take care of the horse. I haven't even mentioned a young horse, like the one you have.

"She disappeared after that and we thought it would be the best for her to learn how to just get back up and get that damned thing back home. So we left her. She didn't come back that evening. She could never figure those things out. Her mother was just the same."

The wine had made Frau Kuni talkative. Katarina couldn't listen to this anymore. She left the merry round of people and made towards the house to wash up the wooden plates and knives they used for the meal. Katarina set some wood on the fire, warmed some milk and fed Isabeau her bottle. Frau Kuni's voice carried on the breeze, telling stories and laughing, finally saying her farewells. Wanting to close the paddock doors to the evening chill, Katarina stepped out into the paddock and saw the old woman leaving the fireside.

The wind blew dried leaves into neat piles along the corners of the paddock as if it was an autumn evening. The trees around the house and the ivy on the wall were so parched they dropped their leaves. Rain threatened but none would come. The wind died down to a hint of rustling in the treetops, the boughs rising and hesitating, gently waving in the slight movement of air.

Katarina went back inside, shut the door and tied a bit of cooked meat into the baby's sucking rag. She cleaned the baby up and put her in the alcove to sleep. She heard Frau Kuni closing the front doors. Katarina grabbed her shawl, slowly climbed the stairs up and out of the kitchen and peeked up the stairwell. The last glow of Frau Kuni's oil lamp narrowed as she closed her bedroom door.

Katarina opened and shut the front doors noiselessly. As she walked across the yard, a sudden gust chilled her, lifting the hair on her arms. She pulled her wrap tighter around her shoulders. A blackbird squawked and flew from the barn's roof as if the wind had rustled his feathers. Herr Tucher was alone on the ground, one arm leaning on a log, his legs stretched out before him, staring into the fire, occasionally following a sudden puff of spark that sailed on the smoke towards the evening sky. He let his hair hang free evenings and it had an appealing effect on the shape of his face. He only tied it back when he was working. Katarina sat down on a log across the fire from him and filled her cup with wine.

"Lovely old woman, your grandmother," he said.

"Yes, wonderful." She searched his face for levity but found none.

"Try some honey cake. Tanner's wife made them."

Katarina couldn't eat another bite. She took a sip of wine. "She does have a name, doesn't she?"

"Tanner's wife? Oh, yes. Of course. Her name is Sara."

The clouds rumbled a warning in the distance and slowly closed together overhead, concealing what was to be a promising sunset. They so desperately needed the rain. The wind teased through the trees, thunder rolling far beyond the hills and calming again. The sun dipped below the heavy overcast lid and radiated an extraordinary pink on the cloud cover and the whole farm took on the gentle glow. His face reflected the eerie evening light. He paused from his staring at Katarina's face to write in a little book.

"The sunset is breathtaking," he said.

Katarina squirmed on the hard log, reached for the ceramic flagon and poured some more wine. He looked up at her, scribbled in his book, dipped his quill in the bowl with brown ink and knocked it over with a hasty, hectic movement.

"Hurry, before that thought eludes you," Katarina said and narrowed her eyes to mock him.

"No thought eludes me."

"There is plenty that you overlook."

He smiled, set his book down, filled his mug and came closer to her. Not too close, but close enough that she could see his eyes in the firelight. They were the color of autumn leaves, not brown, not green; pupils wide and playful like a hunting cat.

"I have something for you," he said. He pulled a blue ribbon from his pocket and held it up. From it, a luminous stone with a thin, silver edging oscillated. "I bought this in Amsterdam last year. Moonstone. Has a strengthening influence on women, or so I have heard."

He got up, stood behind her and fastened the ribbon around her neck. The stone fell cold against her chest and took on the light of the fire. He sat again, a bit closer this time.

"Tell me what it is I overlook," he said.

Katarina decided to take this chance and speak her mind. She noticed that when he'd been drinking, she could say things. He'd laugh, or discuss the point and philosophize, and seem to forget the conversation the next day. She'd been watching him the last few weeks and there was a point most evenings about this time when she noticed the change in him.

"Sir," Katarina said. "How long are you going to keep me here?"

"Keep you here? You sound like I hold you prisoner. Are you not here of your own free will?"

Sitting there with an overfull stomach, a feeling she couldn't ever remember having, guilt doused her like a shower. Was she so ungrateful?

She sat up straight. "No, sir, I'm not here of my own free will. How long must I work to pay off debt that is not my own? I'd like to be with my man. I want to go home."

"My dear Katarina. Prutt's bed is not empty just because you are not there."

"Why should I believe you? I don't. Lies roll easily off your lips."

"Why would you say that?" He raised his eyebrows. "You know nothing about me and you certainly have no reason to believe I lie."

"What did you tell Willi about the baby before you sent him away?" Katarina said. "Now I'll never get him back."

"Why would you want him back? And why would you want to leave this paradise? The city is no place to be right now. There is a devilish power at work here in our fair land. There are opposing forces that are going to clash and I do not want to be in the middle of the conflict."

"You admit you sent him away, then! He would have taken me with him. Or he could have lived here with me and worked with the young tanner."

"And drained my best wine and schnapps dry," he said. "Tanner does not need help like that."

Katarina whispered, "I can't go anywhere with that child anyway."

"So you are in a cage of your own making?"

"You never asked me about the child."

"I believe you will tell me when you are ready."

"It's not my child," she said.

"Yes, that is obvious."

He took her chin between his thumb and forefinger and turned her face towards his. "Do I need to know about this child?"

"Yes, well, no, I...I..." She looked away from his penetrating eyes. "I cannot tell you..."

"But seeing as it is not a stray dog, you cannot turn the baby out. And we seem to have enough to eat. I offered you transportation, you are free to come and go as you please. You are not on the farm alone. You have enough help from the others. You must only ask and they will help you. Where is then the problem?"

She choked back a counterattack. Yes, he was a kind man. But what was hidden beneath this compassionate guise? He would never understand how lonely she was; passed off and left on this farm to toil away the years and grow old alone, like her grandmother. It was a fact she was just beginning to understand herself.

"Katarina, come inside, it is a chilly evening." He took her by the hand and they stood up. "Your hand is freezing."

She pulled her hand away. They walked towards the house and he laid an arm across her shoulder. She leaned into his warmth. His hair smelled like smoke from the fire and a hint of lavender. He squeezed her shoulder. Tears burned behind her face. He opened the door, put both hands on her shoulders and turned her to face him.

"This is your home and I want you to feel at home."

She looked away.

"Good night, then." He climbed the steps.

Katarina heard the door to his sitting room open and shut. She walked down the steps into the kitchen and stoked the fire. She would never consider this her home, ever again. The baby started to cry and she knew this was the end of the road.

Chapter 11

It was past nightfall when Tanner and Herr Tucher arrived in Amsterdam. His uncle's men took the shipment off their hands and were on their way before he even realized what had happened. They found these accommodations quickly but he could not sleep. He read by one candle until the words swam before his mist-covered eyes. After waking with his face on his book—his tears, sweat and drool eternalized within the pages of *Paracelsus*—he decided to join the other guests in the breakfast room.

The other breakfasting guests, mostly men of his standing—merchants and traders—were accompanied by young women. This Amsterdam inn offered every refuge for lonely travelers. He could identify at least four different languages being spoken by the patrons entering the breakfast room. Out on the street were many more.

And never before had he noticed so many friendly women, eager for his companionship. But his heart desired no whore to share his bed, though his loins would have welcomed the consolation.

The door opened and a chilly-morning gust of Amsterdam wind swirled up the dust from the floor about him. A man dressed in red and gold breeches and a red slashed-sleeved jacket with an extravagant lace collar entered the breakfast room, removed his wide-brimmed hat and threw it onto a neighboring table. He spoke something in French to his lackey, a boy that followed him in, shutting the door behind them.

The city was bustling. Every time he came here, the city's population had once again doubled. If Sichardtshof was ever taken from him, he would want to live in Amsterdam. Where Nuremberg was like a moody old grandfather, Amsterdam was young and playful, daring and fresh. After his meeting this morning, he intended to walk the streets until his feet would no longer carry him, to inspect the new canals under construction and what islands had been reclaimed.

He sipped his tea and flipped open his journal to read his last entry, the night before they had left for the Low Countries. Katarina told him not to let his thoughts elude him. He tried not to and read now those equally eluding thoughts. This entry was the first in this journal that had many corrections and deletions. Herr Tucher could hardly concentrate. Thoughts of that woman kept him from putting any coherent ideas of his own together. Every time he tried to write, words came only in verse.

There was a mutual connection there and he knew she felt it too. He had known her the better part of a year now and he had to have her. She was a spirit he wanted to harness, like a wild mare, better yet, a wild pony or a wild what-kind-of-animal? A dragon, yes. She had a spot, too, in her armor where one cleverly shot arrow could bring her around.

His heart was not in trading today. All he wanted to do was write and that meant he needed to be alone. If he could only get that woman off his mind. He had wanted to work on a new essay since they left Germany and being on his own posed the best opportunity for it. Sometimes he reveled in the solitude, other times he detested it. It was the one evil of writing.

Mr. van Diemen was due a good half an hour ago. Herr Tucher did not mind at all that the man was late. He drank more tea and ate some herring. The door again burst open with that fresh sea wind. A very harassed-looking Mr. van Diemen waved a hand at Herr Tucher and dropped down into the chair opposite him. Herr Tucher remembered him as a bold businessman, dapper and daring, whose risks had paid off handsomely. His clothes had once been fine but his lace collar was frayed and his jacket and trousers faded and worn. The wear and tear was appropriately mirrored in his face.

"My dear Herr Tucher," he said in German, "I am so terribly sorry that I am late."

"I have all the time in the world, my old friend," Herr Tucher said and meant it.

"I have put a rather large amount of goods together for you, mostly grain and wine. Do you really think you will get the goods home without being molested?" His hands shook as he picked up the mug of tea Herr Tucher had filled for him.

"I have hired some men to travel with us. German soldier-types. Thank you for your concern."

A young capable blonde with not only a generous smile brought them another plate of bread and herring. She filled a plate for Mr.

van Diemen and slid it across the table.

"There's one problem with our agreement, though," Mr. van Diemen continued. "The prices have fluctuated and I need more money up front. I haven't sold all of your things yet. Those bronze vases, my friend, are you sure you want to sell them? Oh, yes, I have clients, of course I do."

"I have no need for metal objects that serve no purpose. Have you found any paintings for me?"

"I've arranged a meeting at an atelier with a man named Lastmann. We can go together if you like." A man's shout out on the street made Mr. van Diemen jump. "But I really need the money, first."

"Tell me, old friend, how is the business these days? Such trifles like money never worried you before."

"Everything is wonderful! Never been better. What could possibly be troubling me?" He slumped forward in his chair and lowered his voice. "I have one slight problem that I would like to discuss with you. Please understand that I must beg your absolute discretion."

"By all means, you can trust me!"

Mr. van Diemen moved in closer. Herr Tucher could see and smell his tobacco-stained teeth even though Mr. van Diemen hardly moved his mouth.

"I'm having trouble with my son and I may need to ask you a favor," Mr. van Diemen said.

"What? You mean Pieter?" Herr Tucher said. "Has he gotten into trouble?"

"Yes and no. He's playing with fire, that boy, and I need to remove him from a sticky situation before he sinks into a very deep hole."

"How old is he now? He must be sixteen."

"Not yet. He'll turn sixteen in the winter. Which makes the situation all the worse. You know my wife died in the spring, don't you?"

"Yes, I did hear that. I am very sorry for your loss."

"Yes, thank you. I am too, but the loss seems to weigh on Pieter the heaviest. Now he's always been a personable boy, friendly, intelligent. He learned at an early age how to get what he wanted from his mother. She adored the boy and spoilt him terribly. I always had to remind her that discipline was as important as praise. Well, Pieter learned to charm her and he of course didn't stop there. He's a rather tall boy and most women don't realize right away his true age."

Herr Tucher swallowed a mouthful of herring before he spoke. "So the boy is a womanizer? Where is the problem?"

"Well, some women take exception when a man toys with their affections, don't they?" He reflected for a moment and poked at the plate of fish with a crust of bread. "Now my wife was sick for the past few years. She grew weak and deteriorated and I believe the cold, damp winters just sucked the life out of her. This past winter was extreme. She never fully recovered this spring. I tried all sorts of remedies, but we could never fully understand the nature of her illness. I don't think there was much life left in her.

"This drove Pieter out of the house. He couldn't bear to see her like that. My businesses have suffered because I couldn't bear to leave her alone for long periods of time. And I couldn't rely on that damned German maid, either. I must say, I am having trouble building my clientele back up. Other traders have moved right in and taken my customers. You, my friend, many thanks that you are still a true old friend. Without your business, I don't know what I would do. I know you won't take advantage of this information either, to force my prices down."

"I do need the complete order," Herr Tucher said. "Even though my trade affairs are of a purely personal nature today. Amusement, one could say. I am building a nest, you see. How much money do you need?"

"I haven't secured the wine, yet. I need another 1500 taler. We'll hide the goods in your wagon under the inferior fabrics. That will deter any inquisitive glances."

"That will pose no problem, Mr. van Diemen," he said and drained the last of his tea.

"But I still need to ask you a favor. Do not feel obliged by any means. This is just an idea I had last night and please don't feel…"

Two women sitting with two overweight merchants at the table next to them cackled.. Mr. van Diemen cleared his throat.

Herr Tucher smiled. "Ask me, then."

"I'm sorry, my friend. It's about Pieter. He recognized what his charms could bring a woman to do. As soon as he had one woman, he left her and went for the next. By and by, Pieter had a small collection of paramours, like a greedy collector of butterflies. Mostly older women, widows, and the like. But there was one woman, the oldest one. I believe she was forty-five."

Herr Tucher frowned.

"Yes, was." Mr. van Diemen nodded, moved in closer to Herr Tucher and lowered his voice. "Madeleine Hulft, the wife of a respected neighbor. When she became wise to his game, she took her life. She left her husband a note, too, confessing the affair. The husband stopped by our house last night and wants revenge. Pieter hid upstairs and wouldn't come out. He knows his life is in danger, but doesn't say a word. But I found a book of poetry last night."

Herr Tucher couldn't disguise his interest in the book of poetry.

"Yes, that's why I thought of you. I can't interest him in learning a trade of any sort. He has no interest in my businesses, either. But we both need to work. I cannot, no, I will not support the two of us if he won't work…"

Mr. van Diemen coughed and drank from his tea. The very words stuck in his throat, choking him.

"My apologies, Herr Tucher. I even suggested he try to get a job on a ship, get out of Amsterdam. The conditions are atrocious, though, on those ships."

"So I have heard."

"So, my friend," Mr. van Diemen continued. "Here is the favor I'd like to ask of you. Could you use the boy in Nuremberg for the summer? Maybe for a year or so? He's tall and strong. And of late he seems to like to fight. He's taken up with a group of boys who enjoy coercing passers-by. He could be of use on the journey to Germany."

"Oh, Mr. van Diemen! You haven't heard of my latest project. My nest-building, like I have said. I have bought a farm in the country. And, yes, I could imagine I could use the boy for the next year. And one more man on the return journey would be welcome, too."

"Wonderful, my old friend," Mr. Van Diemen said. He allowed himself a moment to relax. "But enough of all that. Come, we have people to see and money to spend!"

Chapter 12

What a commotion Isabeau made! With a look of utter concentration, like the only things that mattered were muscles reacting and energy expending, the baby kicked her feet and thrashed about. She had discovered that she could squeeze tones out of her throat and reveled in her new talent. Katarina could watch the baby for hours, flapping and flailing.

The baby laughed. A real heartfelt, from-the-belly laugh! Katarina never knew that babies laughed. She thought all they did was cry. Isabeau was really a dear little thing. She was only eight weeks old but she was like a real little person. Katarina wished she had written a journal with all her developments. Once the child was older it would be interesting to read back.

Beyond the open kitchen doors, sheep bleated and chickens clucked in the paddock. Various birds sang and chattered on this dry summer morning. Katarina thought she heard knocking on the front doors but dismissed it. Who would knock? She cleaned the baby up, filled her bottle with milk and stood over her, watching her suckle on the cloth nipple. Isabeau's eyelids grew heavy and she was about to drift off.

Pounding on the front doors startled both of them. Katarina hesitated, suddenly aware of how unprotected they were, remotely situated from other villages. Tanner's wife, Sara, wouldn't knock. Tanner traveled with Herr Tucher. They'd been gone at least three weeks now and they wouldn't be back for another four. Frau Kuni and the Old Widow were still in bed. Knecht and Falk were herding the sheep the other side of the North Hill.

Isabeau yawned and Katarina set the baby's bottle down. She walked to the doorway and looked out of the kitchen, up the stairwell to the double front doors. Katarina heard a man's voice calling from the paddock. Her heart jumped and began to thud in her chest. It sounded like Willi. She went back into the kitchen and instinctively checked the child. Isabeau had quieted down by sucking on her finger. No wonder—they'd been awake since dawn. Katarina had fed all the animals at the house, shoveled manure out of the paddock, milked the goat and the one sheep, collected some stinging nettles, set up some peppermint for the Old Widow's tea and fed and cleaned the baby twice now. Not to mention lugging firewood and water.

"Katarina," Willi said, coming through the paddock into the kitchen. "I was passing through. Are you alone?"

Katarina stirred the pottage for the old women and added a bit of salt. Covering the hot pot, she removed it from the fire and set it down on the table before she dropped it. She ignored him for a moment, an attempt to gather her thoughts, slow her breathing, stop her heart from racing.

"When am I ever alone?" she said.

Willi laid his riding cloak on the worktop. His clothes were new—a coarsely-woven shirt with light-brown breeches and new boots. A leather satchel hung from his shoulder. This was the man Katarina had met four years ago. There was that bright smile. As he approached, she fought back the tears. He bent his head, took her slowly in his arms and held her against his chest for a moment. He smelled like rosemary and roasting meat. Katarina's stomach rumbled. She had drunk a bit of milk that morning—nothing else. He ran his fingers down her back.

"You've gotten so thin," Willi said.

Katarina looked up at him. She lost her voice. Her hands trembled. He took her face in his hands and kissed her.

"Are you hungry?" she croaked and cleared her throat.

"Show me around your new country estate," he said.

He took Katarina by the hand and pulled her towards the door. She glanced at the baby and saw she was sleeping. Willi took no notice of the baby. He led Katarina out into the paddock. What a fine day—birdsong, breeze, billowing clouds. Beyond the farmyard, back by the bramble bushes, smoke rose from the worker's house. Sara led a goat and waved at them.

"I've moved out of that horrible house on the Tannery Row," Willi said. "I'm living above the tavern."

"You said you didn't open the tavern anymore," Katarina said.

"I have to live from something, don't I?"

"Where is the loom?"

"I sold it to the family that moved in after me. I never want to sit at a loom again."

Hand in hand, they walked out behind the main barn. Tanner had built a bench and placed it there hidden; a meditative spot overlooking the hollow and the ponds. Heat rose from the dry fields, the grass yellowing, the grain refusing to grow without water. The frogs croaked and the sky was misty blue, clouds whisking along the rolling hills into the horizon.

Willi pulled a bottle of wine from his satchel and, with a flirty wink, offered Katarina a sip. A sweet sloe wine, Katarina's favorite. He took her hand.

Katarina remembered the night they had met four years ago. She had stood by his stand at the market in Lonnerstadt, fingering an intricate tablet-woven band in a russet color with a mustard-yellow pattern. He put the band in her hair. He smiled when he spoke and seemed genuinely interested in what she had to say. He took her by the hand. They walked down to the creek and shared some sweet sloe wine, just like this. That night he had offered her work in Nuremberg and his appeal was enough to coax her to leave the next day with him.

Katarina released his hand. "You could still find customers. You have a good reputation as a weaver."

"I make more money in the tavern," he said. "I'm finished with fabrics. Starvation, that is."

Willi's grandfather had been a flannel weaver. His father, too, but he died some time back, leaving Willi and his mother not penniless, but poor. They were forced to leave their house in the Seven Rows—a row of seven houses built as a Weaver's District in Nuremberg when flannel was much in demand. Herr Tucher's uncle had offered them the smelly, narrow house on the Tannery Row. Instead of producing their own fabrics, they only wove fabrics for private citizens with the raw materials the customers provided—flax or hemp. Wool was hard to come by. The laws regarding what weavers produced were constricting. A flannel weaver was only allowed to produce flannel; a carpet weaver was only allowed to produce carpets. They couldn't keep up with every new law. So, Willi worked odd jobs for Herr Tucher, bought whatever raw materials he could get his hands on, and they made fabrics and rugs, regardless of the laws. He traveled to country markets to peddle whatever they produced, unobserved.

"Katarina, I've been looking for someone like you," he had said. *"We could use some help in the house. Of course, I can pay you. Mother can't manage everything by herself. You'll love her! She doesn't like to be alone when I'm away for long periods of time."*

The moon had reflected in his eyes that night. He took her hand and kissed it. *"Katarina, you'll love living with us."*

The next day, after Katarina's harsh parting from Frau Kuni, they had traveled the four-hour ride with his one-horse cart to Nuremberg to meet his mother. Frau Prutt hardly greeted her son, dismissed Katarina with a wave of her hand and left the two of them in the hallway. She hobbled through the sitting room into the kitchen, muttering to herself. Willi led Katarina into the sitting room with the massive loom, motioned for her to sit down on the chair stuffed in the corner and stay quiet. He followed his mother into the kitchen.

Katarina had heard Willi's muffled voice, soothing, pleading. Frau Prutt cackled like an old goose, *"What's this, young man? Another mouth to feed? Who will pay her keep? Oh, she can work, can she?"*

He came back to the sitting room, set a flagon of tea and two cups on the table, and sat next to Katarina on the other chair. He took her hand.

"She'll come around. Give her a chance." He had winked at Katarina like he still did today. *"She has trouble with her hands and can't work the way she'd like to. She needs your help, even though she won't admit it."*

Frau Prutt never did come around. Katarina wondered if he blamed her for his mother's death. She laid her hand in the crook of his elbow and slid closer to him on the bench. Insects danced on the top of the pond and a frog jumped into the water.

"Lovely bauble you have there." He fingered Katarina's moonstone, a menacing sneer on his face. "You're enjoying this here, aren't you?"

"I want to come home," Katarina said.

He grabbed her hand. He started to say something, but stopped. Katarina sensed his bubbling temper and prepared herself for an outburst. It was a trait of his she had forgotten. Herr Tucher never lost his temper.

"I'll get you out of here. I told you so. Just give me some time," he said.

He pulled her close, leaned her back and kissed her long and hard. Katarina felt like a starving child who'd been served a proper roast dinner. That hole in her soul filled momentarily with this one kiss. She never wanted to let go. He pulled the shirt string at the nape of her neck and her chemise loosened. The baggy dress hung even looser around her shoulders. He slid his hands from her ears down her neck, along her shoulders, under the chemise, down her arms. The breeze made her nipples stand up.

"There's nothing left to you," he said.

Katarina felt like a rabbit on the other end of a crossbow. She wanted him to erase her with another kiss, swallow her whole. His lips were on her ears, her neck, her lips. She willed him to say what she wanted to hear: he loved her. She needed to give him a chance. He pushed the dress off her shoulders, down to her waist, leaned in and took her breast in his mouth. He leaned back and traced his finger across her cheek, over her chin and down her neck.

She stood, the dress fell to the ground, and she threw off her chemise like she was shedding her skin. He stood, too, undid his pants and grabbed her around the waist. He hoisted her up around his flanks and sat back down, pulling her down and entering her with a low moan from both of them. The bench was quite narrow and they weren't exactly in the middle. It toppled to one side and they fell onto the grass. He laughed and his eyes grew wild. He sprung his weight on top of her, grabbed her buttocks and rolled onto his back, pulling her astride over him, entering her again, her sharp breath a melodic, lingering intake of sound. His hips pushed against hers slow and deliberate. Her fingertips felt shivers along his hipbones.

"Are you cold?" she asked.

He kissed her in response, pulling her hair free from the leather cord. He reached behind her head and pulled her mouth to his, sucked her lip and nudged the wet strands of hair out of her eyes with his lips. She buried her face in his long brown curls.

Katarina pressed her hips down on him until it hurt. If she couldn't possess him any other way, she would possess him this way, even if it was for a short time. She pulled him deep into that hole in her soul. She tightened her grip and pressed—slow, small waves, her hips barely moving. She felt him start to shudder, like a dying animal. She bit her lip trying not to cry out. He trembled and relaxed.

"Get dressed," he said.

"What?" Katarina said.

"Let's go. I haven't much time," he said.

"Lie here with me, just one moment. Please." She was pleading, desperation flushing her as if she was losing blood.

He set her aside like a rag doll and stood up. Katarina grabbed for the chemise in the grass. As she pulled it over her head she felt a desperate need to hide under the material, never to show her face again. She'd fallen for his charm again, the ploy he used over and over to get what he wanted. He grabbed her hand.

"Come on, Katarina."

She tried to adjust her dress properly but he pulled her to her feet.

"Now. Come."

They walked out from behind the barn. Frau Kuni sat on the step outside the front doors. Katarina was vainly tying her hair into a messy, tangled lump at the back of her head, gave up and let it fall free. Frau Kuni stood up, shot her a violent, disapproving glare, turned her back and limped into the house.

Vulkan was tethered to the post by the front door. He was saddled.

"You didn't come to take me home," she said.

"I had to sell my cart. I needed the money." He took her in his arms again. "I wouldn't make you ride a horse. You know I love you. I'll be back next week. I need a cart first."

Willi grabbed her hand and led her towards the outbuilding where Tanner stored the tack. He pulled open the heavy wooden door and squeezed in past the horse carts. He tugged on leather straps hanging from nails along the outer walls, inspected the few horse collars hanging alongside, as if trying to guess their size. He rubbed his chin decisively, like a man at a marketplace.

"Maybe I can find something here I need?" One of the three carts earned his approval. "Help me clear a way to get this out."

"Those are Tanner's things. You can't take them."

"What do you care about him? He won't miss it. Your new master has enough money. He'll buy your Tanner another one. You've heard of that Tucher family, haven't you?"

"I know who he is," Katarina said.

"You have plenty of chances to look around here. Go through his things when you're cleaning his rooms. See if you can find where he hides his silver."

"He normally takes care of his rooms himself, Willi."

"Well, do him a favor. I'm sure he won't mind seeing you in his room."

"Willi, I'm not going to search his rooms."

"Silly girl. You're wasting a golden opportunity He's abroad, isn't he? He won't be back for days, will he?"

He winked at her. He dashed back towards the main house. Katarina ran after him.

"Well then," he said. "I'll have a look around myself. You won't tell him, will you?"

Willi ran up the steps and into the house.

Frau Kuni appeared from around a corner as if she had been spying on them. "Have you no scruples?" she asked.

Katarina turned, armed with a retort, but sunk back into herself. She had none.

"He won't ever marry you." Frau Kuni said. "Can't you just accept your place?"

Yes, her best decisions had gotten her to where she was. She felt ruined and stripped and marred beyond repair. She could blame no one but herself. She heard Willi upstairs, opening and shutting doors, the floorboards creaking as he ran from room to room.

Katarina walked back to the paddock and peered from behind the house to watch the barn. Willi came back out of the house, ran across the farm yard and into the barn. Laden with the tack draped over his shoulder, he came back out of the barn and dropped the leather straps on the ground next to Vulkan. He shoved his new cart over to the horse and harnessed him up.

"There's your chance," Frau Kuni said from right behind Katarina. "Go with him."

Yes, here was the cart and the means to take Katarina home. But Willi had no intention of ever taking Katarina back. He also made no effort to disguise the fact that he had again lied to her. Her last bit of hope collapsed and the escape she had hoped for vaporized.

"You need to learn to be alone," Frau Kuni said. "Only a weak woman needs a man. You have to accept that now. No man is worth the trouble."

Frau Kuni carried an empty pitcher to the well. Willi hopped onto the box of the cart, looking straight ahead as he drove the cart out of the gate. He left without saying goodbye. The turmoil in

Katarina's heart peaked and then quieted. Willi died for her right there.

Frau Kuni was right. Katarina must accept the gloom and those long, lonely nights. Still, complete ruin had a soothing side. With nothing left, one could start anew. Katarina went back into the kitchen and found a bundle of dried marjoram and lavender she had dipped in pine pitch. Marjoram calmed a heavy heart and allowed joy to return. She lit the bundle and let the smoke fill the kitchen.

Chapter 13

On the North Hill, Ralf watched the Sichardtshof farm below. His horse jostled beneath him. After eight weeks of searching for Hans-Wolfgang, Ralf and Elis had finally picked up his trail earlier today. They followed him at a distance and then lost him again. Hoof prints led them to this hill above Lonnerstadt. If the prints belonged to Hans-Wolfgang, Ralf couldn't tell but the tracks stopped at this spot where Ralf and Elis now stood.

"I thought this farm was abandoned," Ralf said.

A cart driven by a scruffy, dark-haired man left the farm at a relaxed pace. A young woman hid behind the house as if she was stealing last glimpses of the man as he drove away. She scurried back into the house. Ralf dismounted and relieved himself by the tree. He pulled the cowl over his head.

"Should I follow him, Padre?" Elis said.

"No, we should be off to Bamberg," Ralf said.

As he was about to get in the saddle again, the woman came back out carrying a small package.

"Wait one moment, Elis," Ralf said. "What is she holding?"

That package was a baby judging by the way she cradled it, taking a protective stance only a woman's body took when coddling a child. The woman waved a smoking wand in her other hand. Some sort of pagan ritual. An old woman hobbled towards her carrying a pitcher, exchanging some words before they both went back into the house. Could this be Andra-Angela's baby?

The night Elis had dispatched Andra-Angela, her body was void of child. They'd found a large amount of blood but nothing she may have birthed like the afterbirth or a stillborn baby. Ralf and the men had then collected Andra-Angela's body, covered it in Ralf's riding cloak and rode back to Upper Eierhofen. Friedrich was beside himself with grief. He had demanded to see her body and touch her belly. To feel the absence of the swelling there. He would not believe the child was gone. At least he had not asked why they kept her head shrouded. He did not want to see her face.

Friedrich had then demanded her baby. He would not rest until he had his grandchild. He said if Ralf would not give him the baby, he would inform the authorities. Ralf tried to calm him and had Elis give him a soothing tincture. The tincture rendered Friedrich unconscious and Ralf insisted they get Andra-Angela's body in the ground quickly.

The morning after, Friedrich had awoken in a surly mood. He wanted information regarding the baby and threatened to get it from Ralf with every distasteful and morally offensive coercion, from thumb screws to breaking him on the wheel. He wanted his grandchild and cursed those who stood in his way into *die ewige Verdamniss*!

"At least give me her cloak," Friedrich had said, "the light blue one she had from her mother. And the ring she wore on her finger. Bring me these things now!"

Ralf had ridden back up to the meadow alone to search for those things. He could have sworn Andra-Angela had lain on that light blue cloak. He had been so shaken after Elis had performed the deed and thought of nothing but getting away from this damned place, this unholy orchard of strange happenings, where the trees mocked him and the wind taunted him. If he had won the battle, why was he so tormented?

All that was left on the spot where she'd lain was the pool of blood, brown and buzzing with flies. Yes, now the way was clear and he needed only claim what was his. This was God's way, he was convinced of that. The only thing that stood between him and taking over the Upper Eierhofen estate was Friedrich and his obsession with that damned child and the few mementoes of his lost daughter. It was a test from God, to see if he was worthy.

As Ralf left the meadow to return home that day, he'd happened on a fresh trail of hoof prints. The prints were deep and chaotic, those of a rider who had ridden from the meadow at a crazed speed. Only one person would have taken the child, the cloak and Andra-Angela's ring and fled at a desperate tempo. That would have been Hans-Wolfgang. He was the only other person who knew Andra-Angela gave birth there.

Ralf had followed the hoof prints through the field, up the South Hill, past the Vier Linden. Friedrich once told him of this place, four linden trees planted to form a perfect square, a popular place to hang degenerates. Ralf followed the hoof prints down the other side of the hill. In the Edelgraben at the bottom of the hill stood the Sichardtshof farm, in the base of the hollow lined with carp ponds. The farm had looked abandoned so Ralf continued on.

Ralf now looked down the North Hill at the woman standing in the Sichardtshof farmyard holding a child and saw he had been mistaken.

"Padre, let's go," Elis said. "It's a long ride to Bamberg and we must be on our way if we are to return tonight."

Ralf needed to return tonight. He hated leaving Friedrich alone for even the afternoon. Ralf needed to apply constant pressure on Friedrich in order to wear the old man down. It was only a matter of time until Friedrich gave in to Ralf's wishes. But it was taking too long and Ralf finally had some support from an old friend in Bamberg. Once he had a sealed document from the Catholic officials in Bamberg supporting his cause, Friedrich would have no choice but to give Ralf the estate. And now that Ralf may have found the baby, Sichardtshof needed to be watched. He couldn't trust anyone with this task except himself.

Ralf nodded to Elis. "You are right. We must leave now. We must do this correctly."

He jumped back into his saddle and they rode down the other side of the North Hill until they met the main track heading north. The road from Höchstadt to Bamberg was better-traveled compared to others in the area. Höchstadt was the administrative quarters for the Bamberg Bishopric and the road between the two cities was straight forward and well-traveled.

This July afternoon, the ground was dry and fast and they made good time. The road led them over a ford in the Regnitz river and they continued north along the east side of the river. After they'd ridden a distance along the flat flood plain, Elis pulled his horse to a stop. Ralf pulled his horse around, prepared to reprimand him until he saw the look of wonder on Elis's face. Ralf turned towards the north and gasped himself.

Even at this distance, the Catholic Church's far-reaching and tangible power awed and humbled the mortal eye that dared gaze on Bamberg's hills and the magnificent structures adorning them: the Altenberg and the castle topped with a single round tower; the Michelsberg and the Benedictine Abbey, the newly-rebuilt twin spiked church towers of the Michelskirche; and in the middle, the

Domberg and the four spires of the majestic cathedral.

Ralf's breast swelled as he looked on these great structures that God allowed craftsmen to build on this earthly plane in his hollowed name. Gratitude that he was chosen to follow this divine path filled him, and he was thankful that God saw him fit to be a soldier in the army of the everlasting, almighty, one and only true religion.

Ralf kicked his stallion into a gallop and Elis followed. The river split and they were forced to travel along the river's right arm, on the opposite side of where they wanted to be. The city wall came into view and they headed towards the din collected around what looked like the city gate.

The two men dismounted as they approached the Langasser Tor. A farm wagon pulled by a mangy ox had stopped in the city gate and the guards were heaving against the animal to get him to move on. A barefoot market girl with an empty basket slipped out of the gate unnoticed. Other farmers inside the city gate trying to leave grumbled and complained.

"Should we find another way in? We are pressed for time. We'll have to stay all night," Elis said.

The ox finally agreed to budge. Ralf pushed his way through the crowd of people waiting to enter the city, demanding to be let in before the others. His stallion pranced and huffed, wild-eyed and wound tight from the commotion and the amount of people. This caused the farmers to step aside rather than be trampled by the horse and they let Ralf and his horse through. Elis and his horse muscled in close behind. Their way was now blocked by a guard holding a pike.

"What is your business here?" the guard asked.

Ralf gave the stallion's bridle a violent yank. "We are here to speak to Marius Eberhardt of the Collegium Ernestinum. He is expecting me at the cathedral."

The guard turned away and let Ralf and Elis pass. Ralf passed the guard and stopped abruptly, leaning his weight against his protesting horse.

"You won't shut the gates until sundown, is that right?" Ralf said.

The guard waved him through, his face insolent and bored.

"Don't ignore me," Ralf said. "I want an answer. We will be leaving tonight. I will be allowed through these gates."

The guard showed no interest in Ralf's demand.

Ralf scoffed. "Now how do I get up to the cathedral?"

The guard pointed the way as if it was obvious and Ralf was the fool for asking. "Cross both arms of the river, over the Obere Brücke, pass the Rathaus and up the hill."

The stallion calmed and behaved until they started to ride across the Obere Brücke. The Rathaus was built in the middle of the bridge and one had to pass through a stone archway under the building in order to cross. The horse grunted and backed away. Ralf had to dismount. He whacked the stallion in the nose and dragged him towards the arch but the stallion fought and turned to the base of the bridge. Ralf broke into a run, gaining enough momentum to run through the archway with the stallion in tow before he could resist. The shod hooves clacked on the cobblestones, echoing in the archway, the beast driven close to frenzy.

Ralf stopped and calmed the stallion. He snorted and grumbled and regained his composure as Ralf stroked his neck. The two men looked back to admire the stone and timbered Rathaus built in the middle of the river.

"The story is that the bishop wouldn't give the townspeople land for the city hall," Ralf said. "So they rammed poles into the river and built an island."

They mounted and continued on the Karolinenstrasse. Both horses protested now as the road became steeper, their hooves slipping on the cobbled street. The two men dismounted, hung their heads and climbed the Domberg. They reached the top and stopped to catch their breath under the shadows of the cathedral. Elis looked up at the dominating four spires of the mighty Bamberger Dom.

Ralf swallowed. "Father Marius is to meet us here, he said. There by the Old Court."

They walked across the Domplatz towards an annex built to the north of the cathedral. The stone structure that swelled at its end into a tasteful renaissance facade was once the bishop's residence and served now as the court building. Ralf's face lit up as a man dressed in a similar black monk's cowl and robe came rushing out of the adjoining stone gateway. The two men embraced.

"My dear Ralf. I am so sorry. I tried to get down earlier." The man's German was softened by a Spanish accent.

"Father Marius, so wonderful to see you," Ralf said. "Elis, this man is like my father, my uncle and my brother in one man. He is the one who saved me those years ago and gave me new life."

"Come with me, you two," Father Marius said.

He led the two men through the ornately carved stone gateway into the courtyard he'd just come out of. The courtyard was paved in stone and the building surrounding the courtyard was a stone and timbered structure—a quiet, quaint and happy place. Grooms took the horses from Ralf and Elis. Father Marius led the two men through what looked like a door to the stables. They followed a cool, ground-level passage and came upon a dark staircase. They climbed the stairs and entered a small dark-paneled waiting room. Father Marius motioned for them to wait.

"They have a recent upsurge of those involved in witchcraft," Father Marius said. "Mostly women. The jurists are working day and night. Are you staying here tonight?"

"No, we need to get back," Ralf said. "It is very important we leave tonight."

"How is the school coming along? I have six boys for you here in Bamberg. They are planning on starting as soon as the summer is over."

"We will open on schedule," Ralf lied.

The door to the jurist's office opened.

Father Marius allowed Ralf and Elis to enter the office of the *Rechtsbeamter* and followed them in. The dark-paneled, stifling-hot room smelled of pitch and sweat. A scribe at a lectern poised with quill in hand waited expectantly for the men to present their business. Father Marius handed the man a sealed letter. He opened it.

Father Marius spoke first. "Good Day, Dr. Faber. I have told you of my visitors. I told you about Father Ralf and the lands he is petitioning close to Höchstadt."

Dr. Faber nodded. "Yes, allow me a moment to consult your papers. Father Marius, yes. From the Collegium Ernestinum. My uncle went there too. We spoke about this estate. You are opening a school for us. The need for a Jesuit school so close to Höchstadt amid those heretic villages is of utmost importance. My concern is that these lands can fall into the hands of that Margrave in Dachsbach. We may have no weight or jurisdiction there, but there are still possibilities."

Ralf moved forward and one step to the side like the knight on a chess board. He stood next to Father Marius.

"Yes, and you are…"

"Father Ralf."

"Thank you," Dr. Faber said. "Yes, I am so glad you could make it on such short notice. I will personally push your petition forward. The Margrave can be persuaded. There are ways to free up lands in the area for our cause."

"Well, the way it looks now, we have two problems," Ralf said. "I hope this may also speed up my petition."

"Tell us, then," Dr. Faber said.

"I would like to report a murder in my house," Ralf said. "Friedrich von Obereierhofen's daughter has been murdered by a heretic and he is in league with a nest of witches in the area, not even an hour's ride from Höchstadt. Directly on the lands we wish to farm."

"This is a more serious matter." Dr. Faber said. "According to the *Constitutio Criminalis Bambergensis* I may hear your denunciation. But I need two men to swear to the accusation."

Elis stepped forward next to Ralf. The scribe scribbled, sweat dripping from his forehead.

"We are two men here," Ralf said. "And we saw the man in question kill my master's daughter."

"Have you detained this man?"

"He eludes us time and time again," Ralf said. "His father is a known heretic and eludes us as well. We've observed them both, during most decadent nights of dancing."

"With the devil?" Dr. Faber crossed himself. "And you saw the other witches during these bouts of dancing as well?"

"Yes, we both saw them," Elis said.

Ralf continued, "The father had studied at Wittenberg with the heretics of the Lutheran teachings. That is proof enough of their persuasion."

"Would you bring the man to me and we could question him," Dr. Faber said. "There are strict laws in place in Bamberg."

Father Marius spoke up, "Dr. Faber, we could clear this up quite quickly. These two men are traveling in the name of the Emperor and my Jesuit colleagues at the seminary. Father Ralf, who has taken vows to serve the Pope, is more than able to take care of this problem. According to your Penal Code, we can have this heretic man outlawed, and these two men can bring him to justice. Then we do not need to waste any more of your time. They can also take control of the heretic nest and confiscate those lands as well."

"If there are strange happenings there, I will want these witches brought here for interrogation," Dr Faber said. "They must be dealt with here."

"Thank you, sir," Father Marius said.

"As for your heretic…"

"Hans-Wolfgang von Unterierhofen," Ralf said.

Dr. Faber nodded. "You two men swear that he had killed the woman in question."

"Andra-Angela von Obereierhofen," Ralf said.

"After he raped her," Elis said.

Dr. Faber stood with a book in hand and walked to the scribe's lectern. The scribe finished his sentence and sat up straight. He readied his quill and penned the words as Dr. Faber read aloud, "Based on my findings and the denunciation from these two men, ah, what are your names?"

"Father Ralf and Elis the Swede."

"Based on our laws, the *Constitutio Criminalis Bambergensis*." He paused until the scribe looked up. "In the case of Hans-Wolfgang von Untereierhofen: I now declare the man *Vogelfrei*, as having been lawfully judged and banished for murder. I remove his body and good from the state of peace and rule them strifed."

He paused again. "The man is now proclaimed free of any redemption and rights. He is now free as the birds in the air and the beasts in the forest and the fish in the water, and shall not have peace nor company on any road or by any ruling of the emperor or king,"

Ralf listened with what he thought was the right amount of solemnity. Hans-Wolfgang was now officially outlawed. Ralf could kill him at will.

Part 2

Chapter 14

"Katarina! Help me here, would you?" Frau Kuni yelled from the Old Widow's room.

The sudden damp, rainy weather was taking its toll on the two aged, flaccid women. The temperature had plummeted like an unmanned wagon rolling uncontrolled down a hill.

September began and with one fell blow, the meaning of warmth was forgotten. One could no longer move about freely. An autumn damp settled down on the fields and in the forest. A low, never-lifting fog settled over the countryside and into their bones. The animals showed the first signs of retreating into a winter lethargy. The days were so grey that after they woke up, they considered going back to sleep.

"Katarina!"

Katarina sat on her low stool by the kitchen fire, huddled under a wool shawl, reluctant to leave the fire's side. Her hands and feet were always frozen. When she wasn't working, she hunched over her knees, wrapped up in shawls next to the fire. She stirred the milk that warmed over the fire, threw the shawl aside and set the pot away from the fire to cool. She shivered and ran up the steps.

"Kata...!"

Frau Kuni glared at Katarina as she skidded to a halt, out of breath, in the doorway to the Old Widow's room. The walls that Katarina had freshly whitewashed shone in spite of the dull grey daylight attempting to come through the windows. The scent of lavender hung over a bowl of tincture standing on a cheery crocheted mat atop the chest of drawers. A vase filled with the dried wildflowers Katarina had brought decorated her bedside table.

"I'm right here, Frau Kuni! What is your problem? I only have a few moments before the baby wakes up."

"Widow Hanson isn't well," Frau Kuni said.

Frau Kuni's breath came in visible puffs. She pulled her shawl up around her neck and pulled her cap down over her ears. Katarina walked over to the window that dripped wet with condensation and opened it, allowing a blast of chilly, damp air to enter the room.

"Close the window," Frau Kuni said.

"We need to air the room to get this disease out of here." Katarina said.

Frau Kuni's brow wrinkled with worry. She turned stiffly towards the chest of drawers and wrung a washcloth out in a bowl of steaming water.

"Everything I give her to eat comes right back out," she said. "This is the second time today I have to change the linens. We have no clean linens left. The clean ones won't be dry until tomorrow."

"When did this start up again?" Katarina said.

"Today. Can you bring me that tincture?" Frau Kuni said.

Frau Kuni walked across the creaking floorboards to the bed and sat down. "Margerethe, I'm going to give you something to make you feel better. Can you hear me?"

Katarina shut the window and watched Frau Kuni's uncommon show of affection for Margarethe Hanson. The two women had been constant companions since they were young. From what Katarina could remember, Frau Kuni said Margarethe married the Farmer Hanson at a young age and came to the farm. Frau Kuni had been born on the farm, so the two women were like sisters.

"She hardly comes to. She's incoherent most of the time. She never really wakes up." Frau Kuni removed the Old Widow's nightcap and cleaned her face. "This reminds me of the time I had that fever. After Maria was born. You took care of me, remember Margarethe? We were such silly girls, weren't we?"

Katarina ran down the steps into her alcove. She rummaged in her wooden box, through the scraps of fabric and found the small ceramic flask from Herr Tucher. It was almost empty, but he said a few drops were enough. She ran back up the steps—at least the running warmed her. Frau Kuni took the bottle from Katarina and put a few drops of tincture onto a spoon and dribbled the brown liquid into the Old Widow's mouth. She was unconscious and showed no reaction.

Footsteps on the creaking wooden floorboards passed by the Old Widow's room. Katarina stuck her head out of the door.

"The Old Widow's sick," Katarina said to Herr Tucher.

He carried a shimmering grey fur. "Does she need an extra blanket? Look at this beauty. That Tanner is an artist. And this was a small wolf. He was traveling alone, without the pack. He might have been sick but he already had his winter coat."

"Thank you. I'm sure she can use it."

"Tanner has three more. When they are finished, you can have one, and the baby, too. And I would like to…"

Hammering on the roof interrupted whatever he wanted to say next.

"Tanner is up there with the boy, Pieter. We will have the roof secured and it should not rain in anymore." He pointed to a brown damp stain in the upper corner of the hallway.

Katarina busied herself with collecting the soiled linens and rolled them into a ball. She ran down the steps and out behind the paddock to the small wash kitchen close to the well. Tanner had found that huge old iron pot that was in the kitchen when she was a child and more or less built a shed around it. He'd hung the pot from the central beam and fire could be made underneath. The pot allowed itself to be tipped for emptying into a drainage gully and the dirty water flowed away from the shed and the well. Brilliant young man.

Katarina threw the soiled linens into the pot and ran back towards the house. Descending the steps, the baby called what Katarina interpreted as Isabeau's call for her. It was an inquiring sound she made and the call's effectivity was reinforced when Katarina replied and came to her.

"Are you awake? I bet you're hungry. You're always hungry."

Isabeau smiled and kicked her feet and cooed.

"And you stink, too."

The only light in the kitchen came from the glowing embers of the fire. The wood basket was empty, as it always seemed to be. They tried to keep a supply of wood close to the house but the wood pile in the stable dwindled at a hasty pace. But Katarina was not going to chase Knecht or the boys to run errands. She would take care of herself.

She threw the last of the wood from the pile in the stable into the basket and prattled on to the baby. Isabeau liked the sound of her voice. When the baby was restless, Katarina could talk to her and she calmed.

"Isabeau, I'll be right back in. You're such a good girl. That's a good girl. Where's my girl?"

Katarina came back into the kitchen and Herr Tucher hovered over the basket, looking down at the baby.

"The child is getting big."

"You should see what she eats." Katarina smiled down at Isabeau. "You'll be a big girl, won't you?"

She filled the baby bottle with milk, closed it up, came up beside Herr Tucher and held the bottle for the baby while she drank. Isabeau looked at them both, from face to face, the perfect picture of a happy family. Katarina imagined settling into this way of life, this nurturing, budding garden of idyll.

"I brought some deer meat," Herr Tucher said after a long pause. "The Knecht is also a great shot. Would you be so kind and prepare this for my meal?" He pointed to the large hind quarter lying on the worktop. "I have asked Pieter to join me tonight and I would be honored if you would, too."

"The boy is a bit moody, quite glum. He doesn't say much."

"He is grieving, I imagine. Needs time to adjust. But he is a hard-working boy," he said, touching the various utensils hanging on the wall, large spoons, a mallet, pots and skillets as if he was looking for something. "Do you have a good knife? I would cut this joint up for you, if you like."

"I don't have a good knife. I use my axe," Katarina said.

"I will bring my butchering knife."

He left the kitchen. Katarina watched the baby drain her bottle and picked her up to burp her. She stuck a finger in her mouth, always the index finger on her left hand, gurgled and burped. Katarina cleaned her up and laid her back in her basket so she could make dinner.

Katarina cut up some onions and parsnip with her small knife, threw the onions in the pan with a melted bit of deer fat and let them cook. She had ground some of the grain Herr Tucher brought and sprinkled the flour over the onions and fat and let it brown. The bottle of the sour red wine from Amsterdam would be fine for cooking and she poured some in the pan with a *zisch*! Letting it first cook and thicken, she added a flagon of blood. What a handsome brown gravy that made, even tastier sprinkled with some salt and pepper, rosemary and sage. Herr Tucher handed her the ample slab of meat he cut from the hind quarter and she sank it into the gravy and covered the pot.

"Sara gave me some mushrooms that she collected. I can make them, too," Katarina said. "And, look! Plums from the meadow. I'll make compote."

In his sitting room, Herr Tucher had proper dishes and utensils laid out on a table he erected from planks of wood he had brought back the last time he traveled. Katarina set the platter of meat on the table. Pieter knelt in front of a barrel of beer, expertly manipulating the tap. A long-legged burly boy, he turned his head and smiled with a baby's face framed with long, dark-blond wavy hair. If it wasn't for that fresh slit above his right eye, he would be almost angelic.

"Beer from Nuremberg. Wonderful, though the beer in Holland is also outstanding," Herr Tucher said.

Pieter finished filling his mug and drank deeply, soundlessly. Herr Tucher fed his wood stove a few small logs and lit two tallow lamps on his empty desk. He used the same sliver of wood to light the two candles on the table.

Katarina deposited her wares and went back to the kitchen for the gravy and the sautéed mushrooms. She ran back down the steps for the wine. It took her three trips to bring all the things upstairs. No, four, counting one more trip down the steps for the baby.

Pieter was fascinated by the baby, who was mewing impatiently, like a hungry cat. Katarina propped her up in her basket and gave her spoonfuls of pureed food. She kicked and threw her arms about and when the spoon came towards her mouth, she lay perfectly still and took the mouthful, smiled and flung her arms and legs about again. Peter had to laugh.

"I never had siblings," he said in a heavily-accented German. He drew his articulation from somewhere deep in his gut.

"The meat is wonderful, Katarina. You used that sour wine?" Herr Tucher said, trying to talk and be polite with a full mouth.

Pieter mumbled agreement. His face looked so young, a boy really, but something in his eyes—a knowing, a shadow, a burden— made him appear older and hardened. His manners betrayed a good upbringing although his clothes were tattered and too tight. Katarina turned her attention back to her plate.

"Would you like to hear about Amsterdam?" Herr Tucher asked, leaning back and sipping on the same sour wine that actually went well with the meal. "Or our trip home? Pieter, do you mind if I tell Katarina how you got the slit above your eye?"

Pieter smiled sheepishly and shook his head.

"The roads are not safe, Katarina. Well, they never have been and we know that. So we were cautious. On the second day of our journey home, I overestimated how much distance we had covered. I thought we would make it to the next town, but we were miles away. So we decided it would be the best to bed down along the side of the road. We were, how many were we, Pieter? Counting those soldier-types?"

Pieter counted in his head. "We numbered eight, I believe."

"Yes, eight," Herr Tucher said. "I thought we could post two men on watch and the others could rest. Two soldiers had the first watch and Pieter and I took the second. It must have been a few hours before dawn, still pitch dark and I heard rustling in the trees. I reached for Pieter, but he had left my side. He had sneaked into the trees and as the three bandits tried to assault our party, Pieter came up behind them and swung this tree trunk and struck them down. All three!"

The two men were now laughing and raising their mugs, proudly toasting each other.

"How did he get that slit, then?" Katarina asked, not wanting to spoil the festive mood, but yes, wanting to bring them down to earth.

"Oh that," Pieter said. A few mugs of beer had relaxed him and he laughed. "Well, one of the bandits got back up, didn't he. Two were knocked to the ground, and the third was angry. Really angry. By this time our other companions were stirring. The third bandit pulled out a blade and started slashing in the dark. He could barely see. I jumped on top of him and he scraped my face with the blade. That's how I got this cut here."

He tilted his head forward, touched his forehead, no longer the angel he appeared to be earlier. "I took his knife from him and slit his throat."

The two comrades held high their mugs and drank to fallen friends and foes. Pieter's face was again angelic and the two continued a light and meaningless conversation.

Katarina cleared plates into piles and gathered utensils. There had always been stories of the dangers out in the wide world; bandits, robber barons, mercenary soldiers without a war. Living at the farm, unprotected by city walls, made such stories all that much more troubling for her. The news Herr Tucher brought from his travels, usually in the form of printed flyers, said it was only a matter of time before the rumors of conflict became the tidings of war. Prices were soaring, people were hungry, religious friction was the topic of the day.

Alone, Katarina could fend for herself. But now she had this child in her care and together they were vulnerable. This left her fearful as she had never been before. She heaved the baby basket, leaned it onto that part of a woman's hip designed to carry baskets and children and brought the drowsy-eyed baby downstairs, took off her diaper, cleaned her up, wrapped her in dry wrappings and rolled her in the wolf blanket.

Isabeau yawned deeply and Katarina kissed her. The baby pulled at her hair. Her half-closed eyes opened wide and fixed Katarina with a deep gaze. Katarina felt an overwhelming pressure, like she'd explode. Burning hot tears were rolling down her cheeks. Was this love?

She picked Isabeau up and hugged her so tight and whispered a small prayer of thanks to a God she never trusted that she hadn't hurt this child. She added a postscript, a sudden dire petition to the spirits she did trust, that the baby's family would give up the search and leave them alone.

"You are a dear, sweet little thing," Katarina blubbered through her tears, "I would give my life to protect you."

Katarina held her arms-length away. She was a beautiful child, wispy white-blonde curls circling the round of her cheeks. The wolf blanket fell to the floor and she kicked her legs and smiled. Katarina smiled back, afraid she woke her up now. Her elbows ached under the baby's weight. She laid her back in her basket, covered her up and set her in their alcove. Isabeau cooed and sucked on her finger.

Katarina grabbed the empty wood basket and climbed the stairs to clear the rest of the meal away. The two men rested on the settee next to the wood stove and talked in low tones, heads hunched over a book that Herr Tucher must have fetched from his bookshelf.

The contents of the table crammed in the basket, she lugged the dinner things to the kitchen and exhaustedly climbed once more up the steps to take her leave for the evening so she could finally finish her work and get to sleep. Herr Tucher was alone on the settee.

"Will you be needing anything else, sir?" Katarina asked.

"Katarina, come here, please, I want to show you something." He held out a book. "Would you be so kind as to sit here a moment and, what do I know, maybe have a glass of port?"

"I haven't finished my work yet. I'm sorry, but please allow me to be excused."

"I will send Pieter to help you tomorrow. Just have a seat."

"I don't want anyone to do my work for me. We all have enough work without having to pick up after others who are too slow to finish their own."

"Nonsense. Where would we all be if everyone thought like that? You will never get all your tasks done. The day you are truly finished with your work is the day they close your coffin." He laughed, amused by his own wit.

Katarina sat down on the chair across from him and leaned back. One candle burned on the tiny table next to the settee.

Herr Tucher read aloud from the book he held:

"Faith is a rope swinging from a point unseen
Grab hold and climb always risking a fall
Ambition, a droning motion grinding forward
Fueled by faith—the swinging rope.
Hope—like a pin prick of light that flickers
And dies at the mere touch
Only to repeat elsewhere on the horizon
Never reaching full sheen."

"Not very cheerful, is it?" Katarina asked. "Did you write that?"

"No, I did not. Pieter did. Bright boy. He wrote this whole book of poetry. Shall I continue?"

"I struggle enough myself without carrying the weight of another's struggle. May I be excused?" Katarina could use fine language, too.

He had reached that point in the evening. Wine had slowed his speech and his conversation turned to more philosophical themes. His eyes were distant and tired. Katarina was exhausted and her conflicting feelings churned together, a brewing storm.

"Our struggles can be minimized when we share them with others. We are all struggling together and not one of us is truly alone, if he does not want to be. Share the burden."

"No one wants my burden, sir. You least of all, I assure you." Katarina narrowed her eyes and hoped he realized she was mocking him openly.

"Tell me about your burden, then, and I will be the judge of what I am willing to endure."

Katarina felt the fresh tears from a moment ago well up in the back of her head. So there was more to come. She would not give this man the satisfaction of seeing anything remotely like emotion. If he had been a simple man she could allow a measure of confidence. But there was only one reason a man of his standing would mix with his maid and that was to bed her. There would be no happy family here. He had won her with a lucky dice throw!

Those conflicting feelings culminated into what was easiest for her to express: anger. The flimsy dream of leaving here and going back to her old life and Willi had been replaced by a dream she was afraid to admit. What she really wanted was to be at home here, raise her child and be protected in a committed household. With a man who loved her. But a woman like Katarina could only wish for a man like Herr Tucher. She mocked her own desires, scolded herself for toying with this dream of idyll. She was furious that she'd even entertain the idea.

Katarina thought she saw him crack that wretched self-satisfied smirk. She stood abruptly, her chair toppled over and she turned her back to him. She screwed her face up and clamped her teeth together until her temples throbbed. She was not going to cry! Wanting only to escape now, she made it to the door and grabbed the handle. Herr Tucher blocked her exit. His hands lighted on her shoulders. She shook him off.

"*Ruhig*," he said so quietly it was a whisper. "Shh..."

He gently reached for her again and turned her to face him. She raised both arms in defence, wanting to strike out but restraining herself at the last minute. Any other master would have hammered her.

He grabbed her wrists and shook her. "I mean you no harm."

Katarina pulled her arms free, wrenched the door open and ran down the steps.

Chapter 15

Herr Tucher had left Katarina in peace the past six weeks since their last encounter. He'd been busy with Tanner, Knecht and Pieter, repairing the fencing and the roof of the main barn and preparing firewood. Tanner was responsible for sorting out the workers' chores and for handling discipline and Herr Tucher oversaw that as well during the day.

Katarina had little time to think. Her hours were filled with her work and the baby; the distraction a blessing, or Frau Kuni's griping *meck, meck, meck*, like an old goat. Autumn evenings were dark and eternal, lonely and cold. Herr Tucher kept to his room. Pieter slept in the worker's house with Tanner and Sara. Katarina stayed in her own house in the evening when the baby slept.

Katarina opened the pamphlet to the page marked 'October.' She flattened the page and crossed out the 30 with her charcoal stick. Herr Tucher had left the *Schreibkalender* for her in the kitchen and said she was free to write on the calendar as she liked. Each double page had not only the days of the week and an illustration, it also had planetary movements and the shift of the zodiac. Symbols had been printed on certain days for planting and harvesting advice according to the phases of the moon.

Katarina grabbed a wool scarf, rolled it around her head and shoulders and went to fetch water. This autumn morning, two days before All Hallows, was crisp and chilly but beautiful. The clear, dark-blue sky contrasted against the brilliant brown of the plowed fields, the blue-greens of the spruce and the blond-yellow straw still lying after the harvest. Brush-stroke white clouds paled against the deep shades of the earth and sky, as if an overzealous painter had mixed his paints with too much pigment.

She carried two buckets of water into the kitchen and set them down, scowling at Frau Kuni who sat on the low stool next to the fire that crackled and curled, sparks sailing up the flue. A pile of wood thundered onto the heap in the stable. Katarina peeked through the door at Pieter. He smiled and sneaked back out the paddock door. Katarina filled a pot with fresh water and set it over the fire to boil.

She unravelled the wool scarf wound around her head and threw it on the straw mattress in her alcove. She looked closer at Frau Kuni, silent and morose, staring at the fire.

"Can I get you anything?" Katarina said.

"The Old Widow is dead in her bed," she said, her voice monotone and quiet. "Dead in her bed."

"What?" Katarina ran out of the kitchen, knowing it was a silly reaction. If indeed the Old Widow was dead there was no reason to hurry. Frau Kuni followed her up the stairs, moving more quickly than Katarina thought her capable of.

Katarina pushed open the door of the bedroom. The Old Widow was on her back, her eyes wide open and her mouth a silent scream like she had a fright and left the world in a hurry to escape it. Katarina rushed to the window and ripped it open.

"Oh dear Lord," Katarina said. "I have to fetch the master."

Frau Kuni slumped on the edge of the Old Widow's bed. Katarina ran to Herr Tucher's sitting room. The master of the house must handle this situation. Katarina hoped he'd take the responsibility off her hands. She knocked on the door and it opened as if he'd heard her coming.

"Yes, I heard." His words came out in billows of condensed breath. "Do we need to get a clergyman?"

"Of course we need a clergyman," Frau Kuni yelled from Widow Hanson's room.

Herr Tucher walked to the Old Widow's room with Katarina following behind him. "We will need to get her buried. Today. Do you have a preference? A favorite spot under a favorite shade tree?"

"We both said we want to be buried in the meadow," Frau Kuni said. "Katarina, take care of this."

Before Frau Kuni could hear Katarina protest, she left the room and Herr Tucher followed her out. Katarina hesitated, then hastily wrapped the body in the bed linen, left the room as well and found Frau Kuni in the kitchen by the fire. She was not handling this well at all. Katarina had never seen her grandmother so shaken.

"Please don't leave me alone with this," Katarina said.

"Go fetch that Sara, she can help you," Frau Kuni said.

"She was your friend," she said.

"All the more reason for me not to want to see her this way."

In the farmyard, Herr Tucher conversed with Tanner and Knecht. Tanner finished harnessing the horse, Knecht threw two spades onto the cart and they drove out of the farmyard. They meant to dig the grave. They returned mid-afternoon. Tanner stomped with muddy boots into the kitchen, sweating despite the frosty wind, his cheeks wine red. He told them how the earth would not yield obligingly.

"We had to fight to dig through the roots of the high grass. The soil is full of clay and is wet, too, from the rains. Heavy to move. Strange place that orchard up there—most of the Edelgraben is comprised of a sandier earth, usually easy to work and fertile."

Sara and Falk came into the kitchen. "I've taken care of Widow Hansen. She's ready to go. Give me the baby, Katarina, and get some warm things on. It's icy cold out there."

Up until now, Sara had kept her distance from Katarina. She was a full-figured young woman about the same age and friendly in a neighborly way, much like when they all lived on the Tannery Row, but Sara kept to herself and didn't mix. She inspected Isabeau like she was some new breed of animal.

"Strange child, " Sara said.

Isabeau's white wisps of hair stood on end and Sara tried to smooth them back. Falk plunked himself down onto the new kitchen bench that Tanner had built. He pulled on Isabeau's arm. Still a slight boy, he wasn't much older that six or seven and he looked like his father.

Katarina, Sara and Falk, bundled in warm clothing, waited in the paddock for the funeral procession to begin. Even though they had waited until midday in the hope that it would warm up, the clear night before brought a sunny, clear day and a biting wind. It was too early in the autumn to be so cold. Now that the cloud cover and rains had moved on, the crisp northern wind reached down and froze the tips of their ears. Knecht sat on the coach box of the open horse cart parked in the yard that had the Old Widow's body on it. He rubbed his frozen hands together. The black Friesian stallion pawed at the frozen earth. Frau Kuni declined his offer to let her ride with him. It was warmer to walk than to ride in an open cart. Katarina preferred to walk, too.

Tanner walked towards the group from the worker's house. Herr Tucher came out of the house and motioned for Knecht to begin the procession. A forced, solemn mood settled over them as they set off out of the yard and up the main track.

Knecht drove the stallion along the track and turned up the last hill towards the meadow, the cart jerking and creaking over the uneven path. They approached the sloe bushes around the meadow. Falk ran to the hedge, laden with black fruit, picked a few sloe berries and brought a handful for Sara.

She popped a few in her mouth. Her face crumpled and she mouthed, "Bitter. We should wait a few more days until we pick them—the berries are better when they hang through the frozen nights." She spat out the seeds.

Katarina walked ahead of the cart and found a break in the scraggly bushes big enough for them to comfortably pass. Few such passageways led into the meadow, ever-changing, depending on how the bushes grew. This one was big enough for the horse and cart to get through.

"This is a peculiar place," Herr Tucher said. "Like a garden. Apple trees and plum trees."

"Where do you think we get all that fruit?" Sara said.

The frozen wind could not penetrate the bushes into the meadow. The smell of fermenting fruit hung in the air and they trampled the remaining moldy apples and plums into the high grass as they walked under the ancient fruit trees. Tanner ran ahead and pulled a huge broken limb away from the horse's path.

Katarina searched the trees in the forest around the meadow. She wondered if Hans-Wolfgang was watching them. Isabeau was quiet and Katarina assumed she was asleep, nestled in her sling secured so close to Katarina's beating heart. The sun warmed the spot where Tanner and Knecht had dug the grave and they moved into the warmth of the golden rays as if they were moths circling a flame.

"Look, see these little mushrooms under the trees?" Sara said. "These light brown ones. They have a little dark nib on the top. And these fat brown ones here? They'll be fine, too. And look, a parasol, we can fry that in some fat."

"All you think about is food!" Frau Kuni barked at her. "Stop that prattle and show some respect!"

The sun cast a brilliant reflection off the grass. Katarina shielded her eyes with one hand. They formed a circle around the freshly-dug grave and Tanner and the Knecht lowered the Old Widow's body in carefully. Frau Kuni struggled to keep her face aloof. Katarina moved closer to her, but Frau Kuni turned her back.

"I'm sorry but you will have to be satisfied with my sermon," Herr Tucher said. "I have written her eulogy."

Herr Tucher read from a scrap of parchment. Bits of his speech included: "...today we lay an old friend to rest..." and "...our saddest hour..." and "...will never be forgotten..."

Katarina was distracted by the figure of a man, fighting through the sloe bushes. He could have looked for the hidden path next to the road, and come into the meadow from the Mailacher Weg, but instead struggled amongst the spiny branches. Why would he force such difficulty on himself when the proper path was not impossible to find? He was dressed like a clergyman in a black traveling cloak and pushed himself heavily up the bank with a walking stick. As the monk approached them, he slipped his hood from his head. He could be the same age as Herr Tucher. It was hard to tell.

"Laying a loved one to rest?" the monk asked.

"Clearly," Frau Kuni said.

"Yes, one of our counterparts." Herr Tucher said. "Would you like to say a few words, Father?"

"If our beliefs are compatible," the monk said. "These things cause most uncomfortable situations these days."

"If you wander, you must notice the problems it is creating," Herr Tucher said. "She was a Protestant, though we seem to live precariously on the edge here. The Catholics are trying to press their influence and win back this region."

"The Protestants are protected by the Religious Peace of Augsburg, of course," the monk said. "Though that only applies to the princes. Their subjects must follow the princes' confessions. I myself believe only in tolerance." He smiled what he probably thought was a winning smile.

He took a place among their numbers and mumbled on in Latin. Katarina watched the thin lips on his thin, pointed face form words.

His upper lip curled under, taut against his teeth as he spoke. His pale-blue eyes and pointy nose dripped condensation caused by the cold air. He glanced from face to face as he spoke. Grabbing a fistful of earth, he invited them all to do so and threw it on the widow's shrouded body. The monk whispered on and on what sounded like incantations. Tanner pulled his spade out of the hard earth and rammed it back in, an impatient gesture. The monk finished his speech and Tanner shovelled earth from the heap into the grave.

Herr Tucher spoke after the obligatory moment of silence, "So my good man, come back to ours for a bite to eat and a mouthful of wine." He addressed the group at large. "I would like for you all to join me and we will toast the deceased."

"I would be grateful for a meal before I continue on my way," the monk said.

The sun hung low and they silently moved away from the grave. The only sounds were Tanner's spade scraping the cold earth and each shovelful thudding on the shrouded corpse. Subdued sobs came from Frau Kuni who walked away with her head bent. The baby gurgled from under Katarina's coat.

The monk tilted his head towards Katarina. "Your child?"

He grabbed Katarina by the arm and pushed her coat aside. A wisp of white hair showed out from under her little wool hat. He gripped Katarina's arm tightly and fixed her with a piercing look. The hair on the back of Katarina's neck stood up.

"Yes, she's my child," Katarina said.

"Lovely child," he said, his voice low.

Katarina pulled her coat closed and caught up the cart. Knecht held his hand out to Frau Kuni. Katarina helped her labor stiffly onto the coach box as Knecht pulled her up.

Herr Tucher and the monk strode briskly ahead through the sloe bushes, onto the path and began an animated conversation. Katarina lagged behind and watched a hawk sitting in the stubble field, still as a marble statue. Knecht prodded the black stallion, the cart jerked forward and Katarina followed them on foot. They moved slowly onto the main track, passing by the ponds. The white light of the low, autumn sun dazzled off the water. The two men stood aside and allowed the horse and cart to overtake them. Katarina kept a safe distance but could still catch bits of their conversation as they strolled on a few feet in front of her. Herr Tucher called the monk Ralf and questioned him about his life in general.

"Yes, I had traveled alone for a few years, after my studies," Ralf answered. "My parents died when I was a young man and I was placed in the monastery at Würzburg with the Jesuits. But I always wanted to teach. Spread the word. So I settled down, here in this area. I have tried to understand the differences between Catholics and Protestants. I am trying to study both persuasions. I've little knowledge of the Protestant teachings and need to learn more about them."

"Do I hear a Swabian accent?" Herr Tucher said.

"Yes, I grew up in Donauwörth," Ralf said.

"A Catholic in Donauwörth? That must have been…challenging. For want of a better word."

"My parents were killed by Protestant ruffians after the Markus Procession in Donauwörth. Catholics were supposed to be tolerated in the city but persecuted nonetheless. It is not only the Catholics who are fervently opposed to diversity."

"Hmm, yes. I am sorry. Religion is the breeding ground for brutal abuse. So, where does the road lead today?"

"Today I am out to stretch my legs. I felt the need now that the sun finally shines. Right now I live in Höchstadt but I feel I have settled too long this time. I have heard they are forming troops and I may travel towards Prague and join a regiment."

Katarina's legs were cold and her ears frozen even though her hair hung over them. She stepped up her pace, passed the two men and got back to the kitchen as quickly as she could. She undid the baby's sling, put Isabeau in her basket despite her fussing, threw some logs on the fire and set a pot on the tripod to boil some water. She made some tea and prepared porridge for the baby. Herr Tucher came in carrying three bottles of wine and asked her to please heat it and add some of the spices in the little pouch he held in his hand.

"What an interesting man," he said. "He knows the Aisch valley well. He had lived here for quite some time and is now traveling."

Katarina mixed the wine and the spices in a pot and set the pot over a low flame. "He's a strange man."

"Any man of the cloth will be strange. That profession attracts those sorts."

"Why would he have any interest in what we do?"

"He was stretching his legs," Herr Tucher said.

Katarina snorted under her breath. She flopped a ladleful of porridge on a plate, sat down with the child on her lap and shoved a spoonful into her mouth. Isabeau squeezed her lips together and all the porridge ran down her chin. Katarina stood again, the child on her hip, and grabbed a cloth to clean her face. The wine steamed in the pot and she poured the hot wine into two ceramic flagons, inhaling the smell of warm cinnamon. Herr Tucher took the flagons and two wine cups.

"He is a teacher," he said. "Might be worth getting to know him. Be so kind as to bring up something to eat."

Katarina sat back down with the child and spooned porridge in Isabeau's mouth. She cooed in between bites and laughed every time the porridge dribbled down her chin. She was growing into a solid child. She grabbed the spoon out of Katarina's hand and held it with a strong grip. Katarina pulled it back and the baby laughed. Her eyes were clear as the winter sky, determined and interested. Now they grew tired as her belly filled. Katarina put her in her basket and into the alcove with a kiss to her soft, white-blonde hair.

"You stay here and stay quiet until I find out who this man is."

She put together some dried meats on a platter and arranged halved cooked eggs around the meats. Sara bustled in, chatting to Falk, the two of them surrounded by the mouth-watering aroma of their tray of steaming honey cakes. Tanner followed her into the kitchen carrying a large flask with beer and grabbed some mugs. Fully-laden, they all climbed up the steps to the sitting room.

Compared to the rest of the house, the sitting room was hot as an oven. Pieter wandered aimlessly, examining the shelving that was overfilled with books and picking one out that interested him finally. Books were piled in the one corner and spilled under the desk littered with papers and writing things. Frau Kuni blended into the wall lined with framed paintings. They covered what little wall space was still exposed: a dark picture of a table laden with fruit; a portrait of a woman with an eerie light on her half-exposed face; another arrangement of flowers and fruit on a table. Frau Kuni looked like one more still life.

Herr Tucher had taken off his heavy clothes and was only wearing knee breeches and a loose shirt with the sleeves rolled up. He had taken off his boots and walked to and fro in the sitting room in stocking feet. His cheeks were flushed from the heat. The heavy work of country living was broadening his shoulders.

He recited something. He stopped, shoved a chair out of the way, bent over the open book on the table and continued talking. Tanner stopped and leaned in the doorway, not entering, and muttered a few words to Pieter. Tanner excused himself from the group, taking Falk by the hand, explaining he needed to tend sheep.

"Ralf, this is Katarina. I would never manage without her here," Herr Tucher said as she sat down on a bench along the wall.

Katarina nodded politely and Ralf did the same. He reached up and stroked his shaven chin. He wore a ring with a coat of arms similar to the one belonging to Isabeau's mother.

"Funny place to bury a loved one," Ralf said, filling himself a plate of food. "I've heard that a man killed his lover in that meadow this spring. A sort of execution. They say he thought she was a witch and caught her in the act of some bloody ritual. Tragic."

"Well, Katarina seems to know the fields and ponds and especially the meadow well. Have you heard such a tale, Katarina?"

"Those are all ghost stories," Frau Kuni chimed in. "Lots of people tell of strange happenings there. Superstitions, I say." She sipped at her spiced wine.

"There were witnesses, I have heard," Ralf said and snivelled.

He popped a cooked egg into his mouth. His head moved in a slight jerk when he chewed. He swallowed and dabbed his mouth with his thumb.

"The man in question is a madman, some say," Ralf continued. "He accused his own father of witchcraft and wants him tried for heresy. But another example of divine intervention. Their house was struck by lightning and burned the night after he killed his lover. The two men are now outlaws, free as birds, as they say."

Katarina's mouth was full of honey cake. She responded by shaking her head, claiming ignorance.

Ralf continued, "I knew the young woman well. She went missing and her father sent us to search. We finally found her decapitated in that meadow and had wondered what really happened there. I thought it looked like she'd given birth but we never found a baby. Have you seen this man, Katarina?"

Katarina shook her head again. She felt her face redden and hoped no one else had noticed.

"Her father is heartbroken. He wants justice and he wants to know what happened to the baby, if a baby exists at all. His last living relative. We will continue to search for the child. If you see anything, Katarina, you may tell me." Ralf's eyes were too big for his head. He looked hunted.

Bored with the conversation, Herr Tucher steered Ralf's attention back to himself. An eloquent speaker, Herr Tucher's voice was low and round. He enunciated every word, stopping from time to time to choose them like an actor on a stage. He felt that unfortunates were at a disadvantage and expanded on his ideas on how to alleviate unrest by simply feeding people. In his opinion, religious doctrines were being perverted to serve some political oppressors. Accusing people, especially women, of witchcraft and heresy was only a sick deviation the church devised to seize control over the common people.

"Yes, but 'unfortunate' women are more susceptible to the deviations of the devil," Ralf said. "It has been proven that they possess a perfidy found only in their inferior sex compounded with their inferior social standing. These women mix strange drinks with potent powers. They are witches and need to be cleansed and taught the ways of the Lord. Even Martin Luther had some serious views on this subject. These women should be executed, he believed."

"Here we differ, young man," Herr Tucher said. "Women are not the root of all evil. Those teachings are the spoutings of a man who could not keep his women under control. Now take this book from Paracelsus. Our health and our lives depend on the balance between man and nature, not the violent upheaval thereof. These are not issues of faith, but of science."

"Paracelsus is much disputed," Ralf said. "Many thought of him as a charlatan. His methods are not unknown to me. My point is the sciences need to be studied with the corrective of theology."

"But many a sick man has been helped by his simple procedures. I'll show you some of the books I have. You must see them. Try some of his remedies. The only men calling him a charlatan are the doctors who lose money when Paracelsus' methods prove effective."

Sara stood stiffly and took her leave to fetch more wine. Pieter grabbed a book from the overloaded bookshelf, sat in the corner on a chair and read.

Katarina had heard enough philosophizing. Of course she could appreciate a man like Tucher siding with the less fortunate. But how could he even think he understood what it was like to be underprivileged, let alone a woman? He traveled when he liked, had new clothes that fit, snapped his fingers and his servants did what he wanted. And this man that Hans-Wolfgang had told her about with his dangerous views. Katarina wanted to leave this party. She stood and gathered the now-empty platter and asked to be excused.

Taking what she could carry, she picked her way down the steps to the kitchen, deposited the things on the table and went back up the steps for the wine mugs. Herr Tucher stood at the open front door saying his *adieus* to the monk. He closed the front door .

"Fascinating man, that young monk."

Katarina thought the sniveling man was nervous and suspicious. She caught him looking at her from time-to-time with a mistrusting look in his eye. He knew who the baby was. Terror pricked along her skin like the biting cold.

"I don't like him. There's something peculiar about him." Katarina turned and ran up the steps to fetch the rest of her things.

"Do you like any of us?" he called up the steps, following close behind.

"I can't listen to men like you," Katarina said over her shoulder, walking into the sitting room. She pulled herself up tall and turned to him. "What do you men know anyway about what it's like to be a woman? What do you know what it's like to be poor and…"

"Don't you see?" he said and shut the door behind him. "Katarina, the more men like me try to break the hold Rome has on the Empire, the sooner we can develop our reformed church here in the German language. Young German men like Ralf can be converted, I'm sure of it. Men need to unite and fight against the superstitions and backward doctrines of the Pope. Nuremberg was one of the first cities to embrace the Protestant religion and has thankfully not given in to the poisoned tongues of the witch hunters, but how long can it last? Do you have any idea what is going on in the Catholic cities nearby? Bamberg? Würzburg? Women being persecuted to promote the power of the Catholic Church, for one…"

Tanner burst in the room without knocking and Herr Tucher stopped. "Sir, a messenger has come. Your wife gives birth. We need to leave now if we are to reach Nuremberg before nightfall."

Herr Tucher, without a word, grabbed a leather satchel from his chair and left the sitting room. Katarina was alone to finish clearing up. She stopped and went to one of his bookshelves, ran her finger over the leather bound volumes, read their inscriptions: *Der Bibel*, various books from Paracelsus—something about Frenchmen. She thumbed through a pile of pamphlets: Luther's Catechism, *Sidereus Nuncius*, Erasmus, Copernicus.

Katarina had never been in this room on her own. She only entered when he personally admitted her. Willi said he had scoured it that day in the summer, found nothing of value and left frustrated. He swore at Katarina for refusing to be part of his search.

Come to think of Willi—that was the last time she'd seen him. To think he'd been the center of her world for four years. That's where sentiment and love got her.

On Herr Tucher's desk, amid the mass of papers, lay a large leather-bound book and next to it, the little book he was always jotting his notes in. Katarina opened the larger of the two. It looked like a journal. She thumbed from page to page and noticed a few dated entries in his fine-flowing script entitled *Amsterdam*, *Traveling* and *Nuremberg*. They were carefully written, with few corrections. She turned to the first page. *The Journal of Sebaldus Novellus*. The book's first entry was dated January 1616. It was called *Sichardtshof*. He must have started the book with this project, recording its progress. Katarina turned to another page dated April and one name jumped out: Katarina. She read what she could and it seemed that he'd planned her into his project since the beginning. She turned to May and saw the name again: Katarina. She turned the page and there was verse: Katarina. He couldn't really mean her, could he? What was his wife's name? She bent in closer to read the verse.

The door flew open. She slammed the book shut without looking up.

"Thirst for knowledge, my dear? I thought you could not bear to know what 'Men Like Me' were thinking."

He was carrying the leather satchel and another, smaller pouch. He took the two books from the desk and stuffed them in his satchel. "I need these. Thank you."

He stood for a moment and glared at Katarina as if he awaited her rebuttal. His smirk and his self-praising stance—feet slightly apart, shoulders squared, one hand on his hip, head slightly tilted back and chin high—made Katarina's steam rise.

"You are nothing but a drunken, arrogant bastard," she said.

"Then leave. Go. Nothing holds you here, *Magd*."

"You hold me here," she said. "Like a prisoner!"

He dropped his two bags and rounded on her, grabbing her hair from behind, jerking her head backwards.

"Is this what you need?" he hollered. "Do you want to know what it is like to be a prisoner? Should I throw you on the ground and take you as I please, like any other master would? You know, I could have any woman here at this farm. I could hire ten maids and have one in my bed every night. I do not need you. But maybe I allow you refuge here for other reasons. You seem to take no notice of the sort of life I would like to offer you."

"What could you possibly offer me?" she screeched.

"They are searching for that child. What have you done? You do realize what could happen to you if you are harboring that child from her rightful family? Where will you go? Alone?"

He loosened his grip on her hair and turned away, his voice quiet. "And sometimes I fear this is what all you women really need."

He grabbed his things, turned on his heel and left the sitting room. His bedroom door slammed. A patch of plaster fell from the ceiling and shattered on the floor. She left without cleaning it up.

Chapter 16

October 31, 1616

Herr Tucher had arrived in Nuremberg yesterday as the sun was setting. Tanner had driven the coach through the afternoon at an accelerated pace with no concern to the thrashing Herr Tucher received as the passenger. The ride was atrocious—bumpy, fast and frozen. Herr Tucher's wife had then labored the whole night through and was still full in the throes of childbirth. There was little he could do except be present.

The first light showed outside on the horizon. A knock sounded on the door of Herr Tucher's library in the wing of the Nuremberg house. His Uncle Paul's *Magd* entered, a thin wisp of a girl, set down a tray of bread and a flagon with what smelled like hot spiced wine on the table. A grateful smile and words of thanks spread over Herr Tucher's lips.

Uncle Paul's *Magd* produced a few candles from the folds of her skirts, laid them on the table next to his inkwell and turned to leave the library. The good girl had the sense to set up a space for him here to work. Herr Tucher lit a second candle and picked up his quill, his hands still shaking from the cold.

The scene with Katarina yesterday afternoon played over and over in his mind, a badly-written drama that he wished he could burn. Katarina read malice into his patient and kind handling. Yes, those same attributes he had lost yesterday afternoon. Her assumption that he could want to do her harm pained him. And his pride could not comprehend why she would refuse his advances in the good spirit they were intended. Together, their evenings could be so enlightening, spent in pleasant discourse. Otherwise the winter would be damned to stretch indefinitely if he found no diversions.

He was determined to write down this last setback, even if only a reminder to himself as to what he must change in the future. As he wrote, he found he could only record their conversation, word for word. That would not do. Herr Tucher stood and opened the wardrobe and found two rolls of empty parchment among his wife's old hats and gloves.

He unrolled one and weighted it down with his inkwell and the flagon of wine. The fire burned low so he stirred the embers and threw on a few logs. They were not quite dry and the resin hissed as they caught fire. He sat and began writing a letter:

My dearest Katarina,

Sleep eludes me and I can only sit here and imagine you breathing low in your dreams. How I wish I could be part of them, take you in my arms and bury my weary face into your hair. All I want is for you to accept my love and maybe one day allow me into your heart and love me as well. But for the time being, I must be content with fulfilling your needs.

Dearest, please admit me into the secrets of your soul. Whisper and I will join you there. Take my hand and my love and hold nothing back. I may be detained for a few days, but I long to return. I shall hurry, dear. Please forgive me, receive me and permit me to start anew. I need you more than words…

Rejoicing voices and the scuffling of many feet down the hall signalled that his wife's delivery was a successful one. Herr Tucher set his quill aside, jumped up and reached the door in two steps. He pulled the door open, ran down the hall towards the din and stopped by the closed door to the wife's sitting room. A whistle from below turned his head.

At the bottom of the stairway, Uncle Paul stood smiling up at him. Herr Tucher's father was an only child and Paul was Herr Tucher's great uncle—his grandfather's youngest brother and the same age as Herr Tucher's father. Paul had been more of a father to Herr Tucher, having never married or had children of his own. The two men shared a similar humanistic temperament. Like many of the men on his father's side, Paul had a stocky trunk and slim legs. He dressed more extravagantly than Herr Tucher did, his full maroon sleeves slashed and a lace collar spilling over his chest.

"Congratulations are in order, my boy," Paul said as he walked up the steps.

"Let us see if they allow me in," Herr Tucher said.

Herr Tucher quietly entered the wife's sitting room and rapped on her bedroom door. The door opened and a midwife clutching a once-white towel in her bloody hands wiped the sweat from her brow with her sleeve. Behind her, women clucked excitedly like chickens.

"A healthy son, Herr Tucher," she said.

Strong, new-born lungs wailed behind her.

"You can see him this afternoon," she said and quietly closed the door.

Paul clapped him on the shoulder. "Well done, my boy."

"Yes, my father and my mother will be pleased. I am pleased that both wife and child have survived the first obstacle."

"She and the baby have the best of care, your mother assured me."

"I have done my duty for the dynasty, as far as I am concerned," Herr Tucher said. "The Imhoff family will be pleased as well."

"This is no time for cynicism, Sebald. You must be exhausted. We will have a proper drink later and celebrate. Go get some rest."

Herr Tucher walked back to his library alone. Fatigue dragged at his limbs and he felt let down and empty. His only purpose it seemed was to sire children, to eternalize his family name and the lineage of both his family and his wife's. He had been matched to the aloof and loveless Fräulein Imhoff and married off to her as a young man. They led two completely separate lives and always had done. Their only common ground was the families' business ties and the task he and his wife were entrusted with: the spawning of capable patricians.

Herr Tucher stopped by the shut door. He had left the door ajar, he was sure of it. He pushed down on the handle and slowly shoved the door open. A fresh heap of firewood lay next to the hearth and a breakfast tray had been placed on the table where his letter had been. Heat rose in his face and he chastised his stupidity at leaving written materials open for all to see. How could he be so careless?

He shut the door, locked it and moved to the desk, only to breathe a sigh as he saw the rolled-up parchment set to the side next to his books and his journal. He took the letter and threw it into the fire.

Chapter 17

All Hallows 1616

Katarina pulled her legs back under the blanket. She grabbed her trousers and the scratchy wool jerkin from the floor up under the blanket as well in an attempt to warm the things before putting them on. All the while, the argument she'd had with Herr Tucher yesterday afternoon rang in her ears.

She misinterpreted Herr Tucher somehow. Of course he treated her fairly. She had grown fond of him. But what did he want from her, for her? He spoke of the life he wanted to offer her. What would he want to offer her? Why would he want anything for her? She'd heard all those empty propositions from patrons at the tavern, the wine and the candlelight having made them soft and affectionate.

Her breaths were visible, damp puffs as she stoked the fire and fed the baby. The cold nights now brought a frost that took hold of the kitchen and the rest of the house. She rolled the baby in a second wolf blanket and walked with her under her overcoat across the farmyard. Frozen mud, hard as rock, and the frosted grass crunched under her feet as she walked past the well to the workers' house.

Katarina handed the baby to Sara and Sara gave her a big basket to collect some mushrooms.

"It's quite cold," Sara said. "Would you rather wait until another day?"

"I would like a walk today," Katarina said. "I won't be long."

As Katarina walked along the frozen track, the sun rose higher in the sky without an attempt to warm the air. She came up to the meadow and ducked through the sloe bushes. Where the sun settled on the grass, gentle steam rose. The old trees and the sloe bushes seemed to trap the warmth. Katarina picked a few sloe berries and spat out the still-bitter fruit. She hunted along the outer edges of the meadow for mushrooms, searching among the damp patches of earth that had not yet frozen.

A few open parasol mushrooms grew under the shade of the bushes. Katarina cut them carefully at the base and laid them in the basket. The dark-brown, woody-smelling, earthy-tasting mushrooms that grew among the scattered brown leaves were the *Boletus*. Others, with white caps and tiny nibs on the top, sprouted like grass under the trees. Similar ones, but darker brown, peeked through the grass— fine-stemmed with dark brown caps and the same little nib on the top. Frau Kuni told her to check if they were poisonous first by tasting them. If they were bitter to the taste, they were poisonous and if they were mild, neutral on the tongue, they were not.

The dark ones had a lively, grassy taste, but not really bitter. Katarina ate one, two, three, maybe four. She took a sip from her small flask of spiced wine and continued searching among the trees. Slowly the basket filled.

She found two more parasols. The basket would soon be full and she could return to her fire. Bending to cut them, she felt nauseous, suddenly overcome by a swelling in her stomach. She sank to her knees and heaved out of dry, drained guts. A pressure behind her eyes made her see stars. She felt cold, bare and empty.

As suddenly as it began, it stopped. Still on her knees, she reached out and touched the grass. It felt so warm. The heat flowed from the grass, through her hands and into her body like a sudden rush of blood. Glow worms appeared on blades of grass and they warmed her hands even more when she held them close.

The sun pushed single rays of light through clouds of sparkling dust that rose from the orchard floor. The sparkling dust gathered at the forest edge to form a walking, living being—a tree-trunk of a woman clad in a flowing white gown. A single white braid hung over her left breast. Her outline became pronounced as she walked towards Katarina. The morning glow lit her from behind and she gestured with her head and her hands. She stopped in front of Katarina and spread her arms wide.

"Katarina, I must tell you the truth…"

A loud ringing in Katarina's ears overplayed the strange woman's words. Her mouth moved but Katarina could not hear her. Katarina tried to speak but couldn't hear anything but the loud ringing. She was still on her knees, unable to move. A dark rush of air forced her backwards. She lost her balance and landed dumbly on her back. The ringing stopped. In its place, the wind hummed a calming ballad in the treetops, lulling Katarina to stare as the pines swayed in cadence, moaning and creaking as they rubbed one another. A hawk rose above the trees and called to its mate. Nothing else mattered. Katarina lay in a cradle of contentment.

Another dark rush of air and another sailed over her, leaving a trail of sparks popping over her head. Thunder rolled under the ground and the sun was gone. She felt cold and thought the thunder might mean rain. What seemed to be large insects were whizzing overhead. Men shouted. Now one man shouted. At her. She recognized his face…

The man kneeled over Katarina, fiercely shook her shoulder and tried to pick her up. Afraid she still couldn't move, Katarina sprang to her feet and set all her strength into beating him around the face. He wrenched her arm behind her back, bent her over and, with his other arm around her waist, heaved her up, across a horse's shoulders. Katarina hated horses. She tried to tell him that, but instead vomited all down the horse's front leg. She felt the man sit lightly in the saddle, the reins lying loosely on her back. He whistled and away they rode.

When she opened her eyes, she was lying on her back, staring up into the tops of swaying pines. The same tree-top ballad soothed her aching temples. An acrid smell of cold smoke stung her nose. She lay in a cluttered but once well-maintained farmyard that had been badly burned. The charred beams of an ample sized, half-standing house stood exposed. Dead, frozen weeds grew up out of the foundation of a completely burned barn. Hans-Wolfgang had his back to her and was tending a wound on the horse's flank.

Katarina rolled over and tried to sit up. He turned towards her.

"Come inside and be quiet," he said, grabbed her hand and pulled her up and towards the ruin.

Hans-Wolfgang's brown riding cloak was wet and smelled like horse. The tip of his sheathed sword peeked out from under the hem. He led her behind the house to a small shed. He opened the door and motioned for her to enter. Inside it looked like a smoke house and a small fire still glowed. At least it was warm. Katarina let herself fall on the low stool across from a makeshift sack of straw, where she supposed he slept. He was only a head taller than Katarina but stood half stooped, his head touching the low ceiling. His closely-cut light-brown hair was wet as well. His head moved at every slightest sound, restless blue eyes searching.

"What is this place?" Katarina said. She should have been scared but it all felt like a dream.

"This is my home, what's left of my home. It was my father's home, and my grandfather's. It's a long story."

"Why have you brought me here?"

"What were you doing in that meadow today?" he said. "In the orchard? You could have gotten yourself killed."

"If you hadn't come along and dragged me away, I would be home by now," Katarina said.

"No, you'd be dead by now."

"I just got a mouthful of bad mushrooms," she said.

"No, you got a mouthful of intoxicating mushrooms. You need to be more careful."

"What do you mean?"

"Didn't you see the riders? Those weren't fairies."

"I didn't see any riders."

"Those were real soldiers up there! And real arrows!"

"What soldiers?" she said.

"Ralf and Friedrich have assembled mercenaries!" He shook his head and suddenly grabbed her by the shoulders. "Where's the baby?"

"Why didn't you take me home?" Katarina said. She remembered Ralf's accusation and her eyes widened. "They aren't after me. They're after *you*."

He tightened his grip. "Where is the baby?" he demanded.

"With the tanner's wife. She's alive, healthy, hungry."

"I'm pleased to hear that." He growled, released her and his tone softened. "She's now all the family I have left. You want a drink?"

He poured from a brown ceramic flask and filled two cups. Katarina took the cup he offered and drank. The strong, sweet drink made her sway in her seat. She drank more. It warmed her. He sat down on the straw sack, still speaking. Katarina watched his lips move but heard only the wind outside. Ralf said Hans-Wolfgang's house had been struck by lightning and burned in the spring. Where had he lived all this time? Here in the ruins? Or in the woods? Many who had lost their homes had taken to living in huts in the woods…

"Are you listening to me?" he said.

"What?" Katarina said. She held out her cup. "What is this stuff?"

"Hawthorn wine. With honey. It warms the heart, they say."

"Do you live in here?"

"Yes, together with my father but he couldn't bear to live among these ruins any longer," he said, looking distant. "Or in the forest. He died two days ago and I buried him last night. That was the end of that story. I followed the soldiers to the meadow this morning. You're not safe anymore. Or the baby."

"Ralf said a man killed his lover," Katarina said. "He meant you."

"I didn't kill her," Hans-Wolfgang said. "She meant everything to me. Isabeau too."

"Then why didn't you keep her?"

"I can't raise her. I don't even have a house left. And, she needs a mother."

"I'm no mother to that child. I don't know what I am anymore," Katarina said. "She's right. I don't know my place. I don't ever get these things right."

"It is your task. I was sent to you."

"I am not the right woman for your task."

"You are the only woman for the task. She told me so. You saw her for yourself in the meadow."

"Who? That woman in white?"

"That was Sybilla Weiss," Hans-Wolfgang said.

"She's only a legend, a child's story. I thought it was Hel, you know, mother earth."

"Well now we have both now seen Sybilla, haven't we?" Hans-Wolfgang took a long draught from his cup.

Thunder rolled outside. It sounded like a whole army.

"Soldiers?"

"No, that's real thunder," Hans-Wolfgang said, peering through the door. Rain pattered on the roof. "The air has warmed. I saw that the river was already high when we rode here. There will be flooding. You won't be able to cross. You'll have to stay here tonight."

"Why didn't you just take me home?"

"Friedrich's soldiers were following us. I would have led them straight to the farm and Isabeau." He stood to leave. "I'll find something for us to eat."

"What does he have soldiers for?"

"Probably a private regiment he hopes to hire out. The German princes are gathering troops. So is the Empire. Some are going towards the Low Counties to fight the Spanish. But soldiers are gathering here too. Mark my words. There's going to be a war here too."

The rain thrashed about in the trees and thunder rolled away to the north. Hans-Wolfgang returned after a short while. From under his soaked greatcoat, he produced some dried meats, apples and bitter-tasting flatbreads. Katarina watched him as they ate. He was a man with an air of capability and broad, strong shoulders. He spoke in a hoarse voice, like he used it so seldom he had to clear his throat before any words would come out.

After they ate, Hans-Wolfgang sat on the straw mattress with his quiver on his lap and inspected the fletching on his arrows. He pulled three feathers out from under the mattress, measured the feathers next to the arrow butts and cut fitting replacements. Katarina sipped her hawthorn wine and the warmth of the fire, the after effects of the mushrooms and the smoke made her drowsy.

"Well, tell me the story," Katarina asked boldly.

Chapter 18

"I don't know how much you know about my family," Hans-Wolfgang said. "I'll go back to the beginning and tell you what I know. I'm still trying to find many details."

Hans-Wolfgang's voice had changed, now clear and innocent. He spoke as if reciting from a story book. His faced smoothed, looked younger and took on a regal air. She had the feeling he was relieved to be finally telling someone his story.

"Here atop the hill between Weidendorf and Gottesgab stand two humble country estates, Upper Eierhofen, the estate that receives the morning sun, and Lower Eierhofen, or what is left of Lower Eierhofen, the estate that receives the evening sun.

"There was a young man from Lower Eierhofen, Hans-Wolfgang von Untereierhofen. He, well, I, am or was, the son of Christian von Untereierhofen, a Protestant pastor. The Pastor von Untereierhofen, my father, had studied theology at Wittenberg, but had no parish at the moment because of violence caused by the Catholics in the area over the last few decades."

Katarina's heart sunk. The religions weren't causing the violence. Men were. Intolerant men who worshipped the same gods and the same artifacts and the same sort of books. Power-hungry men who needed a pious cause to hide behind whilst they ravaged, robbed, conquered and killed. It mattered not what they called their order today, there were so many.

"The Pastor von Untereierhofen was a great hunter," Hans-Wolfgang continued. "Known for his tracking skills, he trained hawks and falcons, even had his own falcon. As a boy, I was always on horseback and accompanied my father on the hunt. Yes, you and I met on occasion, I recognize you. I was and am still precise with bow and arrow. I know the woods and fields between the Eierhofen forest and all along the Aisch River like the back of my hand. But we weren't allowed to hunt at will through the region. Oh, no! The laws were strict. But we won't tell."

Katarina squirmed on the low stool. "I'd seen you and your father out hunting. Plenty of times. But I have never seen anyone else from Upper Eierhofen. As a child, I was told not to come up here."

"I'd seen you before, too," he said. "Because my father and I spent lots of time riding out of our way when we needed to go to Lonnerstadt. We had to travel past Sichardtshof often, on our way to see to his affairs."

He held up his flask of wine. Katarina held out her cup and let him refill it.

"And there was a young woman, Andra-Angela von Obereierhofen. She was the beautiful daughter of the landlord Friedrich von Obereierhofen, whose wife had died in childbirth. 'The Influential Friedrich,' my father called him. Friedrich never had time to seek a new partner, so he said. Others said it was because Andra was an odd girl. She had a limpid, fair complexion with white-blonde hair and pale-blue eyes that were extremely sensitive to bright sunlight. She tended to stay indoors during the day and walk in the evenings. She had an extensive knowledge of herbal remedies and this provoked whispering in the Catholic community. People said she would wander in the woods at night."

Frau Kuni had always told Katarina to be careful who she helped with herbal remedies; neighbors who fell ill and asked for help. How grateful and generous they'd be with their blessings and praise. But those same neighbors could turn at the slightest temptation of gossip or opportunity to weave rumors of witchcraft!

"Because of religious differences, Catholic Upper Eierhofen and Protestant Lower Eierhofen were having a feud. Our grandfathers had been great friends but our fathers were at war. In good times, Upper Eierhofen numbered twenty-three souls. We never had more than ten souls.

"And it often came to blows in the neighboring villages when Upper Eierhofener and Lower Eierhofener would meet in the premises of some unfortunate innkeeper. Not to mention, if a Lower Eierhofener wanted to pass by Upper Eierhofen along the road towards Lonnerstadt. We, the sorry Lower Eierhofener would have to ride south, round the forest by The Old Well, cross the Aisch river, then ride north again past Sichardtshof towards Lonnerstadt. What an undertaking!"

"Yes, of course," Katarina said. "There was always problems at the *Mailacher Kirchweih* with the eggheads."

"You called us eggheads?"

"Frau Kuni called them the '*Eierköpfe*,'" she said. "Those men who came to our fest. They had these singing battles of who could sing the rudest song. There was always a brawl."

"The brawls weren't only at those fests," he said. "No matter where we turned up. So I stayed away from all of them. And in my travels, I often passed the secret meadow behind massive sloe bushes set back from the main road. It was there that I spied this strange but beautiful young woman, all dressed in gray. She had white hair and white skin, when she wasn't covered to protect herself from the daylight. When her hood slipped, there in the meadow, and a ray of sunshine touched her, she shone with a silver shimmer. She wasn't involved in the community like the other women. That's why you may have never seen her. She kept to herself, spending time in the woods listening to birds and collecting herbs. Some even whispered that she was a witch.

"I would capture glitters of her there in the forest and finally one day I summoned all my courage, because brave men are usually very shy, you know, and I spoke to her. 'Good Day,' I had said.

"She looked up at me, her eyes gleaming brilliant blue, like a cloudless day in May. I was awestruck that such a beautiful creature could walk the face of the earth. She told me her name was Andra-Angela. When she spoke it was like chimes, a clear bell still ringing in my memory.

"We began meeting regularly in the woods, in the special meadow. She showed me the beauty of the orchard, sang with the birds, collected herbs and mushrooms. We spent delicious afternoons under the old fruit trees, wondering who had planted them, eating the autumn apples. One beautiful autumn day, we were having a particularly romantic afternoon, we gave in to our budding love and I took her. I did not want to take her without marriage but the lush surroundings and the scent of her skin was so intoxicating, that we consecrated our love then and there. I vowed I would marry her and would see her father that Sunday and ask him for her hand in marriage.

"I found out from my father later that, as children, we were purposely kept from one another. I knew I may not be welcomed by

Friedrich von Obereierhofen. But still, maybe the feuding would stop if I offered such a gesture.

"What we didn't know, was that Andra's father was having her followed. He had heard the whisperings of his daughter's herb collecting and nature walks and had sent the Jesuit priest, Ralf, to follow her. Ralf was her teacher and lived with the family the last few years. He always lost track of her. This time he found us together and he thought she was having an affair with the enemy!"

"He wears a ring with the same coat of arms like the ring you gave me," Katarina said.

Hans-Wolfgang looked away. "He still works for Friedrich von Obereierhofen even though they fought bitterly when Ralf brought Andra's body back. Friedrich made Ralf leave so now he is also working for a family in Höchstadt. But they are planning together, those two men. Ralf told Friedrich that I killed Andra."

He sighed, took a sip of wine and shook his head as if he couldn't understand the logic.

"So, after Ralf found us together, Andra was put on house arrest. She wasn't allowed to leave the grounds of the house she shared with her father, except to go to church on Sundays. The Influential Friedrich would not accept a visit from me, either.

"Now I never knew Andra was with child. I rode past the secret meadow a few times a week since her house arrest hoping she would manage to get out. But as I rode up the bank into the meadow that day in May, I was met by a tree-trunk of a woman, clad in white. Sybilla Weiss. My father had told me my whole life that she was a phantom in the fog, an old-hag's tale, a trick of the light. But now the great seer stood before me, grabbed my horse's reins and we were unable to go on.

"She tried to turn me away. She told me she'd been watching Andra through the pregnancy. She'd witnessed the birth in the meadow. We were not to get involved in the mechanisms of fate. But I heard Andra calling my name. She was in trouble!

"I sprang from my horse and ran into the meadow. I spied the scene that would change my life and my opinion of God and the world and my fellow human beings forever. My beautiful Andra was severed on the ground. She was alone. I could not take it in, the bloody scene. I'd hunted, seen many a dead animal, but none of that had prepared me for this heartbreaking scene. Nothing had prepared me to have my heart ripped out like this. My first thought was vengeance at any cost, and I heard a soft cry like a wounded bird. I thought maybe Andra was calling to me, maybe she wasn't really there decapitated on the ground like this. Maybe it was just a trick.

"I saw her cloak crumpled on the ground and heard the soft cry and quickly opened the parcel and saw a child. 'Oh dear Mother of God!' I cried out. 'Our Child.' With slight wisps of silver blonde hair. 'Your name shall be Isabeau. Like my mother.'

"I could imagine what had happened here. Ralf had something to do with it, I'd heard him. But he had gone and the soldiers as well. Sybilla told me there was no time for that at the moment, that the soldiers were coming back to retrieve Andra's body and I must save the child, my child. Our child was born into this world for a reason. My life depended on saving this child! But where could I take the child? I couldn't take her, couldn't take her…"

He cleared his throat.

"Couldn't take her anywhere where someone could see my bastard child. They might kill her, too. Sybilla helped me onto my horse, and secured the child under my riding cloak. She told me to take the child to Sichardtshof, to the maid there. She took the ring from Andra's finger, gave it to me and slapped my horse into movement. I rode off in panic, eyes blinded by hot, stinging tears, not caring what direction Sybilla had pointed me in.

"I realized that the horse traveled up through that fertile hollow, the Edelgraben. Yes, Sybilla had said Sichardtshof. The beautiful country dwelling alongside the ponds from heaven. But my soul did anything but quiet."

He cleared his throat again. His voice had reverted to a hoarse growl. Gone was the regal young man from his story.

"So I brought the child to Sichardtshof. Gave her to the maid there. Do you remember?"

"How could I forget?" Katarina said.

"Well, I told you my version of the story and made you swear to tell no one where the child came from. Have you told anyone?"

"No."

"The only proof of the child's real identity is contained in her mother's ring. Do you have the ring?"

"Yes."

"You remember I told you this, too. You would raise the child as your own. You would protect the child or lose your life. I would be watching. The danger was you were now raising a bastard child, your bastard child. You could fall in disfavor with your master, your family, the authorities. Or you would be found out and hunted by the zealots. This has not changed."

He rose and opened the door. Katarina jumped up and grabbed him by the shoulder.

"You can't leave me like this. The master may be tolerant but if I stay away tonight I will be punished. Tanner is strict."

"Let him punish you. They cannot know about the baby. What if your master turns her over to Ralf or Friedrich?"

"If the baby is in so much danger, let's take her and go then," Katarina said.

"Running away is your solution? Sometimes one must stay and fight for what is right," he said and walked out into the rainy night.

Chapter 19

While she waited for Hans-Wolfgang to return, Katarina paced nervously in front of the fire. She digested Hans-Wolfgang's story and thought about Ralf's story of the man who killed his lover. Who was telling the truth now? The rain pounded the thin roof of the smokehouse and she heard the wind tearing through the trees. Katarina had to stay here the night. Frau Kuni and Sara would have her head on a platter tomorrow. She could imagine what Tanner would do.

The door flew open. Hans-Wolfgang rushed in and slammed it behind him. From under his dripping-wet greatcoat, he produced a skinned rabbit. He removed the greatcoat and went about arranging it on a peg hammered into the wall. He shook his wet head and scratched his ear like a dog. He seemed to be deep in thought, an internal struggle with an unseen foe. He stoked the little fire, coaxed it to flame, skewered the rabbit and hung the skewer to cook. The shed filled with smoke. He opened the door to allow a bit of air in and peeked out into the trees. Rain splashed his face and he closed it again. Water trickled in under the door and dripped from the ceiling.

They ate in silence. Hans-Wolfgang stood abruptly.

"Sleep if you like. I'm going back out."

Katarina slept on and off and was alone the night. She woke as he came in with more of those bitter flatbreads and a bit of meat.

"It's late in the morning but it's still raining," he said. "Have something to eat."

He pulled a candle and a book from a little box in the corner of the shed. "Do you read? You may consider staying here until the rain lets up. The river is overflowing."

Katarina took the book and the candle and thanked him. He grabbed his rider's cloak from the straw mattress, pulled the door open and went back into the rain. She opened the book, charred and smelling of soot.

"It's all in Latin! I can't read Latin," she said to no one in particular.

She paged past the text and found there were wood-cut prints and songs. The songs had the German text, too. Penned up in this shed the whole day, she was grateful for this diversion. The rain pattering and the repetition of words on the page made Katarina's eyes droop.

A blast of thunder woke Katarina from a deep sleep. Peeking out the door to discern the time of day, Katarina found it was quite dark. She would have to try to pass over the river or be in big trouble. Thunder rolled again. Hans-Wolfgang appeared in the line of trees, running towards the tiny smokehouse, the brown rider's cloak billowing out behind him. He ran in, hitting his head on the low doorframe and slammed the door shut.

"Horses!" He crouched now, one hand on his head, eyes squinting from the pain. He cracked the door and peered out. "Soldiers. I can't see how many. I saw them on the hill behind Friedrich's house this morning. They had packed to leave, but were waiting, taking cover from the rain."

He grabbed the greatcoat from the wall and threw it to Katarina. "You must leave now. Don't let them see you. Don't let them follow you!"

Katarina ran out the door, stopped next to the charred house and searched the tree line for an opening. In the yard, hooded riders dressed in black shouted, their horses stamping and fighting against the restraint of the reins. Their torches threw light, causing shadows to play among the trees, creating nonexistent openings in the forest. She ducked down and sneaked to the first path, a muddy gulch streaming with water, a steep descent down from the Eierhofen estate. She tramped through the brush between the trees to look for another path. The greatcoat snagged on some bramble bushes. She tugged and pulled the coat free.

A man shouted and she looked up through the trees. The man's hood slipped as he barked orders to two other riders in the yard. She froze and waited. He slowly turned his head and looked in Katarina's direction. His thin-lipped smile radiated in the torchlight. It was Ralf. He fixed her with a piercing look. The hair stood up on the back of her neck and a chill shook her.

He pulled his hood over his head and rode into the group of

soldiers. Katarina grabbed the greatcoat snug around her body and slowly pushed through the dense brush, not caring about the snagging branches. She barely spotted a broad path ahead in the dark. Garbled shouts and pounding hoof falls echoed behind her.

The sound of metal, like that of a rusty latch, squealed in the underbrush. Rusty hinges squeaked, like a door being opened. Here in the woods? Katarina stopped, turned and listened. A huff of breath sounded behind her. She jumped and turned around. In the dark she could make out the figure of a man. He moved in close. It was Ralf. She had just seen him atop that horse. Or had she? He grabbed Katarina's shoulders.

"I'll help you find your way," he whispered. "Follow this path."

Katarina could no longer see the path in the dark. He laid his hand on her head and spoke strange words under his breath.

"Quickly!" He pointed ahead in the darkness. "Run! That way will take you home. Go!"

Katarina stumbled forward into the brush but stopped. Ralf was gone. She remembered a story that the young nun who had lived with them all those years ago had taught her from the Old Testament. They had sat at the table in the kitchen that afternoon and she had helped Katarina draw pictures. The scapegoat. The sacrificial goat banished into the desert in order to cleanse the villagers of their sins.

Had Ralf picked her to be his scapegoat? Would he send her to her demise to save his own soul? Katarina turned around and pushed back the way she thought she had come. Could she get back to Hans-Wolfgang? Her orientation was lost. She fought on through the brush, finally came across that muddy gulch and followed it right down into the flood plain. Wading through some puddles, the flood was still low enough to pass through the plain on foot.

In the distance the river raged and smelled of dank, fishy water. Katarina thought she could see the mill. She searched in the dark for the bend in the river where it straightened. There she would find the shallow point where she could cross. But the bend was well-hidden. Water spilled out into the plain, covering the water's edge.

She heard horses splashing through the floodwater, following her. She turned abruptly, slipped and fell, soaked now up to her waist. Flapping wings splashed in the water. A startled flock of ducks took flight. Her eyes tried to adjust to the dark. She steadied herself and looked for the best way to get out of here. The flood water was deeper than she thought.

Men whistled now, urging horses forward. Hooves splashed through the water, though she could see no one coming. She rushed forward towards what she thought was the river's edge.

Katarina slipped, suddenly submerged in silence and surrounded by muffled bubbles. Wet, icy-cold water. Her bladder emptied. She couldn't breathe. Oh, dear God in Heaven, she was underwater. Her soaked clothes were cold and the weight of the sopping greatcoat pulled her down. Her feet found no hold, suspended in water deeper than she'd ever been in. She scrambled for the bank, for a hand-hold, grabbing the foliage that was rotting in the cold water.

Paddling like a dog, her head rose above the surface and she tried to calm herself long enough to take a few breaths. The sky was black and she couldn't see the hand in front of her face. Maybe she'd hit her head and was temporarily blind. Her head dipped under the water. Panic sent her hands into a frenzied flaying and slapping against the muddy bank. She grabbed like a crazed animal and ripped at the vegetation. Stinging nettles burnt her hands. They tore out easily at the roots. She grabbed again and again, trying to get a grip on the river's edge.

Katarina dug both hands into the muddy bank and clawed fast until she secured a place for her face above the water's surface. Breathe, breathe, breathe! Holding hard with one hand, the current tried to tear her away from the edge. She stretched her other hand over her head. The bank rose steeply as far up as she could reach.

She didn't dare call out. She was losing her handhold. Her fingernails were full of mud, her fingers were burning and her feet were freezing. This was it, this was how it would all end.

Like a bolt of lightning running through her veins, it struck: she may not deserve to get out of this alive but she was not going to die here. She had a more important task at hand. No one would raise that child but Katarina. These two families could fight all they wanted to. Isabeau was her child. She jammed both feet into the muddy bank and steadied her knees. Shaking from the cold and the fright, she tried to hoist her weight a trace upwards.

She grabbed overhead. A handful of nettles released their rooted hold in the mud. She threw them aside in the rushing water and shoved her feet and her knees deeper into the mud and pushed, raising her soaked body. She grabbed again, this time a bit higher. Up here, the weeds were resilient and kept their hold in the earth. She pushed her body upwards and pulled on the weeds, slipped back down and jammed one foot in the mud for a renewed hold. She grabbed with the other hand, this time a bit higher, and finally felt her shoulders come above the water's surface.

Her legs were still in the water but her hands reached up to a point where the bank levelled off. She climbed higher and higher at a snail's pace. Finally her upper body rested on a surface where she could just get up on her hands and knees. She crawled away from the water's edge and lay a moment, her cheeks in a bed of stinging nettles, hands stinging, body and thick clothes soaked through, shaking. Alone.

Hooves in the distance. She wanted to crawl out of sight but no one would find her. But if someone found her…she didn't want to think of that. She closed her eyes to catch her breath. Just for a moment.

Chapter 20

Ralf touched a second candle to the one burning on Friedrich's desk, hoping the extra light it lent would illuminate the dark November morning. The rains had ceased but the great hall at Upper Eierhofen remained shadowy and chilled even though the day promised to brighten. Ralf shuddered—the dampness in his bones refused to warm. Last night, his clothes were soaked to capacity and having had enough of the chill, he continued home before he could discover the outcome of Katarina's watery misfortune.

Ralf moved his knight to threaten Friedrich's queen. Friedrich snorted and looked up as that ancient *Magd* entered the hall. She walked stiffly to the end of his desk and set the tray down. Ralf could smell spiced wine. She poured two cups. Ralf took the mug gratefully and cupped the steaming drink in both hands. He took a careful sip and his breathe rose in puffs that climbed into one rare and pale ray of morning sun streaming through the high windows.

"Stoke the fire, *Magd*," Ralf said.

She threw a few small logs onto the metal brazier next to Friedrich's desk. The bark on the split logs smoked and slowly ignited. Friedrich winced as the smoke stung his eyes. He moved his queen to hide her behind his bishop.

"You're taking risks, allowing a bishop to protect the queen," Ralf said. "He may have other designs on her."

"Funny, coming from you, a comment like that," Friedrich said.

"I may not always agree with the Holy Father and his cardinals," he said. "But I do believe the Society of Jesus and the Jesuits can restore honor to the deteriorating Catholic Church. We need only educate the people."

"Yes, Ralf," Friedrich spluttered. "Mm, I've been thinking…"

"Oh, have you been thinking again?"

"I have made up my mind, Ralf," Friedrich said.

"I hope you have thought of our work. What we mean to accomplish for the one true religion and our small contribution to the task of uniting the Holy Roman Empire. The Jesuits saved my life. I owe them everything. You've had the papers from Bamberg. Not to mention what you owe the church if you want to ensure absolution for Andra and yourself…"

"My testament leaves the estate to Andra and her child. I have decided to change my testament when you prove to me that a child doesn't exist. I owe that much to my family, even if my soul be damned."

"How do you want to find that out?" Ralf said and toppled two captured pawns. "That a child doesn't exist?"

"I will wait until the child resurfaces then."

"What, just any child? What if the child is dead? That was almost six months ago."

Friedrich leaned back in his chair. "Andra was pregnant. She died. When you brought her body, she was no longer pregnant. I assume there is a child."

"The wolves could have carried the child away."

"I don't believe that. The child is out there. I can feel it."

Ralf stood abruptly. "Now you sound bewitched. A mysterious child reaching out from the other side. That is all superstition."

"Ralf, I can feel the child is out there. My flesh and blood," Friedrich said. "I think we should find Hans-Wolfgang and find out what he knows."

Ralf stood behind Friedrich's chair with his shoulders on Friedrich's shoulders. "He's dead, his father too. The lightning burned their house."

Friedrich tried to turn to look at Ralf. "Ralf, I saw him yesterday. You keep telling me they are dead. But I saw Hans-Wolfgang, sitting in that tree overlooking our garden. He was watching the men in the back."

Ralf turned away, hoping Friedrich hadn't seen the look of shock on his face. Friedrich got around better than Ralf thought.

"I will try to talk to him next time I see him," Friedrich said.

Ralf could not let this happen. He had to get to Hans-Wolfgang, silence him, get to the child. Why could he not find the man?

"Ralf, where is Andra's ring?" Friedrich said.

"I've told you, it is gone," Ralf said.

"I want that ring," Friedrich said. "It has been in my family for generations. My mother wore it. My wife wore it and Andra as well."

Ralf started to protest. Friedrich held a hand up to silence him.

"You have put me off for months. If you bring me what is left of my daughter, we will discuss my testament. Give me her ring and maybe I can begin to accept that I am truly alone in this world without an heir, no family left. No one."

Where was her ring? Andra-Angela always wore that ring, Friedrich insisted on it. Ralf turned and paced under the high windows. A mouse scurried along the wall and under a ball of dust. No matter how Ralf had tried to humor the man the past few months, Friedrich would not forget this triviality. Ralf feared he'd exhausted his possibilities.

"I've told you, it's gone," Ralf repeated.

"Then it could be that my grandchild lives. Get these things for me. You must work for your reward."

Ralf ran out of the great hall, lost in his own thoughts. He ran up the steps into her room as if this space would speak to him. Friedrich instructed the *Magd* keep the room as it was. As if Andra-Angela still lived. Ralf kicked the chest of drawers. The ring was not here, he need not look. He couldn't remember seeing it on her hand. Must he really disturb her earthly remains and see if it was on her dead hand?

Ralf ran out to the back garden. "I need some men to help me dig!"

He grabbed two men by their jackets. One growled like a stray hound. He dragged the two men towards Andra-Angela's grave. "You two. Dig. I will watch."

Ralf paced back and forth, doubt and distress forming beads of sweat on his forehead. He knew this action was unplanned and blind, useless. But he had to do something dark and depraved. The men grumbled and stalled. Ralf cursed their slow and plodding progress.

"Two more men!" Ralf shouted. "Help them. Faster."

Four men dug and reached Andra-Angela's body quicker than Ralf expected. He damned them for burying her so high but was grateful they had done so. He eased himself into the hole in the ground and forced himself to fumble through the muddy shroud and find her hand. His stomach lurched as he touched her cold, inanimate remains. He threw the shroud aside, his fingers combing the mud from the bones. He had to see for himself if the ring was there or not. He could not trust those hired soldiers.

"Allow me, Padre," Elis said.

Ralf looked up at him, aware how corrupt he must appear. He

climbed out of the shallow grave and allowed Elis to take his place.

Elis searched and stood upright. "There is no ring here, Padre."

"My fear or my hope is that the ring is with the child," Ralf said. "Or Hans-Wolfgang has it."

"We should search the meadow," Elis said. "Come, we'll ride together."

"For what, then?" Ralf said. "We've searched, we've found nothing. My time is wasted on such tasks, like this one, disturbing her remains."

Elis turned to the men and gave them a few quiet commands. They began putting Andra-Angela's grave to rights. Elis led Ralf away from the garden towards the front of the house.

"Your stallion needs to be exercised," Elis said. "Come, let us go away from here. It will help you think."

"We'll take some men with us," Ralf said.

The thundering hooves and the speed of his stallion exhilarated Ralf, even though he knew to search the meadow again was fruitless. His frustration with Friedrich blew away as the rushing wind deafened him. The bracing, late-autumn chill forced the tears from his eyes and he was not only deaf but blind. He let the stallion carry him, feeling the freedom a wild horse must feel. As the horse dropped to a canter, he cleaned the tears from his face with his sleeve.

They approached the meadow, rode around the periphery and dismounted. That same intimidation he'd felt here before returned. Fear was lack of faith and it was most certainly the Devil sowing this unease. He tethered his horse, found a small slit in the sloe and ducked into the meadow. He would never forget the exact spot where Andra-Angela died.

Ralf prayed to be a worthy vessel for God's will as he, Elis and the men walked in circles around that spot, heads down, searching, finding nothing.

"Please show us the way!" he whispered.

"Why are we even here?" one of the men asked.

A doubt Ralf had not experienced in a long time began to creep into his plan. Could he be plodding on the wrong path? He waved the men a sign to abandon the search, they found passage back though the bushes and prepared themselves to mount and ride back to Upper Eierhofen. He jumped onto the back of his dark-bay stallion.

Below them on the track leading to Sichardtshof, laboring wooden wheels squeaked and squealed. A bent figure dragged a handcart up the path into the hollow. The bent figure looked like that old woman from Sichardtshof. From up at the top of the South Hill, Ralf heard the squeak-squeak creaking as the woman trudged with the heavy load. The squeaking wheels carried on the fog that settled over the hollow. It looked like the old woman lugged a cart full of soiled fabric. The fabric spilled out over the sides of the small cart.

The old woman stopped and leaned on the handle of the cart. The contents of the cart moved and sat up. Ralf saw a shock of russet brown hair. Aha, it was Katarina! She lived. Who was watching the child?

"I want five of you to go down to the farm and ruffle some feathers," Ralf said. "Get in and cause a commotion and get back out before that old woman reaches the farm with Katarina."

The huffing, impatient stallion danced and turned in circles. Ralf took the leather crop and bashed the stallion around the ears. The thrill of divine intervention sent a cold shiver up Ralf's spine. Ralf dismounted and tied him to a tree. He was on the right path. God had set him on this spot today. He now saw what he must do.

"He's a barrel of gunpowder, isn't he?" the soldier with the black, floppy mustache said.

"I do not care about this horse," Ralf said with a sidelong glance at the soldier. "I know now what must be done. I need to know who that child is. To be sure that there is no proof that the child belongs to Obereierhofen. I need to know if they have Andra's ring or her cloak. That is the only proof we need. Without those things, that is just another baby. This is what is standing between me and my goal."

"What happens if we can't find these things?" Elis said.

Ralf gripped his chin and looked at Elis. His thoughts raced into a deduction of cause and effect. At the moment there was no real proof that this baby was Andra-Angela's, apart from the light hair. Friedrich had a life-long distrust of Hans-Wolfgang, so he wouldn't believe anything that madman spouted. Unless Hans-Wolfgang had Andra's things. So the first thing Ralf needed to do for his own sanity was permeate this farm and gather information. If they had Andra's things, he wanted them. They could keep the baby. Nobody needed to get hurt. If not, they must tell him where those things were. In the end, he needed Hans-Wolfgang dead. That was his ultimate, God-given task.

Ralf moved towards the tree line. From this vantage point on top of the South Hill, he could see the whole hollow of the Edelgraben, from Sichardtshof right to the main road. And he was well undercover, his black monk's cowl pulled over his head, fitting to the mud and the dark, desolate November. After the brief rays of sunshine of the morning, the sky was now an unmovable dome of grey and black cloud and the ground was soggy from all that rain. The clouds kept the air above the freezing point.

"Get down there before that woman does!" Ralf said.

"Then you mean at the pace she's moving, we have all afternoon, Pater," the soldier with the black, floppy mustache said.

"Move, Blackbeard, and be quick about it," Ralf said.

The soldier called Blackbeard nodded to his men. He rode off followed by four men who could have been his brothers: dark, broody faces framed with black hair and black beards.

"I want the other five to come with me. We ride along the hill, around the farm, turn off and go look for everyone who lives here. I want them all accounted for and I want to know where the child is. We comb the surrounding fields. I want to check where everyone else from the farm is, what their jobs are."

Ralf mounted and rode with five other men along the South Hill, dipped into the hollow at the edges of the farm and towards the top of the North Hill. They took up a natural formation as they rode. To Ralf's right or right behind him rode the Swede, Elis.

"Padre, look, you want me to go down there?" Elis said.

Elis's words were flat and monotone much like the personality on that boy. There was no flourish, no sing song, no fire like the Slavs, but a frozen brutality of the Viking people. Now Elis just pointed. Ralf followed his finger and saw the Dutch boy approaching the farm.

"Yes, the Dutch boy," Ralf said. "Don't let anyone see you, Elis."

Elis motioned for the other four soldiers to stop before they reached the top of the North Hill. Ralf and Elis stopped by two oak trees.

"Follow him on foot but don't let anyone see you. Check every gate and remember every path that leads into the farmyard and to the house in the back. I need to know how to get in, how to get out and how many people live in that worker's house as well."

Elis dismounted, handed Ralf the reins and hushed off.

"You," Ralf said, pointing to the next Slavish solider in line. "Warn the others that the Dutch boy comes home."

The soldier nodded and rode off down the hill. Ralf watched the Dutch boy and his soldier approach the farm. The Dutch boy saw the soldier and broke into a run. The other five soldiers had reached the farm and entered through the gate at a leisurely pace.

These Slavish soldiers were veterans. All of them an undeterminable age, they had been exposed to war since they were children and knew of little else in their lives. After the Turkish threat at the turn of the century had shaped their childhoods, often leaving them without families or villages, these men followed the wave of war. Now, with the rumors of war in the Empire throughout the German territories, they had ended up here in Franconia with the promise of something to eat and the possibility to loot and make a fortune. Even though, to these men, a fortune was something one spent carelessly on wine or women or gambled away in a dice game.

Ralf watched as that old barrel-chested farmhand approached his soldiers carrying a pitchfork. He spoke with the soldiers and from Ralf's vantage point, he could only imagine what they were saying. The farmhand seemed to be appealing to the soldiers' better senses.

The Dutch boy appeared in the farmyard as well. He was a large boy and gestured quite aggressively, waving the soldiers to be gone. Ralf could see Elis hiding by the well. Elis disappeared only to reappear back by the workers' house. The tanner's wife appeared at the door carrying the baby.

The baby. His heart leaped and he was surprised at his reaction. Joy, sorrow. Conflict.

He focused on his goal, his school and his need to give back to the society that saved him. He could accommodate up to fifteen children, all looking to Ralf to teach them, train them. Together they would raise food and feed themselves. Ralf would finally achieve some recognition. Maybe he'd mold the child who would have a divine vision and become the next saint. He himself was too humble to have any aspirations like that. He was but a vessel, serving God as best he could and he loved the path he'd been chosen to follow.

He thought often of his parents and his home Donauwörth.

When the city was taken over by Protestants, most of the Catholics fled but his father refused to leave his *Heimat*. His father loved the city and the path he'd been chosen to follow with the few other Catholic families: the fight to practice the one true religion.

They'd assembled a small group led by five monks in April 1606 for the annual Markus Procession. The Catholic minority had the legal right to march but it all went so badly awry. The Protestants would not allow the Catholics to pass through the city with their flags unfurled and insisted they roll them up. Those in the procession refused and a brutal fight broke out. He and his parents got away but behind the Gasthaus Stern, four men descended on his parents and slit them in front of his eyes.

A traveling Spanish monk found Ralf the next morning. Father Marius. The monk was poor, his cowl torn, his face dirty. He shared his last bread with Ralf and brought him to Würzburg, to the Jesuit monastery. Ralf was taken in and admitted to the school there. Even though he was younger than many of the other students, he studied at a starved, accelerated pace. Ralf owed everything to the Jesuits.

Ralf's stallion stamped his hoof as Ralf watched his soldiers tease the Dutch boy and the old farm hand. The soldiers kicked their horses into motion and rode in circles around them. The old woman appeared around the bend. She approached the gate to the farm yard. Ralf whistled like a hawk to Elis. Elis returned the whistle and Ralf saw him climb the North Hill. The four other soldiers returned from their ride towards the back of the farm. Another hawk's whistle and the soldier leading the group in the farmyard raised his hand. The five assembled and rode off out of the farmyard and back away from the main road. The old woman would not have seen them. They approached Ralf's vantage point as well.

Ralf motioned for the soldiers to sit quietly and out of sight.

"Padre, they may be able to see you."

Ralf pulled his hood over his head. He was no longer worried that anyone could see him. He watched for a moment as the old woman wheeled the handcart around. The Dutch boy and the old farmhand hurried to the old woman's side and helped Katarina out of the handcart. She collapsed. The Dutch boy heaved her up and carried her into the house.

Chapter 21

Sebald Tucher's wife birthed him a son on All Hallow's Eve, 1616. Now he had a son with an apple-shaped head covered with foamy yellow down. Very much alive, his lungs screamed and his skin shined rosy pink. Tucher was relieved after all the stillbirths the Tucher family had witnessed in the past. And now three days after the birth, child and wife were both healthy, thank God.

Frau Tucher had miscarried twice in the past. Each incident had driven Herr Tucher farther away from her and she from him. She blamed him for his bad seed and he wanted nothing to do with his family's plan of selective breeding. He was not the community bull.

The particulars, official registration of a live birth and so on would be handled by Herr Tucher himself. This gave him the best excuse today to get out of the house. He'd finally been allowed to view his son, Christoph Bonaventura, until the boy was whisked away into the throng of women, aunts, governesses, wet nurses and the like. There were, he was sure, a correct number of days that a man must stay by his wife and stand the role of the new father. Otherwise there was nothing for him here in Nuremberg and he should like to get on his way, back to Sichardtshof.

He walked down the steep cobblestone street away from the castle. The city's red-tile rooftops sprawled below him, packed together within the confines of the city wall, grouped like an assembly of city fathers amiably arguing some unimportant point. The city itself was like a moody old man, in danger of appearing prudish and old-fashioned. Beyond the impenetrable wall lay plains and farm fields as far as the eye could see. He moved out of the way of a begging group of vagrants and passed behind the town hall and the dungeon, in order to avoid the market square. Even on this November day, the air damp and chill, the sky grey and heavy with moisture, Nuremberg was a stunning charm on the banks of the Pegnitz.

Herr Tucher finished his business in the town registration in a hurry. He followed the river meaning to go straight home but his feet led him towards the Debtor's Tower and across the bridge to The Stork's Nest tavern. The doors to the tavern were open.

He peeked into the nearly empty, dimly-lit taproom. Uncle Paul, the actual owner of the property, mentioned to Herr Tucher yesterday that Prutt still paid his rent irregularly and would he please sort the tenant out. Standing in the doorway, Herr Tucher looked around the sparsely-patroned room, contemplating an uncomfortable confrontation. He could no longer leave this matter hanging. His own debts were mounting and his uncle would only give him money if he could bring some home.

"Lilium," Herr Tucher said as he entered the tavern, damp filling his nostrils. "Just like a flower. A bit of wine for the new father, please."

"Of course, Herr Tucher," Lily said, throwing a log on the fire. She rolled towards his table. "Your wife had a baby, then?"

"Yes, a healthy boy. And is the master of the house available?"

"Willi? Let me see." She turned and swung her expansive hips behind the counter. "Willi!" she screamed up the steps. "Tucher is here!"

Willi mumbled something from the room above.

"He said you should come on up. He's busy."

Insolent boldness. Herr Tucher grabbed his glass from the table and the bottle from the counter. He squeezed past Lily's hips, which did not budge to allow his passing. She seemed to thoroughly enjoy the contact. He rounded the counter and climbed the steps, wondering if Prutt was alone and if he need worry about such things.

Herr Tucher had only been in this upper portion of the building once before. He and his uncle had cleared this space, if one could call it a room, after the last tenant died. The old man had left tapestries and furniture and Herr Tucher adopted many books from that man's collection.

Willi sat at the table and studied a deep crevice in the wooden table top. Dust webs hung from the rafters, a few roof tiles were missing here and there and drafts of cold musty air drifted across the open space. It smelled of caged animal. A large pallet with a straw mattress stood in the corner. Atop the mattress sat a woven basket and from it came a baby's gurgling. Odd fabrics were piled in the other corner and the clothes of a quite large woman were draped over a wooden chair.

"Good Afternoon, Prutt," Herr Tucher said.

He stood in front of Willi, took a sip of the sour brew that was more like vinegar than wine and winced. He set his glass next to Willi's rested elbows and refilled the glass without looking at him.

"What can I do for you?" Willi said.

Willi was thinner than usual. Herr Tucher hadn't seen him in five months. Gone were those boyish good looks. His cheeks were sunken and his eyes were dull and drained.

"Short visit," Herr Tucher said. "My wife had a son."

"Congratulations," he said dully. "My wife has also had a son."

"Married now, Prutt?"

"Yeah, me and Lily. That's our boy," he said.

"You know why I am here, do you not? Like every month."

Willi looked up. "What do you want to take from me now?"

Herr Tucher waved his hand around the meager space. "Does not seem to be much left."

"Business is slow. You know that and you know why."

"Tell me why," Herr Tucher said. "You could not take care of your affairs. You could not keep your woman and now you are going to lose your business."

Willi slowly stood. "I should have killed you the night I had the chance."

"I beg your pardon?"

"You don't remember anything we did to you that night you were here," Willi said. "I could have slit your throat and you would have never known it. You can't hold your drink, friend."

Herr Tucher let it sink it that his assailant that night was this criminal. "Well, I am still alive, friend. But I may have a proposition. My uncle needs extra men to accompany a shipment to Hamburg. Traveling with a shipment of this nature is becoming dangerous. He may be willing to consider someone like you because he would not have to pay you. You already owe him so much money."

"What about the money Katarina earns?" His mouth twisted now, his voice seething. "She has worked for you for two seasons now."

"She earns nothing towards your debt. I won that woman."

"But that was the agreement." He kicked his chair aside. "Why do you keep her there? She can come back and work here."

"There was no agreement, Prutt. You gamed that woman away."

"That doesn't mean she can't work here."

"No, she stays with me. She cannot work here with the child."

"Whose child is that? I know it's not hers. Her naked body shows no signs of bearing children."

Herr Tucher involuntarily widened his eyes in surprise and understanding. So, Prutt had been out to see her since he put a stop to their relationship. He must be more careful.

"She'll do anything for me," Willi said.

"I've told you before. She tends the child as a favor for me."

"Give the child to the bitch that bore it. I'll have Katarina back when I'm ready."

"There you are wrong, my friend. You are a married man. And you are a ruined man—I will see to it that you stay that way."

Prutt's fist slammed so quickly into Herr Tucher's eye that he never saw the blow coming. The force behind that punch nearly knocked him off his feet.

"Get out of here," Willi said.

Herr Tucher regained his composure and shook off the dizzying cloud that threatened to double him over. This was the one advantage of being a practiced drinker; he had to regularly force himself to function in a giddy, staggering state. Already a few steps in front of him and on his way down the steps, Herr Tucher saw Prutt advance out of the corner of his eye.

"Block his path, Lily!" Willi screamed.

Herr Tucher was practically flying down the steps and slammed into Lily's massive form at the bottom of the steps. It was like hitting a feather bed. She flattened against the wall as the air wheezed out of her lungs with a smell of foul cabbage. He shook himself again, smoothed his jacket and turned to see Willi coming again, holding a knife. Comparing their statures, Willi was considerably more man than Herr Tucher. But Herr Tucher was the predominant man and would prevail. Herr Tucher grabbed a chair, held it up and braced himself. In his rage, Prutt crashed into it and tried to swing the knife and cut Herr Tucher. The knife, of course, could do him no harm. Prutt stepped back and Herr Tucher swung the chair. The solid wood collided with Prutt's head and upper body and he fell to the floor, dropping the knife. Herr Tucher threw the chair on top of him, bent down and retrieved the knife, straightened and made his way to the open door. He admired the knife; the bone handle inlaid with silver swirled in an intricate design. He had once had such a knife. No matter: he flung the knife behind the counter. Two men stood outside and must have been watching the display.

"Good Afternoon," Herr Tucher said to the two men as he walked out of the tavern.

He would most surely have *Hausverbot* from the Stork's Nest. He'd go now and try the drink at the White Harp on the other side of the river. There was the birth of his son to celebrate.

Chapter 22

A bustling din and hollers from the farmyard announced the master's return from Nuremberg. Katarina pulled the blanket closer around her shoulders and peeked through the fold of scratchy wool. Sara felt Katarina's forehead, shook her head and stoked the fire on the hearth in the kitchen of the main house.

Katarina hoped Herr Tucher would retire to his room and not bother to look for her. She was in no mood to answer his questions or suffer his stares. To her dismay, Herr Tucher strode into the kitchen, pausing to pull off his riding cloak and lay it over the bench. He came up close to her and she imagined she saw real concern in his face.

"Fish." Herr Tucher said, taking a lock of her hair in his fingers. "I smell fish. You had a little accident, I hear."

"Yes, Herr Tucher, I smell like fish," Katarina said. "I am cold and can hardly breathe. I think I caught a chill. The last thing I care about is if I smell like fish. I'll get even sicker if I bathe."

He felt her face. His hand was cool on Katarina's forehead and smelled like soap. She leaned her cheek against his palm and inhaled his scent. She had missed him and hated herself for feeling this way.

"You are burning with fever," he said.

His eye was blackened, like he'd been struck a blow. His smooth, dark hair hung neatly around his shoulders and he seemed more rested than usual. He took her chin in between his forefinger and his thumb and looked at her long and hard.

Katarina did not look away.

"Please take someone with you if you need to gather anything again. Take Pieter. Someone." He turned and left the kitchen.

Sara and Pieter brought a small wooden bath into the kitchen. It was the size of a large barrel, just big enough for Katarina to sit in. Katarina recognized it as the one she saw in the barn filled with hay and a litter of kittens. Sara was a woman with a mission. She took off her white cap, rolled up her shirt sleeves and put water in the biggest pot to boil.

"I'll get you in the bath," she said. "Yes, we cleaned it."

"Thank you," Katarina said.

Sara held out a small bottle. "I have a tincture of essential oils. Smell this."

"I can't smell anything."

"And some linden blossom tea," Sara said. "It may be a long night, but we'll sweat that fever out of you."

Sara placed Katarina in the bath like she was a baby and washed her hair. Sara was always an ample woman and even though there wasn't much to eat, she had put on a few pounds. She jabbered on and went about her business like it was the most natural thing. Katarina envied her. Sara was loving and strong, happy and free. If Katarina could steal one thing it would be her cheerful disposition.

"I'll take the baby home with me tonight. You try to get some sleep," she said.

She toweled Katarina's hair, smoothed the creases on the arms of Katarina's white night gown and threw a blanket over her shoulders. It smelled like crisp autumn sunshine. Katarina wondered if this was what it was like to have a mother.

"What did you tell Herr Tucher?" Katarina said.

"Pieter found your basket in the meadow. We figured you'd run off with a lover."

"Sara, the baby isn't mine," she said.

"Yes, yes, I know, you found her in the woods or something, yes, so I've heard." Sara gently combed Katarina's hair.

"She's in danger," Katarina whispered.

"If you stay away another night, you will be too." Sara laughed. "Herr Tucher had to hold Tanner back. Next time you get the strap!"

This was what it was like to have a mother, yes.

Herr Tucher peeked around the door frame and addressed Sara as if Katarina wasn't there. "She will sleep upstairs. Not in this damp room here. I can keep an eye on her, too."

"Come, Katarina, I'll help you upstairs." Sara grabbed Katarina's arm and helped her up. "He's too soft with you."

"I can still walk," Katarina said.

Her head throbbing, she walked through the kitchen and stumbled up the first step.

Herr Tucher sat at the table in his sitting room with one candle burning, humming over his book. Someone had made a nest for Katarina on the settee. He looked up from his book as Sara led Katarina to the soft feather bed, laid her down and covered her with another smooth blanket. The heat of the fever, more pronounced now from the warm bath, dropped Katarina into a nauseating swoon. She closed her eyes and felt Sara push the blanket away from her legs. Water dribbled into the small bucket on the floor as Sara wrung out the bits of flannel. She wrapped Katarina's calves in the cool, damp cloth.

"This will help break the fever, Katarina." She covered her legs with another blanket.

Sweating and shivering, Katarina wandered in and out of consciousness. Pungent lavender, mixed with a musky, spicy smell filled her nose and mouth. She opened her eyes, wondering how late in the night it was. Pieter was on his knees massaging her temples.

"Lavender oil. Good for a heavy head. This doesn't hurt, does it?"

Katarina mumbled and tried to nod.

"Don't worry, Katarina," he said.

She fell into a dream of fire, fear and a spinning chaos, woke again in a sweating panic. Pieter was gone. Herr Tucher lit another candle from the one burning low and opened a bottle of wine. She faded into another dream of a tall blond man named Christian, a man she had never seen before. She was desperately in love with him. She wanted to kiss him and begged him not to leave but her mouth was so dry no words came out. As he walked away, a hot, gaping hole burned into her soul. She tried to drink from a well, saw the water spill into her hands but no liquid reached her mouth. She woke up coughing, tears streaming down her face. She tried to sit up.

Herr Tucher closed the trap on the woodstove and wiped the sawdust from his hands.

"Are you thirsty?" he said and handed her a cup. "Have some tea."

Katarina grasped the cup with both hands and sipped the clover tea. The room spun.

"You fall in and out of delirium. You mumble and have said some strange things, dear."

Katarina lay back and he wiped her head with a cool, damp

cloth. He stood and left the room with his empty wood basket.

It must have been late morning when Katarina awoke again. She steadied herself, sat up and drank more tea. Her legs wobbled as she stood up, hands shaking, head pounding. She slumped over a chair, feeling empty. She was skin and bones. Her feet were cold and blue. The fire was burning but she was chilled. She wanted to get dressed in something warmer than this nightshirt. When she opened the door from the sitting room and moved into the cold and drafty stairwell, the house seemed empty, lit with the gray daylight that refused to admit any color.

Katarina walked into the kitchen and was taken aback. It was clean! The floor had been scrubbed. A fire burned. The room was warm. She smelled and heard food cooking in the pot. In her alcove, she found breeches, a shirt, a scratchy woolen jerkin and she quickly threw the clothes on.

She moved over to the fire, grabbed a towel, wound it around the pot's lid handle, lifted it and inhaled the soup. Her mouth watered. She was famished. She pulled a plate off the shelf on the wall, spooned some pottage of unknown ingredients onto it and inhaled it like a greedy savage. Slopping hogs came to mind. In the paddock, a baby mewed. Boots stomped through the stable into the kitchen. Pieter ducked under the door frame and walked into the kitchen holding a pitch-black kitten, about that age when they are weaned from their mother.

"Look what I found in the barn. The mother has deserted the poor bastard. Now he thinks I'm his mother."

Katarina looked up guiltily from her plate and wiped her mouth on her sleeve. "Sorry, I was so hungry."

"Is it good? I made it. I can't cook, but a bit of salt and pepper makes anything taste good."

"It's wonderful. Did you clean, too?"

"And I filled the stable with dry wood. We've been hauling firewood out of the forest this last week. I brought all the dry wood here for the kitchen."

"I'm sorry. That's my duty. You shouldn't have to do that."

"I don't mind. What should I do otherwise? Drink? Fight? Think? That's all I do: think. It's so quiet here and my thoughts are so loud. In the city the thoughts were drowned by the noise. But here…the nights are long and lonely. And quiet."

"Yes, I know," Katarina said, liking Pieter even more. "I thought you liked to write poetry."

"I hate my writing. I never want to write again. I burned those poems."

"It was a whole book, Pieter! The master showed me that book in his room. He read one aloud. Why would you do that?"

"You saw that?" A cloud passed before his eyes and he made that same dark smile she'd seen before. "I took that book and dropped it onto the fire."

Katarina finished her meal and stood. "I need to get the baby."

"Stay here. I'll go get her," said Peter.

"There was some trouble," Katarina said. "I may have some more trouble."

"Yes, it looked like there was a scuffle in the meadow. Just try to stay indoors. Whatever it is…"

Herr Tucher swished into the room from the stairway, his breeches and boots muddy, his shirt sleeves rolled up. He dropped a skinned rabbit onto the worktop. Pieter slipped out of the kitchen.

"That's as fresh as it gets, dear." He scrutinized Katarina's face. "Your color has come back. You are really smiling. I thought we had lost you."

"I feel much better. Thank you."

"Where has Pieter gone? I just saw him…"

"He's gone for the baby. She's still with Sara."

"He is a good boy, Katarina. But that is just what he is. A boy."

What did he mean by that?

He dropped his good knife onto the worktop. "I would appreciate some company this evening. Are you up to preparing the rabbit for the two of us?"

"I believe I can manage that."

"Wonderful. These long, dark evenings are driving me insane. Let me know if you would like some help."

Katarina chopped a handful of smoked venison into small cubes and browned it in fat with some onion. Rabbit had a delicate flavor and could easily be overpowered by red wine or port, so she made a vegetable fond with celery root, sage, parsley and two leaves of lavender. Pieter brought some goat's milk and she mixed that with flour and thickened the gravy. There were oats and beans from yesterday. That would have to do as a side dish.

Pieter's wanderings in and out of the house lightened Katarina's mood on this one-tone gray day. Not knowing who to trust or who to believe was tightening its grip around her capacity for reasonable thought like a dried leather strap. She needed to tell someone the story Hans-Wolfgang had told her, no matter what he said. Pieter had no interest either way and she desperately needed an ally.

"Pieter," she said, wiping her hands on her apron and gesturing towards a stool for him to sit on. "There is something I have to tell you."

He looked alarmed. "Tell me?"

"Not you in particular. But you're impartial and a good man."

"Is it about that baby?" he asked.

Katarina nodded.

He stood up abruptly. "I don't want to know about it. I don't want to lie if someone were to ask me."

"But, I have to tell someone!" Katarina said.

"If you aren't supposed to tell anyone, then don't!" Pieter said. "I don't want to know. I will help you though, don't worry. I won't leave you alone."

She prepared some milk for the baby and he fed her so Katarina could finish cooking the meal. After letting the pot cook for about an hour, she piled the rabbit and the oats and beans on the large platter. Pieter lifted the platter.

"He's going to question me," Katarina said as the two of them climbed the stairs. "I'm afraid of what he'll say, Pieter. I don't want to be alone with him."

"Don't worry," he said. "Just get him to talk about himself. He'll forget everything else."

Herr Tucher had the windows wide open and smoke wafted out of every crevice of the woodstove. "We need to get at the chimney tomorrow morning, Pieter. Seems to be obstructed again."

Pieter nodded and took his leave. The door shut. Katarina stood and looked around the room, like a lost child who didn't want to be seen. Herr Tucher took her by the hand and led her to the table. She sat down. He watched her so intently, she wanted to disappear. She poured herself some wine, feeling his stare burn on her face. Finally, he looked away and carved the rabbit. The meat had simmered in the creamy sauce and it was falling off the bones. Katarina pierced a small piece with her knife and stuck it in her mouth. It melted on her tongue, the herbs rounding the flavor of the celery root. She had to hold herself back from shoveling the food into her mouth.

As they ate, he made short comments about the cooking and asked questions about Katarina's preparations. He was polite, remarking about her condition, about the day in general. But he watched her with an unwavering concentration. She purposely avoided meeting his gaze and glanced directly at him from time-to-time only to find him still watching her.

Herr Tucher set his utensils down, propped his elbows on the table and rested his chin on his folded hands.

"Katarina, do I need to fear for the safety of my farm and my people here?" he said.

"No, not that I know of," Katarina said.

"Do I need to fear for your safety?"

"I'm not sure yet."

"I see enough of the world and enjoy observing its denizens. I must say, people are not as honest as I would like them to be. There is a delicate balance between trusting your friends and suspecting your enemies. And they can turn at any time. Friends become enemies and so on…" He took a sip of wine. "Our intuition can sometimes deceive us. On other occasions we need to heed its warnings."

Katarina speared another piece of meat and put it in her mouth. She knew this only too well. Would Herr Tucher recognize the danger she felt for what it was or would it seem like Katarina's hysterical feminine foolery? Was Katarina even in danger? Herr Tucher seemed to trust Ralf, he knew nothing of Hans-Wolfgang or Friedrich. He brushed conflict away with the wave of his hand and seemed to ignore danger with a careless disinterest. Look at his black eye! Maybe that was the difference between being rich and being poor.

"Is there anything you need to tell me?" he said. "Is there something I should know?"

"No," she said.

The two finished all of the meal. Katarina filled her cup and drank deep the light white wine flavored with sweet elder blossom. She filled her cup again and drank, the thoughts of Hans-Wolfgang, his story, his warnings and Ralf becoming shadows behind an opaque curtain. So full and content after the meal, the conversation lightened. After another glass of wine, Katarina found herself smiling. Relaxed and unconcerned, she chattered on about the baby and Tanner's wife. This feeling could go on forever.

"Ah, Katarina, that was a wonderful meal. I have a lovely brandy from France. Join me on the settee for a sip of this," he said, grabbing a bottle from behind the bookshelf and two small glasses. "I have to hide this even from myself."

Katarina stood and moved slowly to the settee, sat and took the glass he held out. She sipped at the strong, earthy-tasting brandy that reminded her of sautéed mushrooms.

"*Eau-de-vie*, they call this. 'Water of life.' Wonderful," he said, holding the glass up to the candle's flame and examining the amber liquid as he swirled it in his glass.

Katarina sipped at the spirit. She was watching him now but he was intent on the contents of his engraved glass. His smooth, dark hair was caught at the nape of his neck in a loose loop of yarn. His face was unshaven and slightly flushed from the brandy and the heat of the wood fire. The bruising around his eye had faded from purple to red. She asked him what had happened.

"Business in the city. You know, hazardous tenants who do not pay their rent."

Katarina sat up straight.

"I met Prutt, yes. He will be evicted from the tavern. He and his new wife. They need to find somewhere else to live, too."

"Wife?" She sipped the brandy and laughed. "Then I could take back the tavern."

The brandy made that news easier to receive. Besides, the idea of going back to Nuremberg sent a charge up her spine. She perched on the edge of the settee.

"You could rent it to me," Katarina said. "I'll take Pieter to help me. I'm not really one for this country living. What do you think? Sounds like a wonderful idea." She laughed out loud. "I pay my rent."

"I want you here," he said. "I need the two of you here." He set his glass on the table and moved a bit closer. "And no one is traveling any great distances until the spring. The last ride to Nuremberg was much too chilly."

"Hmpff." She laughed again. That warmed her heart like hawthorn wine. "You know you'll find no better person than me." She stopped and smiled wide. "Think of the money I could make for you."

"I can think of no better person than you." He laughed. "And I do not care about the money. That is probably my biggest downfall: I do not care about money. That building belongs to my uncle. It is none of my concern, really." He took her hand. "I want you to stay here with me."

He leaned in and Katarina froze. She smelled a sweet scent, like a freshly-baked honey cake. He smiled like he wanted to laugh, pulled her into a loose embrace and pressed his lips to hers. There was no longer a hole in her soul. It had not been filled but eliminated. Willi's kisses had brought her insane pain: the need to please coupled with the fear of impending rejection. But Herr Tucher's kiss gave her promise of what she could have if only she was the right sort of woman. In short—if she had been worthy. But, alas, she was not and a nagging voice in the back of her head told her to stop. He was the master and she was nothing more than his maid. A *Teufelsweib*, bastard child, farm girl, milkmaid, barmaid. *Magd*.

"Stay here with me tonight," he said, wrapped his arms around her and kissed her: deep, apparent, disclosing.

She would never, could never, never, never. Tears filled her eyes. She ended the kiss, stood and left the room.

Chapter 23

After sitting the whole morning over a blank page that his quill could not will to fill, Sebald Tucher opened his journal to the entries from the spring and summer, trying to extract warm thoughts, bird song and the sound of wind in the trees. Katarina had slipped into a weary melancholy the last few weeks since he had kissed her. She had returned the gesture and kissed him tenderly. But she pulled away and left the room, her eyes filled with tears. Now those eyes had taken on the color of gloomy contemplation. He'd seen her earlier this morning on her stool in the kitchen, staring into the fire, like her spirit was trying to recapture extinguished flames. At first, Herr Tucher wondered if she was still a bit off-color, but she was in good health, Tanner's wife reassured him.

The December days started black, turned an ashen grey and black again. They woke up, ate breakfast, took care of the animals, drank and went back to bed. And that for days on end. It must now be midday. Herr Tucher had to squint to read in the dismal light. Candles were running low and he only lit them in the evening. He scraped his chair along the wooden floor closer to the window, stood and opened the window to freshen the air. He sat back and paged through his journal.

Therein, among silly verses and lists of tasks he had finished leading up to the move to the farm, he stumbled on a forgotten entry, a compilation of what he felt was important. It was undated but it must have stemmed from a conversation he remembered having with Tanner in the summer:

By this time, I am settled in at Sichardtshof. I am 33 and quite established. I feel quite sure that this was a good move. The situation in the city grows dire. People are sick with all sorts of diseases. Prices are soaring. Religious strife in other German-speaking cities is peaking. Nuremberg is Protestant but because the Catholics are trying to gain some control, and proving their efforts are worth it, rumors are sprouting that we could be involved in more strife in the years to come.

My search, then, is to really experience some passion, try to find what it is my soul is lacking and do that before we are all extinguished. I am starting to feel like my days are numbered and it is a good chance to do what I really feel I need to do, that is, write, study art and learn to love. I will repeat that: Write, Study Art and Learn to Love. It seems like a perfect time to start, not to look back and not to look too far ahead.

Because the Germans could never seem to unify on any given front, this problem had him seriously worried. The German Territories had enjoyed a long stint of peace, the longest anyone could remember. Herr Tucher wanted to suck the life out of every minute of the day; read all the books he could, hoping not to miss an ounce of wisdom. Sleep was a waste of time. More than anything, he hated to waste time. Luckily in December, the year's end, the weather held opposing forces at bay. Warring troops had retired to winter quarters. Any group of ruffians looking for a fight was easily deterred when it was cold and frosty.

When Herr Tucher first met Katarina in Nuremberg, her eyes sparked intelligence, her words sprayed spirit, their tone boisterous the later and louder the night became. She was the upper-hand in the tavern. She had that Prutt in check to a point. Herr Tucher hoped that she only grieved the loss of that relationship. Yes, some women needed these men that they had to chase and keep in check. Herr Tucher would keep an eye on Katarina with Pieter. He had the same sort of charming personality and used women's company carelessly. Why do some women need these types of men? He would never understand.

And the reports of soldiers visiting the farm in his absence had him uneasy to say the very least. Knecht and Pieter assumed they were Croatian riders but got no information out of them as to what they were seeking. Katarina would not talk about her disappearance and he feared the two situations had a direct correlation. She had not told any of the others what had happened and she was now on edge and easily frightened.

A horse approached the farm. Herr Tucher set his book aside, leaned out the open window and watched the rider on a slim, dark bay coming up the track from the main road. It looked like that young monk on an elegant, athletic horse. Herr Tucher pulled his overcoat from the peg behind the door and threw it over his shoulders as he walked down the steps. The double front doors were swollen from the damp, winter air. He tugged, lifting the latch and using all his weight to pull those doors open. Ralf was waiting by the closed gate. Herr Tucher descended the few steps to the gate and pulled it open with a massive effort, mud slopping over his boots from that infinite puddle. Someone must fill that hole with something.

"Greetings," Herr Tucher said. "Come in out of the cold, my good man."

Ralf tethered his horse by the house. Knecht came as quickly as those bow legs would carry him from around the barn to tend the young stallion and openly admired the creature as he led him away.

"What brings you here on such a horrible December day?" Herr Tucher asked.

"I fancied a ride and the young stallion needs exercise, otherwise he is unmanageable. I brought a book that we had talked about."

After they entered the house, Herr Tucher pulled the doors closed, turned and saw Katarina peeking up the steps from the kitchen doorway. The baby called and cooed in the kitchen. Katarina turned her back with a "hmpff." She scurried away like a mouse.

The upstairs sitting room was a warm welcome after standing in the frozen stairwell. Herr Tucher admitted Ralf, shut the door and covered the drafty slit between the door and the floor with a tattered wool blanket.

"Wine, sir?" Herr Tucher asked.

"Yes, please."

"I have something stronger against the chill, if you would like."

"Would also do just fine," he said, pulling off his woolen traveling cloak. He hung the cloak on a peg on the wall, pulled on the tattered latch of his saddle bag and produced a worn volume from the bag's innards. "The well-known *Hammer of the Witches*. The *Malleus Maleficarum*. You have no doubt heard of this book, sir?"

"Of course I have. I just question its effectiveness."

"There are women who have gone astray. They need to be cleansed of their wayward habits." He sat on the settee, crossed one leg over the other and wiped his nose on the back of his hand.

"Often all these women need is regular meals and care for their children," Herr Tucher said. "You cannot expect hungry people to sit in a church and think of cleansing their souls when they have empty stomachs. No one can concentrate on salvation when they have no roof over their heads."

"Life is suffering and when one accepts that, salvation will follow."

"I find it hard to believe that God expects people to witness their children dying of starvation in order to find them worthy of saving. What about you? Is suffering your way to salvation?"

"I live by the three vows I have taken: poverty, chastity and obedience. I was ordained into the priesthood quite young. Shortly afterwards, I was invited to take the fourth vow of the Jesuits. My life is led by complete surrender to the visible church. Our universal mission is to insure that our ministries reach to the ends of the earth. I have an advanced intellect and the Jesuits agreed with my assessment that I have been called to teach, a task I gratefully accept.

"Of course, you are a teacher. I wonder if you would be interested in teaching some of my counterparts, here at the farm."

"You may not agree with my doctrines, Herr Tucher."

"Would not matter," Herr Tucher said. "*Was der Bauer nicht kennt, isst er nicht*. What the farmer does not know he will not eat. Just like doctrine. He may nod his head and take your time but he will not believe you."

Ralf scoffed and turned away.

"You had mentioned that you were not wholly convinced of your faith," Herr Tucher said. "That maybe some point east was the next destination."

"I wanted to travel to Prague but it is a city in turmoil. That is no longer my wish."

There was a knock on the door. Herr Tucher opened it for Katarina who was overloaded with two wine bottles, ceramic cups and a ceramic flagon. "Will you need anything else, sir?" she asked.

"Some dried meats, perhaps? Do we have any bread? Maybe a pudding? Do not put yourself out, my dear."

"I'll put something together," she answered.

She walked to the table and set her things down. Judging from the aroma emitted by the flagon, it was his peppermint tea. She took her leave and shut the door.

Herr Tucher opened the wine, poured a glass and tasted it. "I have drunk better wines. My apologies, Ralf, this one is sour."

"Lovely girl," Ralf said, taking the glass he handed him. "Where did you find her?"

"She worked for me in Nuremberg. I brought her out here when I moved."

"With child? Is that your child?"

"No, the child is not mine."

"She must have been pregnant when you brought her out here. Why would you want a pregnant *Magd*?"

"She is a capable woman." Herr Tucher sat next to Ralf and wrinkled his face as he took a sip of sour wine. "That is why I have her here."

"These women with insatiable appetites. Maybe she does need to be educated to resist her carnal lusts. Otherwise you'll have more children to feed than you can handle!"

"I think there is no need to worry about my Katarina, thank you."

"She must leave the child unattended in order to complete her work."

"Katarina usually has the child by her side. She has the child with her in the stables."

"You are very fond of her, aren't you?" Ralf said.

"Of course I am. She is running my household to my liking."

"Overly fond, don't you think?"

"What a strange thing to say to me, Ralf."

Ralf stood, walked to the table and sniffed at Herr Tucher's tea. "These teas Katarina serves you. Do you know what kind of herbs she uses?"

"What are you saying? That she is filling me with some potions? Love potions?" One barking laugh escaped before Herr Tucher could hold it back. "Do you know how ridiculous that sounds?"

"Well, she is nothing special. A man like you could surely have, and please don't take offense, a better woman."

"I am married to a 'better woman,' thank you."

"Wicked are the women that lead married men away from their exquisite wives. Katarina is a farm girl of unknown parentage. Common, if I dare say so. And who is that old woman? The one who looked down from the window when I came today?"

"Katarina's grandmother. She has lived her whole life here."

A knock sounded again. Herr Tucher opened the door and

Katarina set a tray of meats on the table. She left without looking at either one of the men. As the door closed, Herr Tucher caught her scent. He smiled and forced himself to actively return to the conversation.

"It has been done before," Ralf continued. "You are rich, she is poor and has a child to take care of. I've seen your house. It is not clean or well taken care of. The floors are dirty. And that old woman. Why do you suffer such company?"

Ralf stuffed some meat into his mouth and chewed with his mouth closed.

"They suit my purpose," Herr Tucher said. "I choose my companions not because of their lineage. What I value in a person cannot be limited to the beauty of their living form or the quality of their work. I compare it to the feeling I have when I see a painting I must have. There is more to beauty than merely mood, color and lighting. Deliberate disuse of technique can be as intriguing as masterful method. Sometimes a blemish makes the picture perfect, or a scar the woman stunning, not the absence of flaws. I expect a quickening of heart when I look into someone's eyes. A longing, a mutual understanding, one could call it. I either see it, actually feel it there, or not."

"What do you see in my eyes, Herr Tucher?"

Herr Tucher looked into Ralf's eyes and weighed every word. "Indecision and a lack of conviction."

Ralf turned his face sharply away. He blushed like a young girl. Herr Tucher allowed him a moment of privacy and looked out the window. Ralf cleared his throat and ate another piece of meat. He recovered himself quickly and chatted on about Höchstadt and the family he lived with. Herr Tucher responded that he had never had the honor or reason to do any business there. In his humble opinion, they were much too influenced by Bamberg, one of the major cities involved in witch burnings under a very unsavory man, the Bishop von Aschhausen.

"I often travel to Bamberg. Lovely city," Ralf said.

"When I travel north, I make a large arc around the city so I do not become entangled in their diseased politics."

"The natural order of things, Herr Tucher."

Herr Tucher thought it best to steer the conversation away from conflicting dogmas. Ralf would come around. He was still young and unripe like many men of the cloth. Such men had often never had the opportunity to discuss other doctrines than those they had been force-fed at the monastery. In due time, Herr Tucher vowed to introduce him to other thinkers and other philosophies. Ralf seemed wrestle with himself. He could not continue to believe in this course of poverty and self-deprivation once he had been exposed to the other options enlightened men had these days, could he?

They carried on with polite and secularized conversation. Herr Tucher reminded Ralf of his wish to have him come teach. Ralf looked out the window at the failing winter light and prepared to leave. Herr Tucher slipped him a copy of *Medical Writings* from Paracelsus. Ralf thanked him and stuck the book in his saddle bag. Herr Tucher kept the *Hammer of the Witches* book, to better acquaint himself with what he needed to arm himself against.

"On horseback I'll make it back to Höchstadt before dusk," he said and pulled on his cloak.

Herr Tucher threw his overcoat over his shoulders. They left the room and clumped down the chilled stairwell. Herr Tucher tugged on those stubborn front doors. Walking down the few steps into the yard, they made plans to meet regularly and while away some winter days. It was a short ride, Ralf said, and he didn't mind getting out of the walled city now and again for an afternoon.

Knecht came around the barn, as if they had called him, with Ralf's horse saddled and ready to ride.

Chapter 24

After Christmas, the days became noticeably longer, the only promise in the deep winter that spring could return again. An icy chill had permeated every corner of the house and mocked the crackling fire's attempt to alleviate its grip. Steam rising from the boiling pot swirled in the cold kitchen air. Katarina removed the pot from the flame and added a handful of lemon balm leaves, a burst of lemon scent filling the kitchen. Frau Kuni burst into the room as well.

"Bloody monk tried to plow me over with that damned horse," Frau Kuni said. "He's a nuisance, that *Schlappschwanz*."

"Stay here a moment until I come back?" Katarina said. "In case Isabeau wakes up?"

Frau Kuni chuckled, a scary, sarcastic cackle. "Little devil's going to be walking soon. She's restless."

"Let's hope she waits until she can control it. You said if they walk too soon, they only hurt themselves."

"The joy of seeing the young I've raised with their own young." She chuckled again. "I always said you'd get one like you. And that baby is bushels worse than you ever were!"

Katarina filled a jug with beer for Ralf. His visits had taken on a regular rhythm. He used the excuse that his horse needed exercise and, when the paths were free from ice, he liked to take the twenty minutes to an hour ride, depending on the roads and the condition of his young and spirited horse.

She hoped the lemon balm would improve Herr Tucher's mood today. He had gotten into a bit of a sulk, a gray mood that mirrored the frozen, dark days. They were all susceptible to the pensive humor—the cold, dry melancholia—and any diversion was welcome. That was Herr Tucher's reasoning behind assembling all the workers a few evenings a week so they might eat together and have a drink and a laugh. Since he approached Katarina only when others were present, she savored the time they spent together. In the group, the two could banter and joke with one another without the danger of giving in to questionable conduct.

She would catch herself thinking about what could happen if she accepted his advances. After she scolded her sheer foolishness for entertaining the thought, she would give into her version of the dream and let it play through, like a bit of theatre. He would take her into his arms and tell her that, yes, he was no longer married. He and Katarina were no longer bound to their stiff social system and could court and marry as they wanted. There would be nothing stopping them from engaging in anything that would further mar Katarina's honor.

Herr Tucher could engage any woman in anything he wanted. It would do him no harm. But Katarina was not willing to risk the repercussions and reprimands of shameful behavior. She imagined Sara's *tut-tutt-tut* and Frau Kuni's outright: *what the hell were you thinking child!* And there was always Tanner's strap. Oh, if they could just fly away from here…

She climbed the steps to the sitting room carrying the two ceramic jugs. Herr Tucher opened the door as if he heard her coming. The sitting room was flushed with sunlight. Katarina squinted against the unusually bright day and set the drinks on the table. Herr Tucher liked a mild herb tea in the afternoon and she steeped peppermint, lemon balm, elder blossom or stinging nettle from her dried stores. Ralf accepted no teas from Katarina. He neither spoke nor looked at Katarina when he visited.

Herr Tucher prepared himself for these visits with arguments and "researched rebuttals," he liked to say. He read anything he could find and cited passages to underscore his opinions. He seemed to be on a mission to sway Ralf away from the stiff, constricting and, in Katarina's opinion, some downright ridiculous creeds found within some of the documents and books he brought with him. One, of course, was the *Hammer of the Witches*. Katarina couldn't read it in Latin. It was Ralf's favorite book.

Katarina ran back into the kitchen, grabbed two buckets for water, climbed the steps and slowly pulled the front doors open. They were still swollen and scraped on the floor. She would have gone out the back door and stayed away from the front of the house at all but the paddock was muddy and icy and slippery. She walked briskly down the front steps and headed for the well. Pieter had cleared the path of brush and it was now easier to walk carrying buckets, not having to worry about tripping over the scraggly underbrush.

"What is he doing here again?" barked a voice from behind the barn.

Katarina saw wild eyes embedded in the taut and angry face of Hans-Wolfgang. His brown riding cloak was a similar color to the wooden barn. His cheeks looked red and sore from spending a lot of time in the cold, biting wind.

"Visiting the master," Katarina said. "Just like every week. Ask them yourself. I stay away from the two of them. Unless they summon me."

"Did Ralf see the baby?" Hans-Wolfgang said.

"He doesn't approach me at all."

"Don't let him near the child."

"I said: he never sees her. I don't take the baby upstairs when he's here. I usually go to Sara."

"I'd wager it is the only reason he comes here," he said. "You've left her alone right now, haven't you?"

"You're watching me that closely?"

"You have left her alone!"

"She's sleeping!" Katarina said. "I can't sit by the whole day when she's sleeping. And Frau Kuni is with her. When she's awake, I have to watch her like a fox. She's starting to crawl. She can get out of her basket. When she sleeps I have to get my work done."

He turned abruptly without a word and disappeared behind the barn. He stole across the brown field, up the hill out of the hollow and into the distant forest. Katarina assumed he tethered his horse to a tree and snuck into the farmyard. How easy that must be. She searched the tree line and the horizon, realizing how exposed they were here in the hollow. The breeze lifted the hairs on the back of her neck. The whole farm was surrounded by hills where anyone could stand and observe.

As she walked into the kitchen, Isabeau whined and squirmed in her basket. She had turned half way onto her stomach and was struggling either to roll onto her back or get on her knees. The basket was getting too small for her. Katarina set her buckets by the fireplace, freed Isabeau from her twisted position, set the baby on her hip and pulled her in close. With the other arm, Katarina threw a log on the fire.

Isabeau peeped like a baby bird and turned her head abruptly. Katarina turned too, to see what she was looking at. Ralf stood in the doorway dressed in his black riding cloak as if he was leaving already. He stomped into the kitchen and Katarina instinctively backed up against the wall.

"Lovely little girl," he said and stroked Isabeau's cheek. "She's getting big."

Katarina turned to the side, pushing her other shoulder towards Ralf, putting her body between him and the baby.

"Whose child is this? She shows no resemblance to you, *Magd*."

He stroked Katarina's cheek. She tried to turn away but he came in closer and she backed into the corner. He gave off a strange, sour smell.

"She is my child. I am her guardian," Katarina said, looking up at him and trying not to press the baby's body against the wall.

He smiled, his top lip taught against his teeth. His eyes bulged and he looked like a weasel. "I know who this child is. I knew this child's mother well enough. Very well, indeed. *He* gave you the child to care for, didn't he?"

"Who?"

"Hans-Wolfgang. I just saw him. I want that man. You must lead me to him."

"I don't know what you're talking about."

"You spent the night with him," Ralf said. "Maybe two nights. What will your master say when I tell him what the two of you were up to? There was dancing involved. Musicians."

Katarina felt Isabeau's body stiffen on her hip.

"When women are caught *in flagranti* dancing with the devil and there are two men who can confirm the accusation…"

"There was no dancing with the devil!"

"When you are questioned, you will break down and tell the truth. You will name me everyone involved, too."

Isabeau dug her fingernails into Katarina's upper arm. Katarina tried to duck away from Ralf but his elbow shot up and he pushed her and the baby firmly against the stone wall with his bent arm. Where was Pieter?

"Ralf, you're hurting me!"

"If you speak now and give us the names of everyone involved, the implications against you could be reduced."

"Let me go," Katarina yelled.

"Is Hans-Wolfgang in league with the devil?" Ralf crossed himself. "Is he the demon who bewitched Andra-Angela?"

Katarina's breaths came hard and the pressure of his arm on her chest made her gasp for air.

"You work with Hans-Wolfgang, don't you? I know what you are doing to your master, you devil's woman. No man in his right mind would want a *Teufelsweib* like you. You may very well be the succubus who has sown all this unrest. I've seen women like you. I've watched them tied to the burning stake, heard them beg for their souls."

Ralf leaned all his weight on Katarina. She tried to cry out but she could hardly breath. Isabeau screeched with all the air her lungs could emit.

"You have no right to this child, Katarina. Hans-Wolfgang has no right to this child! I want her, to deal with as I see fit."

"Have no right to the child?" Katarina gasped. "I have no choice but to care for her."

Ralf's eyes widened. Katarina realized how that sounded and regretted the words.

"I can give you another choice," Ralf said. "Give the child to me and you are free to go. Decline my offer and you will pay dearly."

"This is my child and I take care of her! Nothing you could say would change my mind."

"*Liebe Holla!*" Frau Kuni's voice boomed through the kitchen.

Ralf howled in pain as if he'd been bitten. Frau Kuni stood behind him with a pitchfork and a murderous look on her face.

"Let her go, Priest, and leave the property!" she said.

Katarina heard two men conversing outside in the paddock. The goat bleated as their voices approached. Ralf straightened, released her and walked quickly out of the kitchen, his boots ringing on the stone floor. Frau Kuni followed him, her pitchfork out first. He stopped on the steps and peeked back through the doorway.

"You have a choice, *Magd*."

Chapter 25

Ralf pulled back on the reins. The horse slowed involuntarily to a canter, tossed his head, laid his ears back and finally stopped at the gate of the Golden Lamb Tavern in Lonnerstadt. Ralf reckoned there was still two hours of daylight. A dull hum of conversation rumbled inside the tavern. A smell of burning fat and stale beer stood like a watchman at the gate. The farmers celebrated their heretic new year, February 2nd being the day they would take up the work in the fields again. For Ralf today was Candlemas.

He had spent another afternoon with that Tucher. Listening to him dissert without end had given Ralf a headache and quite an appetite. He'd spent one or two afternoons with him every week for the past month and was none the closer to finding Andra-Angela's ring, her cloak, Hans-Wolfgang or convincing Friedrich to let him take possession of Upper Eierhofen for the Jesuits.

Herr Tucher had not mentioned Ralf's confrontation with Katarina in January. Either the maid was too dull to register what he meant to do to her or she was too afraid to tattle on Ralf to her master. He needed to be careful: to denunciate a maid of witchcraft was one thing, but accusations against a patrician family from Nuremberg could bring him more trouble than he cared for.

Ralf had to stall Father Marius and the Bamberg Jesuits time and time again. He'd made excuses that the Upper Eierhofen house was not yet ready to accommodate the new students. Of late he had simply not responded to any messages from Bamberg. The last message from Marius read urgent and accusing that the society was not happy with having to feed the extra boys who now numbered fifteen. The boys had only been taken on because Ralf had promised placements at his Upper Eierhofen school. Then, last week, five of the boys had unexpectedly turned up at Upper Eierhofen; thankfully large, older boys who looked like they could fight. He told Friedrich that they were soldiers. They were to be Soldiers of God.

Ralf pressed his thigh against the dark bay stallion's side and the horse walked through the gate of the Golden Lamb and into the yard. The innkeeper and his two daughters bustled around a few women working over a table of meat. The horse shied at the smell of fresh blood. Ralf slapped the horse's ears, the horse jumped sideways and Ralf lost his balance. He straightened himself in the saddle, grit his teeth and raised his fist.

Instead of bashing this horse until it bled, Ralf took a deep breath and restrained himself from expressing his bristling impatience. He knew not to question why the Lord had put so many obstacles in his way for fear of coming up against more. But days like these he felt he could cry for frustration. A draught of beer would calm that. Ralf prodded the horse forward, stopped again in front of the stable, dismounted and led the horse in. A shovel scraped the ground and Ralf searched for the source of the sound.

"Stable boy?" Ralf called. "Would you take my horse?"

The scraping stopped. A man limped out of the horse box and straightened when he saw Ralf.

"You there," Ralf said. "Take my horse."

"Yeah, when I'm done here," the man said.

Ralf tied his horse to the wall. The man in front of him was too young to be bent over like this. His eyes glared with a knowing that was uncommon for a Franconian farm hand. He looked more like a criminal.

"Where's the stable boy?" Ralf asked. "I've never seen you before."

"Nope," the man said. "I'm just passing through. Times are hard."

"Where are you from? You don't speak like the others."

"Yeah, I can hardly understand them myself. I'm from Nuremberg."

Ralf laughed. "A bit of a better man then?"

"Yes I am, a better man that is," the man said. "Just traveling through here. I've had a bit of bad luck."

Ralf touched the horse's shoulder and ran his hand down the horse's leg. The horse lifted his hoof and Ralf inspected the knee and heel and the underside of his hoof. Satisfied, he moved to the haunch and did the same.

"Luck rarely plays any part in our lives," Ralf said. "Divine providence does. What you describe as bad luck is only free will and the consequences thereof. Now you don't strike me as superstitious or simple minded. Surely there is more to life than shoveling shit."

"I'm just waiting for a fair break. A merchant traveling away from here, maybe."

"When was the last time you had a good meal?" Ralf said.

"What, are you going to buy me a meal?" The man wiped his nose. "They just slaughtered the pig. The whole village will turn out for the *Schlachtschüssel*. But they won't let me sit in the tavern and eat."

Ralf's stomach rumbled. "Come, let me feed your body and we can talk about feeding your soul."

"Oh, I don't believe any of that…"

"I ride this horse hard," Ralf said, moving to the other shoulder. "He has only gone lame on me once but I am careful since then."

The man stroked the stallion's neck. "This is a beautiful horse."

"Yes, he serves me well. I am grateful that I have him by my side. My work dictates that I travel. On foot I would not be as effective. But with him I can cover greater distances. This territory is sinking into a morass of muddled morals. They need to learn the Truth, not the tools of doubt."

"The truth is I need some food and a drink," the man said.

"That we meet today is an example of divine providence." Ralf laughed. "Do you want to make some money?"

"Well, yes, I do," the man said.

"What's your name?" Ralf asked.

"Willi. Willi Prutt."

"Mr. Prutt, I need somebody like you to help me. There's a farm out there in the Edelgraben. I need to locate something I lost and I think it may be there."

"You mean Sichardtshof?"

Ralf smiled. "Yes, you know the place?"

"No love lost there," Willi said.

That's where Ralf had seen this man before. Yes, he'd seen him early last summer driving a cart away from the farm. He would feel him out to see what the connection was. Judging from his reaction, it was not a positive one. Ralf loosened the saddle girth. The horse took a deep, cleansing breath. Willi took the saddle away and returned in an instant.

"They have something," Ralf said. "Something that belongs to my master. I believe the master from Sichardtshof has something to do with it."

"Why don't you just kill him?" Willi said.

"No one is to be hurt." *At least not yet.* "I am only searching for what rightfully should belong to my master and the Jesuits."

Willi pulled a brush out of his smock and brushed the horse's back and flank. "It won't be too hard to get in there. I know the area. I know Katarina."

"Oh, you know her? You can get close to her?"

"Yes, I can."

"That's good to know," Ralf said. "We are willing to pay quite a lot, just to find out what she knows. We're looking for a ring that has been in my master's family for generations. I think she stole it. If you can get close to her, you may be able to find out where it is. So, Willi, come join me for a meal."

They walked from the stable towards the back entrance of the Golden Lamb. The yard teemed with bustling women with knives. The two men picked a path between the women and the other workers and ducked through the low doorway into the kitchen. Iron lids clanged against huge steaming pots that hung over the open fire. A greasy cloud smelling of meat and fat and beer and onions covered their faces. Seeing as they couldn't get though the kitchen, they pushed their way through the opposite doorway and down the hall.

Ralf opened the door to the guest room. His nose filled with smoke from the tallow lamps mixed with the smell of sauerkraut. The loud conversation of drunken farmers vibrated off the walls. He picked a path towards a break in the crowd by the front wall. That meant there could be two empty seats. Across from the two empty seats beamed a familiar face.

"The Dutch boy," Ralf mumbled.

The ember of faith and gratitude in the back of Ralf's mind flared and he smiled. Everything happened in the Lord's time, not his. His selfless act of wanting to feed a hungry man would be rewarded. He looked closer at Pieter's face. His eyes were unfocused and his smile a bit lopsided. There mustn't be much farm work right now for this boy to be here in the tavern in the middle of the day. There wasn't much to do in February anyway.

"Hallo Pieter," Ralf said. "Are these seats taken?"

Pieter gestured to the two empty spaces on the wooden bench and nodded his head. "Hallo, Father Ralf."

Ralf turned his head as he sat and saw the Knecht at the next table. "Is everyone here at this fest?"

Pieter smiled. "Just us two, Father. They have this midwinter fest every year and we thought we'd come and have something to eat."

"And drink," Ralf said.

"Here you go," a barmaid slammed two mugs of beer before Willi and Ralf. "You'll be wanting something to eat, Father Ralf?"

"Yes, we would. Thank you, Gerlinde."

"Gerlinde! Another beer for me and the Knecht please," Pieter said.

Gerlinde whirled away and Pieter drained his tankard dry.

"So you boys done with work already then?" Ralf asked Pieter

"Yes, we were looking over some new lands that Herr Tucher has petitioned for. When he gets the land, we'll be able to farm the whole area right up to the main road."

"Has it been decided that he will get those lands? Are those the fields that were being farmed by the cloister in Frauenaurach?"

"Yes, as good as decided. Herr Tucher should take possession right away."

Ralf's thoughts raced to digest this news. He had petitioned for those same lands in the name of Friedrich von Obereierhofen last year. Friedrich had given him the authority to do it in his name. Friedrich's financial situation could not handle the extra expense, but when the school opened, more money would come in. How much money did that Tucher have then in order for the Margrave in Dachsbach to assign him the land instead of Friedrich? The Margrave hated the Nuremberg patricians, he'd thought.

Pieter turned away and flirted with a young barmaid. Gerlinde returned with a plate for both Willi and Ralf. Steaming sauerkraut and slabs of glistening pork that smelled of pepper and ginger were surrounded by *Fleischküchla*, sweet meatballs with cinnamon and sultanas, *Rote Pressack,* collared pork spiced with marjoram and Ralf's favorite *Blutwurst*: inventions intended to utilize every last bit of pig. Ralf grabbed a hunk of gray bread, tore a mouthful off and chewed.

"What do I get?" Willi whispered.

"Wha...?" Ralf stammered, having forgotten everything except the intoxicating, hot, wonderful smells in front of him.

"How much are you going to pay me?" Willi said. "I'm going out to Sichardtshof tonight."

"Eat. And be quiet. Drink your beer. You are coming with me tonight."

Chapter 26

Katarina opened the doors to the paddock. A hint of earthy, green, new-born spring wafted on the midday breeze. The air carried a chill, but the frozen fog had lifted. The worst of the winter weather was hopefully behind them. Herr Tucher had given her a new calendar for 1617. The quote for March read: *Märzen kalt und Sonnenschein, bringt eine gute Ernte ein.* March's cold and sunshine will bring you in a harvest fine. Katarina crossed off March 15.

She stepped into the paddock and looked down the hollow, over the ponds that reflected the blue sky. Sara hung linens to dry. Pieter split firewood back by the worker's house. Sheep bleated beyond the house. She'd gotten in the habit of examining the line of trees on the hilltops, searching the North Hill, the track towards the main road and back along the South Hill. An annoying, low-resonating level of fear nagged at her and would not go away. The last few weeks were peaceful and that made it worse, like watching calm waters and waiting for the flood.

Pieter's boredom the last few weeks had resulted in new things for Katarina and Isabeau. Back in the kitchen, Katarina dropped the armful of wood she'd collected into her new wood basket next to the fireplace. She swept the sawdust out into the fresh straw bedding in the stable with her new broom. The goat munched on the aromatic hay that Pieter had brought this morning. She closed the paddock door as Isabeau stirred in the new bed that Pieter had made for her; a wooden frame with a small sack stuffed with wool.

Isabeau sat up and said, "Mm-mm."

"Are you hungry, Isabeau? What else is new?"

"Mm-mm."

Katarina cracked four eggs into a pan, stirred them and set them over the fire to cook. The paddock door creaked open. Katarina jumped and her heart pounded. She breathed a relieved sigh as Pieter came into the kitchen, followed by a young black cat.

"Peh," Isabeau said.

"Is that Pieter? Look Isabeau, Pieter is here. Muddy boots in my clean kitchen, eh, Pieter?"

"Peh," she said. "Peh. Peh!"

Pieter grabbed her out of her bed and held her high. Isabeau screeched and laughed. "Peh!" Her blue eyes flickered and Pieter swung her up and down and up and down and she screeched again and again until Katarina yelled, "Enough!"

They stopped and looked at Katarina. She felt her face stiffen and she forced herself to relax. She flipped the eggs in the pan, they sizzled ferociously and she slid the mass onto a plate.

"I'm sorry, you two," Katarina said. "Who wants something to eat?"

"I need to check through the outbuildings," Pieter said. "I can't stay. I already ate at the house. Seems something, a rather large animal is getting into the stores. My wood pile has been disturbed and I'm afraid something is getting into our cellar. There are meats missing, a barrel of beer has been opened. Wine is missing."

"What kind of animal drinks beer?"

"There is only one."

Katarina set the plate onto the new table Pieter and Knecht had made and sat down on one of the two new benches. Pieter handed Katarina the child and she swung the baby onto her lap. The cat purred, tail held high, and twisted around the table legs. Pieter tousled Isabeau's white-blonde curls and she grabbed at his hand. He left the room, his musky scent of leather and spice still lingering. Isabeau turned to look at Katarina and stuck her finger in Katarina's mouth.

"Mm-mm," she said.

"Would you like eggs? Or eggs? Or maybe eggs?"

"Mm-mm."

She opened her mouth wide as Katarina raised the spoon. Another new tooth pushed through next to her other upper two. Now she had five. Frau Kuni said she would cry or be feverish with every new tooth, but there was no discomfort. She was actually an uncomplicated child.

"We need to check on Frau Kuni after you're finished eating," Katarina said.

"Gu-ni," she said, with a mouthful of egg.

She'd eaten at least three eggs. Katarina came at her one more time with the spoon and she shook her head, mouth tightly closed. Katarina finished the eggs herself. Isabeau drank milk from the cup Katarina offered her.

"Let's go look for Frau Kuni," Katarina said, set the baby on her hip and they climbed the stairs.

Katarina stopped on the landing outside Herr Tucher's sitting room and listened. She wondered if Ralf was in there. Katarina climbed the next flight of stairs to the upper floor where Frau Kuni had her small chamber under the slope of the roof. She could have moved into the Old Widow's now-empty room, but she refused.

"Frau Kuni?" Katarina said, knocking on her door.

Katarina pushed the door open. Frau Kuni lay on her bed. She always said she was fine but Katarina suspected she was in pain. She stayed in her room, spoke little and had no appetite.

"Frau Kuni, come down and have something to eat. Then we'll go outside for a walk. It's going to be a nice afternoon."

"I'm not hungry." Frau Kuni sat up, her face weary and sagging, gathered the shawl that lay on her bed, slung it around her shoulders and slowly stood.

"Come, let's go. Do you need help?" Katarina readjusted the baby on her hip.

"No, I can manage," she said.

Katarina walked down the steps and Frau Kuni followed. No sounds came from Herr Tucher's room. They descended to the front doors. Katarina jiggled the one door and pulled it open. It scraped on the stone floor. They walked into the farmyard and Pieter walked towards them from the barn.

"I found a sort of nest, I think," Pieter said. "It looks like someone is sleeping in there."

He turned to walk back to the barn and motioned for them to follow him. He pulled open the smaller side door cut into the large barn doors, made for people to enter, and left it open for a small stream of light to shine in. Katarina stopped in the doorway and turned as she heard men's voices in the farmyard. She slipped behind the door, peered around the opening and saw Ralf standing on the front step. He took a look around and walked down the steps. Engaged in animated conversation with Herr Tucher, he strolled towards the stable where his horse must have been tethered.

"Shh," Katarina said to Pieter and watched them from her hiding place.

The two men came out of the stable with Ralf's horse. Ralf mounted and rode through the open gate. Herr Tucher went back into the house, shut the doors and took no notice of Katarina and Pieter. Where did Frau Kuni go? She was right behind them.

"Katarina, don't worry about him. Nothing will happen while I'm here with you," Pieter said.

"This is the first time in weeks that he's come by."

"Herr Tucher won't let him do anything stupid," Pieter said.

"That is a dangerous man."

"Come here, I want to show you this," he said.

He squeezed his broad frame past long stumps of wood, those that still needed cutting and splitting, towards the back of the barn where he had stacked the small bits to dry. Pieter was a tidy boy, with a forced sense of rigidity, judging from the symmetrical sculpture he'd made with firewood. There, alongside the woodpile in a small cleared space, lay a few crumpled blankets, an empty bottle of wine and small animal bones.

"Here's something we should worry about. Someone must have made their quarters here."

Yes, it was possible. There were enough wayward, homeless types who wandered from town to town, looking for food, shelter and loot. Or was it someone familiar? Katarina shuddered at the thought, a chill making the hairs on her arms stand up.

"Go tell the master." Pieter said.

Katarina walked back to the house, her heart pounding. She welcomed any reason to relay the master a message. She settled the sleepy baby down in her bed, covered her and gave her a kiss. Isabeau grabbed at Katarina's hair and then turned onto her side, sucking on her finger.

Katarina pulled the leather cord from her hair, raked her fingers through her curls and tied it back tight. She checked the state of her dress. She scolded herself for being childish, climbed the stairs and knocked on Herr Tucher's sitting room door.

"*Ja, bitte?*" Herr Tucher shouted.

Katarina opened the door and poked her head around the door jamb, not entering. "Herr Tucher, I need to tell you something."

"Wonderful, I need to talk to you, too, dear Katarina," he said, smiling a genuine smile.

"Seems that someone is living in the barn. Pieter pointed it out to me today. Someone has made a camp in the one corner."

"Yes, I have noticed it, too. There is wine missing. I have the feeling someone has been through my things here in this room. Certain artifacts have been disturbed. I am missing a small dagger with a bone handle. It was one of a pair from my father. See, here is the other."

His face and voice softened when he spoke to her as if he valued what she thought and appreciated her friendship. He held out the dagger, the bone handle inlaid with silver swirled in an intricate design.

"I had a hunk of glass," he continued, "nothing special, but that is missing, too. Though I cannot imagine anyone opening those front doors without causing us all to stand up in our beds!"

He stared and awaited Katarina's response.

"Katarina, come here and sit down. I have something else to tell you." He looked out the window. "The spring is coming and I must travel. I expect to head north in the next few weeks, after Easter, towards Hamburg. I may be gone four to eight weeks." He paused. "Come in here and have a seat, please."

Katarina entered the room, shut the door and sat on a chair across from him. He seemed genuinely happy to see her. He sat up and gestured like he wanted to take her hand but he held himself back. He crossed his hands in his lap and leaned back in the settee. The crook of his reclined body made an inviting space. She could imagine curling up there. How she wished the two of them could just fly away from here…

"You will come with me," Herr Tucher said.

"Pardon?" she said.

"Accompany me on my trip."

"Oh, no, I can't do that," Katarina said and looked away, her face burning. "The baby…"

"The baby can stay with Tanner's wife. We certainly could not take her with us."

"Oh, no, I can't leave her, I…"

"Listen, I have also arranged for Ralf to give lessons to Falk. He can also teach Tanner's wife to read."

Katarina jumped to her feet. "No, I can't leave her if he's going to be here!"

"I know you do not like him but he is harmless. Listen to me: I have acquired more land. I would like to sow the fields, as many as we can this year. Trees will be cleared to provide more acreage to plant. The vineyard needs to be pruned and new varieties need to be planted. We have grapes that should grow in this cold climate. I have arranged to bring out more sheep and goats and hire more help. I also have a worker coming who farms carp. He will stock the ponds. Tanner will oversee the workers and the maintenance of the buildings, his wife can care for the workers. Ralf will give lessons to the children. He is willing to stay the weeks that I am away, well, the weeks we are away."

A knock on the door made Katarina jump and Sara came in.

"Herr Tucher, I found a trunk for Katarina's things. Ah, Katarina, there you are. The baby can sleep next to my bed. It won't be any problem. It may do you some good, to get away for a few weeks."

"I don't think I can…" Katarina said.

"Don't worry," Sara said. "Falk is excited for his first lesson. Tomorrow already!"

The blood drained from Katarina's face.

"Katarina, what could possibly happen?" she said. "Pieter might go with you, too. To visit his father."

Oh, no, what if Pieter wasn't even here to keep an eye on Isabeau? No, Katarina couldn't possibly leave…

"Pieter has not yet decided if he is going," Herr Tucher said. "He has become Tanner's right hand. I hate to lose him here. Like I said, we shall leave after Easter, as soon as my new coachman comes with the hired hands."

He stood, grabbed his coat from the chair and threw it over his shoulders. He smiled at Katarina like he knew they both wanted this, and left the room, shutting the door quietly behind him.

"What about Frau Kuni? Oh I can't…"

"You can," Sara said. "You must, if he wants you to. Don't worry so much. I'll have to cook in your kitchen. You have more space than I do in our house. I've heard the new hands are also bringing wives and there are more children coming."

"But what about the traveling? Aren't the roads dangerous?"

Katarina was in a slight panic. How small her world had become this last winter?

"Herr Tucher has hired men to travel with the coach. You never gave me the impression before that you were such a fearful woman," Sara said.

Sara winked and turned to leave, both hands supporting the small of her back, like she was in pain. She'd become quite plump. She pulled the door shut without a sound and left Katarina alone.

How small Katarina's world had become indeed. What had happened to the brazen barmaid this past winter? All of what she thought she was, she was not. From the sitting room window, on this clear afternoon, she could see down the beaten track and the hills beyond. Katarina wanted to leave this place and go to Hamburg. With him. But by leaving the baby here, she was giving up her responsibility. Isabeau was in danger, even though Katarina was the only one who thought so. But was Katarina the baby's mother or was she a woman? Was it possible to be both? She opened the door, went out and closed it quietly and ran down the steps to the kitchen. Pieter knelt next to his cat, feeding him something red and dripping.

"Pieter, are you going to travel?" Katarina said. "Are you going home?"

"No, I don't think so. I can earn more money if I stay here and work."

"Sit down," she said. "I have to tell you the whole story."

Chapter 27

After three weeks of preparations, the new workers arrived. Katarina had divulged to Pieter most of what she knew about Isabeau's story. If he doubted the story's credibility, he kept it to himself. He had assured Katarina that the child would come to no harm if he was here. She was leaving with Herr Tucher for Hamburg in the morning.

Yesterday, numerous carts and coaches pulled into the farmyard, one after the other. Out of them spilled a throng of bleating sheep, shouting men and screaming children. Katarina had watched at the window in Herr Tucher's sitting room and counted five men and three wives. The drove of children flitted around like a flock of pigeons and Katarina miscounted again and again.

Because of the whirlwind of activity and Sara's insistence that she would deal with the new arrivals, Katarina was forced to retreat to the upper story of the main house. Sara and one of the other women named Anna, a woman Sara seemed to know well, took over the kitchen and the chores. Katarina and Isabeau moved into one of the garret rooms in the main house next to Frau Kuni's. The other new woman had brought a trunk of clothing from Nuremberg and deposited it in this room for Katarina to rummage through. Katarina was instructed to pack what she wanted.

Ralf had come and gone the past three weeks but his visits were short and limited to instructing Falk at the workers' house. He'd stayed away from the main house. Katarina and Sara had little time for anything besides turning both houses upside-down preparing for the new workers. Herr Tucher and the men worked to full capacity and they came home late, when it was completely dark.

Herr Tucher told Katarina that they would take the trip slow, no need for haste. They could allow a week to ten days to get there and he would fashion their stay at will. He had appointments, yes, and people to meet, but that would be arranged upon arrival. They were making a delivery for his uncle—that was all. He was mostly in the market for art.

This garret room, directly under the roof construction, had nothing separating it from the elements but the clay roof tiles. Outdoor sounds surrounded Katarina as if she stood unprotected on a balcony. A small opening in the plaster paneling served as a window. The floor was covered with dusty wooden planks. As a child, Katarina had slept here only once. That night, she fell into a wild dream of fire and brimstone. When Frau Kuni found Katarina screaming and blind with panic, she was forced to allow Katarina back into the alcove by the kitchen, that very night. How could Katarina ever escape the burning house here under the roof?

Sara's small traveling trunk with a wood inlay pattern and engraved brass latch stood open on the floor. Katarina folded a dark blue wool skirt and a matching jacket and threw it in. She tried a wide brimmed hat with a long white plume and laughed at herself. She disliked hats but would have to cover her head. Sara told her these hats were the latest style. She was unsure about the seductive wine-red dress and threw it on the lone chair that stood in the corner.

A knock sounded on the door and it opened. Pieter came in with Isabeau in his arms and laughed.

"That hat suits you," he said.

He picked a path between shirts and skirts and boots that spilled out of the two trunks and were strewn all over the floor. He handed Katarina the baby and sat down on the straw sack mattress with a thud.

"Ralf has arrived and is in the kitchen with Sara. I wanted to tell you that. Don't worry. I won't let anything happen," he said.

Katarina sat on the floor and set the baby on her lap. She held a little dress up to Isabeau's frame. The fabric smelled of mold and Katarina threw the dress aside so it could be washed. She grabbed another one and added it to the pile.

"These are still a bit too big for her," she said. "But they will fit this summer."

Katarina stood the baby on her feet, supporting her around her middle. She bobbed up and down and laughed. This all felt so wrong. Katarina should not be leaving her.

"She wants to walk," Pieter said. "And she loves horses."

"Have you put her on a horse?"

"She wants to go into the barn! You love horses, don't you

Isabeau?" He reached out and gently stroked her hair.

Isabeau bobbed up and down. She was getting so heavy that Katarina's elbows hurt to hold her like this.

"I'll take Isabeau back to the worker's house tonight," Pieter continued. "She'll sleep by my bed. Sara is preoccupied with the new workers."

He stood to leave and held his strong, scratched hands out to collect the baby. Katarina pulled Isabeau in close and hugged her. Katarina's eyes welled up with tears. She should not be leaving.

"Don't worry," he said and meant it. "I'll protect this child with my life."

Katarina released her grip on Isabeau, kissed her and handed her up to Pieter. She leaned away from him and reached for Katarina as Katarina got to her feet.

"Ka. Ka. Ka," Isabeau said and started to cry.

Katarina took the baby in her arms again.

"I won't be long. I'll be back, my dear, sweet Isabeau."

Katarina kissed her again, handed her to Pieter and turned away. Pieter laid a hand on Katarina's shoulder and she turned to face him. He kissed her on the cheek and left the room with the sobbing baby. Katarina grabbed the wine-red dress off the chair and threw it into the traveling trunk. It did fit perfectly.

Katarina folded a few undergarments and another dress and placed them carefully on top. She slumped down on the straw mattress and looked at the leather pouch with Isabeau's ring that lay on top of a little book of poetry Sara had given her. She stuffed them both into a larger leather pouch, place it in the traveling trunk and closed the lid. She should not be doing this. Her place was here.

Someone quietly climbed the steps. Herr Tucher stood in the doorway. He held out a dark-green velvet dress.

"You can wear this tomorrow. We need to leave quite early," he said.

Katarina took the dress from him and ran her finger along the row of black wooden buttons that lined the back.

"I'll never be able to button these alone."

"You will not be alone," he said.

He held out a comb made of bone. He ran his fingers through her hair.

"I found this among my things," he said. "I have less use for such a thing as you do."

Katarina took the comb and thanked him with a nod. He kissed her on the cheek, pulled back and held her gaze. Her chest rose and fell and she did not look away. Satisfied with her reaction, he turned and walked down the steps.

Chapter 28

The first light rose in the east, pink and gray, misty and cold. Frosty dew dusted the mounds of tilled earth in the brown fields and an invigorating charge filled the air. Katarina knotted the wool shawl around her neck, grabbed an armful of firewood from the heap in the paddock, dumped it in the wood basket in the stable and pulled the paddock door closed.

Quiet footsteps came down the stairs, crossed the kitchen floor and stopped behind her. Fingers tugged ever so slightly at the shawl around her neck. It loosened and fell to the floor. The fingers got a hold of the bottom black button on the dark-green velvet dress and fastened it. The fingers moved from button to button as if they performed a sacred ritual, fastening, smoothing, tugging. Katarina felt his face in her hair, his breath on her shoulder. His lips brushed her neck and a soft, thick, woolen riding cloak covered her shoulders. Herr Tucher turned her to face him, and without a word, took her by the hand and led her out the front door to their coach.

The party traveled the first two days with no incidence. The pace was slow. Katarina and Herr Tucher's coach accompanied a heavy wooden wagon laden with the goods for delivery. The wheels on the heavy wagon pulled by six grey Austrian stallions creaked and plodded on. They made occasional stops by flowing waters and Katarina watched the horses drink. Twelve men on horseback rode alongside the coach and the heavy wagon. Those rough-looking fellows constantly circled their group, rode on ahead and retraced their route in case they were being followed by bandits.

An occasional traveler waved in greeting and the few farmers out utilizing the warm spring afternoons stopped to watch the wagon pass. Herr Tucher pointed out the villages and towns they passed by, always knowing something about their histories. The swaying of their light coach pulled by Herr Tucher's two Friesian stallions and the cadence of their hooves lulled Katarina to sleep on more than one occasion.

She found herself thinking about the future, a notion that would never have crossed her mind before. As a young woman, she never thought about her own mortality or where she would end up in the years to come. A brisk *"Mir egal"*—"I don't care"—and the wave of her hand kept her from worrying. The casual dismissal of concern for her future was rooted in fear she could now see. But, slowly, the need to ensure a home for Isabeau and herself replaced her disinterest of what would be. She now needed to play a more active role in her destiny.

Sitting so close to Herr Tucher gave her a chance to have a good look at him. He would look out the window and lose himself in his thoughts. Sometimes he seemed pained, sometimes reflective. He reached for her hand often and gave her affectionate smiles. No man had ever treated her like this before.

"One village looks like the next to me," Katarina said.

"Yes, I tend to lose track of time and distance when I am traveling. Here," he pointed to a circular map he had spread out on his lap, "we are here. We are right outside Erfurt. I will find you a comfortable room close to the stables. I want to stay by the wagon tonight."

As they approached the city, he took Katarina's hand and pointed out the coach's window. "Erfurt is a city smaller than Nuremberg in size and significance, housing about 18,000 people," he said. "The city is known for its trade in dyer's woad, a blue dye."

"Yes, I know dyer's woad," Katarina said.

"Their trade is in danger of being replaced by the import of indigo from the new country, you know, the one they have discovered across the ocean. Trade in general is suffering and monies are being filtered largely into arming troops. I feel this is a bad sign. The worst may be yet to come."

The coach stopped in front of a country inn with a deep-sloping thatched roof. Herr Tucher opened the coach door, stepped down and offered Katarina his hand. She stepped off the coach. The guards, Katarina called them, accompanied the heavy wagon further along the street and disappeared around the corner. Herr Tucher led Katarina to the tavern on the ground floor. The tavern was peaceful enough at this early hour.

The smell of roasting meat and fresh bread wafted from

somewhere behind the house. A plump *Magd* with flushed red cheeks and greasy hands brought them two mugs of beer, a plate of meat with two knives and a basket of steaming grey bread.

"Wild boar, that is," the *Magd* said and winked at Herr Tucher.

As the evening wore on, the spirits rose and the level of noise did, too. Katarina decided to retire. She may have worked in this type of tavern but it wasn't the sort of place she would choose to frequent. As the barmaid in her own tavern, the men respected her even if it was because they knew they had to in order to get more drink. But here in this foreign place, she was vulnerable and a bit uneasy. Herr Tucher walked her up the steps to her room, opened the door, bowed and left. Katarina wondered if he was taking turns on the watch with the other men. She opened the window, poured some wine and opened the book of poetry Sara had given to her. The late evening sky lent just enough light for her to read the anonymous verse:

The ponds were calm, the moon shone bright
The wolf, his voice was still.
Your eyes were wide and full of light
You shuddered from the chill.

I took your hand and led the way
You came reluctantly
I kissed your cheek and 'til this day
We love most pleasantly

I need you, Oh, my love don't go
I need you by my side
I want you, though the wind may blow
We'll never have to hide.

Over the rooftops, a cloud front moved towards the city. An uneasy breeze carried the warning of a spring storm. From the street below, a din rose from the entrance to the inn, up to Katarina's window. She stood but could not see the cause of the ruckus.

In the stairway outside the door, heavy boots pounded up the steps. It sounded like an animal scratched on the door. Something thudded against the door, like a heavy sack being left to fall. More scratching unnerved Katarina. She rustled through her pouch and found the sheathed knife that when pulled had a comical, rippled blade as long as her hand. Pieter had urged her to take it, just in case. She turned one of the two chairs towards the door, sat down and faced the door with both feet braced on the floor. She studied the knife's carved silver handle. The door handle rattled as if someone struggled to open it and Katarina wondered if she should give that someone a fright by pulling the door open with a flourish.

The door flew open of its own accord. Herr Tucher dropped a very drunken soldier on his face and caught himself before he fell into the room on top of him. He stepped over him, grabbed him by the shoulders, pulled him face down into the room, stepped over him again and slammed the door shut. Katarina sheathed the blade and stuck it into her pouch before he saw it.

"It is a very unappetizing crowd down in the tavern tonight. A group of Frenchmen—well, a group of men speaking French—settled upon us and the air was so thick and tense I thought it was best to drag my friend out of there. He was sleeping like a baby, poor fellow. Left alone, they would have made mincemeat out of him. I am so sorry to disturb you, Katarina. We will just let him sleep it off and I will get him out of here. Do you mind?"

He poured himself some wine, drank a sip and paced back and forth, the wooden floor creaking. "I cannot sleep myself. I am unsettled. You may sleep if you like. I will not disturb you."

The drunken soldier snored in the corner of the room.

"There seems to be a large, boisterous group swarming through the city like ants." He stopped pacing and took a deep breath. "They had blocked our way back to the stables where the other men sleep. I admit I do not want to come up against these men. I did not want to leave you alone here, either. I left the tavern as nonchalantly as possible. We will depart at daybreak anyway. Do try to get some sleep."

Suddenly very tired, Katarina laid back and covered herself with the surprisingly clean-smelling feather bed. The wooden buttons dug into her skin. She turned over and watched him at the table reading a book. Katarina wondered if he slept at all. He sipped his wine, stood and shut the window to the night chill and rubbed his eyes. Eventually Katarina drifted off. She dreamt a black cat lay on her pillow, purring in her ear and stroking her cheek with his smooth nose. She awoke to the shout of:

"FIRE!"

Katarina shot up to a sitting position. Herr Tucher stood by the window, prodding the soldier with his foot and said, "Get up!"

Katarina pulled the riding cloak over her shoulders, stomped into her boots, grabbed the leather pouch. They bolted out of the room like three cannonballs. Herr Tucher pulled her by the hand. The sky was just beginning to lighten. They dashed along the deserted street towards the stables. They rounded the corner. Herr Tucher stopped before he pulled the stable door open and pointed to black cloud rising above.

"There, that house with the thatched roof is ablaze. It will not take long until the other houses catch fire." He coughed and spoke to the soldier. "Rouse the men and prepare to leave immediately! I will find the innkeeper. Expect to leave as soon as I return!"

Flames danced inside the billowing black cloud, thatch crackled and a man shouted. Katarina coughed as the hot, acrid smell of burning hay caught in her throat. More men shouted now. Wood splintered as a heavy construction collapsed. Katarina covered her mouth and nose against the taste of charred wood. Herr Tucher returned after a few moments. The street was alive with hollering men. Herr Tucher's men were in position and Katarina climbed in the coach.

"Tanner, get on the main road and maybe we could reach Wolfenbüttel this evening," Herr Tucher said.

He got into the coach and pulled the door closed. Smoke swirled all around them as the whole street sunk under the hot, irritating fog. He coughed and took Katarina's hand. Urgent calls of *Hü*! spurred the horses into motion and the coach jerked forward. They picked up speed and the smoke cleared from the coach as they quickly left the burning buildings behind them.

"Tanner?" Katarina said.

"Tanner the Elder. I thought the young tanner's father could use a trip up north. His wife died recently. He'll be staying with us at Sichardtshof now."

After they rode a way in silence, Katarina asked, "Who were those Frenchmen?"

"I am not sure myself. Soldiers, I would assume. I do not speak much French, but what I could understand, they were not just traveling to buy dyer's woad."

They rode for hours. At some point Herr Tucher knocked on the roof of the coach to signal Tanner the Elder to stop.

"I am tired of riding," he said. "I would like to stop for the night and continue on tomorrow."

The coach stopped and Tanner the Elder looked in the coach window. This is what the young tanner would look like in twenty years: robust, ample nose and mouth; those red, glowing cheeks; bright blue eyes; wavy hair, the Elder's considerably grayer.

"We have reached Nordhausen," Tanner the Elder said. "We were slow today, but no matter, let's stop."

"Ah, yes. Nordhausen," Herr Tucher said. "The town had burned badly about five years ago. I have not been back since."

They found a room in a newly built, charming country inn and ate in their common room; a warm, dark-paneled parlor with settees, tables and benches and a fireplace built into the stone wall.

After the meal, Herr Tucher showed Katarina to a simple room at the very top of the house. A large bed was shoved under the slope of the roof in the one corner, a table for two with two chairs stood under the two tiny windows and a wash table stood next to the door under a tiny mirror. Katarina hoped they wouldn't be trapped up here under the roof, should the place burn.

The door could be locked, he said, and told her to do so once she was inside. He left like every other night, leaving her an extra candle he'd gotten from the innkeeper and a bottle of wine.

Katarina locked the door, sat at the worm-holed, dark-stained table, and poured a mug of red wine. With the door closed and the tiny windows open, she heard no sounds from inside. It was as if she was cut off from the rest of the house. The sun was setting, but there was still a lot of activity outside. Two women in the street called to a man riding atop a cart full of hay. A dog barked behind the next house and a breeze rustled leaves in the tree outside the window. A blackbird sang lazily from a rooftop.

She thought she heard careful footsteps climbing the narrow stairs. Or was that a hammer in the house next door? A soft rapping on the door acknowledged someone's arrival. Katarina set down her wine and opened the door. She stepped aside and Herr Tucher came in. She stuck her head out the door and peeked down the steps.

"I'm on my own," Herr Tucher said.

"Where are you staying tonight?"

"The inn is full. And I am not so keen on sleeping in the barn with twelve soldiers. May I come in?"

This place they found themselves in—traveling—was an abstract place where the general rules of conduct did not apply. Katarina dropped her guard like a relieved sigh and let herself slip into the role of this man's partner. And what sort of role did this man play in her plans for the future? She could only imagine her future together with him. Without him, she could go on and would have to, but she did not want to. He was the man she wanted by her side and this was all that mattered.

She felt a pressure in her chest, a feeling closely related to being saved from drowning. Her shoulders rose and fell as her breathing quickened. She swallowed hard. He shut the door, turned back towards her and tugged on the cord that held her hair. It fell free around her shoulders. His hands reached for her face thoughtfully, like he needed to record every curve and crevice.

He picked her up and carried her to the small bed in the corner of the room. He smelled like fresh-cut grass, his breath like the warm breeze gently wafting over a field of grain. He laid her down, studied her face, stroked her cheek. He kissed her lips like he was sampling a costly wine.

"What would you have done if I had turned you away?" Katarina asked.

"I would have gone," he said. He stood and closed the window, came back and lay on his side, propped up on one elbow, staring down into her face. "But you did not. Turn me away, that is."

He pulled her close as if he could not get close enough and kissed her lips, the kiss deepening the tighter he embraced her. She pulled back to catch her breath.

"The only thing keeping us apart is twenty wooden buttons," he said.

She turned her back to him. Starting from the top, he unlatched one button after another, his face in her hair, his lips on her neck. The candle burned low. He pulled her dress over her head and let it fall to the floor. He kissed her neck, her shoulders. His touch made her shiver.

He turned her onto her back, took her hand and pressed it to his cheek. With his other hand he drew a line down her neck and along her breast. He seemed to be memorizing every shadow, his finger tracing her outline. He kissed her neck, slow and deliberate and then her shoulder, his hand reaching between her legs and gently spreading them.

He sat up, hastily undressed and lay back down, one leg draped over her, a protective move. Katarina pulled his face closer and kissed his lips. He responded to her kiss by sliding his whole body on top of her. She opened her legs and allowed him in, a slow sliding secret. He reached behind and grabbed her buttocks and pulled her closer, entered deeper, his weight pressing against her hips.

He eased back and leaned to the side, pressing two fingers between her legs, on a spot hard and engorged with blood. His fingers slowly circled and caressed until her legs began to shake. Katarina grabbed his arm and their eyes met.

He smiled and continued, saying: "You have never had a man who cared if you had pleasure or not, have you?"

Katarina pulled his face to hers and kissed him, a desperate fervor, enveloped wanton wanting. He worked her until she shuddered and relaxed. His hips pounded out a rhythm, his sweating body sliding against hers. He pushed himself in as far as he could, shivered and relaxed.

They lay tangled in each other, his breath in her ear, his lips on her cheek and she drifted off. She slept until the sun was high and the birds chattered in the tree outside the open window. The air was crisp and clean. He sat in a chair reading a book, stood when he saw her stirring and sat on the edge of the bed. He kissed her.

"We have quite a distance to put behind us today. Come! Let us be on our way!"

Chapter 29

Herr Tucher wanted to finish the journal entry and record their arrival in Hamburg before Katarina woke up. He had fallen asleep half way through his writing last night and now sat in the parlor of his uncle's Hamburg house, staring out of the open window at the crooked row of houses, quill in hand, listening to the hooves on the road, the shouts of fishermen and laughter from women across the street.

The morning light shining through the shutters had awoken Herr Tucher early. He stood stiffly from his chair, walked outside and opened the shutters quietly, assuming Katarina slept still and peaceful. He stoked the fire, made a pot of tea and sat back at the desk. As he read back through his journal he noticed that his impressions of Amsterdam and Hamburg were similar, but for many reasons quite different. He compared his two favorite cities to two brothers and relationships between brothers are anything but still and uneventful.

Where Herr Tucher imagined Amsterdam as the younger of the two siblings, he was of course left with only his unspoken impression because his Dutch comprehension and speaking skills were below average. There was a willy-nilly speed in the comings and goings all along the canals. Bustling, energetic movements from the water, from the people, and the rats ticked like time. Recklessness, friendly and fueled by success, Amsterdam's independent and forward thinking would propel the city to greatness, in his opinion.

But in Hamburg there a discipline, like a strict older brother's, that was not as apparent in Amsterdam. Rules were meant to be followed, but they were lovingly enforced. Of late, they fortified the Hanseatic city. A wall was being built and soldiers were numerous in the streets. Herr Tucher read in the weekly newspaper that this endeavor was costing them dearly. But to summarize the citizens by the clothes they wore in one word, it would be "affluent." The atmosphere was festive, the mood positive, the people unaffected by matters unknown. Politics were a policy of neutrality. Maybe because there was more air in the north, the feeling as if one could escape by way of the sea. The sea was freedom and the people were less inclined to close their minds.

He read the journal entry and corrected small nuances. He wanted to remember every moment. After days of unending motion, he and Katarina had disembarked from the coach last night, on the waterfront, on the banks of the Elbe River. Herr Tucher asked her to please put on the wide-brimmed hat and cover her hair. It was inappropriate for her to be in public with a bare head; it suggested a woman of ill repute. And the wide brim and the festive plume suited her.

A refreshing, salty breeze accompanied a few gulls which swooped and swayed. The red setting sun accented the tips of the waving water. The shod hooves of the horses pulling the heavy wagon cracked against the cobblestones and stopped behind them. The chains from the team's harnesses clanked, the wagon creaked and gave an impression of movement even at a standstill. One horse pawed the ground. Another tried to bite the behind of the teammate ahead of him.

Herr Tucher had turned and looked around for his contact. He was only meant to accompany the heavy wagon to its destination here at the waterfront, shake hands with the recipient and receive his papers. The transaction was considered sealed and he was free to go. The wagon was to be unloaded and reloaded with goods for his Uncle Paul and they would embark on the journey back to Franconia. Katarina had asked him what they were delivering.

"Metal, judging by the weight of the wagon and the fact that we need six heavy horses to pull the thing," Herr Tucher answered.

"Metal? Do you mean weapons? Is that why we need twelve soldiers to guard our journey?" she asked.

"I do not ask what I deliver. I do not need to bother myself about any of it. The monetary transaction is taken care of through the banks. And no matter what we deliver, we need guards. We could be traveling with a pile of manure and they would attempt to rob us."

"But it's against your ideals, I would think," Katarina said.

"Yes, I have my ideals. I consider myself a peaceful man. But what the others do will be according to their own philosophy, not mine. Men will fight as long as there is a territory or an opinion or a woman to fight over. On the other hand, one can benefit from a business deal. Business is not the correct stage for morals."

Herr Tucher's contact arrived and gave him a sealed letter. He opened it, read the contents and was satisfied with its authenticity. They shook hands, exchanged a few syllables of kindness and he signaled to Tanner the Elder to jump down from the coach box and talk with him.

"We will walk up to the house, then. You can take the horses to the stable and you are free to go, my friend."

Tanner the Elder smiled and jumped onto the coach box with the vivacity of a man who had not spent the last eight hours driving a coach. He grabbed the reins, snapped the team into motion and was gone.

"There are some very friendly women in Hamburg waiting for the company of a man like him. A man with a full purse, that is. He loves to come here."

Herr Tucher offered his arm and Katarina threaded her hand through the crook of his elbow. He took a deep breath of fresh, salt-laden air and they sauntered off, up the banks away from the water.

"My uncle has a house here, so we have our own apartment," he said. "I would first like to engage in my favorite pastime, though."

"Which is?" she asked.

"Eating and drinking wine. I hope you like fish."

Night had fallen and men moved about the streets like rats coming out of their holes for the evening. Herr Tucher and Katarina passed a few local establishments, but the raucous nature of the din inside shoved him further along the street. They found a small, airy corner hostelry and found a place to sit. He wanted a sweet wine and a bit of whatever they had to eat. They drank their wine, which was expensive, and ate some salty, unidentifiable pottage consisting of salty fish, some sort of grain, root vegetable, what looked like an egg and more salt.

After the meal they walked a few streets farther, arrived at his uncle's uninhabited house and Herr Tucher unlocked the front door. Paul had the door latch made in Nuremberg in order to keep unwanted visitors at bay. They stumbled into the low hallway. The front sitting room was so dark he could barely see the table with a candle on it. He threw his leather satchel on the floor next to the settee and removed his doublet.

In spite of the darkness, he could feel Katarina staring at him. He moved towards her without much thought and pulled her close. She could always refuse if she wanted to. Her chest quickly rose and fell as her breath quickened. She was not going to refuse. He bent his head, kissed her and held her long. He could smell the forest in her hair, imagine the color of fresh-tilled soil in her soft deer-eyes, feel the new leaves flutter on her skin. She was like no other woman he'd ever had. Solid but supple, intelligent but honest, innocent but obscene.

He undressed her. She wore an uncomplicated wine-red dress and it was quickly shed. He would make love to her right here, in this darkened sitting room. He led her to the settee and banged his shins on the wooden frame. An oath escaped his mouth. She touched a finger to his lips. He grabbed her hand, kissed her arm, her shoulder, her neck, sat her down on the settee and knelt before her.

Being robbed of sight he was a slave to his other senses. He pulled her velvet hips close and kissed her knees, her thighs, her warm folds. He lingered there, her body rising and falling, her legs shuddering with every generous kiss. He could love her like no other woman. Her body responded easily, again and again.

Herr Tucher gathered naked Katarina up in his arms, kissed her, lifted her effortlessly, climbed the steep narrow steps to the bedroom and laid her on the clean sheets. Paul had the sense to have the place cleaned before their arrival. He must remind himself to thank him for this courtesy.

He undressed and covered her body with his. Hers was like cool clay that molded itself to fit his contours, taking him in, holding him firm, allowing him refuge.

Katarina whispered, "I am so tired."

He covered her with a blanket. She turned to the side and breathed low.

The house was chilled and he made a fire in the kitchen. He returned to Paul's desk, found a candle in the drawer and lit it. He reached for the satchel he had thrown to the floor, pulled out his journal and his little book, slumped into the chair and opened the books on the desk. He pulled one creaking drawer looking for ink. He had not thought to bring any. The next drawer stuck and wood scraped as he pulled and wiggled it open. Inside stood an inkwell and he reminded himself not only to thank the man, but bring him some port back from Hamburg.

He sat and counted the syllables, tried not to be too soft, but the mood, the flickering candle and the wine got the best of him and he began to write:

Heut´Abend bin ich ganz allein.
Und denke nur an dich.
Du schläfst im Bett, du bist jetzt meins.
Von draußen kommt kein Licht.

Ich sitze seit Momenten hier.
Und lausche dir im Schlaf.
Ich will dich, Oh, du fehlst mir sehr.
Einsam blökt ein Schaf.

Soll ich zu dir? Ich schleich mich rein.
Ich will dich nicht gleich stören.
Mein Herz, Oh! wie es nach dir schreit.
Verlangen wird mich zerstören.

Ich küss dich wach, du drehst dich um.
Ich schließe dich im Arm.
Mein Mund sucht deinen, andersrum,
Verschlingst mich wie ein Schwamm.

Chapter 30

Pieter stuck his head in the barrel full of rainwater that stood next to the workers' house in the shade of a small oak. He shook off his daze and let the cold water drip down his aching shoulders. They had plowed a field on a slope yesterday, Tanner and he, and Pieter had pushed himself harder than those oxen. He splashed himself again with the cold water and rubbed his dirty shirt over his chest. The air was dry and warm today. He and Tanner wanted to get started on the fencing before it got too hot.

Isabeau was awake. She was crying under the eaves where they slept. He went back into the kitchen and threw his shirt in the basket for the women to wash. He climbed the ladder. Isabeau sat right at the top and looked down at him.

"Don't you dare. Get away from the ladder," Pieter said.

She crawled back under the linen curtain. Pieter followed her. She sat on his straw sack and made her eyes big. He had to laugh. Sara had hung these linens to divide the upper floor between all the workers who had to share this miserable little space. Through the curtain, he could see the children who slept on a pile in the corner. They looked like a litter of piglets.

Suddenly Pieter's curtain flew aside and he had to jump back. That new woman Anna grabbed Isabeau off the straw sack. She laughed and poked Pieter in the stomach. Pieter backed away from her. She wasn't married to the man she came out here with, so she told him. They were not even friends and none of the children were hers.

"Just making sure you care for the child," she said.

"The child wants nothing but her peace and quiet," Pieter said and took Isabeau from her.

Tanner coughed downstairs. Pieter climbed down the ladder with Isabeau on his hip and sat down at a chair in the tiny kitchen.

He plopped her on his lap.

"Some tea, Pieter?" Sara said and handed Pieter a mug. She was having trouble moving in the kitchen. Her belly had gotten quite large.

He sipped at the bitter tea and almost spat it out.

"What is this?" he cried.

"Wormwood. Bitters are good for your gall. Clean you out." She set a bowl of porridge on the table.

"Two spoons?" Pieter said.

"We don't want to spoil the child. She can eat by herself."

Tanner squeezed through the opening in the nailed-up boards that separated the kitchen from the small space where he slept with his wife and Falk. The little room was built around the tiled wood stove. He coughed again. Falk sat down at the table, rubbing his eyes. Slowly the two new workers climbed down the ladder, too. Tanner didn't need to call for them. They showed up on their own. No one thought of talking back to the man.

"Anna, take the child from Pieter and tend the fire at the main house," Tanner said. "Sweep the floors, too, and check on Frau Kuni." He pointed to the two blond men who looked more like boys as they climbed down the ladder. "You two, relieve Knecht from the herd of sheep and take the herd towards the west. I'll send Knecht back out this evening. Pieter, you can help Anna with her firewood and then come back here to me as quickly as you can. We have a lot to get done today."

He sipped at the tea and screwed his face up. "What is this stuff?" He took another big gulp. "We'll meet at the main house for our meal when the sun goes down. How are you holding up there, wife?"

She maneuvered her belly around the two blond workers, leaned against her husband and kissed his cheek. "I'm fine. Don't worry about me."

Anna and Pieter left the kitchen and walked towards the main house. It stood still and empty in the morning sun, all the windows closed up tight. Pieter handed Anna the child and grabbed a basket for firewood. There was plenty in the barn.

The barn's main door stood ajar. Pieter listened as he moved slowly back to the woodpile. The blankets had been disturbed. Whoever was sleeping here made sure they were up and out by the time they started moving around. Pieter filled the basket and went back to the kitchen. Anna had stoked the fire. He dropped the basket by the fireplace and walked to the chamber where Katarina slept.

"I thought that other woman was sleeping in here, Anna."

"I think she's gone. The man I came with is no longer here either. I heard that the man fought with Tanner and they left together. The master is away, you know."

"Someone should stay here in the night," Pieter said.

"The other woman who sleeps with the carp farmer said there are ghosts in this old house."

"The world is full of ghosts, Anna. They are poor souls, really."

"The world is full of *gchosts*," Anna said.

She mocked his Dutch accent. Pieter hated it when she did that. She came up really close to him and poked his stomach again. Pieter didn't like her much. She was a crude woman, easily ten years older than he was. She smelled like burning fat. She scratched her head too much. Fleas, he'd bet.

"I'll stay here with you if you're afraid," she said.

Pieter gave her that look. This woman even had the thoughts of a flea. Isabeau's head would be full of insects after spending the day with this woman. He grabbed Isabeau and walked back to the barn. She would spend the day with Tanner and Pieter.

Tanner was standing by the barn's smaller side door, filling a satchel with tools. He wiped the sweat from his brow, disappeared into the dark-planked wooden structure and the door swung closed behind him. The door swung back open and he came out carrying a large sledgehammer. He shook his head and sighed when he saw the child.

"If it must be, Pieter," he said.

Pieter sat the child on the ground and she tried to pull herself up on her feet, both hands clambering on the wooden barn wall. He found his handcart behind the barn door, pushed it out of the barn and loaded it with posts, thick as his upper arm, which they had sharpened to a point. They were building another fence around the paddock to keep other animals out of the property. They had started ramming these sharp posts into the ground at an outward angle, a futile attempt to protect themselves, Tanner and Pieter agreed, but it was better than nothing.

He spread a blanket over the posts and sat the child on top, securing her around the shoulders with a leather harness. He pushed the overloaded handcart and his aching shoulders burned. His thoughts quieted. Pieter no longer heard his father scolding. Or his mother crying.

He pushed on behind the workers' house, along the path that led to the west. The grass in the fields had been shorn from the number of sheep they had grazing. They reached the section of the fence where they had left off two days ago, a gentle upward-sloping field at the westernmost boundary of the farm. Beyond the hedgerow, sheep bleated and a man whistled. A breeze rustled in the row of willow trees.

Some of the posts had been pulled out of the earth. They lay on the ground. Tanner spat.

"Pieter, we may just abandon our free time this evening and try to hunt out this ghost."

"These aren't ghosts," Pieter said.

He undid Isabeau's leather harness from the handcart and tethered her to one of the willow trees in the cool shade.

"No matter, we'll stuff the damn fencing back into the earth, twice as deep." Tanner produced his huge sledgehammer.

Like a rehearsed team, Pieter held the posts and Tanner hammered. The vibrations shook Pieter's forearms. After a few, they switched and Pieter hammered with all the fury he had.

"You've pounded the points in," Tanner said and laughed. "We'll re-sharpen them when we're done."

The day grew hot and Tanner tapped Pieter on the shoulder. He pointed along the fence and smiled. They'd made progress. Pieter heard Isabeau calling from under the tree. He wiped the sweat from his brow. What an empty, dry pit his stomach was. Tanner threw the sledgehammer aside and grabbed a ceramic jug of beer, uncorked it and drank deeply. He handed Pieter the jug. As he drank, he saw a brown form moving on the hill in the trees. A hawk cried.

"Psst. There, among the trees," Pieter whispered.

Tanner's gaze followed his. He nodded. They watched the man in brown on his sorrel steed pick his path through the underbrush. He stopped, turned and rode out into the field. He kept his hair cut short and when he stood still, he blended in with the forest.

"I've seen him before, too," Tanner said. "Do you think he's our ghost?"

"I don't know," Pieter said.

Pieter undid Isabeau's leather harness and sat next to her under the tree. Pounding hooves made them all turn with a start. A beautiful dark bay stallion galloped towards the two men, his coat gleaming in the sunlight. What a fine horse. What an inept rider. The horse's gait was fluid and smooth, but this rider sat atop the animal with the grace of a sack of grain. Even in this heat, the rider wore a heavy, black cloak with his hood up.

"Hallo there, men. I have brought you some food from the dear Tanner's wife." Ralf pushed the cowl back and tried to halt the stallion, which pranced on the spot. "Oh, yes, Tanner, that is you. Your wife sends me with your lunch. Hallo Pieter."

Pieter nodded a greeting.

Ralf dismounted and sat with them. "Oh, the child is here, too." He handed her a piece of bread and she took it.

"Lovely fence," Ralf said his voice carrying a bit of a sneer. "What do you hope to keep at bay?"

Tanner coughed and swallowed his bread. "If we can slow down any charging force, man or animal, then it has done its duty."

"This is part of the new property, then? If the dear Lord sees fit, these lands will yield quite a bit of food." Ralf handed Isabeau more bread. "And look how big this little one is getting."

"It all depends on the weather." Pieter nodded and chewed his dried deer meat.

"Children grow so quickly, don't they? Now, you have a fine boy, Tanner," he said. "Amazing how that child learns."

"He spends his evenings reading. I am impressed that he takes to it so well," Tanner said.

"He has many theological questions. Maybe he is destined for the monastery."

Tanner filled his mouth with bread and took a long draught of beer from the ceramic jug.

"What about you, Pieter? Do you sympathize with your fellow countrymen? They cannot even unite their Dutch Reformed Church without bickering between themselves."

"I never had much time for church," Pieter said. "My mother was sick and I spent my time taking care of her when my father was away."

"I don't think the truce with Spain will be able to hold up," Ralf said. "There is too much controversy between your countrymen. The Spanish will use this dispute to further their campaign."

"I come from Amsterdam," Pieter said. "We seem to benefit from the Spanish. They buy our goods. Even though they are the enemy, we wouldn't turn away good customers."

"The Catholic faith is still the only true faith. Spain will see to it that those Dutch Reformed heretics are stopped."

"I don't go to church. My father doesn't. My mother didn't go to church. She had other needs we had to see to."

"That is precisely the role of the church. To help you in your time of need. Where is your mother now?"

"She's dead." Pieter felt his face redden. He had never spoken the words out loud.

"Do you pray, boy?" Ralf said.

"God has no patience for the likes of me. I am left to be guided by my ghosts."

"A dangerous view indeed. A bit of prayer might cure your malady."

Ralf stood, mounted his stallion and the prancing horse turned in a circle. Ralf pulled much too tight on the reins. That further agitated the animal.

"Well, men, I am finished for the day," Ralf said. "We will continue this conversation. See you tomorrow, then."

Ralf kicked the horse and away he shot. Pieter would not be continuing this conversation. He laid the sleepy Isabeau on her blanket and covered her up. He stood and looked down the hollow. Admired the curve of their new fence. Tried not to think. But thoughts of the nights he left his mother alone intruded. His father would never understand that he had to get out and find some life. He thought about Henrike and Greta and whatever the others were called. He heard his father hollering, saw him throw his mug of wine when Pieter finally came home after three days and his mother had died while he was out. *'Galavanting,'* he said. *'You killed her,'* he said. *'It's all your fault,'* he said.

A hand touched Pieter's shoulder. He spun around.

"It's me, friend." Tanner laughed. "We have work to do."

Chapter 31

Katarina struggled to remember the names of all the landmarks she'd seen. This morning, they'd passed the Wartburg, a majestic stronghold that watches over the town of Eisenach, the castle where Martin Luther had been hidden almost one hundred years ago and translated the New Testament into the German language. Katarina and Herr Tucher's coach, still traveling with the heavy wagon and the soldiers, had then joined the Werra river and traveled south alongside that, the smooth monotony of the rocking coach lulling Katarina into a doze. The coach stopped abruptly and jarred her awake.

"We have reached Coburg," Herr Tucher said as he climbed out of the coach.

After riding in this coach for what seemed like weeks on end, Katarina wished to remain stationary, have her feet on the ground and finally go home. But once they returned to Sichardtshof, Katarina's fantasy would end: she'd be back at the farm and again the master's maid. If he cared to promote her to mistress, she feared she'd be shunned by the other workers as the trollop who didn't have to work anymore because she slept with the master.

Herr Tucher jumped back into the coach obviously excited to have this last measure of the journey completed. "The soldiers will turn south and travel on to Nuremberg with the heavy wagon," he said. "Tanner the Elder will take us farther to the west first before we continue the journey south to Sichardtshof."

He took her hand. "We haven't got far now Katarina. We will be home in the evening."

He pulled her into an embrace and kissed her lips with a passion that Katarina had become accustomed to over the last few weeks. She moved closer to him. Even though it was May, there had been frost last night and a chill hung over this elevated landscape.

"I'll miss being with you," she said.

"You will have me every day. I fear you may tire of me after a while."

"Not when it's this cold."

"Yes, once we get below the southern portion of the Thuringian Forest and Coburg it will hopefully warm a bit. You will stay with me tonight I hope?"

"*Erste Liebe wie der Mai geht selten ohne Frost vorbei*," she said. "First love is like the month of May, seldom without frost they say. Yes, I will stay."

She hoped he would detect what she felt without her having to tell him out loud: that she loved him. Those words would never reach his ears; not by light of day. Maybe a faint whispering in the night when he slept. The words spoken aloud would only fall to the floor, losing their impact, weakened from the sound of her voice traveling through thin air.

After what seemed like hours of rolling motion, the landmarks and the terrain took on a familiar hue as the early evening sunlight deepened. Herr Tucher pointed out the Höchstadt Castle as they rode by. Exhaustion was replaced with anticipation as they finally reached the Edelgraben, rode along the familiar track and pulled into the quiet, seemingly deserted Sichardtshof farmyard.

"Odd, it is so quiet," Herr Tucher said. "They have herded the sheep out to graze, I am sure. We have so much work now, they have plenty to do."

No sheep, nobody working outside, no smoke rising from any chimney. No sound, not a soul. A cold chill ran down Katarina's spine. She opened the coach door. Tanner the Elder unhitched the horses and led them away. She alighted and ran back to the workers' house. A chorus of women screeched a welcome as Katarina opened the door.

"Katarina!" Sara called from her little room. "You're home! Come and see, I've had a baby."

That's why Sara had expanded so the last few months. Katarina chastised herself that she had been so lost in her own thoughts that something so important as Sara's pregnancy could pass her by unnoticed. That new woman Anna came out of the room behind the woodstove carrying Isabeau. She watched Katarina as if she thought Katarina might steal something from her.

Sara walked out of her little room and sat at the table as if it pained her. The other new woman who chopped onions nodded a greeting. Katarina admired the tiny baby on Sara's arm.

"A boy," Sara said. "His name is Albin."

"Kata," Isabeau said and Anna set her down.

Oh, Katarina had missed her sweet little girl! Isabeau took a few careful steps, set herself down with a plop onto her backside and waved her arms. She propped herself onto all-fours and crawled to Katarina.

"Hallo Isabeau," Katarina said, picked her up and kissed her. "You were once as tiny as little Albin."

"How old is Isabeau now?" Anna asked.

"She must be a year old now," Katarina said. "She was born on May 16. It's so quiet here, where's Pieter?"

"Peh-ter," Isabeau said.

"Isabeau loves Pieter, don't you?" Anna said as she came up close to Katarina and stroked Isabeau's cheek. "He and Tanner are out in the fields. They should be back soon. Falk and Knecht are out with the sheep. They'll be back tomorrow."

Sara pointed to Anna. "She's been staying at the main house with Frau Kuni during the day."

"The woman is not well," Anna said. "She eats but she doesn't want to go out much."

"I'll go check on her," Katarina said.

She thanked the two of them, set the child on her hip and took her leave. As she walked towards the main house, a cloud of dust billowed down the track. A horse traveled away from the farm. Herr Tucher stood on the steps by the open double front doors. He read from a piece of parchment.

"That was a messenger from my Uncle Paul bearing news of the affairs of the last few weeks. One forgets the tedium of day-to-day business. One pressing matter though. Pieter's father is very ill. I need to let him know."

"He is out right now," Katarina said and heaved the solid child farther up her hip.

Herr Tucher walked down the few steps and laid his arm on Katarina's shoulder. He took Isabeau's tiny hand in his. "Who do we have here? Hello, Isabeau. Now we are all together again. Our life can resume some sort of normality. As much as I love traveling, I am so glad to be back. I am tired. I must retire."

"Give me a moment. I'll bring the baby's bed upstairs and join you."

A large cup of wine added to Katarina's fatigue. She washed the dust from her hands and face, carried Isabeau's bed up the steps and arranged her things in the room that had once belonged to the Old Widow. She finally got the baby quieted down after singing more than a few rounds of:

Schlaf, Kindchen, schlaf,
Der Vater hüt die Schaf,
Die Mutter schüttelts Bäumelein,
Da fällt herab ein Träumelein.
Schlaf, Kindchen, schlaf!

Katarina heard no sound from Frau Kuni's room so she opened the door and laid her hand on Frau Kuni's shoulder.

"I'm home," Katarina whispered.

Frau Kuni waved Katarina away. She shut the door and walked to Herr Tucher's room. She threw off the wine-red dress, climbed under the covers, nestled into that space next to his heart and closed her eyes. This was home. When she opened her eyes again, day was breaking.

The morning light eased into Herr Tucher's room. Katarina watched his face while he slept. Her gaze woke him. Katarina quietly pushed back the blanket, stood up without a word and opened the creaky door. She had slept solid as if dead. Such sound sleep was rare since she had the baby. She laughed a subdued snort as she shut his bedroom door and crossed the hallway. Isabeau slept on in her bed. It was still early and Katarina crawled into what had been the Old Widow's bed, lay down and listened to the chattering birds nesting in the ivy outside the window.

"Kata. Kata. Kata." Isabeau stood in her bed and impatiently called.

It was well into the morning. Katarina must have drifted off again. She stood, grabbed Isabeau and swung the baby out of her bed, pulled her close and smelled her hair. Katarina sat down on her bed, took the comb from the bedside table and combed the little white ringlets out of Isabeau's eyes. Isabeau took the comb from Katarina's hand and tried to comb Katarina's tangled hair. Katarina kissed her cheek as Isabeau tried to smooth Katarina's hair.

"Are you hungry?"

Isabeau shrieked at that and Katarina carried her down into the kitchen. She would get her chores started and check on Frau Kuni. Someone had already brought in the water. The fire was burning, so Katarina put water on to boil and searched the shelves for something to eat. Isabeau toddled around the kitchen and Katarina startled each time she teetered too close to the open fireplace, even though she never got too close. The door to the paddock creaked and Pieter came in, preceded by that cat. Like the baby, Pieter's cat kept a healthy distance from the heat of the fire.

"Be careful," Katarina said with a laugh, "someone will take you for a warlock the way that black cat follows you about."

He frowned at the remark. "Please don't speak of such things aloud. There are many who take such things seriously."

Something dripped in the fire with a *zisch*, *zisch*, like rain water dribbling down from the flue. Katarina looked away from the boiling water up into the flue and saw a wooden frame with chunks of meat hanging from it, fat dripping from the slabs into the fire.

"Do you like my construction?" Pieter said. "I fastened the frame to nails that I rammed into the flue. I can smoke meats. I rolled them in salt and pepper and hung them to dry."

Pieter was a handsome boy but something dark and morose cast shadows over his face and aged him. His dark-blond hair grew so fast and the days in the sun gave his face a healthy sheen. He tended to a slight stoop, like he wanted to diminish his size. He must be sixteen now. His birthday was after the winter solstice, during the *Rauhnächte*, the twelve days of Christmas. Children born during the days between Christmas and Epiphany were known to have qualities allowing them to see between the worlds, Frau Kuni said.

Pieter was still talking. "The disturbance? You didn't hear it in the night? That's why I like to sleep in your old chamber. I don't hear any disturbance when I sleep back in the workers' house. It's nice here by the kitchen at night. I can tend the fire all night if I wake up, too."

Katarina nodded. "That's what I like about sleeping here, too."

"I heard something scratching at the door to the paddock," he continued. "I thought it was a wolf at first. I heard someone open the front door. That was surely no wolf. I came up the steps out of the kitchen and must have scared him away. The door stood ajar and I heard footsteps outside. Boots. That's why I assume it was a man.

Women don't do such things, do they?"

"Pieter, could it be, well, do you think it could be Isabeau's father, Hans-Wolfgang?"

"No, I see that man. Regularly. He watched me the weeks you were away. I saw him up the hill in the field. He rides a sorrel stallion. The hawks fly overhead when he is near—in the fields or the forest. He is at home in the forest. He doesn't need to live in our barn. He is not a thief, nor a liar. I can tell."

"You can judge his character by how he rides a horse?"

"Well, yes. He seems to be patrolling. Watching." Pieter rubbed his eyes. "Keep your eyes open when you're outside today. Our visitor is getting quite bold. I need to get out into the fields with Tanner. We're out all day."

Pieter stood and stammered like he had something else to say.

"Pieter, what is it?" Katarina asked.

He shook his head and left the kitchen.

Katarina picked up Isabeau and climbed the steps to Frau Kuni's room. Katarina knocked and when she didn't answer, pushed the door open. Katarina went to her bed and shook her by the shoulder.

"Frau Kuni, good morning. Do you want me to bring you some tea?"

She mumbled something and rolled onto her other side.

"Call me when you need anything," Katarina said and left her bedside.

She carried Isabeau outside and set her down outside the paddock on a patch of grass. A window creaked above as Frau Kuni opened her bedroom window. Children screeched and hollered back by the workers' house. Sparrows flew in and out of the ivy on the wall of the main house.

Katarina cleared the manure from the paddock and let the goats out. The ram stayed tied on when she worked. He tended to butt her legs, the little devil. After lugging water back to the paddock, she filled the troughs with water. The goat was giving milk again since she had her kid and she needed to drink. Katarina crossed the yard to the chickens and gave them fresh water, too. A new-found appreciation of physical exertion, almost joy, filled Katarina after weeks of inactivity.

Isabeau made angry calls. She'd pulled herself up and was standing, holding onto to the fence. The goats stuck their noses through the fencing, nudged Isabeau and pulled on her dress. Katarina leaned on the fence and watched Isabeau bat at the goats' heads, causing them to flee.

Katarina grabbed the baby under the arms, swung her up high and pulled her in tight to her chest. They went into the kitchen and she yawned. Katarina put her in for a nap in Pieter's bed and went out to get more water. After she filled the kitchen pot, she went back to the wash kitchen, filled the pot and set a fire underneath so she could wash some linens. She ran back to the house, grabbed a willow basket and climbed the steps.

The door to Herr Tucher's sitting room banged open and he swore an oath. Katarina peered around the door jamb. He had scattered books all over the floor, spilled documents out of two open wooden trunks and strewn pamphlets about the settee and onto the floor. He didn't look away from the papers he searched through.

"My papers for the new properties are gone," he said to no one in general. "I know I had them here with the documents for the house, but someone's been through my papers. I have them organized just so. No one knows how I organize my papers. And they have been disturbed. I need those damned papers!"

"I'm sorry to disturb you, but…"

"Books are missing! The book of poetry from Pieter, a book of my early essays."

He looked away, preoccupied. "I need to find those documents. My uncle wrote that someone is challenging my right to the lands I petitioned. I do not know who and now the papers are missing."

Katarina left the door open and moved down the hallway. His bedroom was much like she left it this morning, twisted linens, stale air. She opened the windows and stripped the bed. As she passed his sitting room, he had closed the door. Books thudded on the floor and his voice swore.

Katarina carried the linens down to the wash kitchen, stoked the fire and when the water boiled, she threw the linens in. Her wrist brushed the iron pot and she cursed when she heard and felt her skin singe. She fetched a bucket of cool water from the well and stuck her hand in up to the wrist. The well-maintained farmyard caught her attention and she was struck with a wave of gratitude. The chicken coop stood in good repair, full of clucking fowl. The ram, the goats and two lambs frolicked about in the paddock. The second, smaller, wood-clad barn full of tack and the main doors of the large barn had been newly stained.

Slowly one of the barn's two main doors swung open. From Katarina's angle, she could only see the large door moving, not who had pushed it open. No one went in or came out. She decided to have a look and wondered at the same moment if she should. She was alone. She had linens in the boiling water. A chill made the hair stand up on her arms. Maybe it was one of the workers. But they were all out in the fields or the forest. Sara was home with Anna and the new baby. Pieter was out all day, he'd said.

As she walked across the yard, a host of sparrows that fed on fallen grain flew off. She rounded the barn door and peeked in. It was dark so she moved a bit further inside. A fury of wings flapped. Planks of wood collapsed down with a hollow *thunk, thunk, thunk.* One plank slammed Katarina's cheek and flung her to the floor. She landed on her face, a great *oaf!* of breath forced from her mouth. The light of day faded as the barn door closed, the hinges squeaking.

Katarina was suddenly enveloped in the darkness. She tried to sit up and shake off the reeling feeling. Straining her ears for any sound, she heard nothing but the wind rustling in the tree outside and humming through the roof tiles up above in the hay loft. She was alone and lay still. The light came back up. Someone was opening the squeaky door again. Light flooded the space where she lay.

Pieter knelt down by her side. "Oh Katarina, you're bleeding, what happened?"

"I don't know. I saw the doors open and I came to see who was in here, but I seem to have fallen."

He stood abruptly. "You've been hit with something. I'm going to round up a few men. We have to find this ghost. I've had it with constantly looking over my shoulder."

"I thought you were out all day," Katarina said.

"Tanner sent me to fetch some leather straps. Ours tore through."

He helped her stand and led her back to the house, into the kitchen. He wrung a towel with cool water and laid the towel over the cut on her cheek. Isabeau was waking in Pieter's bed. Katarina couldn't have been out there too long. Pieter picked the baby up. She cooed and laid her head on his shoulder and yawned. She turned her face towards Katarina and smiled a sleepy smile.

"Mum-mum," she said.

"Can you manage?" Pieter said. "I'm on a hunt."

He set the child on Katarina's lap, grabbed a crossbow from the corner of the kitchen and left without another word.

Pieter returned after dark with the other men and reported that they had found nothing. He brought Katarina out to the others as they stood at the open barn doors. They showed Katarina where they'd cleared the sleeping quarters that the ghost had arranged. They found footprints where none of the others had reason to tread and one of the men had set traps. No, they assured Katarina, not where any of the workers would step in them.

Crackling sparks flew from the fire and they all turned towards the yard. The aroma of roasting meat traveled on the grey smoke. The one new woman turned a pig on a spit over the fire. Pieter told Katarina that during the search, they spied a young wild boar grubbing alone in the spelt field and now he would be prepared for a nice meal.

The evening was warm and all gathered at the fire. Katarina filled a wooden plate with food and began to eat before she even sat down. She tried to count how many souls they now numbered. Tanner and family were four; his father made five. Two new blond men, Anna, the other woman and the carp farmer made ten. Their children were impossible to count because they never sat still. Sara had said there were four. Pieter, Katarina, Herr Tucher, Isabeau and Frau Kuni made fifteen plus the drove of children.

Frau Kuni hobbled towards the fire leaning on a walking stick. Her hips looked twisted somehow and walking caused her pain. She nodded a greeting to the group, filled a wooden board with meat and slowly returned to the house.

Katarina sat down next to Pieter. Isabeau, who sat on his lap, grabbed at Katarina's hand as she held a chunk of bread out for her. Knecht and the two new men who looked more like boys had drunk quite a lot and slurred through their newest song: *Mei Fraa, dei Fraa, sin zwa alta Rosn. Meine ham ihr Hände hoch, deine in meine Hosn.*

Katarina patted her stomach and wondered when she had ever been so plump in the past. She had eaten so much she felt she could burst. All of her dresses were tight these days and the contours of her face felt fuller than last winter.

Herr Tucher sat off to the side and conversed in serious tones with Tanner. Sara spoke to Katarina from the other side of the fire but Katarina heard none of her words over the rollicking children and the singing: "My girl, your girl, both old faded roses. My girl has her hands up high, yours stuck hers in my hose!"

Katarina heard, "A visit the next few weeks…" and "…his uncle," and shook her head to show Sara she could not understand.

Herr Tucher suddenly crouched behind her. "I am having a visitor the next few weeks. He is arriving in the morning. Early. Do we have an extra room? He won't be staying long."

Chapter 32

Herr Tucher quietly closed the front doors that now fit in their frame and graciously extended his hand towards his Uncle Paul. Paul grasped his hand firmly and looked down in amazement.

"Working hard, boy?" Paul said. "Those are the rough hands of a farmer."

"Hello Uncle," Herr Tucher said.

"I came as quickly as I could," Paul said. "What is this all about, Scbald?"

"Have you got the amount I asked for?" Herr Tucher said.

"Yes I do. It is not the amount that worries me, but the amount of money you owe in general," Paul said. "This is a lovely manor, though, I must say,"

Herr Tucher motioned for Paul to take the stairway to the upper floor. Paul had taken to wearing a black hat with a lovely white plume that bobbed behind him. Herr Tucher showed him into the sitting room and shut the door behind them.

"I've been summoned to the Margrave Christian in Dachsbach," Herr Tucher said. "There is some discrepancy about the new lands I am working…"

Uncle Paul removed his hat, straightened the white lace collar over his black jacket. "Yes, he had written to me while you were away."

"…But the documents are gone," Herr Tucher continued. "All of them, except the documents for the farm itself. Just so you know. We need to appear before the Margrave today before midday."

"We need this land and what it yields," Paul said, working his goatee to a point. "Can you think of anyone who might want to play you prank?"

"This is no longer a prank. Someone knows exactly the harm

they are causing."

The two men left the room, descended the stairs and went out into the yard. In spite of any formalities that irked Herr Tucher today, he took a deep breath and savored the air of the warm spring morning like a man enjoying a bouquet of exotic flowers. Knecht waited with their horses.

"One moment, I almost forgot," Paul said, rummaging in his saddlebag. "I found this. Does it look familiar?"

Paul held out a dagger with a bone handle inlaid with silver swirled in an intricate design. Some of the bone next to the still-sharp blade had chipped away.

"Where did you find this?" Herr Tucher said.

"In that old tavern by the Debtor's Tower. What disarray that Prutt left behind! This we found behind the counter in the tavern itself, flung in a corner. I thought it looked like one of the daggers from your father. I am sure Prutt forgot it. He sold everything else he could."

"I had the daggers here and one went missing. But that was last summer."

"Herr Prutt has no reason to cause you harm, does he?"

"Prutt could have easily come out here again," Herr Tucher said. "Of course he has reason to harm me. I have bested him. But what would he want with my documents?"

"Maybe he is working for someone else?"

"Can you still trace him, Uncle? Where he may have gone? Could we still find him in Nuremberg?"

The two men mounted and Paul pulled his horse around. "I will see what I can do."

They rode the hour south to Dachsbach, towards a tall, thin castle that towered above the Aisch valley known as the Wasser Schloss. They rode past the gallows and into the courtyard, where two grooms awaited their arrival. The two Tucher men dismounted and the grooms led the horses away.

A man dressed in a finely-embroidered green doublet with a lace collar and green breeches led Herr Tucher and his uncle through the entrance hall and up a dark wooden staircase. He opened a richly-carved dark-stained door and allowed them to enter a dark-paneled office. The man followed them in, took a seat behind a short lectern, opened a registry and held a quill at the ready. Another man, dressed in the same style as the secretary, came through a door at the opposite side of the office, stood aside and allowed a regal man to enter.

The Margrave Christian paused and regarded the two Tucher men, smoothing his forefinger over his mustache and goatee. The Margrave was a man of indeterminable age, one of the benefits of being raised in a barrage of wealth and nobility. He, too, wore a dark hunter's-green doublet and breeches, though more ornately embroidered and costly than the clothing of his subordinates. A fine lace collar showed from beneath his shoulder-length light-brown hair. He sat down behind his desk in a richly-carved high-backed chair and motioned for the Tucher men to approach.

"So, young Herr Tucher, it has come to my attention that you are farming lands that you have no right to work on. Someone takes offense and would like this wrong righted."

"The lands were written over to me, in this office, by Your Grace, with the agreement that I would pay the set amount four times a year," Herr Tucher said.

"In my books there is no such entry, is there?" He motioned to his secretary who nodded his head in agreement. "Please show me the papers in your possession."

"The papers in question have been stolen." Herr Tucher sniffed. "*Gnädiger Herr.*"

"Now, Herr Tucher, how can we continue with this conversation when you have no proof of the transaction? I have a petition from another man who claims he has the right to the lands, not you."

"I was robbed," Herr Tucher said.

He smiled as if Herr Tucher was to be pitied. "No matter. There is the problem with the price. You have then no proof of the agreed price, do you?"

"No, Your Grace, I do not."

"Then we will agree on a price. Seeing that the fields are already sown, they are worth more. I need 12,000 taler in order to write these lands into your possession."

"Pardon me?" Herr Tucher shouted. "I have sown the fields! These lands are in my possession! Who is this man? What has he to do with our agreement?"

Blood rose to Herr Tucher's head and he felt he was only one word short of an explosion. *"Gnädiger Herr."*

Uncle Paul touched his arm and gave him a sympathetic look. "Not now, Sebald," he whispered.

"The agreement, in this message sent by Your Grace's messenger…" Herr Tucher dropped the document with the Margrave's seal onto the desk, "…was that I pay another 2000 taler and the case would be closed!"

Herr Tucher pressed his lips together so that no wild spurt of words would spray out.

"The lands have been petitioned by Herr Friedrich von Obereierhofen. He is the great-great grandson of the late Peter Truchsess von Treppendorf," the Margrave said.

"I have a rather impressive family tree myself, Your Grace," Herr Tucher said and pressed his lips back together.

"Your family is made up of *Nürnberger Pfeffersäcke*," the Margrave said.

Paul coughed and spluttered.

"Pardon?" Herr Tucher said.

"Pepper sacks!" the Margrave repeated.

"I haven't heard that term for years," Paul said.

"Nuremberger patricians," the Margrave spluttered, "have no business out here in my territory. My family tree is also impressive. My great-grandfather is the Margrave Albrecht Alcibiades who burned this fortress down with his own hands before he would surrender it to the Nuremberger Peppersacks."

Herr Tucher stood still and held his breath. What had stirred up this silly dispute? He had met with this man in the winter and he was amicable, even friendly.

"Herr von Obereierhofen has agreed to pay the price I need for these lands. I will extend you the courtesy of a week to come up with the money. This conversation will now adjourn until next week at this same time. Good day."

The Margrave rose out of his high-backed chair, turned and exited through the door his servant held open for him.

Chapter 33

Katarina followed Pieter out into the paddock and watched him sniff around the buildings like one of the sheepdogs. He jogged off towards the North Hill and returned followed by that black cat.

"The door to the cellar in the barn has been pried open," Pieter said as he followed Katarina into the kitchen. "I found a fresh trail and followed it into the forest. They aren't even trying to hide their tracks anymore. Where is Herr Tucher?"

"He's gone with his uncle this morning," Katarina said. "They'll be back later this afternoon."

"I just saw a man in black run towards the knoll of trees to the west of the hollow. Back where Tanner and I rebuilt that new fence around the paddock. We need to find this man and settle this. Stay inside until I come back, Katarina."

"I have work to do outside," she said.

"I'm going to look for Tanner. He must be back by the paddock. Wait for me to come back."

He walked out of the kitchen. Katarina grabbed her pitchfork and followed him out. She could not wait until he came back. He'd left the paddock gate open so she closed it after him. Isabeau teetered behind Katarina and dropped onto her backside.

"Oh no, Isabeau, it's too muddy out here."

She screeched and held her arms up, signaling Katarina to come back and pick her up.

"Well, then, you get muddy and I'll clean you up afterwards."

Tanner and the men had taken the goats to graze with the sheep and Katarina wanted to clean the paddock before they returned. She spiked a load of wet straw and manure, threw the load on the pile and straightened her aching back. An uncomfortable cramping pulled all around her midriff. Maybe she had worked a bit too enthusiastically yesterday.

Out of the corner of her eye, she thought she saw a shadow turn behind the barn.

Pieter's tales had scared her and now she thought she saw his ghosts. Leaning on the pitchfork, she pushed the hair out of her face and watched for a moment. Then a man in black flitted behind the barn. That was no ghost but a real man. Now she had had enough. It might be foolish, but she was done with hiding quietly like some hunted prey. She opened the gate, went out and closed Isabeau in. Isabeau screeched again, not wanting to be left alone.

"I'll be right back." Katarina marched towards the barn carrying the pitchfork and turned the corner. "Show yourself, coward!"

The breeze rustled the low bushes behind the barn. Down the hollow, Katarina heard ducks quacking, like they were arguing. Isabeau screamed and scolded in the paddock. Katarina walked along the back side of the barn, pricking the bushes with her pitchfork.

She was about to go back when she thought she heard scurrying. She continued around the next corner and stopped behind an elder bush on the north side of the barn. Here she had a clear view of the farmyard, the well, the wash kitchen, and main house, too. Nobody could see her from the farmyard. This was a perfect vantage point for an intruder. Katarina lowered the pitchfork, walked along the back side of the barn to return to the paddock.

She smelled him before she saw him and jumped back with a shriek. Her pitchfork fell at his feet. Before her stood a gaunt and dirty Willi Prutt, dressed in a black uniform like those riders up at the Eierhofen estate. He bent down and picked up the pitchfork. Katarina's initial fright was replaced with a saturated rage.

"Look at you! Tell me you are now a soldier." Her breath quickened. "What do you think you're doing here?"

"Look at *me*?" he said. "Look at you: the master's mistress. I should have killed him when I had the chance. But I'm not a killer. Look here, nobody is here to help you, and you're all alone."

Isabeau cried on in the paddock. Katarina had to get away from here and quickly.

"What do you want, Willi?"

"Tucher said that's his child but he lied," Willi said. "He told me you have to take care of his bastard child. But I know the truth, Katarina. Someone is looking for that child."

"The child is mine!" she said.

"No, it isn't." He took a few steps towards Katarina, the man a chest and head larger than her.

Isabeau wailed. Katarina could not let him near the child!

"You are the bitch in heat, aren't you?" Willi threw the pitchfork aside and grabbed Katarina's upper arms. "The master's bleeding whore, you are. You've forgotten what a real man is like."

He pressed his lips to hers and bit down hard. Katarina cried out, pulled away and screamed. She tasted blood. Willi slammed his closed hand into her face and something cracked in her neck as her head flew to the side. She fought to keep her balance and stay on her feet.

Out of breath, Katarina said, "I'll scream again, someone will come, there are plenty of men here."

"Don't you think I know the comings and goings here? I've been living here for some time myself. You didn't know it was me, did you? I know they're all out of the way. I sent the Dutch boy on a false trail. He'll be hunting a dead end for the next few hours. He's gullible that one."

He grabbed the front of Katarina's dress and pulled, ripping the worn fabric easily. He kicked her foot out from under her with a sweeping movement. She fell on her back. He laid his weight on top of her. She couldn't breathe.

"You want me to hurt you?" Willi said. "Like you hurt me."

"I hurt you? Are you a complete idiot? Admit the truth." Katarina struggled for a breath.

"You left me alone," Willi said.

"I never left you, Willi. I loved you and you gave me away like a bit of old rag, you fool."

"I lost everything," he said.

"You are married!" Katarina panted. "Go back to your wife."

"She had fever, the baby too. They didn't make it."

"Serves Lily right, that slut."

"You're coming back with me," Willi said. "You wanted me to take you home. You can work for me now. This is all because of you!"

Katarina struggled and pulled her arms free. Willi grabbed her wrists and pinned them to the ground.

"Watch me, Katarina. I'm going to make a fortune. I'm going to take that baby back where she belongs. Tucher will regret the day he tried to outsmart me. He'll regret the day he took you away. We'll see who will be ruined in the end."

Katarina stuck her face under his matted curls and bit hard on his neck, on the source of life pumping into his head. He slapped about her head, tried to strike her face, but no blows sat. She was much too close. She felt under his shirt around his waistline to see if he was armed. At the small of his back, she felt a leather sheath with a small dagger sticking out of his waistband. But before she could pull the dagger out, he grabbed her hand and squeezed, causing her to scream out and lose the grip her teeth had on his neck.

A hawk called in the distance.

Willi rolled onto his back and was on his feet with masterful agility. He grabbed the pitchfork like he meant to smash Katarina with the handle when an arrow whizzed over his head. Willi took no notice of the arrow. Katarina looked right and left and tensed every muscle, ready to roll out of the way. He raised the pitchfork over his head to deliver the fatal blow. Another arrow whizzed past his thigh. Katarina felt its soft whisper on her cheek and then another *whizzz*, followed by a growl of rage and pain.

Willi dropped the pitchfork. He sank to his knees and cradled his injured arm with his other hand. The arrow had grazed the wrist of his raised hand. He growled again like a mangy street dog. The arrow was not lodged, but blood squeezed through the fingers he clenched around his wrist. He narrowed his eyes, like he was debating whether to advance on Katarina once again.

"Don't move, friend," yelled a hoarse voice from the field. "Katarina, see to the baby. Leave him to me."

Katarina lay still on the ground and looked from one man to the other. Willi, dark, dirty, mangled, on his knees, blood oozing through his dirty fingers. Hans-Wolfgang von Untereierhofen, the archer in brown, strong, stocky, sure. Hans-Wolfgang needed no words to express his anger. His very person seethed.

"Move!" yelled Hans-Wolfgang.

Katarina stood and ran to the paddock. She grabbed the screaming baby, hugged her tight and ran into the house without looking back. Isabeau had cried herself into a frenzy, gulping between sobs, gasping for air. It took all Katarina's composure to calm her. Katarina rocked Isabeau until her eyes became heavy; the child's face red, blotched, hot and sticky with tears. She sniffled and still took shallow, exhausted, fearful breaths.

Isabeau was finally quiet in Pieter's bed. Katarina sat next to the fire and sipped at a cup of tea with elder blossom schnapps. The front doors banged against the wall. The heated voices of Herr Tucher and Uncle Paul rang in the stairway. They must have returned from Dachsbach and, by the sound of the two men, the meeting had ended on a sour note.

"Intrigue!" Uncle Paul's voice boomed in the stairway. "I hate intrigue."

Herr Tucher's voice said, "Business should be conducted face to face, not in this manner."

Their voices faded amid the stomping of boots up the stairs.

Katarina wrung a rag out in a bucket of cool water, held it against her cheek, took a gulp of tea and set the cup aside. A long twig lay next to the fire and she poked about the embers mindlessly. It caught fire and she let the burning twig go. She grabbed the mug, emptied it and filled it again with half tea and half schnapps. The cramps pulled around her middle again, like she had eaten some spoiled meat, and thought she might get sick. Maybe the tea would settle her stomach.

The door to the paddock opened and a tiny baby's cries foretold Sara's entrance. Katarina smiled and stood as Sara came into the kitchen. Immediately, Katarina's middle was struck with a lightning bolt of pain. She doubled over and threw up on the floor.

"Katarina!" Sara said.

She laid her baby with Isabeau on Pieter's bed. She rushed to Katarina's side and laid her arm around her shoulder.

"I'm so sorry," Katarina said.

"Dear Lord, Katarina, you're bleeding!" Sara said and pointed to the stool.

Katarina straightened and touched the back of her dress. She pulled her fingers back, wet and sticky with dark-red blood. She shook her head, puzzled, and doubled over as the cramps hit her again.

"You need to lie down," Sara led Katarina to Pieter's bed. "Lie still, I'll get some water." She fixed Katarina with a dead-serious expression. "Are you pregnant?"

"I can't be pregnant," Katarina said. "I've never been pregnant. Willi said I was barren. Frau Kuni says that if I've never been at this age, I must be barren."

The bucket slipped out of Sara's hands and thunked on the

floor. She bent down, picked it up and walked to the door. "I'll be right back. Please lie still and try to relax. I know it's not easy, but you'll be fine."

Katarina lay on the bed with the two children and braced herself as the next wave of cramps hit. Isabeau laid her head on Katarina's shoulder. Sara was back and removed both children from Katarina's side.

Katarina must have lost consciousness. She heard Sara's light, quick stride as she came down the steps. Sara peeked into the alcove and laid a clean skirt and shirt for Katarina on the bed. She sat next to her with a grave look on her face. Katarina's head hurt. She sat up, swayed a bit and lifted her dress. Sara had wrapped Katarina in a sort of diaper. It was stained a deathly, dark red. She ran her finger over the soaked, sticky fabric. The smell of blood made her want to retch.

"It seems you were pregnant," Sara said. "Not too far gone, but nonetheless. I'm sorry. The worst should be over. There's nothing I could do. It's sometimes better when these pregnancies don't last. Do you still have the cramping?"

Katarina nodded and bit her lip. She could not allow herself to grieve this loss. Not now.

Sara laid a finger on Katarina's brow and turned her head to the side. "What happened to your face?"

Katarina touched the welt on her cheek. "It was Willi in the barn the whole time. We fought. He hit me. I don't know where he went."

"That is probably why you miscarried, that scoundrel. Can you stand and unwrap the bandages? Try to get dressed. I have to feed my baby. He's back with Anna."

Boots stomped down the stairs. More heated conversation vibrated throughout the stairwell and off the stone walls of the kitchen. The front doors crashed open and Herr Tucher ranted on. The voices moved outside into the yard. Katarina had never heard him in such a state.

"There's some trouble," Sara said.

"Please don't say anything about the miscarriage."

"Herr Tucher has been asking about Willi. He'll want to know that you saw him."

"Don't tell him anything. Please. This is all my fault."

Katarina stood and hastily undid the bandages. Her dress was already ripped so she tore it from her body, wiped the rest of the blood from her legs, dried herself with the destroyed dress and carefully put on the skirt and shirt.

"I'm still bleeding," Katarina said, like a despairing child.

Sara pulled a strip of soft, supple sheep hide from under her apron. "Stick that between your legs. Here are a few more for later."

Katarina sat back on the bed and looked at Sara. "This is all my fault."

"Nonsense. What makes you think it's your fault?"

"Willi was here because of me. I wanted him to take me home. If it wasn't for me, none of this would have…"

Everything went white before Katarina's eyes and she lay back on the bed. "I think I need to stay down here this afternoon. I feel so weak."

"I'll make you some alchemilla tea to help with the bleeding. Get some rest."

"Katarina!" Herr Tucher called from out in the yard. "Where is she?"

"Stay still. I'll tell him something," Sara said and left the kitchen.

Chapter 34

"There's more than one man sneaking around here, Tanner," Pieter van Diemen said.

"We sat watch all night, Pieter," Tanner said. "I didn't hear a sound."

Pieter pointed to the slew of muddy boot prints leading all around the first pond, back behind the barn and up to that elder bush on the other side of the barn. More than one size and type of boot was easy to discern: one boot was large with a forged metal heel much like a horseshoe. One boot was smaller, like that of a boy's.

"Two lambs are missing. I counted them last night," Pieter said. "The cellar door was pried open."

"Someone would have seen them." Tanner coughed and spat.

"No, they are clever." Pieter pointed to the path made of five or more pairs of boots, all with forged metal heels, leading away from the farm into the trees. "They tie their horses far enough away from here. Or more follow on foot."

Tanner hopped back into the saddle of the heavy chestnut gelding he usually used to pull logs. "I have to get back to the paddock. Those two Danish workers are inexperienced and they need help. Make sure the women have firewood and join me as soon as you can."

Peter walked across the farmyard, through the paddock and into the kitchen. Sara thrust Isabeau into his arms.

"Please feed her while I make the meal for the men," Sara said.

Sara looked disheveled. Unnerved. That was a bad sign. The woman kept her composure when all the others had lost theirs. Her baby cried from the alcove where Pieter usually slept. He peeked into the alcove. All he could see was the screaming baby lying next to the lump of Katarina's curls sticking out of the blanket.

"Is Katarina ill?" Pieter asked Sara.

"Yes, I am ill," Katarina said as she crept into the kitchen carrying the baby.

"Katarina, get back into bed!" Sara said and took the baby.

"I'll feel better helping you, Sara," Katarina said. "I'll go mad lying in bed."

"Pieter!" Tanner barked from out in the yard.

Pieter ran into the yard with Isabeau on his arm.

Red-faced, Tanner spat. "Anna! Where is that damned woman? Come and take this child. When I need my men, they should not be tending children!"

Anna ran up behind Pieter and took Isabeau from him.

"The two Danish boys have been ambushed," Tanner said. "The sheep are strewn in the fields. We must all go and round them up. You go on foot. I'll ride ahead. Hurry, please!"

Pieter walked towards the pasture alone. He forced himself to listen to the birds chirping. But thoughts pulsed like a headache, no matter how he tried to stop thinking. He rubbed his eyes and tried to empty his head. The warm spring breeze smelled like Madeleine's perfume, reminded him of one beautiful afternoon they had spent together. It reminded him of something else, too: she had taken her life on a spring day like this one. So, a whole year had passed since she died.

"Hey there, Pieter, need a hand?"

Pieter shook himself out of his reverie. He stopped and turned to see a woman in white following close behind him on foot. She moved silently through the underbrush like a ghost.

"I am...I'm...not," Pieter stammered, lost in his thoughts, and walked on.

"The sheep are scattered," the woman said. "Come I will lead you to the others."

She kept up with Pieter's brisk stride with no show of fatigue.

"Pieter, you seem distraught," she said. "Would you like to talk about what is troubling you?"

Pieter figured there was no harm in talking to a ghost. "She was the only woman who had treated me like a real person, not like a toy. Her name was Madeline. Her husband worked for the East India Company and she was always alone. I would visit her in the afternoons, for tea. My mother thought I was working. I guess I was."

Pieter stopped walking and the woman stopped walking. She brushed the long white braid back behind her shoulder. Could this be the woman in white Katarina had spoken of?

"Go on, Pieter," she said.

Pieter started walking at an even livelier pace. "Madeleine liked to sip tea, maybe some port or brandy and listen to poetry. She would give me a subject and I would write about whatever she wanted to hear. Sea gulls flying over the IJ, children running through the fish market, lovers walking along the Singel canal. Love and romance were her favorites. I wrote for her because I loved her. She had a tender soul, was a passionate love maker, a wonderful woman."

"That is beautiful," the woman in white said.

Pieter broke out in a jog. "But the relationship turned. After my mother died, she started to stick a few coins in my pocket as I dressed. She may have thought Father and I needed the money. We did, really. It became an angry game for me. This woman, thirty years my senior, did not care for me. No more than a toy. Or so I thought at the time."

Pieter slowed his pace in order to catch his breath. The woman in white did not seem to need to breathe.

"She saw me one evening, walking by her house with Henrike on my arm," Pieter said. "She tried to summon me the day after, but I would not come. I was not a whore! The next morning, her husband came home from a particularly long sea voyage. Her body swung from the rafters in the attic. She'd explained why in a letter."

"None of this was your fault, Pieter," the woman in white said.

Pieter ignored that remark. He felt his face twist and that pressure on the top of his head.

"I had been hiding at the top of the stairway and heard the conversation between my father and the neighbor. The rich one. Madeleine's husband. I came down the steps, afraid to face my father. I swallowed hard. And I am a good two feet taller than he. '*Do you know who just paid a visit?*' my father had screamed from the sitting room. '*Mr. Hulft. What have you done to his wife?*'"

"'*This is your fault, boy,*' he had said. Just in that tone," Pieter said.

Pieter heard men whistling and stopped walking. Now his father had fallen ill. He should return to Amsterdam. But he could not find it in himself to leave Germany. He was much too cowardly to face his father again.

"Your place is here, Pieter," the woman in white said. "Your father will wait until you return."

Pieter had not spoken those words about his father aloud, he was sure.

"Protect the baby," she said. "Isabeau is the key."

In the meadow beyond, Pieter saw Tanner on the chestnut gelding and Knecht with the two Danish boys. They had managed to round up most of the sheep. He turned around to look for the woman in white but she was gone.

In a crop of trees in the underbrush, a lamb bleated a forlorn cry. The lamb tried to run away but his foot was tied to a tree with a rope. Pieter picked a path in the brambles. He pulled out his knife and cut the rope. A black figure hushed by, behind a tree. Pieter stood still for a moment. He held his breath. He bent and picked up the lamb. The figure sneaked to the next tree. Pieter set the lamb down and it ran towards the herd.

A man dressed in black with dark, curly hair ran away from Pieter, up the bank. Pieter wondered if he had seen this man somewhere before. The man wore a uniform like those soldiers who had come when Katarina had disappeared. His head was bare and he had trouble climbing up the hill, like he was injured. Pieter went after him. His feet sank into the muddy bank strewn with brown leaves and twigs as he pushed himself up the hill. The man fell, looked back at Pieter, got up and ran along the path through the forest. Pieter gained on him. He could run fast. He grabbed the man by the back of his black tunic and flung him to the ground. Pieter rolled the man onto his back and sat his weight on top of him.

"Don't hurt me," the man said.

The man had bruises all along his face. Pieter pulled his head back as the man's dirty, bandaged fist flew before his eyes. He forced both of the man's arms down on the ground. The man's wrist had been badly cut and bled still.

"Who are you?" Pieter said.

"I am a friend of Katarina's. She is in danger."

"I'm going to take you to Tanner."

"No, please, let me go. I can help you."

Whistling. Men's voices. Tanner and the other men were coming closer, herding the sheep back to the paddock with the newly-repaired fence. Pieter turned to look for them, easing his grip on the man's hands. The man pulled both hands free. Pieter saw the man's fist out of the corner of his eye as it slammed against his temple, the cracking punch resonating in Pieter's head. As Pieter fell over, he saw the man in black run into the trees.

Chapter 35

"Where is Katarina?"

Katarina heard Herr Tucher shout from the yard. She laid the knife and the onion she was peeling on the worktop in the kitchen and wiped her hands on her apron.

"Get Katarina out here!" His voice resonated in the stone stairway.

"Sara, what am I to do?" Katarina said. "I can't go out there like this. I am still so giddy."

Sara shook her head and turned away.

"Where is Katarina?" Herr Tucher bellowed again.

Sara laid her hand on Katarina's shoulder. "I'll finish the meal. Just go."

Katarina whispered, "I must face him, yes I know."

She walked up the steps and stopped in the doorway to steady herself. The two Danish boys carried a long plank from the barn and set it up in front of the house like a table. The carp farmer and the other woman lugged the bench from back by the workers' house and plunked it down next to the table as though they were preparing for a garden party.

"Anna, a few bottles of that port, please, and some cups. Enough of this spouting off. It is time to dissect this problem into solvable morsels." Herr Tucher laughed like he thought he was witty. "I am going to sit here and drink until I come up with a plausible solution."

Anna set three bottles of wine before him and ceramic cups. He poured the wine and with a nod of his head, offered the group at large some wine. Uncle Paul sat on the bench and drank from his cup. Tanner waved his hand, declining Herr Tucher's offer.

"Tanner, stay here, please. First of all, who is this Friedrich von Obereierhofen and why do I know nothing about this man? We will find out. We must confront the man. We shall find him and pay him

231

a visit."

"Sir, I must secure the herd," Tanner said. "We only have the half of them in the paddock. We left the others grazing beyond the first hill. It is getting late."

"Next," Herr Tucher said, ignoring Tanner's request, "where is this Willi Prutt? Paul could not find the man. As if the earth swallowed him whole. We must find him and find out what he has to do with all this." He looked at Tanner, like he just registered his presence. "Of course, dear Tanner, you do what you must."

Tanner waved to the two Danish boys to follow him and they walked away. Anna, the carp farmer and the other woman followed them. Pieter approached Katarina who stood alone by the front step. Pieter now had a fresh slit under his right eye.

"You must tell him what you know," Pieter whispered.

"Where is Katarina? Ah, there you are." Herr Tucher held his hand out and Katarina moved towards the bench. "My dear Katarina, please have a seat next to me. Do you know anything about this situation? Do you know these people? You grew up here."

Herr Tucher set a cup of wine on the table in front of her.

"Have you seen that Prutt since you moved out here?" He finally turned to look at her. "Dear Lord! Are you ill? You are so pale and grey. What happened to your face?"

Tears welled in Katarina's eyes. "This is all my fault."

"What is your fault?" He stopped, pondered the possibilities and turned away from her as if disappointed. "What do you have to do with this? Do you know where the documents are? Please tell me what you know."

A cloud of smoke billowed orange-gold in the light of the setting sun as a horse and rider raced up the track. A reluctant dark-bay stallion danced at the open gate. The cloaked rider coaxed him through with a sharp kick to his flanks. His hood slipped back, revealing Ralf's sneering, sweating face, and the horse shot through the gate and pranced into the yard. Ralf tried to bring the horse to a standstill, but the stallion marched on the spot, snorted and turned a circle.

"I've met with certain men of council in the area," Ralf said. "We know who has been hiding in your barn."

He slammed the reins onto the agitated horse's broad neck and dismounted. The horse tossed his head up and down.

"We have questioned neighboring farmhands and other families who are often in the fields," Ralf continued. "They say it is that madman Hans-Wolfgang who was seen sneaking around here the last six weeks. We have a group out looking for him now. His house was destroyed, he cannot return there, but we will find him. If he is seen here, please have your men detain him for questioning and send word that he is here. He is dangerous and a wanted man."

"Ralf," Herr Tucher said. "Please, share a cup of this exquisite port wine."

Herr Tucher motioned to Pieter to take care of Ralf's horse. Ralf pushed the reins in Pieter's hand and the horse quieted. Herr Tucher poured another cup of wine. Ralf remained standing and took a long, healthy gulp.

Herr Tucher's mouth froze into a strained smile. "Who, for the love of God, is Hans-Wolfgang? Who is Friedrich von Obereierhofen? Please enlighten me. All seem to know the facts but me."

Ralf wiped his mouth on his sleeve. "Herr von Obereierhofen is a rather respected member of the community, the Catholic community. I worked for him for years. It was his daughter who was killed by this madman Hans-Wolfgang last summer. We spoke of this."

"Why would he challenge my petition for the lands?"

"That must be some mistake," Ralf said. "He need not do such a thing. But, you can document all your transactions, can you not?"

Herr Tucher looked up at Ralf as if a sudden understanding lifted a cloud of deception. He stared at Ralf with that piercing precision that always made Katarina so uncomfortable.

"Of course I can, my friend," Herr Tucher said. "I found the documents this afternoon in a secret compartment in my trunk. I will present them to the Margrave tomorrow morning. But I still want to speak to this so-called madman."

Ralf grabbed the reins back from Pieter. "I will take my leave and deliver you this man when I find him. You can question him and then he shall be judged by a higher authority."

Ralf mounted the dark-bay stallion, pulled him around and left at the same speed he came with.

"But…" Katarina said.

Herr Tucher made a motion for Katarina to be silent. "Drink

your wine."

Katarina did not understand. She thought Herr Tucher still sought those documents. She began to question him again but he held his hand up to silence her. He sipped at the thick, sweet wine and she did the same, the fruity aroma filling her nose.

"Katarina, I would like a light evening meal in my sitting room." He stood. "Please bring it up to me."

He turned to Pieter. "Where is Tanner? Oh, yes, out with the herd. Please take the men with you and go find him. Help him secure the herd and have him gather our people together and come back here. I need to speak to all of you about anything you might have seen. I have left this matter go too long now."

Isabeau shrieked when Katarina walked into the kitchen. She bit at her bread and threw it on the floor. Sara sat by the fire and nursed her baby. Katarina put bread and a bit of meat on a wooden platter and took it up to Herr Tucher's room. She knocked. He opened the door and shut it silently behind her. His expression was blank and fixed as if all of his strength was necessary to contain his anger. He took the platter from Katarina, took her by the hand and led her to the settee.

"So, *mein Mädel,* I need to know everything you know. What is this intrigue and what is your part in it?"

He took some bread from the platter and bit into it as if he hadn't eaten all day.

Katarina took a deep breath. "The baby isn't mine. But I didn't steal her. Hans-Wolfgang is her father. He forced me to take the baby. He thinks that Ralf killed the baby's mother. Herr von Obereierhofen is Isabeau's grandfather."

"Slowly. One point at a time."

"That's where I was when I disappeared. I was with Hans-Wolfgang."

"Who is Hans-Wolfgang and what does he mean to you?"

"He is one of the two families from the Eierhofen estates. They have an old feud. It is a long story."

"Is this man your lover?"

"Of course not! The soldiers, Herr von Obereierhofen's soldiers, had been searching for the baby. They would have hurt her if he hadn't brought her here. The night I was with him, the river was flooded and I couldn't cross back over. And Ralf sent me to my doom like a sacrificial goat."

"The baby? You think they are after Isabeau?" he said and swallowed a mouthful of bread. "Why not give her back if that is her grandfather? You would be free of any responsibility."

"I can't send her away. If Ralf really killed Friedrich's daughter, what will he do to Isabeau?"

"You think you can trust this Hans-Wolfgang, then?"

"He saved my life twice now, didn't he?"

"Twice?"

Katarina looked away. "It was Willi living in the barn. I'm not sure, but he wears a uniform much like those from Herr von Obereierhofen's soldiers. Willi and I fought. It's my fault that he came here. I always wanted him to take me away."

"Yes, it could have been Prutt who went through my papers. Uncle Paul had heard from associates in Nuremberg that he may have gone and joined a private regiment, but nobody would confirm it. Prutt knows you and could have come here anytime…"

He stopped. With one finger, he turned Katarina's chin so she was facing him.

"Do you still want to leave with him?" he asked.

"Of course I don't want to leave. I want to stay here. With you."

He took her by the hand and smiled. He rubbed his other hand over his brow, took another piece of meat from the platter and stuffed the whole thing in his mouth.

"But, you say, you have your papers," Katarina said. "What is then the matter?"

Herr Tucher finished chewing. "I lied. I do not have those papers. And Ralf seems to know all about my dilemma. Come, let us join the others."

He stood and offered Katarina his hand. She took it and he pulled her close. He brushed her cheek with his lips, looked down and kissed her lips soft and deep. He led her out of the room. They walked down the steps and into the yard. The evening was mild and pleasant but dark clouds were collecting and slowly rolling together. The workers congregated around the table and bench. Torches had been lit, gaily illuminating the whole throng. It really looked like a garden party now. Paul and Tanner sipped at the port wine. The others spoke among themselves.

A wind picked up through the yard. Thunder rumbled overhead.

Dried leaves and debris whirled around the buildings. The horses snorted in the stable and a cow mooed anxiously. Chickens clucked at the oncoming storm. A droning made them all turn to look at the main road. A dust funnel, hardly visible on the darkened road, twisted and blew like a dervish.

"What kind of storm could that be?" Anna said.

The first horseman appeared and the second. The men whistled to their horses, driving them forward. Five more pounded around the bend; five more after them. At least twenty horses with black-uniformed riders thundered into the yard at a staggering speed. Katarina ran into the house and down into the kitchen.

"Please tell me we aren't under siege," Sara said.

Katarina shook her head in disbelief. Isabeau wrapped her arms around Katarina's legs. Katarina picked her up, wrapped her in a life-saving embrace and whispered a frantic petition to the loving mother *Holla*.

Part 3

Chapter 36

"I'm so afraid that they're going to set the house on fire," Katarina said.

"If they do, we'll have to run for it," Sara said.

Albin began to cry and she ran into the alcove, grabbed him from the bed, hoisted him onto her hip and held her hand over his mouth.

"If we do try to run, the soldiers will easily catch us," Katarina said. "The fields around the farm offer no cover. The forest is a march away from here. We'll never be able to fight against all those men!"

"Kata? Kata?" Isabeau said and touched Katarina's cheek, her lips.

Men shouted outside. Horses snorted, hooves pounded, women screamed. The air burned with a fierce energy and fear.

"How many men are there?" Sara asked.

"I don't know. More than ten, maybe twenty? Thirty?" Katarina whispered. "I'm afraid."

Katarina shifted Isabeau onto her hip, walked through the stable adjoining the kitchen and pressed her ear to the paddock door. Men scuffled outside, scolding and swearing. Katarina and Sara were trapped.

"Did you see Frau Kuni today?" Katarina asked.

"Yes, she came down into the kitchen when you were outside before. She got a bit to eat and some wine and went back upstairs."

Katarina heard Herr Tucher somewhere from the front of the house bellowing garbled orders. A crash echoed in the stairway as if the front doors were being splintered by a massive hammer. Demanding voices shouted outside the door in the paddock. Sara pulled Katarina from the paddock into the kitchen. Sara shut the stable door. Katarina and Sara huddled together like two orphans.

Heavy footfalls rang on the stones in the hallway. Many boots stomped down the steps to the kitchen. Three massive soldiers pushed through the doorway wearing heavy black tunics and black woolen pants stuffed into dirty black boots. A tall, dark man with stringy hair and a full beard barked at his companions. The small, thin blond soldier with a wisp of facial hair sniveled and nodded his head. The squat soldier stared at them with strange slanted eyes, slits on his flat face. More sounds grated from the dark soldier's lips but Katarina couldn't understand him. The blood rushed in her ears and she felt like she was deaf.

"What did he say?" Sara whispered.

The tall dark soldier stood in front of the two women. The grating sounds formed to speak words.

"The baby."

"No," the two women said together, as convincing as the squeak from a mouse.

Two other soldiers advanced on the two women and more soldiers took their place at the doorway behind them. The door to the stable adjoining the kitchen flew open. Sara and Katarina moved closer to the fire. Katarina could not tell how many soldiers were behind them. The beastly stench of these men mingled with a nauseating scent of stale alcohol surrounded her. Isabeau cried.

"The baby!" the soldier demanded.

He pulled the screaming Isabeau from Katarina's arms, turned and disappeared among the throng of soldiers. The soldier behind him blocked Katarina's escape by waving a sword in her face. Sara sniffed and gasped. The other soldier ripped baby Albin from Sara's arms and turned to leave like the other had done. One at a time, the soldiers retreated and the two women stood there, alone, dumb, shocked.

Katarina willed a bit of life into her limbs. "We have to go out there now. We have no choice."

Sara's foot slipped as they ran up the steps. Katarina caught her and pulled her through the splintered wood doors into the yard. Billows of smoke hid the sky. The sound of hooves thundered away from the farm. The soldiers retreated. They had what they wanted.

The smell of burning wood singed in Katarina's nostrils. Dry brush around the main barn was burning. The small fires illuminated the two blond Danish boys and the four children who formed a line to the well. They handed buckets along the line, extinguishing the fire. The carp farmer lay on the ground. A few soldiers, too.

Sara searched the yard. Her eyes fell upon her husband kneeling on the ground next to a fallen child lying in a pool of blood. She cried out and ran to him. Katarina scoured the group, hoping to find Pieter holding Isabeau.

Pieter ran up to Katarina. "Did you give them the child?"

"I had no choice," Katarina said and sank to her knees.

"We have to get her back." He pulled Katarina up to her feet, eyed her skeptically and softened his gaze.

"Where is Herr Tucher?" Katarina said. "Where's Frau Kuni?"

"They are not out here. I'll check upstairs."

Pieter pulled Katarina back into the house and she followed him up the steps. He stopped on the landing by Herr Tucher's rooms and urged Katarina up the steps to Frau Kuni's room. She opened the door. The room was empty. She pulled the door shut and ran back down to Herr Tucher's rooms. Pieter stood in the hallway and slammed the door.

"Nobody here," he said and pulled her back outside.

Tanner stood at the bottom of the steps and held the lifeless form of his son Falk. Both father and son had blood-smeared hands and clothes. Falk appeared to be sleeping. Someone shouted and Tanner turned suddenly. The boy's lifeless head slumped to the side exposing the bloody gash under his ear.

"Those bastards killed my son," Tanner said.

Sara knelt on the ground behind him, her face in her hands. She looked up at her husband, her face smeared with dirt and tears and sunk her head again. Her body heaved with violent sobbing.

"Where is Herr Tucher?" Katarina said.

Tanner knelt down next to his wife without answering. Katarina knelt down next to Sara and laid an arm on her shoulder.

"You have to get the babies back," Sara said. "Find them!"

Katarina kissed her cheek. "Don't worry, we will get them back."

Katarina turned to Pieter and watched him search the farmyard.

"There." He pointed to the barn where the horses were kept.

He grabbed Katarina by the hand and marched towards the barn with her in tow. In the shadows of the torchlight and the fires, Tanner the Elder sat with his back against the barn with Knecht at his side. Smoke hung over the yard with the smell of burnt wood and the sickly, rancid-sweet smell of spilled blood. Both men wiped at bloody cuts along their arms and faces and conversed in low, serious tones. They stopped talking and looked up as Katarina and Pieter approached.

"Horses are gone," said Knecht, his words breathless and hard to understand. All of his front teeth were missing. "They drove the sheep we had here at the house into the forest up there." He jabbed his thumb over his shoulder towards the North Hill. "Tanner has the rest of the herd secured back there."

"I thought they'd burn all the buildings, but that's not what they were after," Tanner the Elder said.

"They took the babies," Katarina said and choked on the words. "Falk is dead."

Tanner the Elder nodded in affirmation. "They took Herr Tucher and his uncle."

"What? Why?" she said.

"Ransom. They took horses because they need them. They drove all the animals they could into the forest to slaughter for food. And they took the master and his uncle because they can get a good price when the family hears that they are being held for ransom."

Pieter grabbed Katarina by the shoulders and turned her to face him. "Let's take this one step at a time. Break this problem down into solvable morsels. Let's see who we have here, who is not too badly hurt and we'll take care of those who are. We need to bury the dead and we have to do that before the wolves come. Only then we can try to find the men and the babies."

Katarina's head was spinning. Pieter dragged her towards Anna who tended the two Danish boys who seemed to have burned themselves extinguishing the fire. The carp farmer lay limp and crumpled in the middle of the yard.

"He's dead," Anna said. "His woman is gone. No idea where she got to."

Pieter pointed to a heap of black cloth as he walked towards it. He bent over the motionless blond soldier, knelt down and rummaged through his pockets. He removed the soldier's baldric and slung it over his own shoulder, grabbed the soldier's sword from the ground and slid the sword back in its sheath. He found a tobacco pipe in the man's pocket and stuffed that in his own pocket. Mesmerized, Katarina watched him wipe the dead man's blood from his own hands on the soldier's tunic.

Pieter prodded her onto the next soldier, his black tunic and red sash soaked with blood. The smell of death made Katarina reel. The ridiculously long red feather from the man's black hat had slipped and covered the man's face. Pieter knelt and removed the hat revealing a blood-smeared face. Pieter grabbed her by the hand. He pointed back to the first pond. In the dark, Katarina saw a black heap in the grass.

"Come with me," he said.

The black heap was a soldier who had taken an arrow in his back and was lying with his face in the water. Pieter pulled the man out of the water by his tunic. He let the corpse drop on its back in the grass with a thud. Katarina looked down at the man and thought she recognized his face. She turned away and retched there on the spot.

"He's been shot with an arrow, look," Pieter said. "His throat's been slit, too. That's what finished him off."

Katarina coughed.

"This is the man I chased in the woods," Pieter said. "The one who hit me in the head."

"It's Willi Prutt," Katarina said. "The man who had been in the barn all those weeks."

Pieter spat on his face and set about rummaging through his pockets. He found a few silver coins, the small dagger Willi usually kept stuffed in his waistband and a blue tablet-woven band. Pieter threw the dagger and the band to Katarina and stuck the coins in his own pocket. He raised the limp corpse, slipped the baldric with the sheathed sword over the corpse's head. The corpse fell to the earth again with a thud. Pieter hung the baldric around his own body with the other sword.

"He hadn't even drawn his sword."

"I need some water," Katarina said.

She fingered the blue band and felt all the blood drain from her head. Her legs ached as she ran towards the well. She threw the band and the dagger on the ground and pulled on the rope to bring the bucket up. She splashed her face with water and tried to drink a draught of sense into this senseless evening.

Her foot kicked against a soft, unmoving pile of fabric that lay at the base of the well. She bent to have a better look. At first, it occurred to her that it was washing that Anna had forgotten here and let lay. She knelt down and the warm pile of fabric let out a small grunt. It was Frau Kuni.

"What are you doing here?" Katarina said. "Are you hurt?"

"I think I fell. I don't know what happened, Katarina."

"Can you get back up?" Katarina moved closer to her, slipped one hand under her upper back and laid Frau Kuni's head on her lap. She pulled her wet, sticky hand back and smelled blood.

"Katarina, I don't think I can get up."

"Don't try to speak. I'll get you up to the house."

"There is such a thing as destiny. And one's place in life. And one will never be able to change that. Never mind what our *liebe Holla* has planned for us."

"Frau Kuni, it'll be fine…"

"Katarina, my mother was the *Magd*, I was her bastard child. I had to serve the Master Hanson and that's where your mother came from. He could be mean. He was rough. Funny that the Old Widow and I were such good friends. But your mother left after the old Master Hanson got her with child. She left. Well, after she had you, of course."

"Frau Kuni, we'll talk about this later. Now try to stay quiet and I'll get you to the house. You'll be fine."

"Katarina, I've had enough and I'm tired. I'm so angry with myself that I couldn't get you married. Get you out of here. And now you're the master's mistress, just like we were. I wanted more for you."

"Frau Kuni, we'll talk about all this tomorrow, I promise. Can you stand up? Come with me, now, get up. I'll get you to the house…"

"I'm so tired. I want to sleep." Her chest heaved as she drew a deep breath. "Oh, my child. Please forgive me."

Frau Kuni's muscles relaxed as a whole and released with a sigh. A breeze whispered up Katarina's spine and swirled to heaven. Silent tears streamed over Katarina's cheeks.

Katarina was finished with this game of Fate or Destiny. She was finished. She could not get up. She would not get up. She would sit here forever until she died. Everything that had once meant anything at all to her had been taken away and there was nothing left to lose.

"Katarina?" a voice whispered. "Oh dear God, are you hurt?" It was Pieter, holding an oil lamp high. "Can you stand? Is Frau Kuni hurt?"

"She's dead," Katarina said.

Pieter untangled Katarina from Frau Kuni's body. He pulled her to a standing position but Katarina's legs gave way after kneeling so long. He embraced her and she let herself melt onto his chest. Katarina cried on and her body heaved and heaved.

"We need to bury the dead," Pieter said. "The wolves will come. Have a drink of this."

Pieter handed Katarina a small flask with a strong drink. She took a long draught and handed the flask back. He dragged her away from the well towards the barn lit with a few torches. The others had congregated there as well. He handed her the small flask again and a spade.

As if in a dream, Katarina dug and dug and dug in the earth. Hours later, she somehow found herself lying on the straw sack in her alcove next to the kitchen. She sank into a dream of fire: hell fire, brimstone, witches, sacrilege, rooftops burning. She smelled burnt skin and heard tortured babies crying.

Chapter 37

Katarina scrubbed the smell of blood off her hands. She ladled more boiling water from the pot over the kitchen fire into a shallow bowl, dunked her fingers in and quickly pulled them out again. She tore a bit of bread from the round loaf, dipped it into a pot of lard and ate greedily. Isabeau must be hungry too. Would they feed her? What about the Tanners' baby? She dried her hands and face, grabbed the rest of the bread and went outside to the others.

The first hint of daylight climbed over the hills. Pieter and Tanner conversed quietly together with Knecht and Tanner the Elder. Their eyes were sunken but alert. Their clothes were dirty and they smelled of alcohol. Anna watched Katarina approaching.

"Where is Sara?" Katarina asked.

"Maybe you could go check on her, Katarina," Anna said.

The two Danish boys walked towards them. They looked like brothers. Their simple clothing was dirty and stained but they seemed healthy enough despite the circumstances. They approached Tanner and slammed their spades into the ground.

"We've finished filling in the graves. What should we do now?"

The men whispered quietly among themselves. Katarina handed them the round loaf of bread and walked back to the workers' house. Sara looked like she'd been awake all night. She held a steaming cup and sipped at it cautiously.

"Katarina, I'm so sorry about Frau Kuni."

"I'm sorry about Falk. And the babies. They must be hungry…"

Katarina fought back the tears.

Sara set her cup aside, stood and hugged Katarina. They embraced in silence, supporting each other like two crooked trees in the forest leaning on each other against a strong wind.

Sara pulled back and said, "Pieter says you know why they took the children."

"Isabeau isn't my child. I've only been entrusted with her care."

"I didn't think she was. You bear no resemblance to each other."

"I didn't always love her like a daughter, either."

"There is no right or wrong way to love, Katarina. We do what we can."

"He wanted her back. Ralf did."

"But why take my son?"

"They may have been instructed to take any children they came across."

"The others say you know where Friedrich von Obereierhofen lives." Sara said. "That Ralf is working for him. That the soldiers were here at his command. Willi, too. Is that true?"

"It is the only explanation I can think of."

"They want to start the search there."

"Yes, we will start there. You stay here." Katarina turned to leave.

Katarina refused to think beyond the moment. She felt like she was standing on a high ledge about to jump. Sara came up alongside Katarina, grabbed her by the hand and walked with her towards the others.

"I have nothing here, Katarina," Sara said. "My son is dead and my other son is missing. We'll all go. If we fail, what do I know? I can't think like that."

The men were gathered in a group, talking in low tones. They stopped talking when Katarina and Sara walked towards them. Aside from dried blood stains on the ground and the absence of animals, the farmyard was as it had been yesterday. Katarina wished she could get on with her chores and return to some normality. The sun was rising today, like any other day. But for some, this day would never be; life would not continue. For Katarina and the others, life would go on and they had a hard day ahead of them.

"It's not far," Katarina said to Tanner. "We cross the river. The Eierhofen estates are on top of the hill. We'll see them from the riverside."

Tanner put his arm around his wife's shoulder. "We may be no match for trained soldiers. No matter what weapons we have. And we are outnumbered. But we have to do something."

"We'll have to use stealth," Pieter said. "We'll have to sneak in. Break in. Like a robbery, except the things we want belong to us in the first place."

Katarina trembled. "Let's go. I'll lose my sanity if I stay here any longer."

The two Danish boys nodded.

Tanner pointed at the two of them. "They want to come, too."

"We have nothing without this work," the younger man said. "Herr Tucher took me and Lasse from the streets in Nuremberg. I'm not going back there."

"After our mother died, our father left us there," the older brother Lasse said. "Went back to Denmark, someone told us. Bjarne and I had to beg. Herr Tucher always gave us something to eat or sent us to the Tucher's kitchen."

And so the group set out on this early spring morning. The birds chirped and a light breeze filled Katarina's head with the scent of all things spring. They looked like a group of field workers off for a day's tilling and weeding. They were clad in an interesting disguise: none at all. The two brothers Lasse and Bjarne, Tanner, Sara and Pieter and Katarina, armed with pitchforks, hoes and spades. Pieter and Tanner had the swords that Pieter had recovered from the dead soldiers. Pieter handed Katarina Willi's dagger that he'd found by the well. As they walked, Katarina stuck it in the folds of her skirt.

They followed the track to the main road, the Mailacher Weg. They passed by a quiet farmyard. No sounds came from the farmyard beyond that one, either. They crossed over the main road and down a beaten path beside the mill that also seemed abandoned.

"Why aren't they working?" Katarina said. "Where are the farmers?"

Pieter shook his head. "Where are they all?" he whispered to Tanner.

Tanner pointed to the last of the three Mailach farms, the one now closest to the river. "They seem to be hiding. I can't imagine that they would leave. But we have no time to check."

They walked along the bank of the Aisch river. Lasse and Bjarne whispered between themselves in their own language. The water was low and Katarina pointed to the spot where sand had formed a passable path. They waded through the shallow current easily and walked along the other side of the river, close to the edge of the water.

Clouds were coming in from the south and covered the sun. A wind picked up and it smelled like rain. Katarina pointed up to a stretch of dense, dark-green forest on the hill beyond the flood plain. A red-tiled roof was barely visible above the trees.

"There is Upper Eierhofen," she said. "That's Friedrich's house."

"We shouldn't go head on, should we?" Pieter said. "Is there a back way?"

"The hill is covered with trees," Katarina said. "No matter which way we go up, we will be under cover. We must see if the soldiers are patrolling the road, though."

"Or the trees," Tanner said.

Hooves approached from behind them. A cloaked horseman gingerly picked a path across the shallow, rocky riverbed. Katarina's heart pounded. She recognized that dark-bay stallion anywhere. The rider pulled hard on the reins and the horse protested. When the horse and rider reached the opposite river bank, he slammed his heels into the horse and they rounded the bend in a fury, heading in the group's direction.

"It's Ralf!" Katarina whispered. "Turn your backs and keep walking."

"No!" Tanner hissed.

He pulled Sara's hand and jumped into the high overgrowth surrounding an ancient willow tree. They ducked down. Pieter grabbed Katarina's hand and they leapt into the dense weeds next to them. Pieter slipped and one foot dipped into the river. Katarina saw the two boys hop behind the willow as she lay down flat in the weeds. Stinging nettles. She stifled a scream.

Keeping her head down, she heard Ralf's horse gallop by and along the road towards Weidendorf. She stuck her head out of the stinging nettles to see him disappear into the trees.

"We have no plan," Katarina whispered. "We have no idea what we're doing. Where is this all leading?"

"If we knew where it was leading, we probably wouldn't go," Pieter said. "Better that we don't know."

They stood and climbed out of the nettles.

Tanner cursed. "We need to be more cautious."

They walked across the flood plain. A hawk called overhead to another. Katarina looked up and saw the two meet in midair, climb effortlessly and disappear. From downriver, the sound of *cuck-oo cuck-oo cuck-oo* floated above the trees.

"Did you know that cuckoos don't raise their young by themselves?" said Lasse to Pieter. "They lay their eggs in other birds' nests and the other birds raise them."

"Be quiet, you two," Tanner hissed.

They walked on silently until they reached the base of the hill and the tree line. Katarina looked up into the dense foliage. Anyone observing from above would have easily seen them approaching. Her legs tensed. There was a deathly silence in spite of the lively breeze. They stopped by a pile of eroding sandstone blocks covered in moss and fern and took cover there for a moment, listening and watching the forest for any movement or patrolling soldiers. The breeze seemed to stop at the forest's edge. No rustling leaves, just a still, empty void.

"Ghosts," Pieter whispered.

The clouds covered the sky now and the absence of sunlight lent the forest a fatal foreboding.

"What do we do now?" said Bjarne.

No one moved. A twig snapped and the sound fell flat among the underbrush. Katarina held her breath. Something scurried behind her. She gasped and turned suddenly. Pieter put an arm over her shoulder and a finger to his lips, motioning her to remain quiet. More twigs snapped. Bjarne and Lasse knelt down behind the sandstone pile. Something was sneaking up on their group. In amongst the trees, a heavy sorrel horse clambered through the forest with a brown-clad man astride. Together they were the colors of the forest. The rider could have been a tree had he not been a man. He approached them slowly.

"You let them have the child," a hoarse voice said.

"No, they took the child with force," Katarina said. "They killed Falk. They killed my grandmother. They would have killed me."

"I told you to protect the child!" Hans-Wolfgang said as he approached, still on horseback.

"Where were you?" Katarina said.

"I was watching from the field."

"Why didn't you help us?"

"I did. I chased enough soldiers away. I killed another. That one who was after you. I finally got that dog. I thought you'd thank me."

"Where did they take the children?" Katarina said.

"They took them up there to the house but I'm not sure if

they're still there." Hans-Wolfgang barked a laugh. "Your lover is among them."

"We want to get in there," Katarina said.

"You'll never get in like that," Hans-Wolfgang said.

"Well what do you suggest?" Tanner chimed in.

"There is a way. Friedrich's father and my grandfather had made tunnels to store food in case they were ever under siege. They connect to Upper Eierhofen's cellar."

"We need to find the way in," Tanner said.

"Follow me. But be careful. They are patrolling the trees."

"They are looking for you," Katarina said.

"They've been looking for me for a year," Hans-Wolfgang said. "I'm right here under their noses the whole time. Those soldiers! They are good riders and probably good in battle, but they drink too much and aren't very clever."

Hans-Wolfgang removed the tack from his horse and hid the saddle and harness under a bush. He explained he would rather set the horse free than have one of those soldiers claim him. The horse would return if it suited him. He struggled half-crouched between the trees and lifted the gnarled growth from time-to-time, like he was looking for something he lost. The bow over his shoulder snagged in some vines and he tore at them impatiently. The rest of the group followed him silently.

Tanner and Pieter unsheathed their swords and hacked at brambles and twisted vines, trying to clear a path. The sound of metal on wood echoed under the trees. Hans-Wolfgang stepped lightly, sometimes running up the hill or back down. Suddenly he straightened. He waved for them to come over and pointed up the hill.

"Do you hear that?" Hans-Wolfgang said. "They always patrol this part of the woods but today they are all up at the house."

Men's shouts, muffled echoes in the trees, were barely audible. A distinct shout made Katarina stiffen.

He ran back up the hill and disappeared. Pieter and Tanner had sheathed their swords and waited for him to return. Katarina heard a whistle like a hawk from behind a tree not far from where they stood. They moved as a group towards the sound.

"See the beaten path behind those brambles?" Hans-Wolfgang said. "That leads to the entrance."

He climbed over some thorny underbrush and pulled tree limbs away from a wooden door pressed into the hillside.

"Here it is," Hans-Wolfgang said. "There is always a guard at this door. Something must be quite important at the house for them to leave this entrance unmanned."

Tanner and Pieter trampled the brambles to join Hans-Wolfgang. Tanner grabbed for the door latch.

"I don't know where it leads," Hans-Wolfgang said, laying his hand on Tanner's. "And I am not responsible for what happens on the other side."

Tanner made no move to retreat.

"Help me clear these vines," Hans-Wolfgang said.

Tanner and Pieter pulled at the brambles with their hands. Hans-Wolfgang produced a small leather pouch from his pocket. He stuck his finger in the pouch and rubbed the hinges with fat.

"Tallow," he said. "I thought they would be rusty and loud, maybe completely unmovable, standing here in the elements."

Hans-Wolfgang and Tanner released the latch and pulled on the door. It creaked open. They peeked through the door into the emptiness, like they were expecting to see something revealing. All that greeted them was a dank, rotted reek and a faint, cool breeze. Compared to darkness above ground, darkness underground was a different animal; final, dead and unmoving.

"I'm not going in there," Lasse said.

"We need a torch," Tanner said. "Or a lamp. Do you have an oil lamp to go with that tallow?"

Hans-Wolfgang was already smearing tallow into a clay lamp, like the one Frau Kuni always used. Lasse squatted down, busying himself with a flint stone trying to light the lamp.

"We're never going to find them like this," Sara said, sniffing "My baby needs to be fed."

She shoved the prongs of her pitchfork in the earth, leaned on the handle and wiped her eyes with the back of her hand. After what felt like an eternity, they got the lamp lit and shone it into the gaping doorway of the cellar. A few dead rats lay by the door.

"Leave your tools here," Hans-Wolfgang said.

"We're going, aren't we, Lasse?" Bjarne asked and grabbed his brother by the arm. "But we're taking our spades. Sharp, they are."

"I'll hold on to my pitchfork, thank you," Sara said.

"I don't even know if this leads into the house," Hans-Wolfgang continued. "This may only be storage. I'm warning you all. If you go beyond this point it is your own choice."

"I'm going in. Give me the lamp," Tanner said.

"No need. I'll go first," Hans-Wolfgang said and led the way.

Chapter 38

At mid-morning a few of the black-clad thugs took Herr Tucher by the arm and led him out of the damp, windowless cellar room up the grand, bowed stone staircase. He could hear bird twitter through the few missing panes of glass. The windows reminded Herr Tucher of his family's country estate north of Nuremberg, where he had spent so many pleasant summers as a child. His mind was drifting and he had to force himself to concentrate on the challenging situation he found himself in now.

The soldiers led him up the staircase into a wide entrance hall. Between the two stone staircases, massive oak double doors stood ajar. The soldiers showed him into a chilled, roomy hall.

Herr Tucher walked across the dusty-yellowish stone floor accompanied by soldiers. A dead mouse lay in a pile of dried leaves. A broken chair lay under the far window. Next to the broken chair was an old brown-velvet divan with Uncle Paul unmoving on top of it. At the end of the hall, a plump, ginger-haired man, a man Herr Tucher assumed to be Friedrich von Obereierhofen, was propped up behind a heavy dark-stained wooden desk in a high-backed chair, as if he was reclining in a throne. Friedrich's breathing was labored and his face was flushed.

"So, Herr Tucher," Friedrich said as if his nose was full. "I am so sorry for the inconvenience, but you must understand my obligation."

"Make me understand, my dear man," Herr Tucher said. "What do you want with me?"

"Ah, the times are changing. Nothing is like it used to be. We were once so innocent. The world changes men like you and me."

"I would like to think that men like you and I are the ones who change the world."

Friedrich snorted at this, his belly heaving like a pregnant woman. "The world is finally changing in a way that I approve of."

He turned his head stiffly to look out of the long window, filled with thick, round, fist-sized panes held together with lead strips. A draft managed to get through the few panes that here, like in the stairwell, were missing. The hall was once a splendid meeting room, but time had left its traces. Plaster crumbled in the high corners. Parts of the room that were no longer used were dirty. An ornately carved chair in the corner was covered with thick, black dust.

"I come from a great family, you know," Friedrich said. "I had but one child myself and she was prematurely and rudely, no, violently taken from me. I tried to keep her away from that Protestant family. From that boy, Hans-Wolfgang. But he was always sneaking through the woods with that father of his. The two of them hunting with their falcons.

"My father and Hans-Wolfgang's grandfather were great friends," Friedrich continued. "That is why our houses stand together on this hill. Their religious differences made no difference to the old men. But the more I studied the work of that man Luther, the less I could tolerate my nearest neighbor believing in such heresy. His work is banned in my circle. I wanted no child of mine being influenced by such devil's work."

He blew his nose into a handkerchief lined with lace.

"I hired my now most trusted servant, Ralf, to instruct my daughter. It was the best move I'd made. Her education was a vivid, lively study of nature, art, and religion. Ralf protected her. He had seen Hans-Wolfgang follow her into the woods and rape her. I should have had him hanged for that then and there. His father begged me to spare the boy. He said they were in love. My dearest Andra-Angela. She would never have loved that boy. But God takes care of such men. Their home burned last spring like a hellfire. Ralf told me that the blaze was caused by lightning. Hans-Wolfgang's father, Christian von Untereierhofen, could never have survived the blaze. But the young Hans-Wolfgang eludes me still."

"I have not yet had the pleasure of meeting this man," Herr Tucher said.

"You may never meet him, if I find him first. But I want to find out why he killed my daughter before I kill him. Maybe because he couldn't have her, because she did not or could not love such a heathen boy? I will have him executed exactly as he killed my daughter. And now I have my granddaughter, to raise in the Catholic faith as I see fit."

"Excuse me, sir." Herr Tucher interrupted. "One of those children you have abducted belongs to my most trusted counterpart. That baby boy is the Tanner's son. The white-haired child is Isabeau."

"Who named her Isabeau?" Friedrich said. "She will be baptized as Waldtraut."

"Penalize the child for life," Herr Tucher said.

Friedrich shot him a most poisoned glare. "That was my mother's name."

"I rest my case…" Herr Tucher said.

"If your family does not react to my proposition, I'll have to kill the two of you."

"Proposition? You are holding my uncle and myself for ransom? How common."

"My troops are hungry and they need new boots," Friedrich said. "Your sheep will only keep them fed for a few weeks."

"If you were my prisoner, I would at least show you some hospitality," Herr Tucher said. "How about a bit of breakfast?"

Uncle Paul groaned from the divan under the window. A ragged old *Magd* had come in through a side door and now dabbed at the scabbing slash on his arm and the welt on his head. Paul stirred, so he was alive, thank God. Herr Tucher shifted his weight from one foot to the other impatiently.

"I'll arrange for a chair," Friedrich said.

As if he had spoken a silent command, the door opened, two soldiers came in and stood a chair behind Herr Tucher, facing Friedrich. One soldier pushed down on his shoulder and Herr Tucher sat. The soldier knelt and bound one foot to the chair leg.

"One moment, sir," Herr Tucher said. "I would like to tend to my uncle."

"Do not worry, Herr Tucher. I have arranged him a safe hideaway." Friedrich narrowed his tiny eyes.

The soldier bound Herr Tucher's other foot. Again the door opened. Three soldiers sauntered towards the divan. Two men heaved Uncle Paul like a sack of flour. He groaned and they carried him out of the hall. The last soldier led the ghost-like *Magd* and the two followed the others out.

"My maid is a silent woman who obeys orders," Friedrich said.

"You could do with such a servant. But you may not be at fault, my good man. Ralf tells me that maid of yours is in league with the devil. Arrangements have been made to take her to Bamberg for questioning. She will confess her real sympathies when my people are done with her."

Herr Tucher laughed. "I am not under the influence of any black magic. And I do not need 'servants.' If my maid chose to, she could leave. She is in my employ."

"A suspicious response that no man of your standing would make on his own. You see, women are imperfect animals. Weak, inferior beings fashioned from a bent rib. Ralf says they are quicker to renounce their faith. That is why they resort to witchcraft. This is cited numerous times in the Scriptures."

"No educated man of my standing would believe such nonsense," Herr Tucher said. "I say you release me and we discuss this further over a bottle or two of wine."

"You have nothing to say that would be of interest to me." A young guard with light-brown hair came in through the door, again as if summoned. "Please tie this man's hands, too. I am not sure what he is capable of conjuring."

Friedrich stood and walked to a square cabinet, intricately inlaid with wood and pearl, that perched on top of a chest of drawers. He drew a bundle of keys from under his doublet and unlocked the door. He withdrew a wrapped package the size of a newborn child, carried it with two hands and set it on his table with a heavy thud.

"I will not allow you to spread like a plague through my lands, Herr Tucher. I will see to it that your influence in this area comes to a sudden halt."

Friedrich opened the parcel and produced an assortment of documents.

"These areas of land you attempt to work will be transferred to me. And I will install the people I see fit to run them."

The guard returned to Friedrich's side after binding Herr Tucher's wrists a bit too tightly behind the chair.

"Please organize the riders, Elis," he said. "I need to finalize this transaction before this situation escalates."

Chapter 39

Katarina and Sara followed silently behind Hans-Wolfgang and Tanner as they moved single-file into the cellar passage. Bjarne, Lasse and Pieter followed them. Pieter pulled the door closed. They stopped for a moment and their faces took on an eerie, disembodied look within the ring of light from the tallow lamp. Pieter rammed a bit of wood into the latch and hammered it with a rock until it was securely closed.

"Nobody will be coming in behind us," he said.

They followed Hans-Wolfgang and the ring of light deeper into this crypt. Fine webs brushed Katarina's cheeks. Roots hung from the ceiling and looked like dead, broken fingers. They snagged her hair. She wanted to bat at them, but there was no room to even raise her arms. The cool, damp air smelled of rodents and mold. They squeezed past the remains of two broken barrels. Something crunched under her foot. Thank God she couldn't see what it was.

They walked on along the unevenly carved floor. At times Katarina had to duck down to pass through, her bent back and shoulders scraping on the moist earth above their heads. Pieter crawled behind Katarina, his shoulders barely passing through the cramped space.

"This is what being buried alive would feel like," someone whispered.

Katarina heard a grunt and a thud.

"Stop!" someone hissed.

In the lamplight Katarina saw that Tanner had slipped in some damp mud. Standing still in this grave-like passage sent a cold chill down Katarina's sweating back. Tanner got up and they plodded forward, more slowly than before. Time became something otherworldly and suspended. Katarina saw white shadows coming up from the ground. She realized that puddles were becoming more frequent, the mud slippery and slimy.

Hans-Wolfgang hissed, "Stop!"

They had come to a door at the end of the tunnel.

Hans-Wolfgang said to Tanner, "Do you want to open it?"

Tanner wiggled the rusty latch but the door wouldn't budge. In the lamplight his face twisted into a ferocious mask like Katarina had never seen on the man. He drew his sword. He wedged the sword between the individual planks that made up the door and broke one out. A breeze came through the fissure. The other side was just as dark. Hans-Wolfgang held up the lamp and Tanner broke another plank out of the door, reached through and rattled the door latch.

"Locked," Tanner said. "Enough of this."

He stepped back and kicked against the door, breaking more planks out, until the way was large enough for the group to pass through. This passage led into a wider tunnel. They followed each other and the path began a descent. The air was cooler. Katarina looked up in the dull lamplight as they entered a large cellar room. Barrels were lined up against the one wall. Crates were stacked on top of each other along the other wall. Three steps led up to an arched door at the end of the room. Lasse rocked one of the barrels next to the door and liquid could be heard swishing inside.

Tanner pressed his ear to the door and jumped back. "Someone is coming. I hear voices!"

Katarina scampered behind the stacked crates and ducked down. Sara landed next to her and her pitchfork clattered on the stone floor, the clang echoing off the walls. Hans-Wolfgang extinguished the lamp. The acrid smoke hung in the air. The door flew open and torchlight flooded the large room. Sara and Katarina peeked from behind the crates. Three soldiers rushed in, all wearing those same black uniforms. One held a torch high and one stood watch by the door. The tallest of them stopped, eyes searching the outer walls of the cellar room.

The tallest of them, who seemed to be the commander, systematically rocked the barrels. He had well-pronounced, rounded features under a mass of black hair, glaring-black eyes and a fresh slit on his high cheekbone. He seemed to be looking for wine. But he stopped when he found an empty barrel. He grunted to his comrades. Two more similarly-dressed men, with the same high Slavish cheekbones and rounded noses, came into the hall dragging a man whose arms had been bound behind his back.

A groan came from the bound man. It was Herr Tucher's Uncle Paul. His black doublet and breeches were dirty, the sleeves torn. His hair was rumpled and, in places, caked with blood. The two soldiers let him fall and he rolled onto his side. A wound bled on his forehead. The commander opened the barrel, laid it on its side and gabbled some words that ordered Paul to climb in. He was unable to obey. The commander uttered some unintelligible commands to the others and they grabbed Paul's feet and loaded him into the barrel, uprighted it and attempted to press the lid back on. Paul struggled against his prison.

A scream echoed off the walls of the hall. One of the soldiers cried out in pain as an arrow stung his right shoulder. The scream reverberated in Katarina's ears as another arrow whizzed by and struck the other soldier in the leg. The lid of the barrel thunked onto the floor. Tanner flew out of his hiding place, sword drawn and charged the commander. The soldier standing watch by the door fell to the ground as an arrow struck him in the neck.

Tanner swung his sword at the commander, who had not only drawn his sword, but had a dagger in his other hand. The commander returned the blow. Metal clanged on metal. The last standing soldier holding the torch turned to run back through the door but Sara stood in front of him with her pitchfork and blocked his way. Katarina came up behind him and rammed her dagger into his arm but it stuck in the bone. Panic paralyzed Katarina as she felt an angry growl form in the man's stomach. As he reached to pull the dagger out of his arm, he dropped the torch and clipped Katarina in the face with his elbow.

He knocked Katarina to the floor. She rubbed her jaw. Pieter jumped over Katarina and slashed at him with his sword and sliced him across the neck. Blood spurted and he fell to the floor. Hans-Wolfgang bent down, grabbed the torch and held it high.

The commander had Tanner backed up against one of the crates. Lasse rushed up behind them, raised his spade and rammed it downward against the back of the commander's thigh, slicing not only his black woolen breeches, but also a large chunk of the man's flesh. The commander sunk to his knees.

"That's for my son, you pig," Tanner said.

Sara stood by the barrel and helped Paul crawl out. He staggered on the spot. She steadied him but he still sank to his knees.

"Oh, you're hurt," Sara said.

"Leave me here," Paul said. "I can barely walk."

"What were they doing to you?" she asked.

"Oh, another trick they like to use," Paul said. "I was to be buried in the barrel among the trees. What will they think of next?"

"Where are the children?" Tanner said.

"I do not know where they took the children, but Sebald is still in the hall with Friedrich. I am afraid of the fate they will decide for him."

Pieter stood next to Katarina and said, "That's the work of Ralf."

Paul shook his head. "I am afraid that Sebald may give him every good reason. He does not know when to keep his thoughts to himself. He is always trying to top anyone with what he considers wit."

Tanner grabbed Bjarne by the arm. "You and your brother get Herr Tucher's uncle out through the tunnel. Break the door open if you have to. We need to move on. The wounded soldiers could get back on their feet."

That shadow passed over Pieter's eyes and a dark smile spread on his lips. He sheathed his sword, bent down over the dead soldier and pulled Katarina's dagger from his arm. He leaned over the one groaning soldier and rammed the dagger into his throat. He pounced lightly on the other one and did the same. He walked over to the commander, looked down at him as the wounded man panted in pain. He finished him off with one quick swipe. He wiped off the dagger and gave it back to Katarina.

"They will not be getting back up on their feet," he said.

"The hall is up the steps there," Paul said as Bjarne and Lasse led him out of the cellar into the dark tunnel. "Good luck."

Tanner, Hans-Wolfgang and Pieter ran through the door. Sara and Katarina followed. They entered a cold, sooty-smelling kitchen; a huge, neglected space. A few embers glowed on the wide, low fireplace with an open flue; a large hearth where a few maids could cook at the same time. Large pots were stacked in the one corner on the floor. High windows draped in cobwebs on the opposite wall lit a long working table. Empty shelves hung on the wall. A cracked plate lay on the floor. They followed a short hallway that led to the base of a curved stone stairwell, leaving footprints in the dusty ash. They climbed the steps to an entrance hall. On either side of the entrance hall, curved stone stairwells led to the upper floor. Between the stairwells, intricately carved oak doors stood ajar and they could hear men in a heated discussion.

Hans-Wolfgang held his hand up for all to halt and they stood still.

"…and if you insist that your maid is innocent, maybe you or one of your men are acting on the persuasions of the Devil. I would never have believed this, had Ralf not warned me about what was going on at your farm. What about that Dutch boy? We have arranged to get them all in for questioning. And you, as well. Our executioner has ways of making you talk…"

Pieter drew his sword. Tanner grabbed his arm and held a finger to his own lips.

Katarina heard Herr Tucher clear his throat. "And you really believe such confessions made under torture? Or could it be that the accused tell the authorities anything to make the pain stop."

"We should go in there!" whispered Pieter.

Ralf's voice came shrill and angry. "…the Archer. Hans-Wolfgang. Do you know what that man did? I had carved a wooden crucifix and erected it in the garden on a pole to mark the grave of Andra-Angela's mother. Hans-Wolfgang perched in a tree, where he had full view of our garden, and shot arrows into the heart of the Holy Cross. Three arrows. That was shortly before Andra-Angela was found murdered. I believe the arrows were symbolic for all three of us, Andra-Angela, myself and Herr von Obereierhofen. Other similar accounts of the possessed Archer have been recorded. I swear he will not rest until he has us all dead and buried.

"I believe, too, that he had Andra-Angela under some sort of spell," Ralf continued. "She would never have acted so carelessly on her own. I knew her too well. A beautiful, pure girl. She was god-fearing and a virgin."

"How did you know she was a virgin?" Herr Tucher said.

A slap. A grunt.

"We have to go in there!" Tanner whispered.

Chapter 40

Katarina watched Hans-Wolfgang run up the curved stone stairwell. He disappeared through a doorway. She prayed that this was part of his plan and not his escape. Katarina gave Pieter a push. He shoved his shoulder against the oak door and the two of them rushed into the large hall. Tanner and Sara followed close behind.

Herr Tucher sat with his back to Katarina, in front of a massive oak table with his hands bound behind his back. His white shirt was soiled and his dark hair fell around his shoulders. He tossed his head in an attempt to shake the hair out of his eyes. Katarina couldn't see his face.

Ralf hovered over Herr Tucher like a teacher trying to prove a disputed point. His simple black monk's robe was damp around the neckline from sweat and his face was red, lips tightly stretched over his teeth. He appraised Katarina, Pieter, Tanner and Sara individually, like he was trying to read their thoughts or influence their actions.

Behind the oak table, a plump, red-haired aristocrat sat in a high-backed wooden chair, his head held at a haughty tilt. Katarina assumed the seated man was Friedrich von Obereierhofen. He shoved his chair back and slowly stood, his large frame precariously positioned atop two spindly legs. He pulled two small hand muskets from under his table. He laid one musket on the table and pointed the other at the group.

"Well, now we have no need to hunt for you," Friedrich said, a fat man out of breath. "The guards will show you to your quarters until we are ready to transport the lot of you for questioning."

"Where is my son?" Tanner spat the words.

Friedrich pointed the musket at Herr Tucher's head. "Turn around and get on your knees and if you dally, I will shoot this man first. You will be next."

Tanner made no move to retreat.

Two soldiers entered from the door behind Friedrich's desk.

They each held the same style of hand musket as Friedrich.

"Men, show our prisoners to their coach," Friedrich said.

The soldiers approached Tanner and took his sword. Two more men with muskets came in through the same door. They grabbed Pieter's sword and relieved Sara of her pitchfork. They physically turned the four of them around, marched them through the door and out of the house.

The soldiers shoved them down the few steps and into the front garden surrounded by a stone wall. Katarina felt the soldier's firm grip on her shoulders. A wagon, much like a cage for transporting animals, with two heavy, light-brown horses hitched to it, stood tethered to the wall. Beyond the wall, the trees of the forest insured privacy for the comings and goings of the estate.

Two black-uniformed guards stood watch at the wooden gate large enough for horse and wagon to pass through. Next to the guards, two exotic-looking trees stood next to the gateway, planted in clay pots double the size of a wine barrel. On the path from somewhere behind the house, a small troop of riders clad in black suddenly appeared, atop their horses and ready to ride. They murmured among themselves.

Katarina heard a whizzing from somewhere overhead.

The soldiers' faces all shot upwards. An arrow flew over Katarina's head and struck the squat soldier with the slanted eyes. He fell from his horse. Katarina turned and looked up. Hans-Wolfgang hung out of the window from one of the upper floors with his bow strung. He shot again. Another soldier slumped in his saddle. He shot again. Another slumped. They fell from their horses.

One rider kicked his horse, broke free from the group and rode like a shot back down the path that led behind the house. Angry shouts and whistling sounded, as if he had summoned reinforcements. Stomping feet confirmed that suspicion.

Hans-Wolfgang's quiver was empty. He only had one arrow left—the one he was holding. He disappeared from his window. Friedrich and Ralf appeared in the doorway, exited the house and marched down the front steps. Ralf carried a baby-sized bundle.

"He has my baby," Sara whispered.

Ralf and Friedrich mounted the horses that two soldiers held for them. The horses protested, agitated now by the shouts and erratic movement in the yard. The mounted guard followed Friedrich and

Ralf to the gate and the two guards pulled the heavy gate open.

A group of soldiers appeared from behind the house, led by the dark soldier Katarina recognized as the baby-snatcher from Sichardtshof. The soldiers swarmed over Katarina, Sara, Tanner and Pieter.

Next to Katarina, Tanner spun abruptly with his fist swinging and pummeled the soldier who held him in the face. Pieter swung at another. A shot rang out. Pieter punched the soldier closest to him, knocking him down and Katarina forced her dagger into his soft, unprotected stomach. Hot, sticky liquid flowed over her hand and the smell of blood made her heave. She took a deep breath, pulled the dagger back out, wiped it off and somehow stuck it back into the folds of her skirt.

Katarina was surrounded by flailing arms, grunting and groaning and a smell of blood so strong she could taste it. They were grossly outnumbered. Another shot rang out and another. Flashes of light and smoke. A soldier raised his sword over Katarina's head. Hans-Wolfgang came up behind her, pushed her aside and swung his sword. She fell and rolled out of the way.

In the middle of the confusion, Katarina saw Tanner had already climbed onto a horse. Pieter hopped into the saddle of another. They both gathered their reins and tried to control the prancing horses. One soldier grappled with Hans-Wolfgang, slashed at him, and Hans-Wolfgang fell. Sara ran up to them and tried to pull Hans-Wolfgang out of the way, but the soldier struck her on the head with his sword's hilt. She fell onto her side.

More soldiers tried to pull Pieter and Tanner from the horses but they kicked the horses into motion and galloped through the open gate. Soldiers ran after them and more shots rang out.

Katarina ran over to Sara and helped her crawl out of the way. They both found a place to hide behind another clay potted tree further along the outer wall of the yard, somewhat out of sight. Blood dripped into Sara's eyes. She wiped at the cut on her head.

"Follow them, Katarina, please. Ralf has my baby," Sara said. "Don't let them out of your sight."

"He doesn't have your baby."

"What was that in the bundle?" Sara said.

"I don't know but it wasn't a baby!" Katarina cried. "You must be mistaken."

"I'm sure it's my baby. Go after him! Look! That horse there, chewing on the bush."

"I can't ride," Katarina whispered.

"Yes, you can," Sara said.

The soldiers had scattered. Two rode past Katarina and Sara and paid them no mind. Three others ran past and out of the gate. One soldier staggered towards them from somewhere behind the house. His leg was bandaged and he was limping. He saw the two women there on the ground and laughed as he limped over to them.

"The spoils of war," he said.

"I can't leave you alone here!" Katarina whispered to Sara. "What about Herr Tucher?"

"I'll be fine. This soldier is drunk," Sara said and sat up. "Follow them. Stay with Tanner and Pieter. I'll go find Herr Tucher."

The drunken soldier stood over Katarina and Sara. He bent down and grabbed a handful of Katarina's hair. She stood and waited for the right moment. He grabbed her hips, turned her around and drew her in close. He smelled like moldy leather and alcohol. Katarina tried to back away but he had a firm grip around her hips. He began to gather her skirt up. Katarina pulled the dagger out from the folds of her skirt and slit across his forehead, his eye and cheek. He gritted his teeth and cried out. As he swung to punch her, she ducked and slid out of his grip. Katarina slammed her bent knee into his bandaged thigh. He cursed and grabbed for her, but she was quicker.

Katarina ran to the heavy black horse that was chewing on the bush growing in the clay pot. She grabbed the reins, closed her eyes and took a deep breath. The horse pawed the ground and tossed his silky black mane. He grunted and pulled away from her, tight against the reins. She held on to them although her hands were already soaked with sweat. He circled Katarina in a threatening dance. Round and round he trotted and shook his head. Her heart boomed in her ears and with shaking legs, she backed up towards the potted bush, trying not to let go of the reins, even though that was all she wanted to do.

Katarina saw the soldier as he ran-limped towards her. He stopped to wipe blood out of his eyes. She pulled the reins in tight, backed up and stepped up onto the edge of the large pot, pulled the horse close and slid one foot into the stirrup. The horse jolted forward. Katarina fell onto the saddle on her stomach, looking over the other side of the horse. Her foot twisted in the stirrup.

She grabbed a fistful of the horse's mane and pulled back on the reins so he would stop moving. He pranced on the spot under her weight. He could feel Katarina's insecurity. Somehow, she swung her other leg over the saddle. The soldier staggered up to Katarina and grabbed a hold of the bridle. She kicked him square in the face and he retreated. Katarina wondered if she was going to pay for this later. She hoped Sara would get out of sight before the soldier got back to her.

Before Katarina could slide her foot into the other stirrup, the horse bolted forward towards the open gate. She closed her eyes. Tree branches whipped at her face. Pumping blood and wind wailed in her ears. She lowered her head down onto the horse's muscled neck and tried to maintain her grip as the precision pounding propelled them forward. The horse whinnied to his companions; his desperate attempt to find his herd. Katarina felt herself thunder out of the trees into an open space. She opened her eyes.

At quite a distance in front of her on the green fields of the flood plain, Katarina saw Ralf and Friedrich on horseback being chased by Tanner and Pieter on horseback. Friedrich's mounted guard followed close behind them. Soldiers chased on foot. The clouds over the valley hung now lower, dark and threatening. The flat, grassy field was fast and Katarina's horse closed the gap quicker than she wanted.

She hunched down low over the racing horse's neck and gripped tighter on the mane. She let the reins relax and he gained speed. She closed her eyes again. One foot still hung free. She didn't dare to look down and search for the stirrup only to see the earth speeding past. She was going to die.

Katarina remembered that Sara believed that Ralf may have the baby in his grasp. Was she to knock him from his horse? Was she to slash at him with her knife? This suddenly seemed so senseless, so hopeless. Katarina opened her eyes again and she was gaining on them. Tanner grappled at the reins of Ralf's horse. Pieter tried to control Friedrich's horse. Friedrich's mounted guard surrounded the whole scene. And Katarina was gaining on them. She pulled on the reins and tried to slow the horse down. He galloped to the rhythm of his breathing. She couldn't stop him. She pulled again but the horse huffed, spluttering like an overheating pot of water. He was heading for the other horses, for the other men. She couldn't stop him. They were going to collide.

Katarina's horse stopped and jumped to the side with a squeal. She continued flying in the direction she'd been traveling in. She hit the ground with an impact that forced the air out of her lungs with a grunt. She rolled and rolled and when she stopped she saw her horse, obviously a stallion, try to mount Friedrich's horse, a mare, with Friedrich still in the saddle. The stallion rammed his hooves into Friedrich's sides, trying to get a better grip. Ralf finally came to Friedrich's rescue and pulled the squealing, biting and whinnying stallion away.

Katarina lay back. Her head was pounding. She blinked her eyes. Ralf stood over her with a rope. He grasped both her wrists and slipped the rope around them and pulled tight. Katarina winced at the pain in her shoulder. He fastened the long rope to his dark bay's saddle.

"On your feet," he commanded.

Katarina stood. Tanner had his hands bound with a long rope that was fastened to one of the guards' saddle. His hair was rumpled, his clothing askew, but he was unhurt.

"Are you hurt?" Tanner whispered.

"Where's Pieter?" Katarina asked.

"Your Dutchman left you behind like the coward he is," Ralf said.

Friedrich snorted. He limped towards his horse. One of the soldiers on foot helped him mount his horse.

Four soldiers galloped up from the river towards them. Katarina looked past the river where they had come from and saw they were right across the road from Lonnerstadt. The men pulled their horses around and nodded to Friedrich.

"We've delivered the package, sir," a soldier with light-brown hair said.

"Thank you, Elis," Ralf said. "And I have these two in my custody. I think we should transport them immediately."

Chapter 41

Herr Tucher stood stiffly after the Archer undid the ropes that bound him to the chair. The Archer's arm bled profusely. Herr Tucher laid a bed sheet on Friedrich's desk and tore the fabric into strips. The Archer fumbled with the material.

"You would like some assistance, Archer?" Herr Tucher asked.

Herr Tucher finished the bandage, left the hall and walked out of the front doors. He gasped as he looked over the quiet scene of slaughter. Some soldiers lay shot with arrows. A woman tended an injured man. Smoke hung low over the yard. Tanner, Pieter and Katarina were gone. Tanner's wife peeped out from behind a large potted exotic tree and blotted the blood from her head with the hem of her skirt. Herr Tucher rushed over to her and helped her to her feet.

"They went after them," Sara said with gesticulating hands. "They aren't even armed. They can't possibly…"

"Where have the others gone?" Herr Tucher asked.

"They followed Ralf and those soldiers. Katarina, Tanner and Pieter." She hung her head. "On horseback."

"They're done for," Herr Tucher said.

"But Ralf has my baby!" Sara cried.

"Are you sure?" Herr Tucher said.

"He was carrying a small bundle."

"Why would they take the baby away from here?"

"To bury him alive, I'm afraid, like they wanted to do to your uncle."

"You have seen Paul?" Herr Tucher said.

"Shh…" she whispered.

"You have no need to be so quiet," Herr Tucher said. "I do not know where the rest of the soldiers are, but they are not here."

Herr Tucher led Sara towards the house. "Should we bandage your head?"

"Bjarne and Lasse led Paul out of the cellar," she said as they walked towards the house. "He is hurt quite badly, but he is in safety."

Once in the hall, Herr Tucher pointed to the chest of drawers and the now-empty cabinet. "That bundle was probably the documents Friedrich produced from that cabinet there. He doesn't have your baby."

Sara slumped onto the chair. "I sent Katarina on horseback for nothing."

The Archer played with his bandage, flinching. "We still need to find Isabeau. I would assume that the other child is with her, too."

"Then you must be Hans-Wolfgang," Herr Tucher said.

Hans-Wolfgang ignored the offer to introduce himself and walked over to the cabinet and inspected it. "I'll start upstairs."

Herr Tucher, Sara and Hans-Wolfgang walked into the entrance hall and climbed the stone stairwell. The walked down the hallway on the main upper floor to the wooden stairway that led to the garret rooms. There they searched from room to room, finding one mustier than the next. Mice scurried away as Herr Tucher opened one door. Finding nothing, they descended the steps to the main upper floor. Herr Tucher opened one room and found what must have been Friedrich's daughter's room.

"Dear Lord," Hans-Wolfgang said.

Hans-Wolfgang pushed Herr Tucher aside. The sight of the girl's effects caused Hans-Wolfgang obvious grief and pain. The room was well-tended and neat, like someone still dwelled here. Her clothes hung in the wardrobe and the bed was done up with clean linens.

Hans-Wolfgang sat on the edge of the bed, absorbed in lost memories. Herr Tucher backed out of the room and allowed him some privacy. He and Sara moved on to the next room.

"There's no one here," Sara said.

"Seemingly deserted," Herr Tucher said. "Maybe we can find that old *Magd*."

Herr Tucher and Sara walked back into Friedrich's meeting hall and looked out the windows. It was hard to make out shapes through the thick, glass panes but he could see a group of thugs lounging in the garden behind the house.

"Some sentinels they are," Herr Tucher said.

He laughed out loud as something amusing occurred to him.

"Come with me, Frau Tanner. I have a brilliant idea," Herr

Tucher said. "Now I need certain things to carry this out."

He grabbed her by the hand and led her into the large kitchen.

"Also deserted," he said and laughed again. "An open door. Let us have a look in the cellar. I am thirsty. Why, I have not eaten, either."

"Herr Tucher, this is not the time to…"

"Come, my dear, I have a plan!"

The two went down into the cellar and, as Herr Tucher had hoped, a few barrels stood about. He rocked one and another. They were full. The rest of the cellar was dark. He squinted around the dank space for ways out into the garden. He imagined he saw more than one opening from this large underground room.

"Let's see where these passages lead," he said. "I want to get into the garden."

"To the soldiers?" Sara said and looked at him as if he had gone mad.

"It's only common courtesy to pay a visit to our hosts."

They felt their way along the outermost wall. They tried one door then another. These doors led to even darker underground passages. Herr Tucher tried the third door and light flooded into the cellar. Men jeering and laughing echoed in the passage.

"What a bit of luck," he whispered. "This passage leads to the garden. Help me roll this barrel out the door, dear."

Herr Tucher and Sara rocked the barrel back and forth and walked it to the door. Once through the door, they laid the barrel on its side and rolled it through the passage and along the path away from the house. They came to an arched gateway in an overgrown hedge. In front of them, on a field of grass and wildflowers, a camp dotted the lawn.

Twenty or so round white tents formed a circle around a merry fire in the middle. Around the circle of tents, a circle of wooden wagons and carts stood parked. A few ragged women tended the fire; one woman stirred an iron pot hanging from the chain of an iron tripod. A small group of older men, workers and a few spare soldiers, sat by the fire drinking from large ceramic mugs. Puffs of smoke wafted from the pipes they smoked. The stone wall surrounded the whole property, Herr Tucher could now see, and beyond the wall, the forest.

"No need to sneak up on them," Herr Tucher said to Sara.

He turned his attention to the few stragglers, "Good day, my good men! Let us open a barrel of beer and salute our fallen comrades, our good luck and this glorious weather."

A few drops of rain fell from the overcast sky. The men looked at Herr Tucher as if *he* had fallen from the sky. But accept the barrel of beer they did in good haste, lest he change his mind. They swarmed towards Herr Tucher and Sara and rolled the barrel away like ants with a honeycomb, hoisting the spoils of the day.

"Let us get another one," Herr Tucher said.

They returned and brought out another barrel in the same manner.

"You would be wise to disappear, I believe, once these men have started their serious drinking," Herr Tucher said. "The same applies for me, actually. Help me roll out a third barrel."

After the delivery, they went back inside the cellar, shut the door and barricaded it with an old wardrobe standing along the wall. Glass clinked as they moved the wardrobe inch for inch. Once it stood in place in front of the door, Herr Tucher stuck his hand inside.

"Wine, I hope. Let us have a look at these bottles in the light."

Herr Tucher grabbed two bottles, found two mugs in the kitchen and they climbed the steps to Friedrich's hall. He sat behind Friedrich's desk in his chair and Sara took a seat on the other side.

"Would you like a drink?" Herr Tucher said, pouring the two mugs full.

She emptied the mug in one gulp.

"Long day, hmm?"

"Is this really such a good idea? I mean, to give those soldiers so much drink?" she said.

"I hope so. I am relying on their indifference. And their lack of loyalty. They will have no desire to do anything this day."

Hans-Wolfgang waved to Herr Tucher from the doorway. "Come with me."

Herr Tucher and Sara followed him out but he had disappeared. The two stood outside the front doors and listened to the soldiers' voices rise and fall, carried on the breeze. Here in front of the house, the air was unnaturally still. The dead lay here still; the soldiers would only bury their comrades if someone commanded them to work.

Herr Tucher felt a strange detachment from the whole battle scene, as though he was watching an outdoor theater. It may have been the wine, but a drowsy sort of calm bathed him as they stood in the overcast afternoon light.

Hans-Wolfgang emerged from behind the house. Sweating, he stuck arrows back into his quiver.

"The ruins of my house are still being watched," Hans-Wolfgang said. "I can't get near the place."

"Have you found the children?" Sara asked.

"If it was struck by lightning last year, where have you been living?" Herr Tucher asked.

"Where? Nowhere. Everywhere. Do you care?" An angry growl pressed through his lips. Hans-Wolfgang's blue eyes were so hard for a man so young.

But Herr Tucher felt as if he had seen those eyes before. The curve of his mouth when he smiled. Had he not heard that angry growl somewhere before, too? Yes, of course. He was Isabeau's father.

"That was no lightning," Hans-Wolfgang said. "After Ralf killed my Andra, he and his men burnt the place down during the night. My father and I got out in time."

He handed Herr Tucher a crossbow. "I have searched the grounds and found no sign of the children. Just some stray arrows. And this crossbow."

"Say, Hans-Wolfgang, you said your house is still being guarded."

"Yes, I did, but…"

"Even though these spare soldiers are here in the garden with three barrels of beer?"

"Yes, but…"

"Come and we will have a look," Herr Tucher said. "Your house, is it there through the trees?"

"What is it, Herr Tucher?" Sara whispered. "Do you think they have the children there?"

Hans-Wolfgang shot up and ran towards the trees. He pulled an arrow out of his quiver. The crossbow was useless without bolts so Herr Tucher laid it back down on the front steps and joined Hans-Wolfgang.

"How many men are there?" Herr Tucher asked.

"I only saw three," Hans-Wolfgang said.

Hans-Wolfgang climbed through dense underbrush, towards a

high hedge, a monument to the years the families had feuded. Herr Tucher and Sara followed him. One could barely make out the ruins on the other side of the green fence.

Hans-Wolfgang whispered to them, "Duck down and crawl through this tunnel I made in the hedge."

Herr Tucher and Sara followed his lead and stayed undercover. From the edge of the hedge, Herr Tucher saw two men dressed like those black-clad thugs, sitting on tree stumps next to charred ruins of the house. Hans-Wolfgang sneaked around a stone foundation littered with burnt wooden beams and covered with weeds that was once a barn. The two soldiers took no notice of him. Hans-Wolfgang positioned himself behind a mighty oak at the edge of the deserted, destroyed property.

No sound came from the bow as Hans-Wolfgang drew it. The arrow flew with a faint whizzing. One soldier crumpled and fell behind his tree stump. The second looked dumbfounded at his fallen comrade. Another faint whizzing. He, too, fell, joining his comrade on the ground.

It was too simple. A third soldier came into view and Hans-Wolfgang shot him, too.

"Why, you could have easily done this before…" Herr Tucher whispered.

Hans-Wolfgang was on his feet, running towards the burnt-out house. Sara and Herr Tucher both waited until he waved them forward. They proceeded cautiously. Hans-Wolfgang practiced no restraint. He threw open the door to what was left of the ruined house and they followed him inside. The sitting room was intact, but unsteady beams creaked overhead in the breeze. Through the doorway at the end of the room Herr Tucher could see that the whole back side of the structure, where he assumed the kitchen had been, was destroyed. The light of the grey sky flickered through the burnt roof among charred beams. His eyes filled with tears from the sooty smell.

Hans-Wolfgang pulled on a trap door in the floor that led to a cellar. He leaned the man-sized trap back, fastened it to an iron latch on the wall for this purpose and descended into the gaping hole. They stood at the top of the steps and peered in. There sat the old *Magd* with the children on her lap.

"He knew this all along," Herr Tucher said, voicing his fears quietly to Sara.

"Here is your son," Hans-Wolfgang said, holding out the unharmed baby Albin to Sara.

She ran down the steps into the cellar, took the baby from Hans-Wolfgang and embraced the child.

"Come here and collect Isabeau," he said to Herr Tucher.

The hair stood up on the back of Herr Tucher's neck as he went down into the dank, earthen-smelling hole. He picked up Isabeau and she tightened her body against his grasp. She squirmed and started to cry. Herr Tucher gave her promptly to the old *Magd*.

"*Nein…*" Isabeau said.

Hans-Wolfgang climbed back out of the cellar. He unlatched the iron hook and lowered the trap door.

"Now stay here," he said. "I have some business to settle. I'm sorry to lock you in but I need to know where Isabeau is. That you are looking after her. I'll send someone."

"If you live to tell, my friend," Herr Tucher said.

Hans-Wolfgang threw the trap door back and it slammed against the wall. He sprang back into the cellar and struck Herr Tucher in the middle of his chest with his fist. Herr Tucher fell to his knees and could not breathe. He was going to lose consciousness. Isabeau cried. Tanner's wife came to his side.

"Of course I'll live to tell," Hans-Wolfgang said. "Now stay here!"

"What have you done?" Sara said.

"Now I know where you are and I know where my child is," Hans-Wolfgang said. "No one will stop me avenging Andra-Angela!"

"We won't try to stop you!" Sara said. "Let us go! We will leave this God-forsaken place!"

"Not until I am sure that my daughter is no longer in danger. Please, just do as I say!"

Hans-Wolfgang ran out of the cellar and slammed the trap door.

Chapter 42

Katarina stumbled and fell, the rope that tied her arms to Ralf's horse pulled taut. This caused Ralf's horse to stop and as she struggled to her feet, Ralf heeled the stallion's flanks. The stallion jolted forward and lurched Katarina into a double-step to keep up.

Four soldiers rode though the flood plain at the head of the group. The guard's horse that pulled the bound Tanner was directly behind them. Friedrich's horse was close to Katarina's heels, his snorts similar in pitch to Friedrich's labored breathing.

They reached the path to the Upper Eierhofen estate and marched up the hill. At the open gate in the stone wall, Ralf's horse protested and pranced. Ralf slammed the horse's flanks with his heels and the horse bolted through. Katarina lost her footing and fell on her face. The horse dragged her a short distance. Tanner bent over her and tried to help her up. He was still tied to the guard's horse, now tethered to the barn wall.

"Let her lay," Ralf said. "She gets only what she deserves."

Ralf dismounted, tethered his horse to the barn wall next to the guard's and left Katarina there, still tied to the saddle. He spoke in low tones with Friedrich, as if they pondered what to do with their prisoners. Elis joined the two men. Ralf shook his head, raised his eyes and scrutinized Katarina with so much loathing that it pierced her heart. How could anyone in the service of God possess that amount of hatred?

The evening deepened. Friedrich and Ralf seemed to disagree over the course they were to take. Their voices became louder. Elis checked the rope that still tied Tanner to the guard's horse.

"We keep them tied," Ralf said. "Lock them away in the cart tonight until we ride to Bamberg."

Friedrich shook his head. "I think we could let the men have the woman for the night. I am behind on their pay."

"The soldiers will only kill her," Ralf said.

"Where are those blasted men?" Friedrich said.

Shouts echoed from behind the house in the garden. Reports of gaiety, reveling, happy drunken laughter.

"Elis, assemble the men!" Ralf said. "No more discussion. I want to leave immediately for Bamberg. If they tarry they will not be paid at all! I will have every last drunken head if they cannot assemble!"

Elis ran towards the garden and returned, followed by a handful of young men. "I am sorry Padre, I have only the boys here."

"My Soldiers of God," Ralf said. "You boys will serve the Jesuits well. Come with me. We will see how quickly I can sober these men up."

Ralf raised his fist and led the boys like he was embarking on some Holy War. Katarina felt a tugging on her rope.

"Be quiet. We can get away now," Hans-Wolfgang whispered in her ear. "Hurry, they'll return with the whole troop. I will take you to Isabeau."

Pieter appeared behind Tanner. He untied Tanner's rope from the horse and drew a knife to cut the binds from his wrists.

"And my wife?" Tanner asked.

From behind the barn, a group of soldiers overwhelmed Pieter. They took the knife from his hand and restrained his arms. More soldiers crept up behind Pieter and Tanner and swallowed them in their throng.

"Alarm!" Elis cried.

Five men attacked Hans-Wolfgang. They closed down on him like a swarm of bees in order to subdue him. More soldiers surrounded Katarina like black ants on an intruder. She smelled an overwhelming stench of alcohol, smoke and onions. She thought she would suffocate.

Katarina's long rope had been freed from the horse, but her hands were still tied. Strong hands now lifted her, other hands brutally subdued her limbs, her injured shoulder burning from the wrenching, masculine grip. Odd words whispered in her ear and she pressed her eyes together, willing herself not to look into the face of the abductors. But she needed to know where the others were going. She opened her eyes and saw a chaos of flailing arms, kicking legs and black uniforms. She wet herself and everything went dark.

Katarina heard Pieter whisper. Tanner whispered something, too. She opened her eyes. It was dark and chilly and felt like the middle of the night. Katarina, Pieter, Tanner and Hans-Wolfgang sat at the base of the stone wall next to the closed cart, back to back to back with their hands tied together.

Torches fixed to the stone wall partially lit the dark yard. The horses had been unhitched from the cart used for transporting sheep. Hans-Wolfgang whispered that the number of soldiers was hard to estimate and that they were going to be transported in this cart to Bamberg in the morning. Soldiers stood guard over them, at the gate and at the front door. Tanner asked if Herr Tucher and Sara were safe and wanted to know where they were.

Katarina's arms were cramping and she had no feeling in her hands. She sat with her legs stretched out in front of her and her back hurt. She felt beaten up, swollen in places and had no recollection of how they came to be here. She was hungry and her mouth was parched. Her skirt was wet and dirty.

Their whispering lulled her into a sort of trance. When she came to her senses again, it was the first light of the new day. She doubted that she could stand up. She was numb and cold, hungry and drained. A hint of that May frost was in the air and a gray mist hung about the property. Unseen crows calling in the back garden sent a chill through Katarina's bones.

Friedrich and Ralf came out of the house. They looked fresh and rejuvenated, clean and wholesome, sharing a conversation they had probably started over a hearty breakfast. They laughed, men preparing for a pleasant excursion. Two farmhands dressed in coarse brown breeches and leather jerkins over simple white shirts led Ralf and Friedrich's saddled horses from the barn and tied them to a post in front of the house.

Katarina, Tanner, Pieter and Hans-Wolfgang were forced to stand, the ropes around their feet cut, but their hands left tied. Katarina's legs wobbled as they stood next to the closed cart. She faintly remembered why she was here. The children. Herr Tucher. They were safe but what was going to become of her? She had heard tales of the Bamberg bishop's methods of inquisition, the brutal *peinliche Befragung*, known for leaving few survivors.

She looked at the other's faces. Pieter's face was resigned, shrouded and dark. Tanner's was tired, drawn and pale but a spark flickered in his eyes. Hans-Wolfgang's face was fuming and red, his eyes angry. If anyone was going to take command here, it would be him.

The two farmhands came out of the barn leading the two horses to the closed cart. The soldier named Elis and a coachman dressed in black helped the farmhands hitch the horses to the cart. Chains clanked, the horses snorted, leather straps snapped. A hoof pawed the earth. A crow cawed. Katarina was loaded first into the cart; Pieter behind her. She pressed herself to his warm body. His cheeks were cold. He looked away from her. Two soldiers prodded Tanner into the cart. He was contemplating a fight, but thought better of it with hands tied.

Hans-Wolfgang fought like a madman. He kicked and screamed. He bit Elis in the neck and Elis slammed his head with a closed fist, a blow that would have rendered another man incapacitated. Hans-Wolfgang sprang to his feet and Elis kicked him in the stomach, sending him into the cart with a thud on top of the others. The cart rocked with fury as Hans-Wolfgang kicked in rage against the cart's now-locked gate.

Rain began to fall. Light, misty pearls beaded on the horses' manes. Katarina shivered against the gentle, cold breeze. Her teeth chattered. Crows cawed, an unearthly, terrifying tone. A man called back in the garden, a hollow, blunt sound in the fog. Another voice called and a woman screamed. Men shouted. Friedrich nodded to Ralf and he sprinted behind the house. Elis and his soldiers followed. Friedrich's plump body moved towards their cart on those spindly legs and he inspected the harnessing and exchanged quiet words with the coachman. He straightened and watched the spot where Ralf had disappeared behind the house. The shouts stopped but Ralf did not return.

Friedrich motioned for the coachman to step down from the coach box and gave him some quiet instructions. The coachman stood next to the team and Katarina watched Friedrich disappear behind the house. Hans-Wolfgang sat still but Katarina expected him to burst the cage with his latent energy.

Two men in black swirled out of the mist, their faces concealed behind black scarves. One man assailed the coachman and threw him to the side. The coachman fell lifeless, stunned and unconscious. The two jumped onto the coach box and cracked the whip. The horses leapt into motion, hooves clattering on the pounded earth, and the cart jerked, throwing the four prisoners on top of each other. Pieter struggled to regain his balance but slammed into Katarina every time the cart hitched forward.

"No one controls my fate except me," Hans-Wolfgang growled. "I will not be led to some destination that I have not chosen."

The cart creaked and rocked as they slowly descended the path from Eierhofen through the trees. Flat, stringy fog wound its way between the trees. Katarina could hear shouting above at the Eierhofen estate.

The cart moved out of the trees onto the flat flood plain. They picked up speed. Hans-Wolfgang let out a growl and kicked at the back gate that enclosed them in this cage. It sounded like crunching bones as the wooden rods splintered. He kicked and kicked until all the wooden rods gave way.

Hans-Wolfgang looked back at the others with a triumphant smile and braced his bound hands on the edge of the cart. He jumped from the now speeding cart, rolled, regained his footing and ran back towards the forest, towards the sorrel horse that stood among the trees. Katarina saw that woman in white greet him, cut his bonds and hand him the reins. Hans-Wolf jumped onto the horse and was swallowed up by the fog and the trees. The woman in white disappeared behind him.

The cart sped across the flood plain and slowed as they approached the river. The coachman pulled the team to a halt next to a concealed patch of reeds. He jumped from the coach box and peered through the wooden rods.

"Hello, my son," the man said, pulling the scarf from his face.

Tanner the Elder smiled at them.

Chapter 43

Herr Tucher sat up. "How long have we been here?"

Sara sat on the earthen floor of the cellar in the burnt-out house at Lower Eierhofen like a tailor and tried to nurse her baby. Albin fretted and whined. A dusty stream of light forced its way between the cracks in the trap door. It must have been morning.

"The one night," Sara said and righted her chemise and blouse.

He tried to get onto his knees. "Is there anything in this cellar? Tools, food, drink?"

"I haven't been able to look," she said. "It is just now getting light."

As he stood, he held fast on the wall as his knees buckled. His head was full and foggy. He stood straight, the cellar high enough for him to do so, shook his shoulders and rubbed his chest. Hans-Wolfgang must have struck a sensitive nerve under his breast bone. The man was brilliant. Herr Tucher would remember that the next time he got in a fight. The blow had winded and lamed him but left him unhurt.

Planks of wood lay strewn all over the cellar floor. Herr Tucher threw the planks aside, any action better than sitting inert. A burlap sack that smelled of rodent stuck to the earthen floor as he tried to pull it up. Underneath, he found a small wooden trunk with an iron latch. He opened it and pulled out a few slivers of dried meat. He bit into one piece and it was terribly salty, unfortunate because they had nothing to drink, but he ate it nonetheless. He handed a piece to Sara, who took it gratefully.

The earth appeared to have been swept along the opposite wall of the cellar. Perhaps Hans-Wolfgang had slept here on occasion? Herr Tucher pulled some planks aside and stacked them neatly along the wall. Amid a pile of soiled fabrics lay what looked like a broom handle, only much more solid. He whistled through his teeth when he pulled on the wooden handle and a heavy hammer appeared.

"Could be useful," Herr Tucher said.

With leaden arms, he stood under the trap door and tried to swing the damn thing upwards. Sara handed the baby to the old *Magd* and came to his side.

"Four hands are better than two," she said.

They held the hammer together, bent their knees and thrust the hammer upwards. The planks of the trap door were old and well-seasoned. But they looked like spruce, not solid oak. They heaved again. He felt dizzy and light-headed. But even if it drained his last dram of strength, he wanted to get them out of here. Together they hammered against the hinges, again and again and finally the iron nails holding the hinges loosened. The wood splintered and the nails fell.

Herr Tucher clambered up the steps and braced his hands on the heavy trap door. Kneeling down, he slowly stood, the door rising as he did so, and secured it to the wall. Sara handed Isabeau up. Herr Tucher set her aside and Sara handed up the baby Albin. Herr Tucher laid him on the floor and pulled Sara up the steps. He clapped his hands to get the *Magd's* attention to follow suit.

Slowly the woman looked up at the two of them. Herr Tucher jumped back down into the cellar and pulled on her arms. Her skin was clammy cold. She opened her mouth but no sound came out. She seemed to be heavily sedated. Herr Tucher had no time to argue with the woman. She was free to go, no longer trapped and would have to climb the steps herself.

Herr Tucher and Sara grabbed the children.

"First of all, we get out from this collapsing house," Herr Tucher said.

Fog meandered in the trees surrounding the Lower Eierhofen estate but had burned off where the sun shone. The shady areas of the yard were still chilly and wet from rain, but it was promising to be a fine day.

"I hear nothing of the skirmish at the other estate," Herr Tucher said. "It is my responsibility to go back and find out how they fare. May I leave you?"

Sara nodded. "I found this dirty swatch of cloth in the cellar and can tie my baby to my front like Katarina does. And Isabeau can walk. It may take me all morning, but I'd prefer to go back to Sichardtshof."

"Alone?"

"I don't want to stay here. I'd rather be moving. I'll go through the fields and stay off the road."

Herr Tucher nodded agreement. Sara busied herself with tying the baby to her front. He turned towards the tunnel in the high hedge that they had crawled through yesterday afternoon. He knelt and the cold, moist earth soaked his knees. He scrambled on a short way when a shot rang out. A man shouted. Two men fell against the hedge, engaged in a struggle. Branches splintered as a black-clad man flew right into the bushes, not far from his right shoulder. Another shot rang out and branches splintered, this time directly over his head. He lay on his stomach, inched towards the opening and peered into Friedrich's yard.

There was a tumult, a chaos of screaming and shouting. Smoke from the muskets hung in the air and the smell of gunpowder filled his nostrils. Herr Tucher could not imagine how many soldiers were scurrying about. The black-clad soldiers in Friedrich's employ brandished swords. Other brown-clad soldiers wearing metal breastplates countered. Wood splittered. Horses hollered.

Herr Tucher recognized the brown uniforms and those metal breastplates. Those were his Uncle Paul's men.

Chapter 44

Katarina flinched with each shot she heard. Knecht, who had been on the coach box with Tanner the Elder, cut the ropes that bound her wrists. She walked around the cart and rubbed her hands. She needed to stand, to move her legs and relieve the cramping. The wine that Tanner the Elder had given her was sweet and helped relax her aching limbs.

The air was warming and the fog was lifting. From their standpoint in the floodplain, where the coach had come to a stop, she could hear shots and hollering from the distant battle at Upper Eierhofen.

"Don't worry about those shots, *Mädel*," he said. "They sound frightening, but they only shoot once. The man has to reload. Plus, they are very inaccurate. It takes too long when you're doing battle. But a sword is always the best for a close confrontation."

Katarina grabbed the extra baldric and sword from the coach box.

"You are not going back up there," Pieter said to Katarina. "Put that thing down. Can you even use a sword?"

Pieter strapped his baldric over his shoulder and took the sword from Tanner the Elder. "Stay here with the horses and Knecht. I'll find Sara and the children."

He and Tanner the Elder started up the path. He hollered back to Katarina, "I'll be right back."

Knecht removed his hat, mopped his brow and set the hat further back on his head. He had an eye patch over the empty eye socket.

"Let the men take care of their silly fights," Knecht said. "Paul's men have been itching to fight. This is just a bit of training for them."

Katarina walked further into the flood plain. The sun warmed her back. In the distant field she thought she saw a figure. She rubbed her eyes. Was it a deer? No, it was moving on two legs and at a brisk pace. That was a woman.

Katarina forgot her stiff, aching joints and her injuries and ran full-out through the knee-high grass towards the woman. Knecht yelled to Katarina and she ignored him. Her lungs burned, her legs cramped and she slowed to a walk, caught her breath and started to jog again. The woman saw Katarina and ran towards her. It was Sara! Katarina doubled over and wheezed a welcome, supporting her upper body with her hands on her knees. She panted and looked up at Sara and smiled—a genuine, joyful smile. Katarina straightened and they embraced, the two being careful not to crush the baby bound to Sara's breast. Tears streamed down Katarina's face. They hugged silently for a moment. Shots sounded amid the trees.

"I told Herr Tucher I would go back to the farm," Sara said. "I wanted to take the children away from all of this..." She tried to finish her sentence through bubbling tears, but choked on the words. "He came. After Herr Tucher left me to join the others. He took her with him. Isabeau. He took her away from me."

"Who took her?"

"Hans-Wolfgang. I don't know what to think of him anymore."

"I have an idea," Katarina said. "Take your son home. I can move freely if I want to. I'm going back up there. I can retrace your steps. You came from that field over there?"

"Yes, and the path is clearly visible when you go back this way." Sara pointed to the position where Katarina had first spotted her.

They embraced once more and Katarina ran on in the direction she had pointed her in. This was the path she had come down last fall in the rain. She knew exactly where she would come out. She ran up the slope. Through the trees she could smell the charred ruins of Lower Eierhofen. Slowly Katarina walked into the abandoned yard and searched the ruins of Hans-Wolfgang's house and the trees behind the old barn's overgrown foundation.

She ran towards the house and hid behind the intact wall. From the Upper Eierhofen estate, she heard the men shouting and metal clanking, but the trees and the menacing quiet here on this desolate property muffled the sound.

Quiet voices echoed close by; an oath followed by a grunt, a shout. The clank of metal on metal. Men argued inside Hans-Wolfgang's collapsing house. Katarina peered around the open doorway. Hans-Wolfgang and Friedrich stood face to face, in a vehement discussion, swords drawn and pointed to each other's chest. They stood on an old wooden trap door and from beneath their feet came a baby's cries. Katarina stood in horror and watched the two men. Not only was she unarmed and disturbing a very heated argument, but Isabeau was trapped!

"Get out of here, Katarina. I will settle this my way," Hans-Wolfgang said.

"There is nothing to settle," Friedrich said. "I will kill you and take my granddaughter out of this wreck."

"Where's that parcel? Where are the documents? The locked cabinet was empty."

"I will kill you and throw your stinking remains to the wolves," Friedrich said.

Friedrich advanced on Hans-Wolfgang, his body clumsy and top heavy, as if those spindly legs would at any moment give way. Hans-Wolfgang, only half Friedrich's size but agile and young, pushed Friedrich away and jabbed straight towards that massive belly. Friedrich turned to the side and Hans-Wolfgang spun around, his sword barely missing Friedrich's face.

Katarina moved into the room and they took no notice of her. She inched along the outer wall towards the trap door. Their swords slashed and met in midair, the metallic scraping making Katarina cringe. Hans-Wolfgang stabbed again at Friedrich's unprotected middle. He gasped, tried to swipe at Hans-Wolfgang and teetered on the spot. A deathly, dark-red stain grew on Friedrich's ornate doublet. Isabeau cried on under the trap door. Katarina inched closer to the door and spotted the latch. She could try to pull the door open. The men scuffled around the room. The scorched beams and the charred floorboards overhead creaked and rubbed against each other as if the fight further disturbed their instability.

The two men were in a clinch in the small doorway. Katarina could imagine Hans-Wolfgang's father coming home, taking off his boots and presenting his mother with some small game that he had brought home for their evening meal. She wondered if there ever was a peaceful time like that in this house. Rage boiled up inside of her. She cursed all this senseless feuding and fighting. She wanted no part of these stupid fights. She was going to get Isabeau and get out of here.

"Where's the parcel?" Hans-Wolfgang gasped.

"You will never find that, you thief," Friedrich said. "All you were after was our gold and property!"

Friedrich disarmed Hans-Wolfgang with a lucky counter. Hans-Wolfgang rammed Friedrich unexpectedly with his head and Friedrich dropped his sword. Friedrich slapped at Hans-Wolfgang and Hans-Wolfgang punched him straight in the face. Blood streamed out of Friedrich's nose. Hans-Wolfgang jumped on him and they rolled over a burnt settee and onto the floor. The baby's cries peaked and raged under that wooden door.

Katarina took her chance. She ran to the trap door and heaved with every last bit of strength. The door was not attached to any hinges but it was so heavy it hardly budged. She pulled and pulled until the momentum of her forceful movements raised the massive door. She leaned it on the wall. A glance over her shoulder reassured her that the men paid her no regard.

"Kata!" Isabeau said.

Isabeau was alone in the earthen floored cellar littered with wood and fabric. She held both arms out to Katarina and her mouth formed silent sounds. Katarina motioned for her to stay quiet. She wailed. Katarina looked back at Hans-Wolfgang who fixed her with a burning stare. Katarina jumped down the steps in one motion, grabbed the child and ran back up the steps. Hans-Wolfgang blocked her way.

"Stand against the wall," he said and held his sword to Katarina's chest.

She backed up against the wobbly stone wall. Friedrich lay motionless on the floor behind the settee.

"Stand right there and don't move. I'll kill you if you do."

"Kata. Kata. Kata," Isabeau whispered.

Isabeau's eyes were red rimmed and she sniveled. She stroked Katarina's face with her finger, her sharp fingernail cutting the side of Katarina's nose.

Hans-Wolfgang dragged Friedrich's lifeless body around the settee, towards the cellar. He laid him at the top of the steps and gave him a push with his foot. Friedrich rolled down the steps.

"Oh, he is alive," Hans-Wolfgang said. "I'm not killing him. You are my witness."

He easily lifted the battered trap door. The clanking hinges hung like some creature had pounded its way out. With a great emission of breath, Hans-Wolfgang let the trap door fall. It slammed over the cellar hole with a whirl of smoky dust. Hans-Wolfgang politely motioned for Katarina to walk ahead of him and leave the house.

They walked out into the fresh air. Katarina breathed deeply and hugged the child close. Hans-Wolfgang stood for a minute and looked at the two of them.

He smiled, devilish and pleased. "Hello, Isabeau. You are going home. Just one more thing to settle and then you may go."

With a running start, he slammed his body against the walls of the unsteady, burnt-out house. A few sandstone blocks swayed and wobbled from the impact. Again and again he threw himself against the structure until the topmost blocks toppled. He growled with every impact until he hit the central supporting point of the house. Blocks broke and stones tumbled. Beams and floor boards all came crashing down into a pile of rubble. A dusty, moldy cloud rose from the wreckage and filled Katarina's mouth and nose with a bitter taste.

"Buried alive, the old pig. I may let him out if I don't find that parcel."

He stood in front of Katarina, feet spread in a fighter's stance, drawn up to his full height. Dirty sweat glistened on his cheeks. His shoulders were bleeding, his leather tunic was full of blood and dust and mud. He smelled worse than she could describe. He stroked Isabeau's cheek carefully with his grimy finger.

"Take her home. Get out of this place. The score will be settled."

"Was this whole fight over gold?"

He snorted. "Among other things, that parcel probably holds the documents for all of Herr Tucher's petitioned lands and both of the Eierhofen estates. Eierhofen shall be Isabeau's property. Not Ralf's. Not the church's. I will see to that! I did this for her."

Hans-Wolfgang left Katarina standing there, turned and ran towards the high hedge separating them from the still-raging battle at Upper Eierhofen. He bent down, got on his knees and crawled into the bushes.

Chapter 45

Katarina awoke with a start and tried to loosen the choking grip Isabeau had around her throat. In the half-light, she could see that it was still very early. She took a deep breath and savored the smells of the little alcove next to the kitchen at Sichardtshof: a hint of mold, animal, and peppermint. And that unmistakable scent of Pieter.

Sara stood in the doorway of the little alcove. "I haven't slept all night."

Isabeau's grip tightened around Katarina's throat again. She stroked Isabeau's fine hair and tried to coax the child to relax.

"Come, Isabeau, everything is fine now." Katarina stood and Isabeau still hung from her neck.

Katarina pulled her close and hugged her. "You're choking me."

Isabeau's world had been shaken. She had a permanent look of shock on her face. Katarina walked into the kitchen still trying to soothe the child.

Sara poked around in the embers in the fire. She had changed into a clean white shirt and a clean-but-torn brown skirt. Her dark-blonde hair was hanging loose around her shoulders and she wore no cap. Katarina had never seen her hair this disheveled. She'd never seen Sara this out of sorts.

"They aren't back yet!" Sara said, her voice an unnaturally high pitch.

Sara's fear was infectious. Katarina had believed the men would return. Now she was not so sure.

"Should we go back up there?" Katarina said and poured some tea. "Where are Lasse and Bjarne?"

"Oh, they're here, brilliant young men they are. Lasse told me that after they brought Paul back, well, Bjarne rode like the wind to Nuremberg and summoned Paul's men."

"Paul's alive?"

"Yes, but badly hurt. He fades in and out. His wounds are

287

infected. Anna has been caring for him."

Anna walked through the door from the paddock carrying a skinned lamb.

"Make enough food for everyone," Sara said and sniffed.

Sara and Katarina worked silently at the table. Katarina peeled an onion, chopped it up and began peeling a second one. Anna carried two buckets of water in from outside and put the largest pot over the fire. She filled the pot with water. Sara cut the meat from the bones, cut the bones apart and put them in another pot of water over the fire. She sniffed and Katarina saw tears running down her face.

"Anna, help me bring a barrel of beer up out of the cellar," Sara said. "They're going to be thirsty."

Anna looked at Sara as if to pity her. "What if they don't come back?"

Sara grabbed Anna as if to strike her.

"Go on, Anna. I'll finish up here," Katarina said, standing in between the two women and shoving Anna away.

Katarina turned to Sara and took her in her arms. "Should we go back up there?"

"Who will watch the children?" Sara said. "Anna? And what if we don't come back?"

The savory smell of the lamb stew made Katarina's mouth water. Anna carried the wooden barrel into the kitchen, stood it on the wooden working top and hammered the tap into it.

"Anna, fetch another barrel." Again Sara's voice took on that unnaturally high pitch. She shook with the effort of controlling herself. "I hope we have enough mugs for everyone."

Anna and Katarina gathered some wooden bowls together, a big bowl of lamb stew and a pitcher of beer each and took their things outside. They set their things down on the table.

"Lasse put the table back together for me this morning," Anna said.

They sat down on the one bench that was still whole. The few children playing down by the ponds came running and joined the women.

The midday sun warmed Katarina's back. Sara fed her baby bits of meat from the stew and he opened and closed his mouth dubiously, not knowing what to do with the solid food crossing his lips.

Sara spoke softly to her boy. "That's why I named you Albin. That was Tanner the Elder's name. He was such a good man. Is a good man."

Katarina sipped at her beer and suddenly stood when a flock of ducks flew up from the ponds. She looked down the track for a tell-tale billowing of dust that would precede someone's—anyone's—arrival. She sat back down. Sara set down her spoon and fixed Katarina with a serious stare.

She spoke, her voice barely a whisper. "What are we going to do if they don't come back?"

Down the road, one man on horseback rode at a trot. A sorrel stallion ridden by a man the color of the forest. Katarina and Sara ran to the gate. It was Hans-Wolfgang. He steered the horse into the yard and in front of them. He remained atop the horse and pulled the reins in tight. The horse tossed its head.

"I've come to collect you and the child, Katarina," Hans-Wolfgang said. "You will come and live with me at the Eierhofen estate.

"Are they alive?" Sara said. "Where are they?"

"I am taking Isabeau to legally register as my child," he continued. "Since Friedrich is gone, she is entitled to his land. Give her to me so I can do this."

Sara grabbed the horse's bridle, her eyes bulging, the veins in her neck throbbing. "Tell me where my husband is! Are the others alive?"

Faint swirls of dust curled up from beyond the bend on the main track. Faint swirls became billowing clouds. A man whistled to a horse. A wagon came into view as it rounded the bend. Wagon wheels creaked and a man's voice drove the two heavy brown horses forward.

"There are your men," Hans-Wolfgang said. "They are for the most part unhurt."

The wagon driven by Tanner the Elder trundled into the yard. Tanner jumped down, ran to his wife and held her long. He kissed her and stroked baby Albin's cheek. Herr Tucher alighted from the back of the cart. His white shirt was filthy and his one arm was covered in blood. He limped over to Katarina. Pieter followed him. His once-white shirt was the same muddy brown as his pants. Hans-Wolfgang dismounted and rounded on the two men. Herr Tucher stood with his feet apart and his chest thrust out.

"Where's Ralf?" Hans-Wolfgang demanded.

"He left on horseback before you came back to the fight," Pieter said. "He and his Soldiers of God."

"Coward," he said.

"Friedrich is also missing," Herr Tucher said.

"So he is," Hans-Wolfgang said. "I will go tomorrow and register my daughter's birth. The granddaughter of The Influential Friedrich von Obereierhofen. And we will take residence in the house that will belong to Isabeau. Katarina will come live with me and take care of my child."

Herr Tucher glanced over at Katarina. "She should decide where she wants to go."

Hans-Wolfgang grabbed a pitcher of beer from the table. He raised the pitcher and drained it in one gulp. He handed the empty pitcher to Herr Tucher.

"Are you challenging me to a duel?" Herr Tucher laughed.

"That may very well be what I will do. I am off to search for the parcel with the documents. I will keep Friedrich alive long enough until I retrieve them."

"My documents are among them," Herr Tucher said and seemed to regret the words as they came out.

"I'll have something you want, and you have something I want. We won't have to duel at all. It will be a fair trade."

"No more trades!" Katarina yelled. "I will decide where I live and where I go!"

"This is not yet settled," Hans-Wolfgang said.

He mounted his horse in one leap and rode out of the yard. Tanner the Elder pulled a shrouded body from the cart and Pieter came to his side. Together they carried the dead man back behind the barn.

Herr Tucher limped to Katarina's side. "Knecht was a good man. I regret losing him terribly."

"I'm sorry," Katarina said.

Herr Tucher stroked Isabeau's cheek. "See what kind of commotion you have caused? You will never remember any of this, thank God."

He walked to the table and sat on the bench. Katarina sat down beside him. He picked up another pitcher of beer, inspected the contents and drank from it.

"Hans-Wolfgang *is* mad," he said. "He fought like a dervish, full of energy. In the end, the men just got out of his way. He engaged with those dark foreign-looking soldiers, one after the next. Hans-Wolfgang easily laid them out. Some were twice his size."

He drank and continued talking, reliving the day before.

"Some men had fallen. Some injured soldiers had crawled out of sight. Other soldiers had given up and were retreating. Some were leaving the grounds with packs. Whispers of Friedrich's disappearance spread like the plague between the men. I sat by the garden wall next to Pieter and clasped a rag to the slit in my arm. Tanner sat next to me. Tanner the Elder sat next to him. Before us, lay the body of my Knecht we had pulled out from the fighting mongrels."

He stopped, took Katarina's face in his hand and studied the bruises on her cheeks. "How badly are you hurt?"

"Nothing broken. This will heal." she said.

"A relief." He took a long draught of beer and let out a heavy sigh. "Even Hans-Wolfgang ran out of steam as the night closed in. No one wanted to fight him anymore, even though he was trying to provoke them. My uncle's men tried to reason with him. He finally gave in and stopped. He brought us all food and beer. We spent the night burying the dead."

"Your uncle is here, he is hurt," Katarina said. "Anna has tended his wounds."

He nodded wearily. He got up from the table and walked towards the front doors. He stopped like he had forgotten something, walked back to her and took her hands.

"You are free to go wherever you want," he said.

"I want to stay here. With you," she said.

Pieter walked back from the barn. He had changed into leather breeches and a leather doublet and wore a riding cloak. Tanner the Elder handed him the reins from one of the heavy brown horses he had unhitched from the cart. He walked towards Katarina and Herr Tucher with the horse and tethered him in front of the house.

"I must leave," Pieter said to Katarina and Herr Tucher. "I must get home to my father."

Herr Tucher nodded. "Yes, I know. Pieter, if you ever need anything…"

"There is one thing I have to tell you first," Pieter said. "I know where those documents are."

Herr Tucher raised his eyebrows.

"I followed the four soldiers on horseback. I saw where they took the parcel."

"And does Hans-Wolfgang know this?" Herr Tucher said.

"I don't believe so." Pieter paused.

"Well? Where are they?" Herr Tucher said, suppressing a laugh.

"There's a tavern in Lonnerstadt. Ralf knows Gerlinde, the barmaid. Elis, his soldier, brought the package to her. I saw them."

"Brilliant boy you are, Pieter," he said and clapped him lightly on the shoulder. "Brilliant."

"I know the barmaid's daughter. Quite well, as a matter of fact. Mother and daughter have no love for those Slavish soldiers. Or Ralf. I told her Ralf had stolen the papers from you. She's holding them safe until you come."

Herr Tucher kissed Katarina on the cheek, turned and carefully climbed the steps to the double front doors, laughing to himself.

Pieter turned to Katarina. "I'm off, then. It's going to be a long, lonely ride."

"Are you going alone?" Katarina said.

"Yes. Why?" He smiled. "Would you like to come along?"

"I am not going anywhere!" she said.

"What a pity." He pushed a curl behind his ear. "I would also prefer to stay here. But I must ride the waves, wherever the wind guides my sails. I'll miss you."

"I'll miss you, too, Pieter," Katarina said and hugged him.

She stepped back and Pieter stroked Isabeau's cheek. Isabeau grabbed at his finger and leaned towards him. She reached her arms out to him. He took her from Katarina, kissed her softly on the head and gave her back. He put an arm around Katarina's shoulder and pulled her suddenly back to his chest. He kissed Katarina on the lips like a lover would.

"What was that for?" she felt her face redden.

"In case I never see you again." He untied his horse, sprang lightly into his saddle and rode off down the track.

BIBLIOGRAPHY

English
1. Holborn, Hajo. *A History of Modern Germany: The Reformation.* Princeton, NJ: Princeton University Press, 1959.
2. Harrington, Joel. *The Unwanted Child: The Fate of Foundlings, Orphans and Juvenile Criminals in Early Modern Germany.* Chicago and London: The University of Chicago Press, 2009.
3. Deursen, A.T. van. *Plain Lives in a Golden Age.* Trans. Maarten Ultee. Cambridge, UK: Cambridge University Press, 1991.
4. Mak, Geert. *Amsterdam: A Brief Life of the City.* Trans. Philipp Blom. London, UK: Vintage, 2001.
5. Kramer, Heinrich. *Malleus Maleficarum: Hammer of the Witches.* Trans. Montague Summers. Calgary, CA: Theophania Publishing, 2011.
6. Wilson, Peter H. *Europe's Tragedy: A New History of the Thirty Years War.* UK and USA: Penguin Books, 2010.

German
7. Hörlin, Rainer. *Lonnerstadt: Spuren der Vergangenheit.* Ipsheim: Medien-Service Winter, 3. Auflage 2009.
8. Haas, Nikolaus. *Geschichte des Slaven-Landes und den Aisch und den Ebrach-Flußchen.* Bamberg, 1819. Neustadt a. d. Aisch: Verlag für Kunstreproduktionen Chr. Schmidt, 1985.
9. Bedürftig, Friedemann. *Taschenlexikon Dreißigjähriger Krieg.* München: Piper Verlag GmbH, 1998.
10. Wölker, Anton; Schmidt, Sebastian; Eppel, Wolfgang. *Aus der Geschichte der Stadt Hochstadt a.d. Aisch.* PDF Version Herausgegeben von der Stadt Höchstadt an der Aisch zum 1000-jährigen Jubiläum der unkundlichen Ersterwähnung Höchstadts im Jahr 1003, 2003.
11. Bartelmeß, Albert. *Die Patrizierfamilie Tucher im 17. und 18. Jahrhundert.*
12. Sakuma, Hironobu. *Die Nürnberger Tuchmacher, Weber, Färber und Bereiter vom 14. bis 17. Jahrhundert.* Schriftenreihe des Stadtarchivs Nürnberg, 1993.

13. Stöber, W. *Ein Held in Kirchenrock: Aus dem Leben des Pfarrers Veit vom Berg.* Neustad a. d. Aisch: Verlag Ph. C.W. Schmidt, 1960.
14. Peters, Jan. *Peter Hagendorf-Tagebuch eines Söldners aus dem Dreißigjährigen Krieg.* Göttingen: V & R unipress, 2012.
15. Huch, Ricarda. *Der große Krieg in Deutschland, Band 1 - 3.* Leipzig: Im Insel Verlag, 1914.

ABOUT THE AUTHOR

Laura Libricz was born and raised in Bethlehem PA and moved to Upstate New York when she was 22. After working a few years building Steinberger guitars, she received a scholarship to go to college. She tried to 'do the right thing' and study something useful, but spent all her time reading German literature. She earned a BA in German at The College of New Paltz, NY in 1991 and moved to Germany, where she resides today. When she isn't writing she can be found sifting through city archives, picking through castle ruins or aiding the steady flood of Höfner musical instruments into the world market.

Her first novel, *The Master and the Maid*, is the first book of the Heaven's Pond Trilogy. *The Soldier's Return* and *Ash and Rubble* are the second and third books in the series.

www.ingramcontent.com/pod-product-compliance
Lightning Source LLC
Chambersburg PA
CBHW020237180626
46810CB00006B/2239